BONDED BY LOVE

By the light of the moon Valerian admired her body, the full, firm breasts, long legs, small waist and well-rounded hips. Wynne was perfect; Venus herself could not have been more beautiful. His mouth came down on hers and Wynne closed her eyes, shuddering in delight as his warm, soft mouth explored every inch of her being.

"We were made for each other. My flesh, my heart, my soul, belong to you," he whispered.

His body was warm and hard and the feel of his rising manhood filled her with excitement. Any doubts she might have had about this Roman were forgotten as her body responded with a will of its own. . . .

Love's Blazing Ecstasy

LOVE'S BLAZING ECSTASY

KATHRYN KRAMER

A SIGNET BOOK

NEW AMERICAN LIBRARY

NAL BOOKS ARE AVAILABLE AT QUANTITY DISCOUNTS WHEN
USED TO PROMOTE PRODUCTS OR SERVICES. FOR INFORMA-
TION PLEASE WRITE TO PREMIUM MARKETING DIVISION, NEW
AMERICAN LIBRARY, 1633 BROADWAY, NEW YORK, NEW YORK
10019.

SIGNET TRADEMARK REG. U.S. PAT. OFF. AND FOREIGN COUNTRIES
REGISTERED TRADEMARK—MARCA REGISTRADA
HECHO EN CHICAGO. U.S.A.

SIGNET, SIGNET CLASSIC, MENTOR, PLUME, MERIDIAN AND NAL BOOKS
are published by New American Library,
1633 Broadway, New York, New York 10019

First Printing, January, 1985

1 2 3 4 5 6 7 8 9

PRINTED IN THE UNITED STATES OF AMERICA

To my family, past and present, without whom I could never have undertaken to write this novel. May the family of man learn to live in peace with each other and walk in the light of the dawn.

AUTHOR'S NOTE

The Celts were a race of separate tribes rather than a nation. Of their antecedents we know little. Central Germany appears to have been their point of origin, yet they wandered far north into Britain and Ireland and as far east as the Ukraine and Poland. Because they did not keep written records, little is known of them today except through legend and through archaeological findings. But by these means, their legacy lives on.

The elemental powers of fire, water, air, and earth were the gods and goddesses of the Celtic tribes. The early Celtic Britons were conquered by the Romans, and under Roman rule their way of life changed. Dress, customs, and religion all became Romanized.

The Roman Empire embraced with open arms the local gods and goddesses of these conquered peoples and attempted to identify Celtic tribal deities and nature-spirits with gods of their own. The Romans put no bonds upon religious thought. The Druids, however, priests of the Celtic religion, represented challenge to the authority of the government of Rome in much the same way as the Christian Church. Because of this, many of the Druids and their followers were killed. Little is known about the Druids in Christian times except from fairy folklore. The elemental powers of the Celtic religion reduced to local elves, fairies, and water spirits are with us still in legend and stories. We can only guess what mysteries the Druids possessed; we may never know the contents of this ancient mystical lore.

I have tried to imagine in this story what it must have been like in those days long ago, what might have happened to two lovers when their cultures were at odds with each other.

Kathryn Kramer

How is it under our control to love or not to love?

—Robert Browning

I

THE DOVE AND THE EAGLE

Northwest Britain

Oh that I had wings like a dove! for then would I fly away and be at rest.

—Psalms, 4:6

One

The sky was dark as the full moon struggled to escape from the clouds which covered it like a shroud. Beneath the heavens, nestled in a grove of small trees, stood the circular dwellings of the tribe of the Parisi, looking like mushrooms with their round thatch roofs.

In the center of the village stood the home which belonged to the tribal bard, Adair. Within the wooden walls it was silent except for the soft moaning of the young girl called Wynne, who tossed and turned upon her bed of furs.

"No. No. Please," she murmured softly, speaking to the images in her dream. Her flaxed gown was wet with perspiration, and her blond hair tangled around her neck like a golden rope. With a start she sat up, her blue eyes wide with fright. Anxiously she looked around, her hands shaking. She was alone. There was no sign that anyone had been in the room. The fire was still carefully banked in both fireplaces, the door shut. Yet she had the feeling that something was very wrong.

Trembling, she got down from her bedshelf, built from hardened clay and covered with furs, and walked to the door of the lodge to look out upon the night.

"It was only a dream," she whispered. But it had seemed so real. Her heart was even now beating rapidly, her breathing heavy.

The only sight which met her eyes beyond the lodge was the glowing embers of the tribal fire, the fire of life, which shone brightly in the distance. All seemed peaceful, but Wynne still felt uneasy; she could still feel the presence of danger, not for herself but for another.

The large communal room was dark, with only a small shaft of light from the fire. Wynne wandered around the room as if in a trance, wondering where the rest of the household was. Her father? Yes, she recalled now, he was preparing himself for the morrow's hunt, and was sleeping this night in the lodge of Cedric, the chief of the tribe. But, she wondered, where was Brenna? More than likely on another of her late-night walks.

As Wynne returned to her bed, a fierce desire to be outside suddenly overcame her. How she wanted to be away from the stifling air and close walls surrounding her. Perhaps outside she could get away from the feelings that were tormenting her.

Wrapped in her cloak, Wynne stepped out into the fresh cool night air, feeling soothed by the soft breeze which caressed her face.

She quickly made her way past the darkened lodges of her tribesmen to the edge of the forest and searched for her stallion. The large black animal nearly blended with the night. Putting two fingers into her mouth, she made the shrill sound which always brought him to her. When he approached, he nuzzled her hand and nickered in greeting. Wynne patted his head and then sprang upon his back with expert nimbleness.

The black stallion tossed his head fretfully, eager to run, and Wynne decided to let the animal have his way. They sailed through the air, the rider and horse becoming as one with the racing wind.

Onward Wynne rode, past the shallow stream, beyond the steep incline. She thrilled at the feeling of freedom she always experienced on the stallion's back, as if all her troubles and worries had vanished.

"Sloan, what a fine animal you are!" she exclaimed. The powerful horse responded to the softest of whispers, the lightest touches on his mane.

When at last they came to the far side of the forest, they stopped for a brief rest. Now, again, Wynne sensed danger, heard the warning voices within her. Again she remembered her dream and wondered at its meaning. Who was the dark-haired stranger whose face she had seen so clearly? Even now she could see him as vividly as if he were standing before her, could feel a power beyond herself pulling her onward.

The wind chilled her to her very bones as the stallion galloped on. Or was it something else which made her tremble, a touch of the fey, perhaps, or the sense of something fatal about to occur?

Reining in her horse, Wynne paused and looked up at the moon, so beautiful with its pale golden glow. Her people worshiped all the great forces of nature: moon, sea, sun, wind, earth, and fire.

Again Wynne was struck by a feeling of danger and strained her ears and eyes to the night. Were her senses deceiving her or did she in truth hear a soft chanting sound carried by the wind through the forest? Perhaps it was the spirits of the woodland. But she smelled smoke and now she could see the glow of a fire in the distance.

Cautiously she urged her horse forward until they came to a small clearing where the oak trees rose majestically against the sky. It was there that she saw him—the man in her dream. He was nearly naked, wearing only a loincloth, and his bare feet were bound.

He was tall and powerfully built; it would have taken more than one warrior to subdue him. He was tied securely to one of the oak trees, his arms bound above his head. It appeared that he was unconscious, for his head drooped to one side and his eyes were closed.

Again she could hear the drone of chanting, and an icy chill of dread traveled up her spine.

Overcome by curiosity, she dismounted and made her way cautiously through the foliage until she was near the stranger. A warning echoed through her brain as she heard the snap of a twig; she stopped quickly and ducked into the undergrowth just as three dark-cloaked figures brushed by her and came to the side of the dark stranger, forcing him to drink from the wooden cup that they held to his mouth. The man lifted his head, snarling his defiance at his captors. Wynne could sense his rage as if he had spoken to her. His suppressed passion touched her very soul. She knew at that moment what awaited him. He was to be a sacrifice to the cult of Domnu, burned alive in the wicker work cage as an offering to the old gods.

No! she thought violently. She could not bear to have him killed in this manner. As if sensing her presence, the stranger stared in her direction, and although she knew he could not see her, her eyes were fixed upon him.

If only I had my dagger, she thought with frustration, for to try to rescue him barehanded was sheer folly and she had run out into the night so quickly that she had taken only her cloak.

A gleam of metal caught her eye. As soon as the hooded figures were gone, she carefully made her way toward it, holding her breath, not daring to hope. She found a sword hidden in the undergrowth. Did it belong to the stranger? Perhaps he had barely had time to conceal it before his captors fell upon him.

Her fingers caressed the weapon like a lover. It was not at all like the swords of her people. It was heavier, of a different metal. *A Roman sword?*

Wynne waited, watching from her hiding place as the three figures returned. She could see that the stranger was not one of her kind, he was a Roman; still she knew she must help him.

When at last the prisoner was again alone, she ran forward, lifting the gleaming object up by its hilt. She must cut the prisoner's bonds before the cloaked figures returned, or she might not get another chance.

"May the gods be with me," she said softly, feeling the strength of their presence.

A sudden noise behind her alerted her to danger. Instincts guided her reflexes as she turned around and stepped aside just in time to avoid being crushed by a large rock hurled at her by one of the cloaked men. With a start she realized that the huge man was completely naked under his robe, with symbols painted on his bare flesh. She did not have time to ponder the meaning of this, however, for the man was coming toward her, intent on killing her.

Gripping the sword tightly in her hand, Wynne made ready to defend herself.

Looking up toward the heavens, the Roman said a prayer to his gods. He was not afraid of death, he was a soldier. Yet to die like this, to be burned alive, was a gruesome end. To meet his end trussed up like a chicken on a spit was more than he could bear. He had heard tales about these heathens and their human sacrifices, but until this moment he had not realized they were true. His eyes strayed to the huge basket. Was this to be his prison or his funeral pyre?

His hands worked feverishly at his bonds until his wrists were blistered and bleeding. He would not give up until every ounce of his strength was gone. Closing his eyes, he cursed these shrouded figures whose singing was nearly driving him mad.

What potion did they force me to drink? he wondered fearfully. Certainly it would not be poison, for that would take all the fun out of their ritual. He felt light-headed, dizzy. He shook his head to clear it of its spinning. Was it the brew that had been forced between his lips which caused him to think that there was someone watching him from the bushes? Had it been only his imagination that had made him believe that he had heard a woman's voice cry out in anguish a few moments ago? No, there had been someone there. He was sure of it.

"Minerva, Goddess of Wisdom and War, hear me," he pleaded. "Save me from this doom and I will forever serve you!"

As if in answer to his prayer, he saw her. It was Minerva herself grappling with one of the hooded heathens. Strange, he had always thought that the goddess would have dark hair, and yet her hair was so light, like spun gold. She was beautiful. More beautiful than he could ever have imagined.

He tried to watch, but the drug was overpowering him. Trying to control his strength, he closed his eyes and with one final pull sought to free himself, but the ropes held him tight. He felt himself fall into unconsciousness.

Whirling around and around like partners in a dance, Wynne and her opponent fought each other. The man was three times her size, but she was armed with a sword. Still, he seemed to be able to dodge her blows, coming closer and closer to her each time.

"You are tiring, eh?" the huge man asked with an evil smile.

She shook her head and lunged at him again, but she didn't know how long she could go on. Another fear gripped her heart. What if the others returned? She must strike a blow at him now, before she was outnumbered.

Encumbered by his cloak, the man removed it and now stood naked before her. Wynne's gown and cloak threatened to trip her, yet she did not have the time or the desire to face this giant in all her natural glory.

Wynne thrust again and again with the sword, but the giant of a man was more than a match for her. A sudden idea came to her.

"Sloan!" she called. The horse was by her side in an instant, pawing the ground before him. For a moment her huge opponent was distracted, but it was just enough time for her to strike a strong blow to the side of his head.

Looking down upon the unconscious mountain of flesh, Wynne found that she could not kill him—murder was not in her blood. She would let him live, but she must make certain that he could not warn the others. Taking off her belt, she tied him securely to a nearby tree and stuffed the end of his discarded cloak in his mouth to keep him from calling for help.

I hope that my kindness will not be my undoing, she thought. Still, she had never killed anyone and did not want to do so now.

Jumping once again upon the horse's back, sword raised upward in her left hand, Wynne started toward the captive. As she rode, the hood of her cloak fell once again to her shoulders, her blond hair glowing nearly golden in the moonlight.

Drifting in and out of consciousness, the Roman watched his rescuer. Cloaked in black, riding her magnificant black stallion, hair billowing wildly about her shoulders, she indeed looked like Minerva. She was a breathtaking sight, yet he felt no fear of her, knew that she had come to free him.

He saw her jump from her horse, felt the swift thrust of a sword as she quickly severed the ropes which bound him. He felt the softness of her hands as she touched him, and then he sensed nothing more. He slumped upon the hard ground in a swirl of darkness.

Two

The first rays of sunlight gently caressed her face as Wynne welcomed the dawn. She looked down at the sleeping form of the Roman. She could see him clearly now in the light. He was handsome, this stranger, perhaps even more handsome than her father, if that were possible. He was powerfully built, perhaps a few inches shorter than her father, but whereas Adair was tall and lean, this man was muscular. His hair was short, cropped close to his head in raven-black curls; it was unlike the long loose or plaited hair of the men in her tribe. She had the urge to touch the shining curls but quickly drew back her hand as the man sighed heavily in his sleep.

Who are you? she wondered as she studied his features, the high cheekbones, fine chiseled nose, the long dark eyelashes which cast a shadow on his face. She couldn't help but wonder what color his eyes were. He had a small cleft in his chin, which fascinated her. This time she couldn't resist the urge to reach out and touch him, to feel the warmth of his skin against her soft hand. She ran her finger lightly over his face as if memorizing it. The man again stirred in his deep slumber, and Wynne drew back her hand.

It was chilly without her cloak, but she had relinquished it to the stranger, fearful that after his ordeal he might become ill without its warmth.

Wynne rose to her feet, hoping that by moving around she could bring back a little warmth to her body. As she walked, back and forth, she thought about what had happened during the night, and was amazed at her bravery, at her skill in fighting the dark-robed giant. She was thankful now to her father for training her in the handling of arms, a practice not unusual among her people, for women were even known to sit among the men in the war councils. Yet, if not for her father's badgering, she would not have become as skilled as she had at wielding a sword.

Wynne shuddered, this time at the memory of the hulking giant she had been forced to fight. Again she could see his face. It had been vaguely familiar to her, but she could not place where she had seen him before.

The sound of the stranger murmuring in his sleep interrupted her thoughts and she hurried to his side. It had been a struggle for her to lift his body and put him on Sloan's back after she had cut his bonds. Somehow she had managed to do so, as if aided by some unseen force, some inner strength. She had ridden to this spot which was very precious to her, her childhood hideaway.

"Minerva . . . Minerva . . . so beautiful," the stranger moaned in his language. She reached out to soothe his brow, thankful that there appeared to be no fever. She wondered what he had been forced to drink. Most likely belladonna made from the nightshade plant. It was often used by those who practiced the dark arts. It was even said that the evil ones could fly when it was rubbed on them as an ointment. Why had he been forced to partake of their drink? Was it part of their ceremony?

The dark-haired man's eyes flew open as Wynne gazed upon him. She was surprised by the color of his eyes. They were not blue, nor gray, but almost golden in their hue, an amber brown.

"You're here . . . Minerva," he breathed. He reached out his large hand and captured a few strands of her soft golden hair. "I never dreamed that I would ever be able to touch a goddess."

His eyes raked over her. She was tall, but of course a goddess would be. Her hair framed her oval face and tumbled down around her shoulders, ending far below her waist. Her face was beautiful, with a straight, perfectly sculptured nose, firm chin, large blue eyes surrounded by thick brown lashes, full sensuous lips. His eyes took in all of her—the full firm breasts, long legs, small waist, well-rounded hips. She was perfect. Even the shapeless blue gown that she wore could not hide that fact.

"You are beautiful!" he exclaimed, longing to feel her body next to his own. He remembered stories from the days of old which told of goddesses who loved mortal men and mated with them. He knew at that moment that above all else this was his desire, that Minerva would love him. He reached out to touch her, gently taking her arm and pulling her toward him. She smelled of violets and early-morning air. His eyes caressed hers.

"Oh, sweet goddess, let me touch your lips," he breathed. His strong arm encircled her waist, pressing her close against him. His lips brushed against her lips, light as the stroke of a butterfly's wing. Then he kissed her again, this time his mouth devouring the honey of her lips.

Wynne opened her eyes wide with astonishment. What was this touching of mouths? It was not a custom of her tribe. His lips had captured hers so suddenly, but she liked the feel of his mouth on hers. Closing her eyes, she accepted the gentle pressure, the exploration of his lips and tongue. A spark went through her. A flicker of flame, coursing through her veins. She was not sure how to react, what to do, but when his lips parted once more she mimicked the caress of his mouth upon hers and gently moved her lips on his. He groaned and tightened his arms around her until she could scarcely breathe.

The warm sweetness of her kisses made him throb with desire. Forgotten now was all else but her nearness. The fragrance of her skin and hair tantalized him, the softness of her skin and hair enchanted him. He reached out his hand to touch her hips, moving upward to cup the fullness of her breast, his hand stroking the taut peak in a lingering touch.

Wynne froze, the spell broken, and moved away from him as if she had been burned. She trembled at the unexpected fire which had coursed through her body at the touch of this stranger. She was fearful of his power over her and confused by the reaction she'd had to his touch.

The dark-haired man was surprised at her actions, at the shocked look on her face, the fear written across her perfect features. Wasn't it natural, after all, for a man to desire a beautiful woman, goddess or mortal? Why, she acted almost like an innocent or a virgin. So it was true, then, what was said of Minerva, that she was untouched and pure. The Roman was suddenly afraid that he had offended her. Would she strike him down in anger for his boldness?

"I'm sorry," he apologized, looking into her wide blue eyes. "But you are so beautiful. Are you angry with me?"

Wynne looked at him, still aroused by his nearness, feeling awkward and shy as he stared at her. She shook her head, wondering what he was saying in his Roman tongue. Her father had dealt with the Romans and knew many of their words. He had taught her some of their language—Latin it was called—but not enough for her to understand what this stranger was saying to her or to talk with him. She motioned with her hands, telling him to lie back, not knowing if he should exert himself after his ordeal.

"Why . . . why, you don't understand a word I'm saying!" The truth of this struck him like a blow. No wonder she had kept silent all the while he had been praising her charms, and had not denied him the kiss. His words had been just so much gibberish to her ears.

The irony of the situation hit him and he laughed softly. He, Valerian Quillon, who could have any woman, could charm the wings off a dove, was here alone with a highly desirable woman and could not make her understand his words of love.

At the sound of his laughter Wynne smiled at him. Her teeth, he noticed, like the rest of her, were perfect, white and even.

The image of the young woman's daring rescue of him came again to his mind. He remembered her golden hair in the moonlight, the upraised sword, the black horse, but realized that she was human, after all. In a way, the knowledge pleased him, for a goddess would be difficult to woo, but a woman of flesh and blood was another matter entirely.

"So, you are no goddess at all, lovely creature. You are merely a mortal like myself," he said softly.

Wynne cocked her head and listened for words which were familiar to her. But there were none. Her father had not taught her the words the

Roman was uttering. For the moment she remained a silent vision of loveliness.

"I know that you don't understand what I am saying," the Roman began, "but you will soon." He longed to bed this beauty, but knew he must conquer the language barrier before she would be his.

Reaching for her hand, he held it firmly, looking deep into her eyes. "Thank you for saving my life," he said earnestly, and was rewarded with another of her smiles. She had understood his meaning, knew the words "thank you" and "life."

Feeling suddenly tired, Valerian lay back upon the hard ground and closed his eyes. Wynne too felt spent. It had been a long night and her exertions had finally caught up with her. Crawling over to where the man slept, she lay down beside him and fell fast asleep.

Three

Waking from her slumber, Wynne rose and glanced about her, taking in the untamed forest with its mossy floor hidden from view by a curtain woven of hundreds of treetops which shivered in the breezes of the early-morning air. The wild, beautiful music of hundreds of wakening birds serenaded her as they flew from bough to bough, flying over the hills and plains and the mountains. She felt safe here in the forest and felt assured that the dark-haired man would also be safe.

Thinking about the Roman brought chills to Wynne's flesh as she remembered his touch, the caress of his mouth against hers. She turned around and found that he too was awake, looking at her with his amber-brown eyes.

"By the gods, you are real after all. Not just a vision of my imagination," he said to her, smiling.

The smile faded as he looked down at his body, clothed only in the loincloth. The memory of his near-death came back to him. His tunic and armor had been taken from him by his captors.

"Where in the name of the gods are my clothes?" he cried in frustration. How could he have allowed himself to be captured, he who was a centurion, leader of many soldiers?

"Clothes?" Wynne repeated, looking at him with a gleam in her eyes, remembering the word.

"Yes. Yes. I need clothing. Clothing," he repeated, excited by her response. Perhaps she knew a few of his words after all. He put his hand to his chest, speaking his name.

"Valerian. Valerian . . . me . . . my name," he said.

"Val-er-ian." Wynne repeated with just a trace of an accent. Taking her small hand in his, he touched her chest and lifted his eyebrows in inquiry.

"Wynne," she answered, understanding what it was he wanted of her.

"Wynne, a beautiful name. It suits you, you know." Valerian knew a little about the languages in this land, but each tribe had its different dialect, which made it hard to communicate with her in this tongue. He did know enough about the Celtic tongues, however, to know that her name meant "the fair" or "the white."

Valerian found that he could communicate quite well with the young woman by a mixture of hand signals and single words. When he made her understand that he was hungry, she went out for a short walk and came back with a breakfast of fruits and berries for him. Together they ate and enjoyed each other's company.

"Go!" Wynne said, suddenly standing up. "Wynne must go back." She gestured with her hands.

Valerian didn't want to let her go. Instead he felt the desire to gather her into his arms and make love to her, but something in her eyes told him that she spoke the truth, that she must get back to her people. She told him with her eyes and by hand gestures that she would return at dusk.

"Good-bye, my fair one," Valerian said to her softly as she departed. He had known this beauty for less than one full day and yet when she left it seemed that a part of him had left also.

Wynne rode back through the forest, not daring to stop to let the horse rest. If the gods smiled upon her, Adair would be gone from the lodge by now after spending the night in the dwelling of the chief of the clan. They were off to hunt the wild pig which lived at the edge of the marshes to the east.

Sliding from Sloan's back, she approached the lodge with caution, feeling relieved to see that her father's weapons were gone from the front of the porch. Wishing herself invisible, she walked softly through the doorway.

"So, you have seen fit to return," a voice she knew all too well said behind her. Turning, she saw Brenna sitting at her wooden loom, her arms moving gracefully as she went about her work.

"I . . . I was out riding Sloan," Wynne whispered, avoiding the woman's eyes. Brenna was her father's second wife. Adair had married the buxom dark-haired woman after the death of Wynne's mother a few years ago, but she and Wynne were always at odds. Wynne knew that this woman bore her no love and wondered if it was perhaps because of the closeness she and her father shared. "I took a spill," Wynne went on, to explain her disheveled appearance.

"Out riding that horse again, instead of helping me to do the household work. When are you going to realize that you are a woman, not a man? You are your father's daughter, not his son!" Her voice was venomous, perhaps because Adair so wished for a son, but Brenna had yet to conceive. Her eyes told Wynne that she longed for the day when she could have Adair all to herself, when Wynne left to live at the fire of her own husband.

"I'm sorry, Brenna," Wynne apologized, wishing to avoid an argument today of all days.

Brenna did not answer her, but merely stared at her with dark brooding eyes as Wynne set about changing her clothes and then tidying the large room of the round house. Wynne touched the wall of wattle and daub with its colorful pictures painted upon it. Her father had been so proud of her artistry, as had her mother. Even then she had shown promise of her many talents.

"Are you going to spend the entire day in the land of dreams?" Brenna's voice questioned scathingly.

Wynne resumed her tasks, feeling Brenna's eyes upon her as she moved about the room. She shook out the furs covering the sleeping shelves against the wall, filled the water jugs from the well, and gathered up the old straw rushes from the dirt floor, scattering new straw in its place.

The hours seemed to drag by. Her thoughts were on Valerian the entire day, worrying about him, wondering what he was doing. She even tried her hand at weaving, but her hands seemed to be all thumbs, her fingers shaking as she tried to weave the soft threads.

"Here, let me do that!" Brenna snarled. "You are totally worthless to me today!" The woman's beady gray eyes searched Wynne's face, as if drawing her thoughts from her. "Something is wrong with you. Something more than a fall from your horse. Something has happened."

"No. No, I'm just a bit shaken, that's all," Wynne lied, hoping that Brenna would believe her.

Giving her a little push away from the loom, Brenna shook her head in frustration. "Oh, all right. But get out of my sight. I can't bear to have you around me when you are so clumsy."

Wynne hurried outside, anxious to be alone with her thoughts. She watched several slaves busy at work digging a hole in the west ditch. A palisade ran round the inside of the ditch except at the entrance, and she could see several workers channeling their cows into the compound. She felt a twinge of pity for these people. What would it be like to be *owned*? she wondered, and shuddered at the thought as she gazed upon their iron neck shackles. Why was it that some men should have a life of hard work and poverty while others were more favored? She had asked her father this question many times, and always heard the same answer. It was so among all the Celtic tribes. The divisions were clear: Druids, learned men and equites, the warriors and nobles, were the ruling classes, and the peasants and slaves were the toiling classes.

Seeing two dogs fighting over a bone in the open area near the fire of life, Wynne was reminded that Valerian had not eaten much this day. Surely he would be starved. Anxious to find food for him, she made her way toward the grain storehouse. She would take some barley back with her for the Roman.

Drifting smoke carried the aroma of meat and vegetables steaming in cooking pots heated by stones from the firepit. She would take a little out of each to carry back with her to the cave.

Hoping that Brenna would be gone, Wynne made her way back to the lodge, but the woman still sat at her loom.

I'll return when it is dark, when Brenna is asleep, to gather clothing for the dark-haired stranger, she thought.

Reaching up to touch her hair, she was dismayed to find that it was a mass of tangles. For the first time in her life Wynne longed for a mirror in her hands, but there was none available at the moment, not unless she went back into the lodge, which she was not inclined to do.

Suddenly Wynne—until now the least vain of young women—wanted to make herself more attractive. Was it because of the stranger? Walking to the edge of the pond near the village, she paused to look at herself. What did the stranger think of her? she wondered. Was she pretty? She hoped so. She wanted him to like her. She combed her unbound hair with her fingers, then carefully plaited it into two thick braids. Kneeling at the edge of the pond, she splashed the clear water on her face. It was icy cold and refreshing.

Will he do it again, that touching of the mouths? she wondered, looking again at her image in the water and touching her lips with her fingertips.

Wynne went on to wash her legs and arms, then remembered that Brenna always wore a concoction made of rose petals and honeysuckle on her skin when she wished to find favor with Adair. Gathering a handful of honeysuckle clover, Wynne wondered if their charm would work for her as well.

By the time the blond-haired girl had finished grooming herself, the sky was welcoming the night. With a feeling of happiness she had seldom experienced before, she realized that soon it would be time to see Valerian again. She returned to the lodge. Brenna was now gone. Going over to her clothing chest, she raised the lid to look for something suitable to wear. She decided upon a green gown with an overtunic of checks in fawn and black, clasped together by a bronze brooch. The garments made her feel very feminine, almost pretty. When she was finished dressing, she looked carefully around her to make certain that Brenna was nowhere in sight and rummaged through her father's clothing trunk, hoping that the stranger would not be too muscular to wear her father's clothing. Wrapping the garments in one of her father's fur cloaks, she made her way toward the fire.

Ah, good. The family has left plenty of food from dinner, she thought, taking a large portion for herself and Valerian and putting it into an earthenware jar. She would have to find a small keg of mead or ale for Valerian too. No doubt there would be some near the meeting-house.

So anxious was Wynne to return to the stranger in the forest that she did not notice the eyes which watched her every move—cold, cruel eyes.

"So," said a voice when Wynne had left, "the Roman barbarian is still close at hand and the bard's daughter shields him. So much the worse for her. She will learn obedience." The figure in the shadows smiled and went back into the lodge.

Four

Valerian scowled as he looked around him. He paced back and forth, wearing a path across the floor of the small cave which had become his home. His jaw was clenched, his arms crossed in front of him. Where was she? Had she come to harm?

Reaching up, he felt the stubble of his beard and swore beneath his breath. What he wouldn't give for a hot bath this very minute, though in this godforsaken land this luxury, as well as many others, was denied him.

A chill ran up his back as he remembered what fate had almost befallen him, if not for the beautiful Wynne. Wynne! His countrymen would call her a heathen, a savage. The fierce Celtic warriors believed in the immortality of the spirit and in reincarnation. They were unafraid to die in battle, for they had been told by their Druids that they would come back in another body.

Valerian had also been told that they were head-hunters who openly displayed the heads of their enemies as trophies. He had not believed all these stories while living safely in Rome. He had laughed at the fears of his cousin Marcus, who had cringed at the thought of being sent to Gaul. And yet wasn't it true that these people made human sacrifices? Hadn't he nearly been a victim of their priests?

"Oh, Wynne, there is so much that I must learn about you, about your people," he sighed.

Perhaps all of these people are not savages, he thought. Surely Wynne was not, although he knew nothing of her tribesmen or of their ways and customs. Of one thing, however, he was certain. The lovely blond beauty was not like the chanting, naked, painted heathens who had fallen upon him as he rode through the night in search of his fellow soldiers, who had become lost to him in the dark mists of the sudden storm. She had come to his rescue out of the darkness like a golden flame.

His thoughts in turmoil, the Roman shivered with the sudden chill of the air and picked up the cloak from upon the ground, touching it reverently as one would something holy, remembering the face of the woman whose touch he could still feel upon his brow. Her touch had been gentle, yet strong. Her lips had been so soft, her skin so smooth. The goddess Minerva herself could not have so inflamed his senses, and yet she had been frightened of his kisses.

Throwing the cloak around his shoulders, he

clutched it tightly around him as if by so doing he could bring back the woman whose image was emblazoned on his mind's eye. Again fear overcame him. What if she had been captured by those naked savages and forced to pay for coming to his rescue? What if at this very moment she were being held prisoner? He longed to go in search of her, but she had made it clear that he was to wait for her and not leave the sanctuary of the cave.

Valerian waited until the sky turned dark gray, and then had not the patience to wait longer. Visions of Wynne lying injured somewhere assaulted him. What if she had been thrown from her horse and even now lay bruised and bleeding upon the ground? Or worse yet, had been captured?

"If anyone harms her, he will answer to me," he vowed, picking up his sword and leaving the security of the cave.

The night was warm, the sky cloudless. Valerian loved the forest; it was a paradise, thick with greenery and tall trees which stood against the sky like centurions. Clear springs bubbled forth from the earth, and he stopped to cup some of the cool water in his hands to refresh himself.

A sudden rustle in the undergrowth put him on his guard. Valerian drew his sword and rose cautiously. Then he saw the small fawn in search of its mother. With a sigh he shrugged his shoulders and continued on, careful to mark his trail so that he would be able to find his way back to the cave.

A vine hidden by the underbrush caught around Valerian's ankle and he fell to the ground with a thud. His hand brushed something soft, material of some sort, perhaps linen. With a feeling of dread he gathered the garment in his hand and held it up to see it in the moonlight. It was a woman's gown, similar to Wynne's. A sob tore at his throat as he drew the gown to his chest and closed his eyes, praying to his gods that she had not come to harm. He rose to his feet and like one demented fought his way through the thick vines and bushes until he came to the edge of a huge lake.

She was standing there, her arms outstretched toward the sky, her blond hair falling in two braids to her waist, twin ropes of gold. She was like a glorious marble statue in the moonlight. He could not control his desire, and his manhood responded to his need for her. He yearned to come to her, to join with her, to make love to this magnificent young woman on the mossy bank. As if in a daze, he started walking toward her.

"O Mother of the Water of Life, hear me," Wynne chanted in her language. "I thank you for the power you have given me. May my eyes be strengthened to see the glory of your bounty, my ears attuned to the sound of your voice, my heart be joined with you. I give myself to you now. May my spirit be cleansed from all evil." Thus having spoken, Wynne dived into the cold waters, swimming around in the still pool, feeling peaceful.

Valerian stopped in his tracks at her words, for although he did not know their meaning, he could sense that she was performing some kind of ritual. He ducked back into the foliage so that she would not see him.

Valerian, you are no better than a rutting animal who would force himself upon his desired mate, he swore to himself. Well, from this moment on you will learn to control your passions. This young woman is no mere slave upon whom you can quench your lust as you see fit.

With an effort he turned away and ran back through the forest as if the gods of Hades were on his heels. His heart was pounding in his breast, but not entirely from his exertions, as he entered the cave and made his way to his bed of moss. Covering his face with his hands, he could see her still, so very beautiful, and knew what torture it would be from now on to keep from touching her, making love to her.

If only I could stay here forever, he thought sadly. Woo her and take her back with me. But he knew that he could not. Wynne was not a woman who would be happy to be a concubine or camp follower. Instinct told Valerian that she was pure. No doubt that is why she reacted to him as she did that first time he kissed her. No, he must leave the girl untouched so that she could go about her life once he was gone, marry, and mother many fine sons. Yet the thought of her bearing another man's children caused an ache in his heart. He closed his eyes against the pain.

Wynne quickly gathered up her garments and dressed. She felt calm, serene, and very happy. Was it because she would soon see Valerian? She knew the answer was yes. The handsome Roman made her feel giddy and lighthearted as none of the young men of her tribe did. Always before now the young men Wynne kept company with had been like brothers. She rode with them, fished with them, frolicked with them, as if she too were a young man. When one of them tried to caress her or touch her in any way, she promptly scuffled with the bold aggressor to teach him that she was his equal and to keep his distance, but now she felt differently. The Roman made her feel soft, feminine. She did not want him to be her brother. She longed for something else, for him to look at her again as he had when first he had opened his eyes and gazed upon her.

Wynne thought about the ceremony she had just performed. She had purified herself in much the same way a young bride would before joining with her chosen husband. The thought of belonging to the Roman made her blush with pleasure. She had thanked the Goddess of the Waters for the Roman's life and for her own strength in rescuing him, but it was much more than that. Now their spirits were joined together as one. She had offered herself to the goddess in exchange for Valerian in the ancient way. Yet, the goddess had let her live, surely a sign that she had found favor with the Mother of the Water of Life, that although the Roman did not believe in her gods, he was still worthy.

Wynne made her way through the trees, tingling from the lake's icy water. Her mind was filled with dreams of the Roman's touch, his nearness, but when she arrived he was fast asleep. Little did she know that he was only feigning slumber, afraid of what he might do if he set eyes upon her tonight.

Walking quietly over to him, Wynne was filled with the urge to reach out and touch him, waken him, cover his mouth with hers as he had done to her. Even at the lake she had felt the strange sensations flood over her as she had thought of him. She reached out her hand, but in sudden fear pulled it back again. She did not want to waken him, to risk angering him. Disappointed, she placed the food she had brought with her and her father's garments on the floor of the cave and tiptoed out into the darkness of the night.

Five

Wynne awoke the next morning before the rays of the sun touched the earth. She had spent a sleepless night, tossing and turning upon her bed, wishing with all her heart that she had been able to spend the night again with the handsome stranger. She knew this was impossible, Brenna would have wondered where she had gone, and she could not take the chance of Valerian being discovered by her tribesmen. The fear and hatred of the Romans was still too strong. Stories of their cruelty, were well known, and where they traveled, they brought burnings, rape, pillaging, destruction. Once she too had felt hatred toward the newcomers from the South, but no more, not since meeting Valerian.

Stretching her slim arms above her head, Wynne gave in to her dreams about the Roman, remembering his strong arms about her, the warmth of his mouth upon her own. Perhaps tonight she would find out what it was to truly become a woman. She had not been deaf to the groans of pleasure which came in the dark night from the bedshelf her father shared with Brenna. Surely what a man and woman did together must be enjoyable to bring forth such moans. Nevertheless, the ceremony which had made her a woman, when her virginal membrane had been severed by the knife of the hooded Druid, had brought her such pain!

Now the sound of her stepmother's footsteps caused her to quickly leave her world of dreams as she bolted up from her bed to come face to face with the dark-haired woman. The dark eyes seemed to bore into her very soul, as if to read her thoughts.

"What ails you, Wynne?" Brenna asked with a frown. "It is not like you to stay abed once you are awake. Perhaps it is your horse. Is Sloan lame?"

Wynne shook her head. Usually at this time of morning she was already upon the stallion's back, galloping in the early-morning air. No doubt Brenna thought her either ill or her horse injured. Still, she could not tell her the truth. She longed to be able to talk to the woman as she would to her mother, but caution prevailed. Brenna would not, nor could not ever, take her mother's place. Sorrow for the loss of her own mother overcame Wynne and her eyes filled with tears. Why had her mother been called to another life so soon?

"So, I was right. You are ill!" Brenna said, standing with her hands upon her wide hips, studying her husband's daughter.

Wynne was touched by her stepmother's concern. Usually the woman seemed not to care what happened to her. Was there still a chance for some sort of friendship between them?

"Let me gather some herbs for you. I don't want to be burdened by a helpless invalid. You are useless enough when you are well," Brenna added, shattering all hopes that Wynne had for a truce between them. "You know I can't stand to be around weaklings."

Wynne fought against her anger. It took all her self-control to keep the promise she had made to her father to obey his new wife as if she were of Wynne's own flesh and blood.

"I am not ill. Thank you for your concern," she mumbled, averting her eyes, lest she betray her feelings or her thoughts. Before Brenna could say another word to her, she donned her tunic and cloak and hastened out into the crisp morning air. She walked from dwelling to dwelling, breathing the aroma of cooking porridge, until her anger had cooled.

I'll bring the Roman some breakfast, she thought, a sudden smile coming to her lips at the idea of pleasing him. She would bring him cereal along with honey and milk. She filled an earthen jug then made her way to where Sloan waited. As before, Wynne was unaware of the hostile eyes that watched her.

*   *   *

Valerian opened his eyes to the harsh light of day streaming into the cave from the rocky opening. At first he was bewildered by his surroundings, looking for the familiar signs of his camp, his soldiers. Then he remembered.

"I fear it will be a long while before I see my companions again," he said aloud. At the sound of his voice the small brown ground squirrel stopped gathering its breakfast and looked at him with black eyes. Deciding that he posed no threat, it again began harvesting its hoard of nuts and then scampered off.

Valerian rose from the hard ground and flexed his limbs, stretching and bending to bring life back to his aching body. He was thankful for his training as a soldier, which had accustomed him to hardships—scant food, hard beds, constant travel.

As he groomed himself, Valerian smiled, knowing the cause of his vanity. The young Celtic girl. The clothing on the ground reminded him of how much self-control it had taken not to reach out to Wynne the night before. Yet he had been strong, and had not given in to his desires, all the while yearning to bury himself deep within her golden beauty.

"Oh, if only she were a Roman. I would not hesitate to make her my wife!" he said aloud, letting himself imagine how envious all other men would be of his goddess wife. But the truth remained that Wynne was a Celt, considered a heathen by his people, as he no doubt was to hers. A gulf as wide as an ocean separated them.

Still deep in thought, Valerian began to dress in the garments his blond protector had brought, wondering at the strangeness of the clothing, further proof of the wall between their worlds. The tunic was much the same as his own, only the sleeves were much longer, falling all the way past his wrists. With a laugh Valerian realized just what a poor fit the tunic would give him, the former owner being much taller and more slender of limb. It was an amusing sight to see the sleeves hanging down nearly to the tips of his fingers. With a laugh he rolled them up so that he would have free use of his hands. A sudden feeling of anger overcame him as he wondered who the garments belonged to. Were these the clothes of her husband? After all, he did not know for certain that Wynne was unmarried; perhaps her virginal air was merely that of a shy young married woman alone with a man she did not know. Gone now was his laughter as he imagined Wynne in another man's arms.

"Fool! You have no claim to her!" he exclaimed, pounding his open hand against his fist and closing his eyes against the pain the thought brought him. "She is merely a very beautiful young woman who saved your life. She has her own life to live, a life which does not include you."

Valerian tried to wipe all thoughts of Wynne from his mind, although the nagging thought which tortured him kept coming back: soon he must be gone and would see the woman no more.

Pulling the tight-fitting trousers over his muscular thighs, Valerian fumbled with the unfamiliar drawstring at the waist. It was difficult to maintain his balance as he struggled with each leg, thrusting his foot through the opening and then pulling the pants up. In confusion he stared at the strips of material upon the ground. What were they for? A belt? A baldric? He did not know, yet supposed them to be a belt. Tying the strips around his waist, he was surprised by the sound of laughter behind him. Turning, he found Wynne standing there.

"No!" she said, pointing at the shred of cloth he held in his hand, preparing for its place around his waist. She shook her head and came toward him. Their hands brushed as she grasped the strips of material, and caused a shudder to sweep through Valerian's body. He hungered for her, but looking into her eyes at the innocence, the trust written there, he could not resolve himself to betray that to satisfy his own wanton desire.

Wynne gently wound the straps around Valerian's leg from knee to ankle, showing him how to do the other leg, crooning her strange language to him in her sweet voice. He understood few of her words and realized how futile it would be to talk to her in the dialect he had been taught in Rome.

"If we are going to communicate, I will have to teach you Latin," he said to her with a smile. Her eyes met his, and he was confused by the look he saw there. If he did not know better, he would think that her eyes were mirroring his own longing.

Wynne stared up at the Roman from her kneeling position on the ground. The feel of his firm legs under her hands was pleasant and stirred her emotions. She was embarrassed by her feelings, and afraid that they were not returned. In confusion she turned her head, rising to her feet and walking away from Valerian. The gesture returned Valerian to reality again from his fantasy of bedding the young woman. Obviously he had misinterpreted her feelings. She was merely being kind to him. No doubt she read his mind and knew his intentions. No wonder she had moved so hastily away. She must think him bold indeed to stare at her so. Again he resolved to keep his distance and to resist the temptation she presented with her soft blue eyes, golden hair, and wondrous curves. Still, for now her nearness was more than he could bear. Cursing, he ran from the cave, leaving behind a confused young woman who wondered what she had done to anger him.

"Come back, Roman!" she cried, eyes filling with tears. Running her fingers through her unbound tresses, she tried to bring some order back to her unruly mane of golden hair, as if by doing so she could win his love. Picking up the jar of food which she had put down upon the floor in order to help him dress, she followed him. Her mind was a jumble of worries, for now she knew that if the Roman did not love her, somehow a little part of her would die.

*   *   *

Riding back to the village, Wynne reflected on the day she had spent with the Roman. He had been polite but distant. Had she offended him? she wondered. Was it because she was a Celt? She had heard that the Romans considered the people of her land to be barbarians. The thought caused her pain and anger. It was the Romans who were the barbarians, coming from their land far to the south, across the wide span of the waters, gobbling up land as they marched like some great beast. Her father had seen with his very eyes the atrocities these foreigners were capable of, when Boadicea, Queen of the southern tribe of the Iceni, was defeated. Was it any wonder he hated them so? Valerian was her enemy, her people's enemy.

"No," she whispered. She could not consider him that. He was not her enemy, no matter what the others of his kind had done. She had sensed a gentleness and a kindness about him. He had praised her quickness in learning the words he had taught her today. He had smiled at her, had touched her hair in a gesture of farewell when she took her leave of him. Had called her "Minerva" again and had explained to her about the goddess of his people.

The sound of hoofbeats behind her startled Wynne out of her thoughts. Panic overcame her. She would be in danger if it were the dark-robed ones. Nudging Sloan into a full gallop, she fled, pausing only once or twice to glance back over her shoulder. Her intuition had been right—dark-cloaked figures on horse-back were following her. She must hide, using all of her instincts for survival.

Dodging in and out among the trees, Wynne retraced her tracks in order to confuse her pursuers. There had been three horses behind her; now there was only one. Guiding Sloan to a clump of trees by a small stream, Wynne quickly ducked behind a large bush, blending with the thick foliage just in time to escape from a cloaked figure who sped by on a dark brown horse.

Fear overtook her, not for herself, but for Valerian. She realized the danger he would be in if he were found, but on reflection was certain that the horsemen had not witnessed her departure from the cave. Valerian would be safe for the moment. Wynne could take no more chances, though, in coming to the cave by daylight. From now on she would have to wait until dark to see the man she was falling in love with.

"Valerian," she cried, as worry overcame her. She felt driven to return to the cave to protect him, yet knew that to do so could cause his death, for no doubt the riders were still in the forest watching for her. There was nothing to do but return to her village and wait until night-fall to go to him.

Six

Valerian stared into the light of the fire. It had been five days and nights since his capture by the heathens and his rescue by the woman called Wynne. He'd had more than enough time to regain his strength, but somehow he could not force himself to leave. He looked forward to seeing the woman each night when she brought him food. Yet he could not stay here forever; soon he would have to find his way back to his own people.

"Why is the thought of leaving so painful to me?" he asked himself, as if he did not know the answer. The fair-haired Wynne had bewitched him.

She learned so quickly, this lovely blond woman. He had taught her many words in his language, and she in turn had taught him words

53

in her native tongue. Their conversation was primitive, but it was improving day by day.

Since that first night Valerian had made no move to touch or kiss Wynne. He was afraid of frightening her. She was so shy, and he didn't even know if she liked him or not. No, he would not take the chance of offending her, not now. If he were honest with himself, he would have to admit to a certain fear, as he had never felt this way before. Women had come and gone in his life; he had sampled their charms and then said his good-byes. With Wynne he wanted something more.

A sound behind him startled him, but turning, he saw that it was Wynne. She had brought him a leg of mutton, bread, and a small keg of ale.

"Ah, Wynne. You know how to please a man," he said with a laugh, and began to eat greedily. By evening he was always starved, since Wynne now came only at night.

Valerian's hunger for Wynne's visits, however, had little to do with the food she brought. As a centurion he was used to keeping himself alive by foraging on the berries and small fowl in the forest. No, it was her company that soothed him. Looking up, he caught her eye and smiled. She shyly returned the smile, then glanced away, fearful lest he be able to read the longing in her eyes. Much to her disappointment, he had not tried to kiss her again. Perhaps he already had a wife, she thought sadly, or did not find her appealing. Yet she had tried so hard to make herself beautiful. As always, she anxiously watched the Roman for his reactions.

After quenching his thirst with the ale, Valerian stood up. How beautiful she looks tonight, he was thinking as he feasted his eyes upon her. Like many of her people, Wynne was nearly as tall as he, only about two inches shorter than his six feet. Her stature made her appear truly regal in her scarlet gown, which reached to the ground, her midriff bare. Her waist was so small that it could no doubt be spanned by his hands. Her breasts were full and he could see the tips straining against the linen of her gown. It took all his self-control not to gather her into his arms. Her slim arms, revealed by the sleeveless gown, were decorated with large gilt bracelets, twined around them. He wondered at the engraving which adorned not only these bracelets but also her necklace and brooch.

"You look lovely," he whispered.

"Thank you," she answered, knowing that he was complimenting her. Her heart quickened as she noticed his eyes savoring her body.

Valerian looked hastily away. The sight of her was too arousing. Frantically he searched for something to say to her to fill the stillness in which his own heartbeat seemed deafening.

"The food was good!" he blurted out, feeling like a fool as soon as the words had left his mouth.

"Yes. Good," she answered, wondering why he would not look at her again. She was becoming used to his language, found it pleasant to her ears. Indeed, she liked everything about this man and looked forward to their time together, although she could tell that her step-mother was becoming suspicious about her whereabouts. She looked at Valerian as he trembled. Was there something wrong with him? What if he felt ill? Worried by his strange behavior Wynne gently touched his arm.

It was if he had been burned by fire, so quickly did he draw away from her. Her touch was nearly more than he could bear, so many nights had he dreamed of her, wanting to make love to her, though he did not wish to shame her. He could not stay here, he thought again, he must leave now very soon. Besides, she had been merely kind to him. There was nothing in her manner which told him that she wanted to bed him. She had clothed him, fed him, and saved his life. Was it any fault of hers that her beauty inflamed his manhood? Overcome by feelings which were a turmoil in his heart, Valerian put his hands to his head, battling with his emotions.

"What is wrong?" Wynne whispered, hurt by his reaction to her touch. Was the Roman offended by her nearness? Did he find her ugly? She wondered what the women of his world looked like.

Seeing the hurt in her eyes, Valerian cursed himself for his stupidity. He did not want to ravish her, yet he did not want to insult her either.

"Nothing is wrong. I . . . I . . ." Searching for

words to say to her, he idly looked down at his clothing, and was struck again by this unfamiliar dress, the leg coverings bound with criss-cross strips, the tunic ending just above the knees and worn with a stout belt.

Noticing Valerian's glance at his garments, Wynne giggled, thinking that this was the cause of his distress and strange behavior. In truth he did look strange in her father's clothing, which somehow looked all wrong on the Roman.

Her laughter made Valerian relax, and he too gave in to mirth, laughing at himself and the sight he must make. "I would surely frighten my men if they were to see me now," he said. The thought of his soldiers suddenly sobered him. He had an obligation to them, too long had he let himself linger in this place.

A slight frown passed over Wynne's lips as she understood what he must be thinking. The Roman naturally wanted to return to his own people. Tears threatened to spill from her eyes at the thought of his leaving. Lest he see them, she turned away and hastily wiped at her eyes.

"Wynne, can you help me find my people?" he asked softly, wondering at her tears. Could they be for him? Was it possible that she cared for him? He felt a shiver of pleasure at the thought.

"I . . . listen . . . for any . . . word . . . of your people," she said, struggling with her emotions and slowly choosing the right words. "Not far."

"My legion not far away from here?" he questioned. "How far? A day's ride? Two?"

"Perhaps three," she answered, feeling such a sadness well up within her at the thought of his leaving that she could barely speak. Again she turned away to hide the tears which trembled on her thick lashes.

"Three days," he repeated. "If only I had a horse!" He pounded his fist against his open palm. "But they took everything away from me."

As painful as the thought of his leaving was, Wynne knew that Valerian's duty lay with his people, and the danger they would both be in if he stayed in hiding much longer was grave.

Gently she touched his shoulder. This time he did not move away from her. "Wynne will help," she whispered.

Valerian looked at her, feeling that he could happily drown in the blue pools of her eyes. To stay here with her would bring him joy; but no, he could not do so. He must return to his own kind.

"You have helped me a great deal already," he said, smiling. "I am deeply grateful. I will never forget you. Never!"

"Wynne will not forget Valerian," she answered shyly.

It took all the restraint he had ever possessed not to take her in his arms right then and there, pull her down upon the floor of the cave, plunge into her honey-sweet softness, and make her his own. Instead, he managed to move away from her once more, finding his voice. "I will need a horse."

"Valerian *has* horse," she said with a smile.

"I have a horse? Did you find my mare running loose in the woods?" He gripped her shoulders in his excitement.

Wynne did not move away from him, though his hands seemed to brand her with their heat and strength, making her tremble as her heart quivered in her breast.

"You . . . you may take Sloan," she said, fighting the tears. The animal was very dear to her, almost like a part of her, yet she would give him to Valerian in order to save his life.

It was no secret to him just how much she loved her black stallion, and the thought that she would give the horse to him overwhelmed Valerian. No one had ever given him anything before without strings attached, not even his own father. He was touched by her gift and loved her even more than before, but he could not take such a precious gift from her.

"I thank you, but no. No. I could not take from you that which you love so dearly." His voice was no more than a choked whisper.

"Take Sloan!" she insisted. "I love him. I love you also. There is danger for you . . . if . . . if you stay." She had difficulty in saying all the words, but he had understood her perfectly. *She had said that she loved him.* These words alone made his senses whirl.

"By the gods, I love you too," he groaned. He was no longer able to control his desire for her. His mouth descended upon hers, full of passion, drinking in the dew of her lips. He picked her up and carried her in his arms to the pile of furs which had become his bed. She offered no resistance as they both moved as if in a dream, touching, tasting, exploring each other, wrapped in each other's arms.

With trembling, fumbling fingers Valerian began to undress her, untying the drawstring which held up her skirt and slipping it down over her hips. He removed the short overtunic and caressed the soft warmth of her skin. Venus herself could not have been more beautiful to his eyes. Impatiently he removed his own clothing, and held her in his arms.

Valerian bent his head to the crest of her breast, suckling it with his tongue. "You taste as sweet as honey," he whispered, looking into her large blue eyes. She did not know the meaning of his words, but smiled at the loving sound of his voice. He molded his mouth to hers, and instinctively Wynne wound her arms around him, holding him tight against her, lost in the cloud of contentment which swept over her. His tongue thrust against hers as their mouths explored each other's sweet nectar.

By the light of the moon shining down upon them, Valerian admired her body, her smooth and pale breasts. He bent down and kissed them, again running his tongue over their tips until she shuddered with delight.

"I love you," he said softly.

Wynne closed her eyes and allowed herself to be consumed by his warm, soft mouth as he explored every inch of her being. When he touched her most secret place, stroking her velvety softness, she gave a start of surprise at the torment of longing she felt, wanting something, but not knowing what. Remembering the ceremony she had undergone, the pain as the Druid had severed her maidenhood to make her a woman, she tensed with fright. Would he hurt her too, this man she scarcely knew? She drew away slightly, and her eyes swept over him; his manhood was erect with his passion, a large menacing sight. Sensing her fear, he held her tightly against him. She tried to push away from him.

"No," she murmured, eyes wide with fright.

"I won't hurt you, I promise," he whispered. Valerian's kisses soothed her, made her quiver beneath his touch. His body was warm and hard and the feel of his risen manhood filled her with excitement. Any fears she had were now forgotten as her body responded with a will of its own. Instinct took over as she returned his caresses, exploring his body, feeling joy at his groans of desire.

Kneeling beside her, he kissed her belly, his mouth traveling down to the golden curls nestled between her thighs. Oh, how he longed to bury himself deep within her, but he would hold back his passion until he was certain she was as filled with fire as he.

Wynne moaned at his touch, feeling herself give way to a wild abandon. He opened her legs with gentle probing fingers, stroking the very core of her being. Again Wynne felt the longing in her loins, and her hips writhed to his touch.

"So, my golden-haired goddess, you are ready for me," he breathed as he replaced his hand with his throbbing staff. Slowly he began to thrust, igniting such a searing pleasure that she was shaken by an explosion of rapture that sent her into an abandoned frenzy. Their bodies seemed to blend, to become one.

"Val . . . Val . . ." she cried out as an aching sweetness became a shattering explosion of pleasure, the warmth spreading to the very core of her being.

Valerian gazed down upon her face, gently brushing back the hair from her eyes. From this moment on she was his. He would never share her with anyone. If only they could be together like this forever. The sadness of their parting gripped his heart.

Wynne opened her eyes and looked up at him, smiling. It had ended too soon, that exquisite blending together. She hadn't wanted him to leave her body, not ever. She felt that she had found the other half of herself, her mate for life. She reached up and traced the cleft in his chin with her finger. In answer he bent down to kiss her, his desire for her again building.

"So, goddess, you enjoy this lovemaking," he whispered. "I swear by the gods that you were meant just for me."

He began to kiss and caress her, bringing back the now familiar fire as his hot, moist mouth traced a path from one breast to the other, leaving her weak with desire. Suddenly he was inside her once more and she felt a throbbing ecstasy. This time Valerian held himself back, for he wanted Wynne to experience the full joy of her newfound womanhood. He was amply rewarded for his patience as she dropped all inhibitions, giving herself to him fully, in joy and wonder. At last a spasm shook her whole being and she seemed to be thrown into the very heavens.

Through the night they held each other, and made love again and again. It was with a heavy heart that they waited for the dawn.

Seven

When the two young lovers parted the next morning, both knew that their lives would never be quite the same again.

Valerian kissed Wynne good-bye, holding her close and fighting to hold back his own tears as he brushed away the moisture from her cheeks.

"I love you. I will come back. I swear that I will!" he vowed. "If the gods are merciful, we will meet again."

"Walk in sunshine," she said in her own language, parting from him. Her heart seemed to be bursting inside her chest; the pain seemed to be almost too much to bear. She had the impulse to run to him again, to throw her arms around him and beg him to stay, but she could not be so selfish. Perhaps someday when the animosity between their peoples was past, he would return and they could be together.

Valerian mounted the black stallion, who pawed the earth, unused to this man on his back. Wynne hurried over to whisper to the horse, to pat his head and assure him that all was well. The animal understood what she wanted and became gentle once more.

As the horse and rider galloped away, Wynne watched Valerian through the flood of her tears until he was completely out of sight. Feeling as if the end of the world had come, she sat down on a rock and sobbed her heart out. When at last her emotions were spent, she stood up and began to walk the path which would take her back to her father's lodge.

Valerian raced through the forest on Sloan's back, marveling at the animal's beauty and strength. Not even the finest horses of Rome were the black horse's match. Sloan's mane and tail streamed in the wind like a royal banner; his eyes flashed fire in the sunlight, muscles rippling under his silky hide. The Roman had no doubt that he would be able to catch up to his companions if he rode day and night, pausing only to let the animal rest when necessary. He realized that his senses must always be alert to any danger. He would never again be taken as easily as he had been that fateful night after becoming separated from his legion.

His thoughts were at war as he rode on, anxious to catch up with his legion, yet yearning to look upon Wynne's lovely face again, to hold her in his arms. She would be forever branded on his heart and soul. No other woman could ever take her place.

"Wynne!" he cried aloud. The blending of their bodies had been a forging of their hearts as well, strengthening them both in the process.

Onward the horse and rider traveled, Sloan's hooves thundering upon the ground, taking Valerian farther and farther away from the woman he loved.

Eight

With his powerful arms folded across his chest, Adair greeted his daughter upon her return to the lodge.

"And where have you been, my daughter?" he asked sternly. "Your bed was not disturbed last night. Brenna tells me that when the fire was banked you were nowhere in sight. Is this true?"

Wynne looked up into the face she so dearly loved. She could not lie to him, she never could. His blue eyes, so similar to her own, stared at her. His expression told her that he wanted her to tell him that he was wrong.

"It's true, Father. I was not in the lodge last night."

Anger flamed across his face. "Where were you?" he asked, his brows furrowed in fury.

Before she could answer, Brenna seemed to

come out of nowhere, her face set in a treacherous smile. "Adair, I'm sure Wynne has a reason. After all, this is not the first time she did not sleep with us in the lodge. There was another night as well." She swept toward her husband's daughter, standing between Wynne and her father.

"So, you disobey my laws and shame me before the entire tribe!" Adair growled.

"No, Father. It was not like that. I did not willfully disobey you. I had to do what I did."

"For what reason?" He looked into Wynne's eyes, compelling her to bare her very soul to him.

Wynne knew that she must tell him everything, make him understand her feelings. Hadn't they always been of like mind? Didn't her father also abhor unnecessary killing? And yet something made her hold back her words from him; a voice inside her head warned her to keep silent.

"I believe your Wynne has become a woman," Brenna whispered. "No doubt it was to meet her lover that she stole out into the night."

Remembering the night she had shared with her Roman lover, Wynne blushed a deep crimson.

"A lover!" Adair sputtered, grabbing his daughter's arm. "But you have been promised to Edan, son of Cedric, our chieftain. Tell me that it is not so. Tell me that you would not bring such dishonor to your father."

Wynne could not answer, for she could not lie to her father; thus her silence betrayed her.

Brenna walked over to where her husband's clothing chest stood and slowly lifted the lid. "My husband, where are your ceremonial crys and your favorite tunic? Did you take them with you to hunt?" Her eyes were all innocence.

This time Wynne could not remain silent. "I took them, Father, along with your braccae and your foot coverings."

He looked at her a long time before he spoke, his eyes full of misery. "Ah, Wynne, thus you would steal from me too, you whom I have loved beyond reason, my golden-haired child." His voice held such sadness that Wynne's heart beat in her breast like the thundering of the war chariots.

"I did no wrong. I only meant to give help to one who was in great need of aid. Father, I have seen the evil darkness cult at the edge of the forest. They sought to offer human sacrifice to their hungry god." Her eyes pleaded with him to believe her.

Brenna's shrill laughter broke the spell as Adair took his eyes from his daughter's face to look upon his wife. "Darkness cult? They have long been gone from this land. Now I fear that Wynne has been partaking of the yarrow leaf, for what else would bring such fantasies to her mind?"

"It's true. I saved a Roman from their bonds!" Wynne cried in desperation, regretting her words as soon as they had passed her lips.

"A Roman? A barbarian!" Her father was incredulous. "Is it he who has become your lover?" When she nodded, Adair raised his eyes toward the heavens. "Better that you would bed a serpent than one of our hated enemies, enemies who even now seek to strangle us, to tear our dignity from us. I will not rest until every Roman has been pushed into the sea. They will not do to us what they did to the Queen of Iceni." He clenched his fists and began to beat his breast like one demented, in the age-old gesture of mourning.

Grieved at his suffering, Wynne put her arms around his shoulders. Angrily he shrugged them off. "Father, please listen to me. Hear my story," she pleaded, tears running down her cheeks. "He was not like them!"

"They are all alike, animals!" he exclaimed. "And now you have defiled yourself with the filth of such a beast." At the sight of his weeping daughter, Adair felt a pain of remorse, and reached a hand out to comfort her.

"A Roman!" Brenna shrieked, seeing that Adair was softening. He quickly withdrew his gesture. "May the gods be merciful to us. May they protect us as the full moon descends upon us." At her reminder that the summer solstice was nearly upon them, a time of purification, Adair's anger returned in full.

"Get out of my sight. I cannot bear to look upon you," he said to Wynne.

She stared at him in horrified disbelief. Never had her father talked thus to her. Slowly she looked from her father to her gloating stepmother and then walked toward the door. Where would she go? What could she do to regain her father's love? She gathered her courage and turned toward him again.

"I have done no wrong," she said. "I have saved a human life. I have given shelter to one who was in need, and I have loved. I can find no shame in that. Be he Roman or Celt or heathen Pict, I still would love him, do love him."

"Go to your cousin's lodge until I decide what must be done," he ordered, moved by her speech and not wanting to risk any harm befalling her alone out in the forest. "I will confer with the council to decide."

Somewhere deep inside her soul, Wynne had the feeling that although she suffered anguish at this moment, all would be well on the morrow. The gods would not turn their backs on her as her father had done. At the door she hesitated and looked back at him. He would not meet her eyes, but she could tell that he was as grief-stricken as she at their angry parting. Still, being a man of pride, he could not call her back.

Feeling as if her heart had stopped beating in her breast, as if she were one of the dead, Wynne walked out into the dark of the night.

Perhaps it would be better if I *were* dead. Then I could return again quickly to this earth and not have to bear this sorrow, she thought, then shook her head. No, she must face tomorrow with bravery. Whatever happened, she would show courage, like a warrior. She made her way softly toward the lodge of her mother's sister's son.

*   *   *

Wynne spent three nights in the dwelling of Tyrone, her cousin. It seemed that to her father she had died, for he sent no word to her concerning her fate. Then, when she had begun to fear the worst—that she was never to be forgiven—he sent word to her that no judgment would be made until after the festival of the sun. That she would be allowed to attend set her mind at ease. At least she was not to be banished from the tribe.

Isolde, her cousin's wife, was a pleasant-enough companion in the days she spent away from her own hearth. Although woman's work had never much interested her, she found that without Brenna there to constantly berate her efforts, she could tolerate the spinning, weaving, and cooking.

She had a fondness for Isolde, for it was she, not Brenna, who had been with her at the ceremony which had taken her maidenhead and made her into a woman who could now be betrothed. Isolde had calmed her fears, held her hand when the membrane had been severed, and dried her tears when it was all over.

Now and again she could see a questioning look come into Isolde's eyes, a look of sympathy, and she knew that no matter what she might have done, no matter how much she would be cursed in others' eyes, Isolde would always be her friend.

"You always have a home with us. I want you

to know that," Isolde said to her one evening as the family sat around the fire.

"I know that, and I thank you, Isolde. And you too, Tyrone," Wynne answered. She was holding the couple's son Llewellyn. The baby tried to suckle at her covered breast, and she laughed. "No. I think you must have your mother for that," she said with a smile. Cradling the baby filled her with a longing to have a child of her own, Valerian's child.

She thought about the Roman, wondering what he was doing, if he were safe.

"Valerian," she murmured, forgetting for the moment where she was.

"What did you say?" Tyrone asked.

"Nothing . . . I . . . I was just thinking aloud," she whispered, looking down again at the child she held in her arms.

· Her quiet reserve, the faraway look in her eyes, unnerved her mother's sister's son. What had happened to the boisterous young woman who frolicked about laughing and joyful like a lad? Somehow she seemed more womanly to him now. Was it true, then, what was being said of her?

"I do not understand you, cousin. You are not as before," Tyrone said sternly. Looking up, Wynne found him staring at her with his piercing eyes, eyes which nevertheless held kindness. She wondered if he had been told that she had bedded a Roman. How could she make him understand that love knew no boundaries or tribes, that she could not help loving the Roman any more than she could stop herself from breathing in the air of life?

"Leave her alone, Tyrone. Wynne has suffered enough these last few days. It is not for you to judge her," Isolde interrupted, gently taking the baby. The tone of her voice told Wynne that she understood and knew herself what it was to love beyond reason.

Tyrone answered his wife's words with an angry glare at being rebuked, and stalked out of the lodge, pausing only to remind them about the coming festival. "Tomorrow night is the eve of the full moon," he said. "When the ceremony is over, Wynne must be chastised for her transgression. It is the law of our people." With that he was gone from the lodge.

A shiver of fear ran through Wynne's body at his words. She wondered just what her punishment would be. Yet, no matter what happened, she must be brave.

"So, tomorrow the festival begins," Isolde exclaimed, breaking into Wynne's reverie. Her gently hand touched Wynne's shoulder. "Do not fear, your father will see that you are treated fairly. The laws of the Druids are just."

Wynne knew that Isolde spoke the truth, and she also knew in her heart that no matter what happened to her, what punishment she was forced to suffer, she would not trade for one moment that night she had spent in Valerian's arms. It was worth a lifetime. Someday she would see him again.

Nine

The sky was a blaze of light as the gods threw down their lightning bolts like spears from out of the heavens. Valerian looked up at the dark clouds with a feeling of frustration. What else could go wrong to hinder his journey? Already he had been riding more than a week and still had not been able to catch up with his cavalry. It was as if they had vanished from sight. And now once again he would have to stop.

"Easy, Sloan," he commanded. He still marveled at the beauty, grace, and strength of the horse. Like Wynne, he was now able to control the animal with the lightest of touches on the reins.

Coming to the shelter of a ruined building, Valerian guided the horse inside. The roof was in disrepair, but it would shelter them for the night. He looked inside the leather sack that he carried to see what was left of the provisions that Wynne had given him and was not surprised to find that he had only a small piece of bread, most likely moldy by this time, a half flagon of ale, and a morsel of dried deer meat.

Wynne had done what she could for him; it was only that neither one of them had envisioned such a long journey.

"Wynne." He said her name reverently. How many times these dark cold nights had he dreamed of her, ached to hold her in his arms. If only he could have taken her with him. He smiled to think of what an impression she would make in Rome, where blonds were rare. Surely the emperor himself would think her a goddess, as he had done that magical night. No woman could ever compare with her. Her beauty was breathtaking. Someday he would return for her, take her to see the splendor of Rome. He wondered what she was doing at this very moment— talking and laughing with her tribesmen around the fire, no doubt, listening to the tales of valor and legends of the gods.

Valerian wolfed down the food. He had become spoiled while in Wynne's care, acquiring a taste for meat. The food in the legion camp was simple—bread or porridge, some vegetables, sour wine; rarely did they eat animal flesh. He thought about the days he had spent as a soldier. They had been a bittersweet experience. It had been his father's choice for him, as the third son. He had been educated for war from childhood, had studied military art, and spent ten years of his life in the field, yet he would never get used to the killing. It was not in his heart.

"Perhaps when this business with the Britons is over I can think about another life, a life without constant battle," he said aloud.

Self-consciously he tugged at the hair at the nape of his neck. It had grown quite long. He felt his now bearded face. He had not had a chance to shave himself, and as for bathing, why, surely he would offend the vilest heathen.

"I must look just like a Pict," he thought with a grimace. How he loathed those barbarians of the North. Had they not been almost more than a match for Caesar himself? Well, at least he was warm and dry in his braccae and tunic. Reaching for his cloak, he fashioned himself a bed and lay down to catch a nap before he must start out again.

The rain pounded upon the roof of the dwelling, lulling him to sleep. The air was damp, chilly, and brisk. Drawing his cloak around him, he fell into a deep slumber, seeing again the flawless face of his golden-haired lover.

Valerian was rudely awakened from sleep by the pressure of something on his chest. Through the veil of awareness he could hear the whinny of Sloan and reached for his sword.

"Not so fast, barbarian!" ordered a gruff voice. He found himself staring into the faces of several Roman infantrymen. His sword was kicked aside and picked up by a grinning youth who looked to be just barely out of the schoolroom.

In anger he struggled with his captors, three brawny men who held his legs and arms to the ground.

"My, my, my, our heathen friend certainly can put up a fight, eh, Darius?" said a tall soldier, laughing. Valerian realized how he must look to their eyes, dressed as he was, and with his straggly beard and uncut hair.

"I'm not a barbarian. I'm a Roman soldier," he answered angrily, seeing for the first time just how ruthless his countrymen could be.

"And I'm Julius Caesar come back to life!" said another soldier sarcastically, giving Valerian such a hard kick to his ribs that he cried out in pain. "Let's see if he is carrying anything of value on him."

While Valerian watched in outraged silence, they searched his possessions, very meager to say the least. Only his sword was of any value.

"I see you killed a Roman and stole his sword!" growled a leathery-faced man with small beady eyes. He looked at him as if he would murder him right then and there.

"I am a Roman soldier, I tell you. My name is Valerian Quillon Tullius, son of Publius Quillon Tullius, a senator of Rome!" Valerian met the man's beady eyes with blazing anger in his own.

The tall soldier looked him up and down and let go of his legs. "He does speak perfect Latin," he said loudly, "but why is he dressed the way he is?"

Seeing that their attention was diverted for a moment, Valerian kicked viciously with his legs, knocking both his captors aside. Reaching out for his sword, he took the young beardless youth by surprise. Brandishing his sword with a grace which spoke of his prowess, he held the small band of men at bay.

"Now, listen to what I say to you. I am Valerian Quillon, centurion of the tenth century. I became separated from my men and came into the hands of a group of barbarians. I escaped with my life and my sword and that is all, and I consider myself fortunate to still be breathing." All eyes were turned toward him as he talked. "I want you to lead me to Severus Cicero. Do you understand me?"

All heads nodded their assent, fearful now, for they knew him to be telling the truth and dreaded his anger, for a Roman officer was able to demand the most severe of punishments.

"We were to join with him ourselves," piped up the youth, who now viewed Valerian as a hero.

The leathery-faced soldier tried to smile, but managed only a grimace. "Pardon us for thinking you one of the Picts, but you must admit that you look the part. However, let's let bygones be. We are, after all, each of us Romans. We'll take you where you want to go."

"Let's get on with our journey then," Valerian replied, lowering his sword but keeping a firm hand on it as he mounted Sloan. He had learned a lesson well this day. He had found out what it was like on the opposite side, to be a Pict or a

Celt. Surely these men had posed just as real a danger to him as the members of the darkness cult had. He had no doubt that it was still possible to end up with his throat slit from ear to ear. As long as the journey took, he would be forced to sleep with one eye open, listen to each and every sound, and always keep his guard up until he reached his destination. Somehow Valerian now felt less Roman, and for the first time began to question their way of life and the empire he was fighting for.

Ten

Wynne awoke early the next morning before the first light. She quietly got down from the bedshelf so as not to waken the others and moved on soundless feet to the doorway. She had the overpowering urge to run to the forest, to greet the golden rays of the sun alone in the place which was so special to her, but to do so might fire her father's wrath once more.

The thought of her father filled her with a mixture of emotions. Fear of his anger, love for the gentle man he had always been until she had angered him, and most of all pride. Her father was one of the Druids, the Bard, a poet of great renown among her people for his singing and storytelling. Among her people, eloquence was valued as highly as bravery, for just as the warrior protected his tribe, so the bard protected the tribal history in his memory.

Had I been a male child, I too would have become a Druid, she thought, learning the laws and mysteries of the sky, the force of the moon and stars upon the fate of men, or perhaps I would have been chosen like my father to sing the glories of life. Lost in her dreams, she closed her eyes. Had it not been said that she had inherited a voice of much beauty from her father? Many times she had wished to be a male child, but no more—not since meeting Valerian. Shrugging her shoulders, she turned away from the open door.

"I am not my father's son, but his daughter, and for that I am glad!" she said aloud. She gloried in her womanly body as she dressed. "For I have what no man possesses, the power to create life within me. Surely there is no power greater than this." She touched her stomach and again said a silent prayer to bear a child as the fruit of her love for Valerian. At least then she would always have a part of him with her.

Hearing a rustle behind her, she turned around and was greeted with Isolde's warm smile. "Sunshine on your head, cousin."

"Thank you, Isolde. May the goddess touch your eyes with light," she responded, in the ceremonial words always spoken on this day of days.

Together they prepared the morning meal, which would break the fast, putting together in a large caldron a mixture of grains that had been ground together in a hand mill. No meat had passed their lips for several days, nor would any again until after the ceremony. In this way they purified their bodies. Nevertheless, the aroma from the cooking pot caused Wynne's mouth to water; she was starving.

"I'll go gather some berries if you will milk the goat," Isolde said with a toss of her blond curls. "You seem to have a way with animals. Me, I always seem to get my toes stepped on, or worse yet, bitten."

With a laugh Wynne went about her chore, which, far from being unpleasant to her, made her feel closer to the goddess, the bringer of life.

Wynne returned to the lodge with the warm milk, which she poured into large earthenware cups for Isolde's two older children, who drank greedily. When Isolde returned with her berries, the two women spread a large cloth over the floor so that they could honor the earth goddess. Upon this cloth Wynne spread the fine brass utensils with the intricate designs and animal figures etched on the handles. She always marveled at the work the artisans had done.

They placed the huge silver caldron containing the grains mixed with special herbs in the center of the table. This urn too was ornamented with curving tendrils, entwining plants, animals, and faces of the gods and goddesses. Silver was the most precious of metals, treasured even more highly than gold.

Tyrone came to join in the feast, greeting his wife and Wynne with a smile. Forgotten were his harsh words of the night before, yet Wynne knew by the look in his eyes that in his heart he still condemned her for causing her father's anger.

Seated on either side of their father, Selma and Farrell grinned impishly, knowing that since the women would be occupied with preparations for the evening ceremony, it would be Tyrone's duty to look after them. It amused them to witness his frustration at their antics. They looked longingly at the tempting berries in the basket, then at each other, and they quickly stifled a giggle as their father began to chant over the food.

Tyrone closed his eyes as he gave thanks to the gods for the bounty of the grains before them, for the nectar of the water of life. It was at this moment that Farrell could wait no longer to taste the tart fruit and stretched out his hand to snatch a handful of the bright red berries. Without pausing, Tyrone glared at his errant son, who, seeing the fire in his father's eyes, quickly replaced the fruit.

When the family had finished eating, both Isolde and Wynne went to dress in their finest gowns of gold and blue, colors that symbolized the summer sky.

"You look so lovely, Wynne," Isolde whispered. "Oh that I had your beauty."

Wynne wore a midnight-blue undergown that almost reach her ankles, and a sleeveless overgown of gold. She had braided blue ribbons into her two plaits. Her belt was of gold, as was her neck torc and finger rings and many bracelets. Like many of her people, she would go barefoot so that there would be nothing between her and the mother earth.

Again Wynne thought longingly of her father. "This will be the first festival in which I have not helped Adair don his white robe, nor anointed him with the sacred oil from the leaves of the oak tree," she said to Isolde. The anguish at their parting still tore at her heart.

In sympathy Isolde gently touched her shoulder. "Give your father time. He will again welcome you to his fire. The punishment will not be severe. Our people are just. It is only his hatred for the Romans which blinds his eyes and causes him to shun you."

"Yes, his hatred is strong. He fears that they seek to destroy our ways. Oh, if only he could see as I do that they are not all evil."

"You are thinking of your Roman," Isolde answered with a smile. She too feared these people from the South, yet if Wynne loved one of them, they could not be too fearsome. The memory of whisperings she had heard came to her mind. "Tell me, is it true what I've heard, that they worship their gods inside large lodges?"

Wynne nodded her head. "Valerian told me that their gods are kept in dwellings they call . . . temples." For a moment Valerian's face came to her, the look on his face when first he had seen her bending over him. "He thought *me* to be one of his goddesses. Minerva," she said softly.

"Minerva," Isolde repeated, then shook her head. "How could these Romans believe that the gods are in human form or believe the great forces which created this world and the stars beyond could be worshiped in manmade dwellings? It is strange." Isolde laughed and picked up her comb, running it through her blond curls. For the moment each woman was silent as they continued in their preparations for the night's ceremony.

When at last the night descended upon the earth, Wynne followed Isolde to the sacred oak grove. In the clearing Wynne could see the white-robed Druids assembled and wondered which of the figures was her father. Each Druid carried the golden sickle, which was used to cut the sacred mistletoe, and which had become a symbol of their power.

Wynne felt Isolde taking her hand, and grasped it firmly, joining in one of the three circles of worshipers in the grove. Three was the magical number to her people, symbolizing birth, life, and death, a never-ending circle which continued throughout eternity. Death was only a sleep, and when that sleep came upon one, it would be but a brief time until the spirit would be born again in a new body.

"And so it begins," Isolde whispered reverently.

"Never-ending. One eternal circle . . . today, tomorrow, yesterday, and forever," Wynne replied, feeling as if she were being joined together with all the powerful forces of nature. She could hear her father's voice, clear and strong, as he began his singing.

The seasons are never-ending.
The circle of life flows on.
The mysteries and miracles of wisdom
Encompass us with the dawn.

Wynne gripped Isolde's hand tightly and felt another worshiper grip her other hand. The ritual continued with songs of transformation and rebirth, the summer solstice, the festival of Lugh, when nature attains perfection. The bare and cold ground of winter now wreathed in the bright new green was bejeweled with the dew of life.

"Everywhere man turns, he sees the blessing of rebirth," the congregation echoed.

"The wheel of the heavens turns and brings seedtime and harvest, heat and cold, light and darkness," her father sang out.

Wynne's senses were dulled to the rest of the ceremony, for as she looked toward the huge hand that held her left hand, she gasped. It was he, the man she had grappled with the night she had found Valerian. Even without his strange symbols, she could recognize him, so strongly was his face etched on her memory. Now he was staring at her with hate-filled eyes.

Wynne opened her mouth, but before she could speak, the man fled. Fear touched her heart. The circle had been broken by his departure; the omen bade her tribesmen no good.

Eleven

"*Quickly, take my hand,*" *a voice intoned in her* ear. She looked up into the eyes of Edan, the man her father had betrothed her to. She was relieved that the broken circle would not now be noticed, for it would greatly trouble the worshipers. Isolde still clung to her right hand, her eyes closed as she chanted.

I am not an object to be given away! Wynne thought vehemently. I should have some say in who I take to my bed. Yet such was the custom of her tribe.

Edan's hand was warm and strong. She turned to look upon him, her childhood friend. With his red hair and gray eyes, he was so different from Valerian. Like all the men of her tribe, Edan wore his hair long and had a long moustache. Even his skin was different from the Roman's, not golden, but ruddy, freckled. Edan was handsome in his own way and she was fond of him, though she had long resented having her future bound to a man without her consent. But that didn't matter anymore—now she belonged to the Roman.

Wynne breathed a sigh of relief that the circle was again intact, but the question still echoed through her mind. Who was the giant of a man who had so frightened her, and why was he at the ceremony? Was he from a neighboring village? He was not one of her own tribesmen, of that she was certain.

Whoever he is, I must tell my father what I have seen. They must find him. Perhaps he can lead us to the sacrificial worshipers before the dark ones cause trouble for my people. It was because of such as they that the Romans believed that the Celtic peoples practiced human sacrifice. In truth they had not done so for generations, but still the lies persisted, the flames of hatred fanned by the bloodlust of the evil ones.

"With every bit of strength I have in my body, I vow I will stop them," she said beneath her breath, closing her eyes in a silent prayer to the gods.

The ritual continued long into the night, until Wynne was exhausted and longed for sleep. Yet it was always thus, for the worshipers must meet the dawn, welcome the light of the sun. Soon it would be time for a symbolic sacrifice to be made. The one who had been chosen as the bridegroom for the Goddess of the Water of

Life would be placed on a raft, arms outstretched to greet the goddess. He must be a chaste young man who had never lain with a woman. His life would be his own after tonight, but there was a time long ago when the sacrificial victim had been given to the goddess for eternity, to sleep the slumber of death within her arms. Symbolic sacrifices were also made for other festivals. At the winter ceremony of Samhain, a young man would again be chosen, this time to be buried in the earth, for earth and water were feminine powers. At the spring equinox—the ceremony of fire, called Beltaine—and at the autumn equinox—called Imbolc, the ceremony of air—the symbolic sacrifice would be a virgin girl, for both fire and air were masculine powers.

Wynne felt Edan's hand tighten on her own. "Ah, it is to be the son of Regan," Edan said with pride, for the young man chosen was his nephew.

"He is a strong warrior. You should be proud," Wynne whispered, clinging tightly to his hand.

"I remember when it was I who was given the honor," Edan reflected with a faraway look in his eyes, "the bridegroom of the goddess, though I yearn to be your husband now, Wynne." His eyes bored into hers and in sadness she looked away.

Like a leaf in the wind, the raft floated on the rippling lake as the sound of singing filled the stillness. Wynne smiled for the first time since the ceremony had begun, happy for the young boy. She was filled with a sense of peace. Now all would be well. Forgotten for the moment was the face of the evil man.

The ceremony came to an end and Wynne's heart leapt in her breast when she was called to stand before the Council of the Druids.

"So, daughter of Adair, you have lain with a pagan, a Roman," one of the Druids began, an old man with white hair and mustache. "Do you deny this?"

"I have lain with the man that I love," she answered boldly, meeting her father's eyes. She could see his anguish.

"Do you not repent of this folly?" the old man asked with a scowl.

"I do not repent, nor am I sorry. I gave my body and my heart out of love. There can be no stronger law than the law of love. The gods themselves must surely find favor with what I have done," Wynne answered unflinchingly.

The seven Druids were silent as Wynne stood before them with her chin up, her shoulders back. She would go to her fate with courage.

"Of course there could be a child," one of the younger Druids murmured. Wynne closed her eyes as if willing it to be so.

"I have promised my daughter's hand to Edan, son of Cedric," Adair exclaimed, looking so crestfallen that for a moment Wynne felt pity for him. She had not meant to cause him pain and had always been a dutiful daughter, but she could not help falling in love.

The old Druid pulled at the ends of his mustache, deep in thought. "We will have to first find out if there is to be a babe," he said. "If not, after she is purified she will indeed wed with Edan. If there is a child, that child will be raised in the house of Adair as his own."

"And my daughter?" Adain asked anxiously. "If there is a babe?"

"She will remain unmarried for the rest of her life," the old Druid answered. "In the meantime, daughter of Adair, you are to live in the small lodge at the edge of the village as an outcast for one month until the moon is full again."

Wynne gasped. One entire month of solitude.

"You will see no one except for those who will bring food and water to you during your confinement, nor are you to go outside in the light of day nor darkness of the night. When sufficient time has passed, we will know your fate concerning the fertileness of your belly." The old Druid's eyes were devoid of pity. The laws must be obeyed.

Wynne put her face in her hands and wept. She would be as a caged animal for one full cycle of the moon, away from her own lodge, away from her people, from Isolde, her father.

Yet if I bear my child, it is not too much to suffer, she told herself. Wiping the tears from her face she again lifted her chin, proudly, defiantly. She would endure this punishment with dignity and grace. For just a moment her eyes met those of her father again and she knew that he wept for her in his soul. She managed a slight smile for him which told him of her forgiveness. It had been his duty to do what he had done. She could not have asked him to do otherwise.

"I am ready, Father," she whispered. Together they walked the path to the lodge, where he left her. With a sigh she began to make preparations for her confinement.

"Wynne. Wynne," she heard Edan call to her, and looking up, she saw him running toward her. He came to her and reached for her hand, bringing it to his face as he had done when they were children.

"No matter what may have happened, know that I will marry you. I will wait for you forever if necessary. You have been promised to me. I have always known that you would be my wife." Edan knelt before her as if to seal his pledge.

Wynne looked down upon him. She had never meant to hurt him and hoped that he would understand. "I cannot marry you, Edan. I love another," she whispered, pulling her hand away.

Edan shook his head, undaunted by her words. "I will not listen. You will be my wife, the gods have told me so." With this spoken, he turned and left her. She felt so lonely and so forsaken. Closing her eyes, she could see Valerian's face before her eyes and said a prayer for his safety. If the gods willed it, she would be with him again.

Twelve

From the highest point of the hill, the Roman military tribune could see the approach of the small band of men, still so far away that they were no more than dust clouds.

"If they be Celts, they have not long to live!" he vowed. He had never liked the blond barbarians, nor this cold country of Britain. Until these rebellious heathens were subdued, however, he would have to be satisfied with mere dreams of the land of his birth.

The tribune's cold blue eyes again looked out across the land. Riding beside one of his centurions, he urged his horse onward, back to the camp. He had still not had time to write a letter to his old friend Publius informing him of the tragic fate of his son, Valerian, missing after being separated from his men during a storm in the northwest. No doubt by now his head was adorning some Celtic wall as a trophy.

"Ah, well. Such is war!" he said to himself.

Dismounting from his horse, he walked around the tents of the camp. The camp was celebrating victory over one of the Celtic tribes. The soldiers were allowed to share in the booty from the defeated peoples—including, of course, women.

Going to his own tent, the tribune ran greedy fingers through his new treasures: fine tall ornamented bronze helmets, a fine wrought sword, several bracelets and rings of silver, as well as several pieces of fine cloth. These wild brutes were skilled in making many things.

Suddenly a young soldier rushed headlong into the tent. "Tribune! A band of soldiers is approaching. They have a Pict with them!"

"A Pict? Where on earth would they find one of those savages so far south?" Severus Cicero exclaimed. The tribune was clearly annoyed at the interruption, still he followed the young man out of the tent to where the horsemen even now were approaching. So these were the riders he had seen from the hill.

Severus eyes the ragged band with distaste. They looked like deserters. If that were true, he would have them returned to their general, who would most likely have their right hands cut off, the usual judgment against deserters or thieves. One rider impressed him, however, on a magnificent black horse. The man was dressed as a Celt but his black hair bespoke Pict heritage. Of all these men he was the only one who sat tall and straight in the saddle.

The band was close enough now that the tribune could make out their features. A hard stare from amber-colored eyes, eyes Severus remembered so well, met his own.

"Valerian," he exclaimed.

With a grin Valerian dismounted and strode forward.

Severus grabbed the dark-haired man firmly by the shoulders. "So, you young stallion, you have come back to us. Unharmed, I see, except for perhaps a little change in your clothing." His eyes raked over Valerian; then he laughed. "Well, welcome back!"

Together they walked back toward the tribune's large tent. "I thought you were lost to us." Again he looked at Valerian. "Please tell me what you are doing dressed like that."

"I . . . well . . . borrowed these clothes," Valerian said rather sheepishly. "Remind me to tell you the entire story sometime. It is unbelievable."

"You were forced into battle with a heathen, and when he was the loser, you stole his clothes so as to provide you with a safe journey?" Severus questioned with raised eyebrows.

Valerian shook his head. "No. Let's just say that I was aided in my return by a beautiful Celt woman who puts Venus herself to shame. I thought at first that she was Minerva. She was magnificent! You see, she—" He had no chance to continue.

"A Celtic woman. No doubt a dirty unwashed

heathen. Did she have heads hanging from her belt?" the tribune asked sarcastically. "Ah, well, not all of us are fortunate to find Romanized barbarians who have come to appreciate our tradition of the bathhouse, eh, Valerian?" The corners of his mouth turned up in a smirk.

Valerian was filled with rage. To have this grinning fool talk so about his Wynne, his sweet Wynne, who smelled of violets and summer air. With enormous effort, he wisely kept his temper in check, calming himself with the thought that he would one day bring Wynne here and let this Roman see real beauty.

"She was not a heathen," Valerian said quietly.

"They are all oafish and unkempt barbarians, unable to speak a civilized language or to write any language at all," Severus barked. How he hated them.

Valerian remembered the enchantment he had felt listening to Wynne's sweet voice. No longer could he restrain himself. "You call them 'barbarian,' and yet as I recall, the word itself was coined by the Greeks from the stammering ba-ba-ba sounds uttered by those they considered too uncouth to learn Greek—including, I might say, us Romans." He forced a smile.

Severus gave Valerian an icy glare. He had been long envious of this young centurion's looks and bearing, but after a time he smiled. "Ah, Valerian. Always the wit. At times I think that you are too educated for this soldier's life." Taking his arm, he guided Valerian into his tent. "We are going to have a real feast tonight, a banquet to welcome you back. And right now, how would you like a nice hot bath?"

"Need you ask?" Valerian chuckled. For the moment his anger at the tribune was gone.

"Tonight you may have anything you want," Severus promised with a sly smile. He left the tent to Valerian and sent for slaves to see to the centurion's needs.

Fresh from his bath, Valerian stretched his arms and breathed deeply. It felt so good to be clean. He had been shaved, his hair had been cropped to its usual length, and he felt Roman again. Standing in his loincloth, he reached for the cup of wine brought to him by one of the slaves, a young boy black as ebony with teeth like ivory. Severus had found him during his campaigns in Egypt. Valerian felt pity for the boy, who had the bearing of a prince and no doubt had been royalty in his own country. To be reduced to slavery must be a bitter cup to drink.

Valerian had always been uneasy about keeping slaves, human beings treated as objects, possessions over whom the slave owner had the legal power of life and death. Still, Rome had been built on the backs of these slaves.

The slave boy handed Valerian his short tunic, but before he had a chance to put it on, he heard the sound of footsteps behind him. Turning, he saw a young girl standing before him. She was barely more than a child, though beautiful, with red-gold hair and eyes like jade.

"I have been sent by Tribune Severus Cicero to please you," she whispered in a trembling voice. As he looked at her, she cast her eyes toward the ground.

Valerian studied the girl. She was lovely, her breasts just beginning to blossom, her hips curved, her waist small. She was wearing only the sheerest chiton, which clung to her slim body.

Hesitantly the girl started toward him, remembering what she had been told to do to please him. She started to wind her arms around his neck, but stopped when he held her away from him.

"What is your name, child?" he asked gently.

"Meghan," she answered softly.

"Where do you come from? Are you of the Celtic peoples?"

"Yes," she answered, trying to control the tears which threatened to spill out of her large eyes. "My people have always been friendly to you Romans. My father was made chief of our tribe by your soldiers because he spoke your language."

"Then how did you become a slave?" Valerian asked.

She shook her head sadly, and this time could not control the tears which rolled down her cheeks and sparkled like diamonds in the firelight.

"My father attempted to save his wife from being ravished by a drunken soldier, and for that he was punished. When the soldier died of his wounds, my father was beheaded and my mother and I were sold as slaves."

The story was not an unfamiliar one. Valerian had heard of such things happening before, for Rome protected its own and felt that the death of a barbarian did not matter.

The girl looked at him again and dried her tears. Something about her reminded Valerian of Wynne. Perhaps it was the full mouth or the shape of the nose or her graceful bearing. What if this were Wynne standing here before a soldier, awaiting her doom?

"Go back to your tent, child," he ordered.

Meghan threw herself at his feet, weeping hysterically. "I do not please you. Oh, what can I do? I will be whipped and then given to that brute Gallus."

Valerian lifted her gently from the floor. "You do please me. Very much. But you are so young and, I would guess, a virgin." She nodded. Severus was generous with his gifts, he thought sarcastically. "You deserve better than to be used merely for a man's lust. Someday you will give your heart to a man and will want to give him your body," he said, thinking of Wynne again. Until he had met her he had not believed that love existed. Perhaps had he not met her, he would have lain with this girl, like the callous soldiers of his army. But Wynne opened his eyes to what was going on around him, and his love for her had shown him how to know right from wrong, love from lust.

"Then you will not say that you were not pleased with me?" she asked.

"No. I will tell Severus that you pleased me a great deal. As a matter of fact, I intend to buy you, lovely Meghan, to keep you from harm until you grow into the beautiful woman I envision."

Her eyes glowed with happiness at the thought of belonging to this Roman, who seemed to be a man of honor. He was gentle and pleasing to the eyes—not old and cruel and ugly like the tribune Severus. She reached for his hand and rained kisses upon it.

"Thank you," she breathed.

Valerian bid her to rise, embarrassed by her display of gratitude. Gently he pushed her away from him. "Go now, Meghan!" he ordered. She ran on silent feet out of the tent, pausing at the opening to look back at him and smile. Then she left.

Valerian finished dressing, putting his cuirass over his red woolen tunic. It was strange to again feel the weight of the gilded overlapping metal scales, to feel the stroke of the leather strips against his thighs. He bent down to lace his white leather boots over his woven hose and slung the baldric of studded leather over his shoulder. Picking up his bronze helmet, he walked toward the opening of the tent. He would talk with Severus this very moment about the girl Meghan.

On his way out of the tent he noticed a small

fire and made his way over to where it crackled. He could smell the odor of burning cloth.

"What are you doing, soldier?" he asked in curiosity.

"The tribune ordered us to burn the clothing you were wearing when you came here," the soldier answered.

"No!" Valerian shouted, and he dashed forward, reaching into the fire like one demented. He felt that in some way these clothes brought him closer to Wynne, that their destruction would injure her in some way. It was as if burning them was a bad omen.

It was too late. The clothes that had belonged to his beloved's father were now no more than ashes. Valerian clutched at his burned hand, but the real pain was in his heart. He had planned to bring these garments back to Wynne when he returned.

The two soldiers eyed him warily. One motioned with his finger, moving it in circles around his temple to indicate that he thought the centurion was crazy, but Valerian didn't care what they thought. He cursed them beneath his breath.

A sudden scream tore through the stillness, sending shivers up and down Valerian's spine.

"What in the name of the gods was that?" he asked one of the men.

"Nothing. Merely the rantings of our Celtic prisoner. The noble Severus has ordered that the heathen be tortured slowly, so that we can make an example of him for all those who would fight against Rome," one of the soldiers answered with less emotion than if he were talking about a dog.

"And we call them heathens!" Valerian exclaimed in shock. He had not been in this land long, but he was fast learning. He wondered if Nero in Rome knew what was happening. Surely this was no way to bring about peace, and yet he remembered hearing of brutalities done to the Israelites and to those called Christians. "Does Nero know what is happening?"

The soldier looked warily at him again. This centurion was a strange one. What did he think war was all about—pleasant conversation and marching all day long? But then, coming from a wealthy family, how could he know what life was all about? His father had no doubt bought his son into his present position. The dark-haired centurion had probably never even been in battle. In disgust he spat upon the ground.

"Severus knows what is best," he said coldly, his eyes glinting dangerously. He wanted to keep this young upstart in his place. "*He* is the ruler of this land, not Nero. Why, the general himself has left the tribune in charge while he is gone to the North. Severus doesn't have to answer to anyone!"

The truth of the man's words hit Valerian like a stone from a catapult. Why had he not realized before this just how power-hungry the tribune was? He looked in anger upon the soldier, yet his true anger was with Severus and even more with himself. How could he have been so blind? How could he have misjudged the man so? Severus was cruel, unthinking, and dangerous. Valerian wondered what would happen if he himself were to get in the tribune's way.

He would not hesitate to remove me from his path, father or no father, he thought.

Now more than ever, Valerian longed for Wynne and the days they had spent together. With her he had been happy and at peace.

Thirteen

That night, just as Severus had promised, there was indeed a banquet to welcome Valerian back. They feasted on wild boar, steaming soup with a pungent herblike odor, pheasant, and even oysters. Rich wines ran to waste as cups were overfilled. Severus had ordered a special tent set up for the festivities, and Valerian could see the remains of the spoils his legion had awarded themselves. Severus lounged on a pillowed couch like royalty, clapping his hands for the slaves to appear and leering boldly at the dancing girls. Like Meghan, these were often mere children who had been abducted from their families for the purpose of quenching the lust of the soldiers and keeping their passions finely tuned with the swaying of their luscious bodies to the music of harp and flute. Valerian was given the seat of honor near his host, and he could not help but wonder if all of this was really for him or for the purpose of Severus ingratiating himself with Valerian's father, a powerful senator in Rome. It was no secret that Severus was very ambitious.

"So, you liked the young girl I sent to you, eh?" he asked, grabbing the wrist of one of the dancers, a dark-haired girl with blue eyes. He pressed her close to him for a kiss and then returned his attentions once again to Valerian. "For the right price I might be persuaded to let you have her."

"What price is that?" Valerian asked cautiously.

"That black stallion of yours. Perhaps I would consider it an even trade. What do you say?" Severus gobbled greedily on a drumstick.

Valerian shook his head. "Ask anything else of me but that. It is not really mine to give."

"That is my price," Severus demanded. "Here, have another cup of wine."

Valerian frowned. This was going to be more difficult than he had imagined. But already Severus was half-drunk, and perhaps this could work to Valerian's advantage. He must be careful not to allow himself to drink too much, while all the time making it appear that he too was far from sober.

"Wine, wine," Severus demanded, flinging out his arm and causing the poor black boy to spill the flask all over the tribune. In outrage he struck the boy hard across the face, sending him sprawling to the dirt floor. "Take this black dog out and have him flogged within an inch of his life!" Severus screamed in rage. The boy was grabbed from behind by two soldiers and dragged from the tent, much to Valerian's consternation. He wondered how he could have been so blind to such happenings before. He knew that this was not an unusual occurrence.

"Tribune, are you certain that you want to have such a fine specimen ruined by scars?" he asked, trying hard to save the lad. "If you do so, he will cease to have as much value to you."

Severus eyed him with half-closed eyes. "Value? Ah, yes, I suppose you are right. However, the dog must be punished." He motioned the men back. "Turn the slave over to the centurion here for retribution." Again he turned to Valerian. "I sense that you are changed somehow. I hope that you aren't getting soft, Valerian. Oh, well, we shall see . . . we shall see. It will amuse me to see what sort of discipline you can wreck on Ibu."

Valerian sensed danger in his words. He was being tested. It would be difficult to be merciful to the boy and yet appear to be masterful, but somehow he would manage it.

"My father has always taught me that hard work and responsibility are the keys to discipline. Give him to me for a few months to act as my stable boy, and I promise you that his arrogance will turn to worthiness."

"Agreed, after he receives at least ten lashes."

Valerian was disappointed, but he let the matter rest. "Now . . . about the slave girl, Meghan.

Is there nothing I can do to convince you that I must have her?"

Severus laughed. "She must be a lusty one in bed. I will have to try her charms myself."

Valerian nearly choked on his wine, biting his tongue to keep from lashing out at the tribune. It would take all his cunning to get the girl out of the old goat's clutches now. He cursed himself for ten kinds of fool. Seeing several soldiers involved in a game of dice, he had an idea.

"Would you give me a chance to gamble for the girl?" he asked with a wry smile.

Severus chuckled in reply. "Only if your stake in the game is your stallion."

Wynne, forgive me, Valerian thought, and answered, "All right." He said a prayer to Venus. Meghan's destiny was in his hands now.

Together he and the tribune sauntered over to where the soldiers played their game. Severus walked with the unsteady gait of the intoxicated, which Valerian did his best to imitate. The tribune held out his hand for the ivory cubes and Valerian held his breath. So much rested on his winning. With a confident grin Severus took his turn, swearing beneath his breath at the turn of fate. With hands atremble, Valerian took his turn, closing his eyes tightly as if afraid of the outcome.

"Damn your heathen heart, centurion. You have won!" he heard Severus scream in his ear, and only then did he open his eyes to see the truth of those words. "I will have her sent to your tent tonight."

The evening progressed with the drunken brawls which always occurred when the soldiers imbibed too much of the grape. Valerian's stomach started to rebel at all the rich food and wine. As he looked around him at the unconscious bodies of the soldiers, the thought ran through his mind that were they now to be attacked, they would be as helpless as children. Naked bodies of lovers, male and female, sprawled over the floor, and he could not help feeling disgust with his countrymen. At his side Severus kept silent, no doubt still upset over losing to Valerian. But finally the tribune spoke.

"You are a brave and a good soldier, Valerian. You have proved that many times already. I wonder if perhaps you are also ambitious." In his drunkenness his speech was garbled and slurred.

"I don't think of myself as ambitious," Valerian answered cautiously, wondering what Severus had in his devious mind. "Why?"

Severus laughed. "Come now, Valerian, every man is ambitious. We all want power. It is the only thing that is really important on this earth."

Valerian did not argue, but he could not help but feel loathing for this man he had once thought of as a friend. Severus looked at him, gesturing him closer, as if to tell him something meant for his ears alone.

"I'll let you in on a little secret. I have the answer to Rome's success with these heathens here in Britain. It is all so simple, really. Now that you have seen with your own eyes the Celts in the North, perhaps you will understand. They are not at all like our docile tribesmen in the South, who mimic our ways."

"Perhaps they can learn from us," Valerian said.

"No, no, no! We have given them every inducement to become Roman. They are too savage. Even our fine friends in the South are not truly bent to our yoke yet. Oh yes, they mimic our dress, language, gods. Even let us set up Celtic chiefs over them, yet for all of their temples to Roman gods, they still cherish the Celtic deities and feasts."

"There is no crime in that," Valerian said, wondering what Severus was getting at. "The empire has never put shackles on philosophic thought, nor on religion. We have embraced with open arms all local gods and nature spirits. Why, look at how the Celtic tribes are beginning to identify some of their own deities with those of Rome."

Severus angrily pounded the arm of his couch with frustration. "You don't understand! It's not the common people we have to fear. It is the Druids. They challenge the very authority of the government. They influence their people not to accept Roman laws and Roman peace. If we can rid ourselves of them, this constant warfare will be over and you and I can return to the warm climate of Rome. Much richer and more powerful!"

Valerian felt cold chills running up and down his back as he realized just what Severus was telling him. "But the Druids are not warriors, they are priests. They are religious men. We can't wage war on them!"

Severus turned with a sly smile. "Oh, can't we? I intend to wage a ruthless campaign against these bloodthirsty savages. We'll cut and burn down their sacred groves and then see how powerful their magic is."

Valerian could not help but remember that Wynne's father himself was a Druid. Although he had nearly lost his life to a sacrificial cult, he knew that this was an outlawed sect and that the Celtic peoples were peace-loving. After having met Wynne, he had a new respect for her people.

"We set out tomorrow for the northern lands, where they refuse to listen to our words or lay aside their native habits and warlike ways. Valerian, my boy, I intend to reward you highly with lands and wealth beyond your wildest dreams. You will be my right-hand man." With this Severus slumped in his chair and was out cold, the wine finally having its way.

Valerian had a sinking feeling deep in the pit of his stomach. They were heading in the direction from which he had just returned. Severus planned his warfare not far from where Wynne and her people lived.

Wynne, if only I could warn you, let you know what is going to happen, prepare you for the danger! But he knew that he could not do so without danger to his own life, for the punishments were severe for those who rebelled against their generals or tribunes. Cowards were flogged to death; generals were empowered to behead any soldier or officer for any deviation from orders, no matter what the outcome. And Severus had clearly taken on a role as general.

I am helpless, Valerian thought in frustration. Still, what value would his life hold if anything were to happen to Wynne? She had given him his life. He must give her her own life and the safety of her people as well.

I will march with Severus, Valerian thought, until I find a way to thwart him. He put his head in his hands. "Wynne, Wynne!" he cried aloud in agony. "I wanted to see you again, but not like this. Not like this!" This night all of the light had gone out of Valerian's world.

Fourteen

The wind blew fiercely through the trees surrounding the lodge where Wynne lay tossing and turning upon her bed, unable to sleep. It was as if a voice called out to her from far away, warning her, crying to her. Her father had often told her that she seemed to have a touch of the sight, and she used to wonder if it were true.

It is my imagination, nothing more, she told herself listlessly. Somehow she seemed to have lost faith in such things now. She had been so certain that she was going to bear Valerian's child, but her monthly time had come and shattered all her dreams. How she had cried that day.

The force of the wind rocked the small dwelling in which she was confined, but Wynne was not afraid. The Goddess of the Wind could not harm her, and would not wish to do so. Turning over on her back, she lay as one dazed, feeling as if all life had been drained out of her. How many days had she spent here? Twenty, twenty-five? She had ceased to keep track. One day was much the same as another here in this small round cell-like structure. She felt caged and longed for her freedom.

Wynne sat up at the sudden sound of broken wood. Her instincts warned her that she was not alone, but she ignored them.

"I'm going mad!" she cried, putting her hands to her temples. "Imagining things." She slipped off her bedshelf and made her way slowly to the doorway of the small dwelling. It was a strange night; along with the wind, there was a mist, a fog, surrounding the village, hiding the stars and the moon from sight and making it impossible to see more than an arm's length away. Even so, Wynne knew every inch of the village with its pits, granaries, and working areas, and the palisade with its fence of stakes that guarded it. She longed to go out into the night, but she could not. Although there was no one here to guard her, to keep her from going from the door, it was a matter of honor. She had given her word, and she would not break it, no matter how much she wanted to leave.

"Valerian," she murmured. She wondered where he was right now. Had he found his soldiers? Was he alive and safe? Would he come back to her as he had promised?

She stepped out onto the porch and let the cool, moist air blow against her face, and felt refreshed. It was so cold for summer, this night. A chill ran up her back, and she wondered if it were from the cold or from the strange feeling of doom which had come over her.

"I am being foolish," she scolded herself. "All will be well."

Her eyes turned toward the inside of the lodge, remembering the now familiar poles and support beams with their carved figures. Again her ears perceived a sound. She stood as still as those carved figures which adorned the posts.

Something brushed her outstretched hand. She started to cry out, but before she could make a sound, a huge hand was clamped over her mouth, muffling her scream.

Wynne fought desperately to free herself, but found her arms pinioned behind her back by a hand as strong as iron.

"So, I have you at my mercy," came a voice she recognized, mocking her. "Without your sword or that black stallion of yours, you will not be so fierce an opponent this time, eh?"

She did not have to see her enemy's face to know who held her so tightly. It was the same man she had fought in the forest and had seen at the festival of Lugh.

"The gods will strike you down for your violation in coming here!" she exclaimed, having struggled with every fiber of her body to shake his hand from her face.

"Your gods are not my gods!" he answered, yanking at the tresses of her hair brutally to still her squirming.

"I am thankful for that!" she spat at him. "My gods do not demand the blood of men to appease their appetite. They are kind, not cruel. They are bountiful and do not ravage all that they touch."

He grunted in response, not bothering to reply to her words. Wynne felt a wooden cup being touched to her lips, and screamed, remembering the potion which had been given to Valerian. Her screams startled her adversary and she was able to break free, spilling the liquid to the ground as she did so. She thanked the gods now that it was dark, for the darkness would be her friend. She looked anxiously toward the door, but her way was blocked by the giant's hulking figure. In desperation she sought shelter beneath a small wooden table across the room, her eyes staring at the man as he made his way in her direction. Only the embers of the banked fire shed any glow. She prayed that it would not aid him in finding her. Holding her breath, she awaited her fate.

"Wynne, Wynne," she heard a male voice call. No sound had ever pleased her ears more.

"Edan!" she called. A loud scuffling sound alerted her to the whereabouts of her captor. The sound of footsteps and the crash of wood told her that the giant was making his escape. This she could not allow. Bounding to her feet, she followed in frantic pursuit, but it was of no use. The hideous man burst through the door, vanishing like the mists.

"Are you all right, Wynne?" Edan asked, stepping forward out of the shadows. She ran to him, seeking the comfort of his familiar arms. "I heard you scream."

Breathlessly she told him all about her encounter with the huge man, about having fought with him to save Valerian from being sacrificed and seeing him again at the ceremony of the summer solstice. She poured out her fears for their people.

"We have to stop them!" she cried, trying to still her trembling hands. Awareness of his presence suddenly dawned on her. "You should not be here. If it were known that you had disobeyed the law, you too would be punished," she chided him.

He gripped her shoulders in his large strong hands. "I don't care. I had to see you. I came here tonight to tell you that the wise ones have given permission for our marriage. You have been here already five days short of the cycle of the full moon. Upon the day that you are again made ready to join the tribe, we will be bound together as man and wife!"

"No!" The word was a sob which tore from her throat. Gone now was the adoration from Edan's eyes, and in its place was anger. He was a man, a man of importance to his people, and although he had vowed to be patient, to try to understand Wynne's feelings, he could not be made the fool in front of the tribe. Women were esteemed and allowed many freedoms in the clan, but disobedience could not be tolerated. If Wynne found him lacking once they were married, then by tribal custom she would be free to take a lover, but not until she had given him a son.

"You cannot undo what has been done," he said firmly. The room was silent except for the sound of their breathing. Edan fought with his emotions, his jealousy. Wynne was his; he would not give her up to a stranger.

"It *must* be undone," Wynne finally whispered. "I love another."

"That . . . that *Roman*." He spit the word as an insult. To Edan too the Romans were a hated race.

"Yes," she answered. Her eyes met his and did not falter. It took him by surprise to have her look at him so boldly, as if she were a warrior.

"I love my people, my father, my life, but my heart has already been pledged elsewhere. I have made a vow to another and I will not break it. As you must honor the words you have spoken, so must I."

He laughed contemptuously. "I suppose you believe that this Roman will return for you. Oh, yes, it is whispered that he left you to face your shame alone. These great pagans from the South think of us as heathens. You will never be allowed to marry a man from the Southland, nor is he likely to be willing to suffer the scorn of his people for you."

"He loves me as I love him."

"Perhaps. He may bed you, but marry you . . . he will not. You will be nothing but his whore, his concubine!" Edan turned to walk away, and Wynne hurried to catch up with him before he walked through the door. She caught the sleeve of his tunic and he turned around to look at her. His eyes filled with pain.

"I hear your words, but my heart will not listen. My love is strong for this man. I would be with him among his people or mine, I care not what I am called, only that I cannot live without him!"

It took all of Edan's control to maintain his dignity. "So, you would rather live with him as his whore than live with me as my honored wife. Is that what you are telling me?"

Wynne's face grew soft as she tried to make him understand. Never had she wanted to wound him so. "Someday you will feel as I do about someone, and then perhaps you will understand," she said softly. "I love you as a brother, Edan. I do care for you and it was never my intent to cause you this pain. Please let there be friendship between us, for I need your love and your trust."

Edan looked at the face of the woman he had known since his boyhood. There was no guile there, only truth. She was a woman to honor and respect, as well as to love. Slowly he held out his hand to her in a gesture of brotherly comradeship. "So be it," he said, taking her hand in a firm grasp. For a moment they stood looking at each other; then Edan turned to leave.

The memory of her late-night visitor returned to Wynne, and she put a hand on his arm to stay him. "My father must know of the danger I am in here," she whispered, "of the danger to us all from the forces of darkness."

Edan nodded. "I go now to tell your father what has transpired this night. You cannot be left alone here when there are those who seek to harm you. Perhaps he will see to it that you are freed."

Wynne shook her head. She knew the ways of the Druids. They would not let her go until the time of the full moon, as they had said. "No, Edan. I must stay here."

"Then I will see that you are guarded night and day," Edan said. For the first time that night, he smiled. "You are brave, Wynne. What a wife you will make. I only hope that the Roman has sense enough to know the treasure he holds." This said, he left Wynne alone, staring hard out into the night, with her dreams of the man she loved. It was said among her people that if one thought hard enough about a loved one far away, one could have the power to bring that loved one back. With all her heart she wished it to be so.

"Valerian," she breathed, then carefully closed the outer door of the lodge.

Fifteen

Wynne woke up safe and warm in her own bed furs, a feeling of happiness overwhelming her. She was home, her confinement had come to an end, and she had been purified in the ceremony of fire and water by the white-robed Druids of her tribe. She would never forget the heat from the flames of the torches as they walked in a circle around her, singing their melodious poetic songs, nor would she forget the chill of the night as she had been carried to the edge of the lake and submerged until she thought her lungs would burst for want of air. When she emerged from the waters, she had been greeted as one reborn, all forgiven, and her father had reached out for her hand, saying, "Now, let us go home."

Leaving her bed, Wynne hurried to get dressed, and went in search of her father. There was still much that needed to be said between them. She found him just outside, sharpening his javelin, deep in thought.

"Father."

He put down his spear and motioned for her to have a seat beside him on the ground. It reminded her of so many other times when she had been seated beside him, watching him at his work.

"I have missed you, daughter."

All the bitterness she had felt the last several days vanished with his words. "And I, you," she said.

There was a silence between them as each struggled to find the right words to say.

Finally Adair broke the silence. "Edan told me about the danger you were in while confined to the lodge," he said. "I don't think I slept a wink all of those five nights, after I heard his words. If anyone were to harm a hair on your head, I swear to you I would strangle him with my own two hands!" He clenched his fists in anger.

"I know who sought to harm me, Father. It was one of the priests of the darkness cult. The same man who sought the death of the Roman."

"You can identify him?"

Wynne nodded.

"Then perhaps all is not lost yet."

"I am safe now," Wynne answered, laying her hand on his arm.

"Yes, you are safe, but I tremble to think what might have happened had Edan not come along in time."

The mention of Edan's name was like a wall suddenly come between them. Wynne got up from the ground and walked a few paces away from her father. She had to tell him of her determination not to marry Edan, and feared that this new peace between them would be shattered at her words.

"Edan has told me that there are plans for our forthcoming joining," she began, turning her back to him. "I will say to you what I said to him: I cannot marry him." She waited for his anger, but it did not come. Instead he walked over to where she stood and touched her shoulder so that she would look into his eyes. She was so like him, the mirror image of his own soul.

"I have learned a great deal this past month. I made many mistakes which I would seek to rectify. I will never lose my temper again with you, Wynne. You are too precious to me."

"Then you are not angry. You will not force this marriage upon me?"

He shook his head, looking suddenly old and tired to her eyes. Had he suffered as much as she during her month of solitude?

"I believe that you should have a right to your own life. Were you a man-child you would have the choice as to what path you would choose, be it Druid or warrior. The choice of a mate also would be yours. I have sought only to protect you, not to bind you against your will. I will give you the choice of marrying Edan or of foreswearing the marriage vows. I will not, however, give you permission to marry a Roman.

As long as I am alive, you must obey me in this."

She would not have to marry Edan. His words filled her with bittersweet joy, for neither could she be given in marriage to Valerian. To become his mistress, she must again trespass against the laws of the tribe to which she had just been welcomed back.

"I hear you, Father, and will obey your will. I will not marry." She could never marry Valerian, but she could not give him up.

Wynne left her father and was setting about her chores when a sound behind her caused her to start. It was Brenna coming up behind her like a dark spirit. She looked at Wynne with eyes full of malice. From her hiding place in the shadows she had watched father and daughter.

"I could not help hearing your words. So you refuse to obey your father and marry a fine man. We are to be burdened with your company until you are old and useless," Brenna whined.

Wynne fought to keep her composure. At times Brenna's sharp tongue was more than she could bear.

"I will not be a burden to you. I will find a way to make myself useful," Wynne answered.

"Doing what? You *are* useless." Brenna took a step toward Wynne as if to strike her, but before she could reach out to her, Adair approached with a scowl. In his presence Brenna was as sweet as nectar, but Adair was beginning to sense that there was discord between the two women.

"Close your mouth, woman. It is I who decide who will and who will not live under my roof. My home is Wynne's home for as long as I live. She is my daughter and I will not permit you to treat her thus."

Brenna turned angry eyes upon him, and for a moment Wynne thought that she would lash out at Adair. She hoped that it would be so, for long had she wanted her father to see what kind of woman his wife really was. Brenna, however, held her tongue and obediently lowered her eyes. "Forgive me, Adair," she murmured. "I was only thinking of you." Returning to the lodge, she shut the outer door, leaving father and daughter alone.

"Brenna will never understand your ways, my daughter. But you mustn't be angry with her— she means well. But enough talk of this matter. Come, I have something I want to show you."

Wynne smiled and complied, knowing that her father was nearly bewitched by Brenna's beauty and charms. And though her stepmother was unfailingly cruel to her, Wynne was reluctant to add further to her father's burdens by revealing this side of his wife's nature.

Adair took her arm, and together they walked away from the lodge toward the outskirts of the village.

Sixteen

As the first rays of the hazy dawn touched the earth, Valerian awoke with a start. Where was he? Had he been dreaming all that had happened? No. The ache in his bones from being on horseback so long attested to that. All the events of the past few days tumbled through his brain. Would he ever be able to forget?

Rising upon his stiffened limbs, he found Severus' eyes upon him, watching, always watching. Could the man read his thoughts?

"The man is insane," he said to himself, and knew it must be true. The Roman Army under Severus Cicero had swept across the land of the Celts, leaving in its wake such destruction as had never been seen before by warrior or Druid. Orders had been given to torch or cut down the sacred oak groves, and the Druids and their followers had been put to the sword or sold into slavery.

"Hurry up, centurion!" one of the soldiers playfully mocked, bringing Valerian out of his thoughts. It was a young brown-haired soldier named Burrus, who spoke in jest, mimicking the tribune Severus, who was now already mounted upon his horse and ready to ride. A friendship had sprung up between the beard-less Burrus and Valerian. A voice deep inside told Valerian that this young soldier abhorred the killing as he himself did.

Hurrying with his armor, Valerian mounted his horse and rode up beside the soldier. Ahead of them they could see the tribune scanning the horizon for any sign of the Celts.

"It seems we will have another day of constant traveling," the young man said wistfully.

"Our tribune seems to enjoy being uncomfortable," Valerian answered dryly. "As for me, I am in no hurry to meet any more of the Celtic warriors. They are fearsome in battle. Never have I seen their equal."

His words were confirmed by Burrus. "I can't help but admire their courage."

"Even our fearless tribune must be at least a little awed by them," Valerian answered. "They are enough to frighten even the most experienced soldiers, the way they ride into battle, long fair hair flying about their shoulders. And their chanting!"

His words were true. The Celts seemed to take on an unearthly form as they rode, their

clear white skin ghostlike in the sunlight. They
rode tall and proud, chanting with their harsh
voices or playing discordant music on their horns
and beating their swords against their shields.
Before a battle they would incite their war spirit
with ritualistic imitations of battle, dancing and
leaping about and often working into such a
frenzy that they threw off their chain mail and
helmets and went forth in all their naked glory,
fearless and terrifying.

Severus turned back toward his men. "We
ride until we reach the crest of that hill," he
ordered. "Onward to the old hill fort, then we
rest."

The bitter winds raged about them as the
soldiers rode. Valerian pulled his cloak tightly
about him to keep the chill from him, cursing
Severus all the while beneath his breath.

"Damn! Can't we Romans learn to live in
peace? Damn Severus and his infernal quest for
territory. One would think him to be Nero
himself." The fear nagged him that Wynne would
be one of the innocent victims of this senseless
violence. He had to find a way to save her, or
there would be no reason to live.

Valerian gazed about him at the rich greens
and browns of the hillsides as they passed by.
The gently rolling hills were covered in golden
grass and dotted with gnarled trees.

Once at the hill fort, Valerian walked around
to stretch his legs. From the hill fort he could
see a great distance. He would never forget that
first battle, the furious rush of the horsemen,

the grace of the horse-drawn chariots. No wonder Wynne had been such a fine rider—it was
part of her heritage. The wheeled chariots of
the Celts were manned by two warriors, one
driving the horses and the other flinging javelins at the enemy. Then, when all the spears
were gone, the javelin thrower leapt into the
conflict on foot, while the charioteer turned the
horses around. Their horses too were manned
with two men, one to manage the horse, the
other to fight.

We fight an entirely different mode of battle,
he thought. The front ranks of the Roman infan-
try hurled a volley of javelins at the foe, while
archers and slingers attacked with arrows and
stones. Then the cavalry charged with pikes and
swords.

"Ah, Valerian," a voice exclaimed. Severus
stood behind him, gazing out at the land like a
vulture. "We must eat and quench our thirst as
quickly as possible. We have much to do this
day."

Much carnage to bring with us, Valerian
thought, but held his tongue. He wanted to end
this killing and make peace with these peoples. "I
think we should stay here the night," he said
instead. "This hill fort is strongly built." The
massive structure had squared ramparts facing
front and back, with upright timbers, tied by
cross-beams, and overlooked a precipice with a
sheer stone wall.

"Stay?" Severus said scathingly. "No doubt
this structure provided security against attack

once. These heathens are skilled in their building, yet were we to face the Celts up here, we would be as ants fighting against a swarm of bees. This hill fort could be easily taken. No. No. We have to strike first."

Valerian could see that it was senseless to argue. "Why can't we try to make peace with these peoples?" he muttered beneath his breath.

Severus heard and squinted at him. "An interesting idea, peace. Peace indeed." Putting on his helmet, he gestured to Valerian to follow him.

The sun was shining like a bright torch as the Romans left the fort. Near the end of the day they left behind the wide meadows and gently rolling hills. Now they had to wend their way slowly over steep rocky hills bordered by swiftly rushing streams.

Valerian looked behind him as they fought their way over the stones and rocks in their path. So intent was he on avoiding injury to Sloan that he did not see the danger until he heard Burrus' cry.

"The Celts!" he shouted. "They are behind us!" Turning, Valerian too saw the sight of spears shining in the light.

"So much for your *peace*, my friend," he heard Severus say sarcastically, then order, "Attack! We will show these heathen bastards the might of Rome!"

Across the rocky hillside the horses ran, toward the oncoming throng of riders. The sounds of the horses' hooves echoed in Valerian's ears, coming closer and closer. He was drenched in perspiration from the exertion of his ride, his heart beating like the wing of a dove in his chest. Suddenly a piercing fire tore through his shoulder.

"Wynne!" he cried, knowing that he could not let death take him without seeing her again. Falling from his horse, he raised his sword to defend himself.

Seventeen

Valerian lost all track of time as he recovered from the shoulder wound. Burrus had carried him off the battlefield and saved his life. From a distance the two men had watched the blood and destruction before them. The senselessness of war had washed over them like a tide. All the death and destruction for what? The glory of a few men, an empire?

At first it had appeared that the Celtic tribes with their superior numbers and brilliant individual warriors would be victorious, but in the end Roman strategy won the day. For the Celts had nothing but their death-defying courage to pit against the steady advance of the legions. It seemed only a matter of time before the Celtic way of life would fall apart against the might of Rome and their culture cease to exist.

Valerian could hear the howl of a wolf nearby

and squinted his eyes for any sign of the animal. It would be pleasant to have a warm wolf fur to bed down upon. He wondered if the Celts heard the cry of the wolf too in their camps. He supposed that they did. Even though he had been wounded by one of them, he could not feel hatred toward them. He settled back upon his hard bed of earth and leaves and waited for the dawn, images of a lovely golden-haired woman haunting his dreams.

When the sun touched the earth with its first glow, the legion again mounted their horses. Valerian reined in his horse, his wound still hurting him. He looked out across the fields, gazing at the land that rolled before them, at the lush woodland with its greens and golds, birds, wild game. He daydreamed of what might have been. Now all too soon this land too would be reduced to ashes.

"Hail, centurion," Valerian heard a voice say. When he saw that it was Burrus, he rode over to the young cavalryman.

"How goes it, Burrus?"

"Well. Severus is well pleased with our victory. No doubt there will be several Druids put to the sword." His eyes mirrored his disgust, as did Valerian's. War should be between warriors.

Valerian knew that in order to appear justified in his actions, Severus had spread rumors concerning his enemies, trumping up falsehoods that the Druids committed human sacrifice, sending messages to Rome of the brutalities of the Celtic warriors, as if Rome herself did not commit atrocities.

"Tomorrow we march to the lands of the North, to the land held by the Parisi," Burrus declared with a scowl.

"Tomorrow we march?" Valerian asked, trying to maintain his composure before this young soldier. So he had run out of time. The day was approaching when Wynne and her people would be in danger. Damn Severus!

"Sometimes I wish that I had never become a soldier," the young Burrus confessed.

"I too feel that way. This campaign is not to my liking," Valerian answered, trying to calm the younger man's fears.

"At night I ... I see the bodies. I dream about the horror of what is happening. Yet, we must be right in what we are doing. There has to be some reason for all of this death. If I thought it was all for nothing, I think I would go mad! But the tribune says that we are bringing unity and strength to the empire." Burrus' eyes looked haunted. Valerian did not have the heart to tell him about his own doubts.

"Yes, we are building an empire, though I wonder what the future will record of our deeds," he said dryly.

Pulling away from the young soldier, Valerian led Sloan down the hill in search of Severus. The time had come to act upon those doubts. No longer could he march blindly to the tune of another's ambition. Not when those ambitions might lead to the destruction of the woman he loved.

"Severus must let me do as I ask," he exclaimed, galloping down the hillside.

Eighteen

Severus looked at the handsome centurion with annoyance. "You want to do what?" he asked.

"I would like your permission to take my soldiers on ahead of your legions," Valerian blurted out. "Give me two days' head start...." He could feel the cold eyes of the tribune studying him.

"And just what is your reason for this request, centurion?" he asked in a tone which warned of danger. "Perhaps you would like all the glory for yourself."

"No, it's just that I have already visited that area and know it quite well."

"And, as I recall, you nearly got yourself killed, became separated from your century. Not a very impressive record, centurion!"

Valerian's face flushed with anger. "I was following your orders, tribune."

The silence between them was unnerving. Severus turned his back for a moment, then faced Valerian, looking him up and down as if trying to read his mind. Valerian's heart sank. He had hoped to convince the tribune to let him go ahead of the other soldiers to warn Wynne and her people. Now he feared that Severus knew his intent.

Severus smiled broadly, baring his protruding front teeth, which always reminded Valerian of a squirrel.

"Of course, now I know why you make this request." He began to laugh, a laugh which chilled Valerian to the bones. "You seek retribution for your near-death. You want to be the one to spill the blood of those heathens who thought to give you to their gods."

Valerian was aghast to think Severus could think such a thing of him. But no matter what Severus thought, if he were allowed to do as he wished, then all would be well in the end.

Severus pounded him on the back. "I knew you were a man after my own heart. You understand the importance of making examples of these heathens." His voice lowered. "Perhaps crucifying them would be the best lesson!" He picked up his cup of wine and drained it. For the moment his interest in Valerian waned as one of the slave girls entered the tent. He cupped one of her breasts in his hand and planted a slobbery kiss on her lips.

"Tonight in my tent," he whispered as she scurried away. Again he turned to Valerian.

"Let me think about your request." Again he smiled. "Oh, and if you do go, Valerian, save at least a few of those savages for us to slaughter, eh?"

You murdering swine, Valerian thought. You call them savages, yet you are not worth a hair on Wynne's lovely head. "I do not believe them to be savages," he said, as he gained control of his emotions. "Fighting is the heart's blood of the Celts, to be sure. Yet with all their savagery as warriors, they are an honorable people imbued with grace and honesty. I have seen this with my own eyes."

Severus eyed Valerian warily, wondering just why the centurion was speaking so adamantly about a people who were not his own, but he held his tongue and merely listened.

"They value their freedom. Can we fault them for that? Should we spill their blood just because they refuse to surrender to the Roman eagle and to lay aside their native habits to become our pawns? I think not. We may be able to enslave others, but I feel that we will never subdue our Celtic foes," Valerian continued. If Severus now sought to punish him for his words, so be it.

Severus studied Valerian, trying to understand just what had come about to so inflame the man. He did not believe that it was really peace that the centurion sought. No, there had to be something else afoot. Valerian waited, thinking that he had gone too far, but the tribune merely smiled.

"Perhaps if we do as we have done in Londinium, where the Celts are not slaves, but tribal chieftains, vassals of Rome . . ." he mused.

"Yes, those tribes have accepted our ways!" Valerian exclaimed, hoping against hope that he could make Severus see reason.

The tribune laughed. "I doubt not that when our backs are turned, they revert to their old gods and customs," he chided, shattering Valerian's hopes. "Leave me. I must think on this." Curtly he dismissed the centurion.

I will not let that bloody murderer kill Wynne and her people. I won't! he vowed. *If I have to steal away without the permission of Severus, I will.*

Valerian was not unaware of the danger to himself. He could be sentenced to death for any deviation from orders, but it was worth the chance. He would act now and worry about the consequences later. After all, his father was a powerful senator. Perhaps he could call on him to recall Severus. If it were known what the tribune was doing to further his own power . . . He made up his mind to send a letter to Rome right away. Severus had taken upon himself the role of a general. Surely the emperor himself would censor this power-hungry swine.

"Oh, Wynne, Wynne," he murmured. "I give you your life." His heart quickened at the thought of seeing her again. For the first time since the campaign against the Celtic people began, he smiled as he saw her face before him. Suddenly he felt that all would be well. The gods would surely be with him.

* * *

Several days later Valerian was summoned to stand before Severus. It was a somber tribune who greeted him.

"Tell me, centurion," he said, "do you still envision peace in these lands?"

"I do," Valerian answered. "I believe that there could be peace between our peoples, that there need be no more bloodshed, yes." He wondered just why he felt like a mongoose before a cobra.

Severus raised his eyebrows. "I see." He thought for a moment. "And just how would you go about bringing this peace of yours to this country, besides killing every Celt in the land?" he asked with a sadistic laugh.

Valerian could see no humor in his words and wondered what the tribune was up to. "By talking with them, proving our good faith. This revolt of the Iceni and our brutal punishment of them has done us no good." He did not add that Severus' brutal warfare also had alienated the Celtic peoples.

"And this ... this ... scouting party you wanted to take with you. Was the purpose then to try to bring peace?" Severus rubbed his chin with his bony fingers.

"I would like to try to make peace between our two peoples, tribune," Valerian answered.

Severus seemed again to be deep in thought, pacing back and forth in the small tent. Finally he grinned. "If you can bring peace to this land and enable us to return to Rome, then more power to you, my boy. You have no idea how sick I am of this country and this constant killing."

Valerian looked at the man before him. Could he have misjudged him? He was one of his father's friends; perhaps he did want to bring about peace. What reason would he have to lie?

"Then you will let me go?"

"You have permission to do as you ask. I will wait two days before setting out, but no longer, I warn you. Hopefully I will not have cause to regret my decision. It would pain me to have to inform your father of your death by heathen hands."

"You will not regret this, tribune. I will do everything in my power to bring peace. By the gods I so swear."

"So be it," Severus said, giving Valerian a friendly pat on the shoulder. "I fear you have condemned me in your heart these past weeks. Being a tribune is never an easy task. Someday you will understand. I want the best for you, Valerian. Your father is like a brother to me, I admire him greatly. I know that a great future awaits you." He turned his back. "Now, go before I get sentimental. Go!"

Valerian ran out of the tent with wings on his heels. The gods were surely with him, as he had prayed they would be.

"We shall see what you are planning, centurion, we shall see," Severus said beneath his breath as he watched Valerian leave. "For I doubt that it is peace you really seek." He would give Valerian the freedom to do as he wished, but he would be following close in his tracks with the entire legion at his command.

He would strike a blow at these heathens such as had never been struck before. No doubt Valerian sought his own glory, thought to bring himself to the attention of Nero and Rome, but he, Severus, would outwit him. He felt drunk with power. Soon, soon he would be General Severus. He had all but that title now.

"Ha! You are a fool if you think that I intend to wait two days before setting out, Valerian. I will be right on your heels, and when I am through, I will prove you to be the traitor you are!"

Nineteen

Life settled back into a normal routine for Wynne as the days passed. As usual, Brenna maintained a kind manner while Adair was in the lodge, but when he was gone she never hesitated to belittle Wynne's efforts, finding fault with everything she did in an attempt to make life miserable for her. Wynne, however, did not let the woman's words upset her. She had the love of her father, and that was all that mattered to her.

In moments when all the work had been done and Wynne had time to sit and let her thoughts wander, she always thought of Valerian, hoping to see him again someday. The Roman was thus in her thoughts as Brenna approached her one day before the evening meal.

"Well, I see that you are lost in your dream world again," she said bitterly. Wynne ignored her icy remark. She would not let her father's wife goad her any longer.

Brenna flew into a rage at being ignored, however, grabbing Wynne's arm so hard that she winced with pain. "Look at me when I'm talking to you!" Brenna said in anger.

"I warn you, Brenna," Wynne retorted, "if you touch me ever again as you did just now . . ." Wynne fought against her fury. "What do you want, Brenna?" she asked finally when her anger had calmed.

"I need some of the wild berries that grow at the edge of the forest. Since you are not busy and I have my hands full preparing our food, I wanted you to pick them."

"But there are plenty of berries nearby. Why go all the way to the forest?" The knowledge that the worshipers of the darkness might be roaming the woods made Wynne shudder, remembering the night in the lodge.

"Those berries aren't what I want. I can't use the red sweet berries with all the seeds. I need the tart purple ones." Making her way to the wall where her cloak hung, Brenna clenched her fists in anger. "If you are afraid to go, if you are a coward, I will go instead."

Wynne shook her head, letting her step-mother's words cause her shame. "I will go," she answered, keeping her chin up and her eyes looking daggers at Brenna.

Picking up a basket, she started on her way. She didn't really mind going to the forest; it would be a pleasant walk. Passing by the common, where the horses were kept, she thought about Sloan. How she missed the magnificent black stallion. So many times they had ridden to the forest. Her father had given her another horse, but none could ever replace Sloan in her heart. Still she was looking forward to training the white horse. Her instincts told her it would make a fine mare.

It was a cool day, the air filled with the scent of flowers and earth smells mixed with the fresh crisp fragrance of the spruce and oak trees. Wynne looked up at the gray clouds in the sky, which might signal the approach of a storm. She had an urge to forget about the berries and go back, yet her pride would not let her. She would get Brenna her berries. With quick strides she walked the steep hill toward the woods, determined to finish her errand and be gone.

Stopping by a cool spring, she bent down to refresh herself, letting the cool water soothe her parched throat. It seemed strange that the forest wildlife had hidden themselves from sight this day. Usually they scampered about, much to her pleasure. Again she had a feeling that she should return to the village, but she was nearly to the forest, and continued on her way.

Breathing a sigh of relief, she saw the clearing at the beginning of the thick part of the forest and ran the rest of the way.

Wynne filled the basket to overflowing, eating a few of the tart and fresh morsels herself. She reached for the basket to pick it up, but paused, hearing a sound behind her. She looked around. Had she seen a shadow behind that tree? Yes, she was certain she had. She sprang to her feet prepared to run as fast as her legs could carry her. Forgotten now were the berries, which rolled over the ground like the glass beads from her father's gameboard. An arm lashed out from the darkness of the forest, winding around her like a snake, halting her flight. Wynne tried to free herself, but another hand covered her mouth, brutal in its strength, and her mind knew that it was the hand of her giant opponent. How many were there now? One hand over her mouth, one pinning her arms, and she thought she could hear a woman's voice in the distance. . . . Three?

Silently, desperately, she fought against her captors, but she was as helpless as a rabbit in a snare, all her kicking and twisting to no avail. A piece of cloth was stuffed into her mouth. Her attacker quickly bound her, bruising her slender wrists. Then to her horror a sack was pushed over her head and down over her body, plunging her into total darkness. The sack was tied around her ankles, and like a sack of grain she was thrown over one of her captor's shoulders. Struggling to throw him off balance, she hit her head on something hard, but still fought like a wounded wildcat. Her bravery was useless, for the more she kicked and squirmed, the tighter the arms clamped around her.

"Oh, Father!" she cried, realizing that her only hope lay in Brenna. Surely when she had not returned, Brenna would tell her father what had happened and they would come to search for her. It was her only hope. She cursed her stupidity and stubbornness in coming alone to this place without her dagger.

Wynne could hear voices muttering; then there was laughter.

Where are they taking me? Oh, Goddess of the Forest, help me. I don't want them to kill me. I don't want to leave this world yet, there is too much I have to do in this life.

She heard a horse whinny, felt herself flung over the animal's back. Her head throbbed and the coarse sack was blocking the air from her lungs. A black fog enveloped her.

Regaining her senses, Wynne wondered how long she had been unconscious. She had lost all concept of time in her darkened void. She felt her hair tangled in a matt around her face. Her whole body ached except her legs, which were numb. Never had she been so miserable. Where was she? She knew only that she was a prisoner. She fought again to loosen her bonds, but only exhausted herself in the effort.

When at last the sack was removed, she found herself face to face with her enemy. She had spared his life once; would he do the same for her?

The light hurt her eyes, blinding her, and she realized that she was surrounded by torches, thirteen flickering flames. How long had she been here? she wondered. Looking up at the fading moon, she knew the answer. No doubt her father would have missed her by now and sent a search party.

The grinning face of the giant looked down at her. His hair was thinning, a sign of his age, and his face was fat and pale, with eyes which reminded Wynne of a snake's, cold and cruel.

"If you are going to kill me, do so now, for I will fight you with every breath I take," she spat at him. She had saved Valerian's life; would she now take his place upon the sacrificial pyre?

The smile faded, replaced by a frown. "We will not kill you, nor will you be sacrificed," he said. "We have something much better in mind for you."

Now that Wynne's eyes had grown accustomed to the light, she could see that she was not alone with her captor. By his side stood two other figures—more of the dark ones. Like the giant, they were clothed in black. She could not see their faces, just a shadow. One was tall and well-muscled, the other short and small of frame. Was it the woman whose voice she had heard?

The small dark-robed woman moved toward Wynne, gliding like a spirit, her bare ankles entwined with silver bracelets in the shape of snakes.

Attempting to shake off her dread, Wynne tried to speak, her voice shrill and choked. "Who are you?" she asked. "Why have you brought me here?" Her voice seemed to come from afar, as if another was speaking.

The woman did not answer. Wynne strained her eyes for a look at her face, but it was painted a ghastly blue with white markings covering the cheeks and forehead, obscuring her features. Yet her eyes were clearly visable, eyes which shone with hatred.

Why does this being hate me so? Wynne wondered. Was it because she had taken Valerian away from them? She did not know. All that she knew was that she must escape from these blood-thirsty savages. Somehow. Some way.

The three figures began to chant, the small figure moving far away from Wynn, shedding its clothes until she was naked, then swaying to the music of their singing. Wynne had been right—it was a woman, her body supple and glowing in the light. Like her face, the woman's body was painted with woad. Flinging back her head, she closed her eyes, arms upraised. Faster and faster she whirled, turning circles until she was nearly flying in the air. Throwing off his robe, the tall man joined in the dancing. His bare arms bulged with muscles and he was covered with scars. He moved with grace for one so big, dancing until perspiration ran down his body like rain from the sky. Wynne watched in fascination as if in a trance. The night seemed cloaked in a shroud of black, and with a feeling of terror Wynne realized that were she to break free, it was not a night in which she could easily find her way home.

From the distance Wynne could hear chanting as more dark-robed figures approached. Now she knew the reason why the two dancers had worked themselves into such a frenzy. There was to be a ceremony tonight. With dread she remembered the words the giant had said to her. They had something planned for her, but what? In panic Wynne tugged at her bonds. It was no use, she was tied as securely as a colt for its first breaking. She felt degraded and helpless. Anger and frustration kept her from thinking clearly; still, she knew that she must do something before it was too late.

Like a snake about to strike, the male dancer moved in closer to Wynne, bringing with him a wooden bowl filled with liquid and holding it to her lips.

"No!" Wynne cried, turning her head to avoid the brew, which she feared might be the potion given to Valerian. She would need a clear head if she was going to escape.

Issuing a curse, the man slapped her so hard that she feared she would lose consciousness. The liquid spilled on the ground, seeping into the dirt.

"You will wish for the potion before we are through with you!" he snarled. His laugh rang out in harmony with the chanting.

"What are you going to do?" Wynne asked, her voice merely a whisper.

"Bury you alive in that pit," he said, pointing to the remains of an old well. "It will take time for you to die, and your death cries will be as music to the ears of the mighty Domnu!"

Wynne had heard tales of such things being done, and knew that she would rather die any death than this one. To be thrown into that abyss where no doubt the serpents which were so revered by these foul creatures lived, was too horrible to imagine.

"You are lower than the snakes you worship," she hissed at him, her blood burning with poisonous hatred. Ignoring her words, the man turned and walked away to join the woman. Together in all their naked glory they walked to greet the worshipers, and Wynne found herself left alone with the huge hulking giant. If only she could somehow convince him to unbind her, there was a chance that she could escape. She had been the victor in their combat once before.

"My hands!" she cried out. "Can you not untie my hands?" The man merely laughed and turned to gaze upon the departing forms of the dancers. She would get no pity from him. With every fiber of her soul Wynne wished for her dagger. How could she have been so foolish as to leave it behind? If she could cut her bonds, at least she could take her own life. Fighting the black waves of despair which clouded her mind, Wynne slowly edged toward a part of the ground where it was rocky. At first she felt nothing but the smooth earth beneath her groping hands, but then she found what she sought, the jagged edge of a rock. Rubbing her bonds up and down, bruising and scraping her wrists, Wynne fought to free herself. Calling on all the gods to help her, she worked feverishly to escape. Now was the only chance she would have to break free, for once the others returned, all would be lost.

The giant stood with his back to her, threatening as he loomed before her. As long as he stood there, he would act as a shield to hide her from the eyes of the others.

When at last her wrists were free, Wynne worked her hands to bring the feeling of life back into them. Slowly, so as not to alert her captor, she dragged herself farther away from where he stood, hiding in the undergrowth. With her legs bound, she could not go far; she must free her ankles too.

As if sensing her thoughts, the man turned around and started toward her with a growl like that of a wild beast, but a sound from the bushes made him turn around. A large wild boar stood staring at him, snorting in rage as the giant moved. Wynne tore at the ropes around her ankles. They were bruised and bleeding, but at least she was free. With a bellow of rage the giant started toward her, but his movement caught the attention of the wild boar and it surged forward to attack. Wynne watched as the two creatures rolled over and over on the ground in battle. The gods had been good to her this day. They had aided her in her escape and sent the boar to help her.

Bounding to her feet, she ran for her life, stopping only to look back at the swirl of blood and death behind. Her hair blew wildly around her shoulders as she ran, blowing into her eyes, obstructing her vision. She knew beyond a doubt that by now she was being followed, the dancers and their followers close behind her.

Onward she ran, not daring to look back. Suddenly she tripped over a large tree trunk in her path, tumbling head over heels onto the hard ground and twisting her ankle beneath her. Pain shot through the injured foot, but still she managed to get to her feet, limping as she struggled to run. She could not afford to stop or slow her pace, no matter how great her agony.

Wynne could hear a shout behind her and knew that the human animal had been the victor. He too was coming after her, closer and closer. Fear drove her with superhuman strength, for she knew what awaited her if she were to lose this race. Dodging between trees, using the blessed cover of the darkness as her hiding place, Wynne traveled on until she could bear the pain no longer. Her lungs felt as if they would burst as she paused, gasping for air. Looking up, it was then that she saw the fires of her people. Truly the gods were watching over her: Wynne fell to her hands and knees and with a last burst of energy crawled over the hard ground back to the safety of her tribe and to the welcoming arms of her frantic father.

Twenty

Wynne stood before the fire of life, rubbing her hands together to restore feeling in them. Her ankle still hurt and no doubt she would have to walk with a staff, at least for a while. But nonetheless she was alive and basically unharmed. For that she was grateful. She looked around for Brenna but could not find her face among the women of the village. Strange. Where could she have gone? Ah, well, at least she would not have to parry her sword-sharp tongue.

"Wynne!" Isolde cried, coming toward her, arms outstretched. She embraced her cousin, feeling the love she bore her envelop her like a cloak. "I was afraid you were lost to us, that we might never see your face again."

"Nor I yours," Wynne replied, breaking away from her cousin's arms. She touched the handle of her dagger. "No more will I leave without

this at my side. 'Tis a cruel lesson I have learned."
The dagger had been thrust into her hand by
her father, who had made her promise not to
leave the village unless it was in her possession.
He had been beside himself with apprehension
when she had not returned to the village, quite
certain that he would see her no more.

"Nearly every man in the village went in search
of you, even those too old to wield a sword.
Have you any idea just how beloved you are by
our people?" Isolde said proudly.

Wynne's eyes moistened with unshed tears.
"Perhaps now I know," she said. She added
more wood to the fire. The crackling flames
reached up to the sky. Even now her father was
riding in the forest with Cedric and Edan and
others, only this time it was the giant they sought.
At first there had been talk of war, for many
had been certain that Wynne had been taken by
members of a neighboring tribe, but her father
had stilled their anger.

"We have had peace with our neighbors for a
long time now. We cannot let this happen," he
had arqued. "We must be united, now more
than ever, or the Romans will sweep over us
and conquer us. We cannot fight among ourselves like jackals over a hare. Besides, we have
no proof that these worshipers of the darkness
are of the tribe of Monroe. We do not know
that there are not those among us who bow
down to the powers of Domnu."

So wise, her father. He had stilled all those
tongues who argued that an eye for an eye was

the only way. After almost an hour, peace had been restored. Nearly a generation had passed since blood had been spilled at the hands of the Parisi, and none of the warriors was anxious to end that peace.

Isolde left Wynne's side and when she returned brought her a steaming bowl of stew, which Wynne wolfed down quickly. It was the third such bowl she had eaten. Would her hunger never be satisfied?

"It is good that I am not taken captive every day," she joked, "lest I eat so much that I grow out of my gowns."

"It would be a pity," Isolde retorted. "How surprised your Roman would be when he returns, to find you twice the woman he left."

Wynne smiled sadly. She had heard no word of Valerian, did not even know if he still was alive. "As long as he does return, I do not care. If he returns."

"He will return," Isolde replied softly.

"Mother, Mother, look, look!" came the joyful voice of Farrell. He ran to Isolde's side, scattering the glass gaming pieces from the board of two old men who sat beside the fire. In their anger they scolded the boy, who took refuge behind his mother's skirts.

"Farrell, what have you done?" she chided. Wynne bent to help the two men pick up the rolling balls, but winced with pain as she moved her ankle.

"Father's home," the boy continued, oblivious of the havoc he had created. All that he cared about was that his father was riding up with Cedric, Edan, Adair, and the others.

At his words, Wynne looked up. With a gasp she saw the returning party with one she knew so well now in their midst. It was the giant. They had captured him.

Adair bounded off his horse, dragging his prisoner by the chain around his neck, which held him tightly. "Is this the man who has sought to harm you, daughter?" he asked, certain of her answer.

"Yes. It is he." Wynne's eyes were drawn to the captive's face. He was grinning at her as if to prove that he did not fear his punishment.

"It is for you to judge his penalty, Adair," Edan said.

Adair knew this to be true. For as family patriarch it was for him to seek retribution on this man for the injury he had done to Wynne. Yet he would not do so.

"I leave it up to my daughter to decide," he said. "It was she who suffered at his hands." He turned to face Wynne. "Well, daughter? Will you seek this one's death?"

Wynne's eyes met those of the giant. Once he had sought her death and she had spared his life. Again he had sought to harm her in the lodge of solitude, and then once more in the forest, where he had taken her captive. He posed a threat to them all, it was true; still, Wynne now knew that it was another's orders that he had been carrying out. To kill him would end forever any chance her people would have to

find out the identity of the leader of the darkness cult.

"I do not seek his death. Life is too precious a
gift from the gods to take away from another.
To shed his blood would make me no better
than the master he serves. Let him live!"

All eyes turned her way, surprised at her
decision. This man had tried to harm her. Didn't
she know the danger in sparing him? Nonetheless, the choice had been hers to make.

Adair knew his daughter well and was not
surprised by her decision. As if reading her
thoughts, he spoke. "Wynne is wise. We will
question this one. There is no doubt much that
he can tell us." At his words the giant's eyes
blazed hatred. "We will let him live, but he will
be made a slave. We will take him to the tribe of
the Brigantes, where he will toil with a shackle
about his neck until death takes him to another
life," Adair thundered. At these words the giant
gave a bellow of rage and pulled at his chains
like a mighty beast.

Wynne didn't know if it was seeing him with
her father or his shout of anger, but in that
instant she recognized him. It was one of Brenna's
kinsmen. She had seen him at the wedding feast,
brawling with another of the wedding guests.
Wynne was certain it was he. For the first time
she felt sorry for her father's wife. To see one
of her kinsmen reduced to slavery and to know
that he had done such evil would surely cause
her great pain. She watched as her father and
Cedric took away the man she had come to

know as the giant, and she resolved to tell her father about his identity.

"So, it is over!" Edan said softly, coming up beside her and taking her hand.

"Is it?" she asked. His words had been meant to comfort her, but Wynne could not be certain that the matter had been ended once and for all. There were still others of the giant's kind. She would never forget the woman and man who had danced together in the forest in their frenzy, who had meant to kill her in the most gruesome of ways. As long as they were free, her entire tribe was still in danger.

Twenty-one

Valerian drove his men onward at a furious pace as they set out upon their journey, heading west. He felt compelled to reach his destination as quickly as possible, before Severus changed his mind. The soldiers stopped only long enough to rest the horses and to take time to eat. Long into dusk they rode into the hills, continuing onward until the horses were just too tired to go any farther; then they made camp for the night.

Valerian lay down on his hard bedroll, so exhausted that he did not even have the energy to eat the bread and dried meat Burrus offered him. His slumber was filled with tortured dreams of destruction, as if reliving over and over again those days of blood and death.

He awoke the next morning to the sound of rain against his tent. "We cannot stay here," he declared sternly to Burrus. "Tell the men to make ready for travel."

"Travel? Surely you cannot be serious," the young soldier responded with surprise. It didn't seem to him that they could travel in such a torrent, the sky echoing with the noise of thunder and flashes of light as Jupiter vented his wrath on the world below.

Valerian put a hand on the young man's shoulder. "You are a man that I feel I can trust," he said. Burrus nodded. "I requested that our soldiers be given leave to travel ahead of the legion so that I can try to bring about peace between us and the tribal chieftain of the Parisi. I am weary of this bloodshed." Quickly he told Burrus all that had transpired with Severus.

The young soldier looked doubtful. "Do you think you can trust Severus?" It was no secret that Severus was power-hungry. Within the legion, there were already rumblings of that fact, however much the man was feared.

"No, I'm not. Before now his only thought has been to kill and thus gain the attention of Nero. Perhaps Nero himself has ordered him to stop all the bloodshed," Valerian answered, deep in thought.

"It's possible. That would explain his sudden change of heart," Burrus answered.

"Perchance Nero orders a halt to this warfare, fearing that Severus will climb to power and threaten his throne." Valerian took an urn of rainwater and poured it into a bowl, splashing the water on his face. Burrus handed him a woolen cloth to dry his eyes. "If Nero has commanded peace, then I have no doubt that Severus will claim the reward if I am successful, but I do not care. The only thing I seek is peace."

"Peace," Burrus intoned, as if the word was sacred. "But will Severus himself keep that peace? Will the chieftains accept Roman ways?"

"I must try. I must try." Valerian donned his laena, the large rectangular cloak of thick soft wool, and drew it over his head. It would offer some protection from the gale.

Burrus grinned. "Well, if we are to win this peace of yours, we cannot stand here talking all day. Let us move on."

Valerian again braved the storm, signaling to his men that they were breaking camp and to move on. He could see the scowls of the soldiers and hear their muttering, but he knew that no one would dare defy him.

Their journey had become a perilous one as they were forced to wade in mud up to the ankles. Valerian walked beside Sloan, guiding the horse through the blinding sheets of rain. As he walked, he pulled his cloak tightly around him to keep from being soaked to the skin. As they turned northward, trudging over the high rolling ground where the rain was turning the hillside into a waterfall, Valerian heard some of the men say, "Let us go back."

He answered stubbornly, "Why go back when we can go forward, closer to our destination?"

As he walked onward, his thoughts were of Wynne, wondering what she was doing at this very moment.

Wynne sat at the hearth in Tyrone's lodge, holding Llewellyn on her knee. She enjoyed her visits with her cousin. The baby always delighted her and Isolde was a good companion. Sensing the change in the weather, the sudden dampness, she asked Isolde, "How does it look outside?"

"It's raining," came the reply. "How I hate this dampness. It cuts through to the very bones."

Wynne laughed at Isolde. She always exaggerated so. "Ah, yes, I keep forgetting how very old you are. A whole two years older than I. Yet already the affliction of the bones affects you?"

Isolde snorted in reply, running her hand through her hair, which was now a cluster of tight ringlets framing her face. "I just prefer the warmth of the sun, that's all."

Just then Isolde's other two children, Selma and Farrell, came running up to their cousin. Whenever it rained, she treated them to songs and stories. Isolde took her baby from Wynne's arms for his feeding and sat to listen as Wynne began.

"How about the story of the bull and the cranes?" she asked. The children nestled about her, sitting at her feet as she began the story which told of the symbolic meaning of the bull as the power of the spirit. "What do the three cranes stand for?" she asked them.

"Intelligence," Farrell answered, his eyes bright.

"That's right," Wynne said. "The first crane stood on the head of Tarvos Trigaranos. 'I am wisdom,' the crane said, 'the wisdom of the gods.'" As she told the story, she used a different pitch of voice for all of the cranes, much to the children's delight. "The third crane said, 'And I am the knowledge of man.' The second crane also spoke to the bull, saying, 'I am the interpreter of knowledge and of wisdom. I make it possible for the gods to understand man and for man to communicate with the gods. Without knowledge there can be no wisdom, and without wisdom all our knowledge is lost to us.'" Wynne knelt down and smoothed the dirt of the floor with her hand, picking up a stick and drawing a picture for the children, of a bull standing near a tree with the three cranes on him, two on his back and one on his head.

"What does the tree signify?" she asked.

"It is the tree of life," Selma replied, eyeing her brother as if to say that he was not the only intelligent one in the family.

"Yes, that's right. The tree of life gave immortality to Tarvos Trigaranos. He was very powerful, begetting many ancestors, this bull. But he was so puffed up with his own importance that he forgot to thank the tree for giving him the breath of life, and without life itself, no power on earth is of any use."

Isolde finished feeding her baby and put the sleeping infant down in its bed and came to Wynne's side so that she could hear the story more clearly.

"For his trangression the gods ordered the three cranes to attach themselves to the bull for all eternity as a reminder to us, his children, of the blessing of life which we have been given. And to make certain that we keep in tune with nature and these sacred spirits. The cranes symbolize our contact with these blessed ones, our link with the gods."

Wynne finished her story and smiled at the children. "Now it is time for your nap," she said, taking them over to their bedshelves. When she returned, her cousin put a hand on her shoulder.

"You are so talented in storytelling," she said. "You too should have been a Druid."

"I have dreamed often of that calling, but our tribe does not admit women to the priesthood as other tribes do. Besides, my heart is elsewhere now." Her eyes took on a faraway look.

"You are still thinking of your Roman," Isolde stated sympathetically.

"Yes," Wynne admitted.

Isolde smiled. "I feel in my heart that you will see him again. The gods favor you." She returned to her weaving and Wynne walked to the doorway to stare out at the rain. Why did she suddenly feel so fearful, as if something terrible were about to occur? Was it the rain?

Usually the rain soothes me, she thought. The sound of the rain tapping on the straw roof is so pleasing. But today I want suddenly to banish the rain, to call upon the Goddess of the Wind to blow it to the four corners of the earth.

She shook her head in puzzlement, then stepped outside to let the cool rain fall upon her, nearly colliding with Tyrone, who strode through the door with an angry frown on his face. Wynne could see that something was wrong.

"What is it?" she asked, shutting the door behind them as Tyrone entered the lodge.

"It's our captive—the one you call the giant. He is dead!"

"Dead?" Wynne cocked her head so that she could see into his eyes. "Who . . . ? Why . . . ? How did he die?" she asked. Surely it had not been by the hand of one of her people, for the judgment had spared him.

"We found him this morning with a knife in his back. I didn't like the man, I hate his kind, and yet to die in such a way . . . only a coward would seek to take a life in such a manner."

Wynne nervously paced the room, her hands atremble. "So it is not ended!" she exclaimed. "Perhaps now we will never know the power behind the force of darkness which threatens us all."

Twenty-two

Wynne stood outside in the sunshine, welcoming its warmth. It had rained for three days and nights. Her father said it was an omen, but now all the rain was gone, leaving only the fragrant breath of the goddess in the air. Wynne filled her lungs with the fresh air, then turned her attentions once again to the antics of the young horse she was training.

"Tara, I'm so proud of you. You learn so quickly," she said in praise, giving the animal its reward of a bit of chopped apple. The animal took the piece of fruit gently from her hand. Wynne had grown fond of Tara while training her. The white horse was graceful and gentle, whereas Sloan had been powerful and strong; yet Wynne loved them both. Tara promised to be the envy of the tribe, just as Sloan had been, for her nimbleness and speed made her impossible to surpass, and on her back Wynne felt as if she were racing with the wind.

Wynne gently stroked the animal's mane, speaking softly into Tara's ear. "Shall we ride together again, you and I?" she crooned, climbing on the horse's back. Round and round the clearing they galloped, giving Wynne the feeling of freedom that had not been hers for a long while.

At long last she reined in the horse and slid gracefully off her back.

"Good work, daughter," she heard her father's voice say in praise. "You have done well with the filly."

Turning around, she saw the pride in his eyes and smiled at him. "I fear it is Tara who has done the work. I have simply guided her." She left the animal and came to her father's side, taking his hand in her own small one. He pressed it tightly in his usual gesture of affection.

"You are a blessing, Wynne," he said softly. "You have brought me much happiness. If . . . if . . . anything were to happen to me . . ."

Wynne looked at him with eyes wide with fear. "Don't speak of such things. I can't bear it."

"No, I must. I will soon be an old man. At the next full moon I will be one-and-forty. Therefore I must speak of such things." Together they walked to where a large rock lay embedded in the ground and sat down. "Death is just a pause in the cycle of life, but still I would so hate to leave you, Wynne."

Wynne put his large strong hand up to her face, caressing it with her cheek. "I love you so, Father. I could not endure life without you."

"Yes, you could. You are a strong woman. I could not love you more if you were a son. Perhaps if you were, I would have less cause to worry, for then you would have your own hearth. Don't think I haven't seen the way it is between you and Brenna."

Wynne started to speak, but he silenced her.

"And I know whose fault it is. Brenna has been a good wife to me, but she doesn't have a mother's heart. She has never stopped being jealous of you. But her sharp tongue has not gone unnoticed by me. If I do not intervene more often, it is because I know that you can fight for yourself. As I said, you are strong. However, if I were gone, Brenna would then be the head of the household, though not of the hearth, and I fear that she would cause you much sorrow." He reached up to stroke Wynne's silky hair in a gesture she remembered well from her childhood. "Would that you had married Edan ... Ah, but I will speak no more about it."

He rose quickly to his feet and offered her a challenge. "Shall we see just how well you have trained that white filly? Are you of a mind to race me? To the tree and back?"

With a laugh Wynne sprang onto Tara's back and issued her own challenge as she looked back at him. "To the clearing at the edge of the forest and back," she shouted.

"To the clearing!" he called out, giving his horse free rein and easing up behind her. He was proud of the way Wynne and her horse seemed to move as one. He was struck anew by his daughter's power and skill. Man or woman, there was none her equal.

Wynne felt immortal on Tara's back as she rode like the wind, laughing and looking over her shoulder as she outdistanced her father. She guided Tara over fallen logs and boulders, making certain that the horse did not endanger herself. She galloped on and on, faster and faster.

Adair came within a length of his fair-haired daughter, urging his horse to go even faster. He could not lose without a fight.

"What a warrior she would have made!" he said aloud, feeling as if he would burst with pride for having sired this lovely woman.

So engrossed was he in watching Wynne that he did not see the snarl of roots which loomed in his path. His horse stumbled and Adair felt himself falling to the ground. With a cry of pain he hit the earth like a star fallen from the sky. He gave himself up to the darkness which descended upon him, and thanked the gods for sparing him any more agony.

Wynne turned, meaning to goad her father with her victory, but to her alarm could see him nowhere. Had he given up so easily? That was not his way. In panic she raced back through the maze of pathways, her eyes searching for him. When she at last beheld him lying on the ground, as one dead, her heart ceased beating in her breast.

"Father!" she screamed out, leaping from her horse and coming to his side. She buried her face in his tunic, her ear to his breast, remembering his words about death only moments before. Had he had a premonition of his own end?

Frantically she sought the beat of his heart. He looked so pale, so still. She forced herself to remain calm, and could hear the faint pounding of his heartbeat and thanked the gods for his life. He was not dead! Not dead! With gentle hands she examined him, noticing the blood trickling from his head. Tearing off a piece of cloth from the sleeve of her gown, she carefully bound his wound.

"Father. Wake up!" she entreated him. "Please, open your eyes!" She scolded herself for having caused this accident. Had she not been so vain, so anxious to show off her horsemanship, her father would not now be lying here like this—hurt, broken, bleeding.

"Oh, Father. I'm sorry, so sorry," she sobbed, letting her tears fall freely. She pressed her face close to his, wetting his own cheek with her tears. Was it the feel of those tears which finally caused him to regain consciousness? Struggling, he managed to open his eyes and look up at her.

"Wynne," he called out so weakly that she could barely hear him.

"Father," she murmured, stroking his face with her hand. He was so precious to her.

"The pain . . ." he moaned, closing his eyes in torment. "My back."

Wynne knew that she must get him back to his hearth, for she had no healing herbs with her, yet she was fearful of putting him on her horse and risking further injury to him. And she could not leave him alone out here at the edge of the forest with the wild animals prowling about, or worse yet, the members of the darkness cult roaming about.

She tried to think clearly. Then it came to her—when Cedric had been wounded in the battle with their warring neighbors the Brigantes, he had been brought home on a litter fashioned from leather and wood. She would have to do the same now for her father, for his life depended upon her skills.

She slipped his sword out of his scabbard, hacking feverishly at two straight tree limbs which would serve her purpose; then she removed her linen underskirt which was held up by a drawstring, stretching it tautly over the makeshift braces and fashioning a sort of litter.

Soothing her father with her words, she struggled to put him on this contraption, being careful lest she injure him more.

"Me legs . . . Wynne. I cannot feel my legs," he groaned.

"You'll be all right, Father. I promise you," she answered, trying to hide her tears. She could not stand seeing her strong, powerful father so helpless.

Her eyes turned toward her father's horse, shrieking in agony, its leg broken. She had been so busy with her father that she had been blind to the animal's suffering, but now she swiftly slit the animal's throat to end its misery, the blood flowing on the ground like a sort of sacrifice.

Tying the litter to Tara's harness, Wynne began the journey back toward their village, stopping along the way only once to gather some herbs to ease her father's pain.

It was a slow, agonizing trip back to the lodge. She could see that her father was in misery, yet he never once cried out.

When at last they arrived back before the hearth of their people, Wynne hastened to bring the Druids with their healing hands, who finally quenched the fire raging in her father's tortured frame.

Twenty-three

Wynne was by her father's side morning and night as he struggled to live. She soothed him with poultices as well as with soft words, and administered her herbs—rosemary for the pain in his head and yarrow for the fever which had taken hold of him the night of the accident—but there was little she could do for his fears, for Adair had no feeling from the waist down. The Druids had visited the lodge with their remedies and prayers, but it appeared that Adair was to spend the rest of his years tied to his bed.

Wynne tortured herself with blame for her father's condition, wishing over and over again that she could control time and return again to that day of their race.

I will never leave him, she vowed. Even were Valerian to return for her, she now knew that although she could love him, give him freely of her body, she would never leave her father. She would spend the rest of her life by his side as an atonement for her vain foolishness.

At first Brenna had been full of concern for her husband, seeing to his every need like a dutiful wife, but as it became apparent that Adair would never walk again, she began to spend so much time away from the lodge that Wynne suspected that she had a lover.

Let her stay away forever. I could hardly care, she thought. But seeing the hurt in her father's eyes, knowing that he too suspected Brenna, her heart went out to him. There was nothing that could be done to censor Brenna, for if a husband could not please his wife, it was her right to go elsewhere. Still, Wynne could not help the scorn that flowed from her lips after Brenna returned one night.

"You are foul! My father is tied to his bed while his loving wife plays the whore," Wynne said scathingly.

Brenna's eyes flashed with hatred for her stepdaughter. "And what would you have me do? Sleep in my bed alone? That I will never do. 'Tis not my fault that I am now tied to a helpless cripple!"

Wynne put her hand over the hated woman's mouth, fearful lest her father overhear them argue. She would do anything to shelter him from this woman's cruel words, anything. "Quiet. Or by the gods, I will not be responsible for my actions," she warned.

But Brenna would not be stilled, as she vented her anger and self-pity. "Who is to hunt for us?

We will have to depend on the charity of the tribe," she wailed.

"I will do the hunting. I am as skilled as my father in bringing down the deer and the boar," Wynne promised.

Brenna gave a harsh laugh. "You? You? So your wish is granted and you become your father's son after all!" She put her hands upon her ample hips and snarled, "Well, I will not be dependent on you for my food. I will go elsewhere. To another lodge."

"You cannot do that!" Wynne whispered in fright, aware of what such an insult would do to her father's pride. He would have no will left to live were such a thing to happen. Brenna was his wife, and even though Wynne herself would have liked to see the last of her in their lodge, she would never allow her father to be hurt that way.

"Oh, can't I?" Brenna replied with a cold smile.

"If you ever leave, you will have me to answer to," Wynne said fiercely. But then her eyes welled with tears. "Have you no pity at all, no love in your heart for my father?"

Brenna laughed cruelly. "Better for me that he had died from his fall. At least then I would be a widow and free to marry again, and not be tied to a useless lump of flesh and bones."

Wynne could control her temper no longer and lashed out, striking her stepmother full across the face, sending her reeling across the floor.

"You will never speak that way of my father again. Do you understand?" she said menacingly. "Say what you want to me. Do as you will. But at least show a little decency and kindness to my father or you will regret it!" With that, Wynne turned on her heel and walked out the door, feeling the night air cool her flushed face.

"You will pay for this. You will pay," Brenna hissed beneath her breath as she watched her husband's daughter leave. "I will see that I am revenged. I swear it will be so."

Twenty-four

Valerian and his men stood at the far side of the forest. It had been a long and difficult journey through mud, over hills, and through rivers, but Mars had guided them and Minerva had guarded their steps. Now Valerian had the strange sensation that he was home, that this was where he belonged—here, with Wynne. If only they could be alone together and shut out the rest of the world.

He had spent part of the morning washing off the dirt of the road in the river. It could not compare with the bathhouses in Aquae, but for now it was pure ecstasy. He remembered his first sight of Wynne's lovely body, that day by the lake. Soon, he thought happily, he would be with her again. The very idea of joining with her body sent waves of desire coursing through him.

"Centurion, are we to rest and make camp here for the night, or move onward?" he heard Burrus ask. He put on his bronze-crested helmet and turned to greet his young confidant and friend.

"We will make camp here for the night. I . . . I have someone I must talk with before we go any farther."

"Shall I go with you?" His voice sounded eager, his youthful desire for adventure underscoring his words.

"No. This is a journey I must make alone. I ask only that you attune your ears for my signal—if there is any trouble, you may have to come to my aid. However, I do not foresee such a necessity." He gave Burrus a comradely slap on the back. "You have been of much help to me. I shan't forget it."

"But you can't go alone. Remember the last time? What if you should fall into enemy hands?"

Valerian held the other man's eyes with his own. "This is something I must do. I must take the chance. The one I am to see, I would trust with my life. Indeed she once saved this sun-burned hide of mine from being burned by a different fire. I will go alone."

Burrus looked with surprise at the man he so admired. He had said "she." A woman? No wonder he did not want him tagging along. So the centurion, the brave and mighty Valerian, was not immune to the powers of Venus.

Valerian started off through the forest, his hand poised on his sword, his red cloak flung over his shoulder like a royal robe. Burrus could not help thinking what an imposing figure his friend was, walking beside the magnificent black horse.

As he walked, Valerian was assailed by worries. How would he find Wynne? How was he to speak with her without making himself vulnerable to the warriors of her tribe? Dare he hope that she would be at the cave, that secret hiding place where first he had possessed her lovely marble-white body?

"Sloan, we must hope that your mistress will sense my thoughts and be there to meet us," he said to the horse. As if in answer, the horse snorted and shook his head no.

"And so we know your answer, Sloan." He laughed. "Well, I will dare to imagine that you are wrong, that my lovely golden-haired Wynne will indeed be there.

Wynne shaded her eyes from the midday sun with one hand, while in the other she tightly clutched her spear and worked her way through the foliage in search of her prey. She had always abhorred the killing of deer, that graceful and gentle creature, but now it was her duty to do so. She had vowed to Brenna that she would keep the lodge well provided with food.

A rustle in the undergrowth behind her nearly unnerved her. Whirling around, she saw that it was only a small wolverine, also in search of its dinner.

Wynne laughed. "Fine hunter I am, frightened out of my wits by such a harmless animal."

Again she scoured the bushes for sign of her quarry. Her pulse quickened as she caught a glimpse of a small buck ducking into the undergrowth ahead of her. Clutching her spear and holding it out from her body, she scurried after the animal, thanking her father for suggesting that she wear his braccae instead of her gown under her tunic. Tripping over a long gown, she would have had no chance at all to catch the deer. Even so, the fine animal led her a merry chase through the forest. But when she paused briefly to catch her breath, the buck eluded her. Disappointed, and yet half-relieved, she sat down upon the hard ground to plan anew.

She reached up to adjust her pointed cap, which held her long flowing golden locks secure. This too was her father's suggestion, partly to make it easier for her to hunt and partly as a disguise. Adair had tried to talk her out of her resolve to go out hunting, but she had remained firm, insisting that she enjoyed the challenge. At last he had given his approval on the condition that she dress as a man.

Dressed like this, I will no doubt frighten the poor creatures to death, and I will not have to even raise my spear, she thought with a laugh. Looking about her, she could see that she was not far from her childhood hideaway. It had been so long since she had been able to visit the cave. Memories of Valerian flooded over her. It all seemed so long ago. Life was so different now. Putting her hands to her face, she gave in to her tears, not for herself but for her father. She had tried to be so brave in front of him, but now that she was alone, she could not control the flood. When at long last she had spent her emotion, she got up, determined to go again in search of her prey.

"I will never shed tears again," she vowed. "I will not give in to this womanly weakness. I will be strong, for my father and for myself." Somehow her words were a comfort to her, though she knew that it would be a difficult promise to keep.

Wynne set out again on the trail of her deer, pausing from time to time to watch and to listen. Once she thought she heard the sound of horses' hooves in the distance, yet her people seldom rode their horses out this far.

"I'm imagining things!" she scolded, moving onward through the woods.

A sound up ahead of her in the foliage told her that her quarry was nearby. Indeed she could see the tip of the buck's horns, hear his very breath. Taking careful aim, she let the spear take flight, racing off to the spot where the deer would be lying. She had a feeling of pride at her first kill, mixed with sorrow for the animal. But it would live again. Life was everlasting.

Wynne stepped through the bushes, her eyes searching for the wounded buck. She would put it out of its misery quickly so that it would not have to suffer. Such were the laws of her people.

But she could see no trace of the animal and stepped back, confused.

A hand grabbed at her from behind, clutching at her, grasping, pulling her down to the ground. Wynne fought like a wounded bear, biting, scratching, and flailing out at her attacker. She looked up expecting to find the hulking man who had tried to subdue her once before, but it was not he.

Wynne let out a gasp as her eyes beheld her assailant. The armor gleamed in the sun, as did the sword poised to strike her. The creature's head looked like a huge bird with its horsehair crest and the glittering cheek pieces. She could not see the face, but she imagined it to be cruel and savage. It was one of the hated Romans.

In spite of herself Wynne let out a scream, which bubbled forth from her mouth in terror as she sought her escape.

"So, you young savage. You try to murder me as you tried to do last time," she heard a voice say. Eyes wide with disbelief, she stared up at her captor.

"Valerian?" she whispered, not daring to believe her senses. Their eyes met and held.

He bent down and gently lifted her up. "By Jupiter. Wynne. I might have killed you!" he exclaimed, trembling all over from the shock of seeing her beneath his sword. "I would have died myself had I done so."

Wynne reached up and tugged at her hat, her hair falling down upon her shoulders in a cascade of gold. "Hunt . . ." she said with a slight smile. "Wynne dress like man." She made him understand that she had been tracking a deer and had thought him to be her quarry.

Valerian went to the spot where the javelin was embedded in the earth and shuddered as he pulled it out and brought it back to her.

"Why are you hunting?" he asked, for the women of his world would never do such a thing and he did not know of such a custom among the Celts.

Wynne's face was so filled with grief that he held out his arms to her, yet she could not come freely into their comforting warmth. Seeing him in his Roman garments, his soldier's clothing, made her feel uneasy. She began to realize for the first time the gulf which separated them, like the great sea between their lands. It was as if she did not know this soldier standing before her, and yet it was her Valerian.

As if sensing her thoughts, Valerian reached up and took off his imposing helmet, removed his baldric and scabbard, and gathered her into his arms, murmuring her name over and over as he kissed her hair, her lips, the softness of her neck. Wynne clung to him like one drowning in a raging sea, her emotions battering her like waves. He was a Roman, a soldier, but he was Valerian and she loved him more than anything in the world. She belonged in his arms.

Breathlessly she told him about her father, her capture by the darkness cult, her punishment and isolation, Brenna's wrath, and her promise to keep food at the hearth of her father.

Valerian listened patiently, brushing back the hair from her beautiful face, murmuring words of comfort and sympathy, controlling the desire which threatened to engulf him. It was as if the whole world beyond them ceased to exist, as if they were the only two people alive, as if there were no warfare between their peoples, only this fire which burned in them whenever they were near.

When Wynne had finished her story, Valerian told her about his reason for coming back, his warning.

"You must either leave, flee this land until the Romans have gone," he said, "or put down your arms and make peace."

She looked at him with anger. "This land is our home. We will not run. The Romans must make peace."

"But you must understand. My chieftain has sent me to do so. If you do not, he will have you killed!" He forgot for the moment all gentleness as he shook her roughly by the shoulders, trying to make her see what must be done. In Wynne's eyes he again became the enemy, a hated Roman. In anger she turned her back on him and stalked away.

"Wynne! Wynne! Can't you see that I don't want any harm to come to you? I love you," he cried. Helplessly he stood there, not knowing what to do or to say.

"You and your people—enemies!" she exclaimed bitterly. Turning toward him again, she looked into the depths of his amber eyes and saw his sadness. *He* was not her enemy. This was Valerian, who had taught her the joys of love.

With a sob she ran into the circle of his arms, felt herself engulfed within the cloak of his passion, as all her resistance ebbed. Her lips found his, her body arched against him. With a tormented cry he crushed her in his arms, kissing her hungrily, fiercely. Sweet Venus, he loved her. All the weeks of worry, of misery, of nightmares, dissolved. Forgotten were Severus, the legion—everything but his longing to love her.

Picking her up in his arms, Valerian headed for the cave, unaware of the eyes which watched them from afar, the cunning eyes of Severus Cicero.

"A little bedsport, eh, Valerian?" Severus whispered beneath his breath with a chuckle. "Well, you had best enjoy it while you may. Before I get through with you, a woman will be the last thing on your mind." Turning his horse around, he galloped over the crest of the hill to his camp to plan for the coming battle.

Twenty-five

The ground under Wynne and Valerian was hard, but they didn't feel it. Their thoughts were only on each other. He moved his mouth on hers, pressing her lips apart, seeking, exploring the softness. His kisses made her dizzy, they sparked such a fire within her.

Valerian undressed her slowly, reverently. "I want to look at you," he whispered. "You are even more lovely than I remembered." His eyes were so warm. She had no thought other than that she was in Valerian's arms and he was embracing her. He was finally here and he belonged to her.

He kissed her neck, her shoulders, the swell of her breasts, then caressed the sweet softness of her body.

"I love your touch!" she whispered.

188 / Kathryn Kramer

"I love you. I love the taste of you, the feel of your body next to mine."

Wynne watched him remove his cuirass, his boots, his tunic, his loincloth. She had forgotten the beauty of his lean muscular body. He was so handsome, her Valerian, so strong yet so gentle.

She reached out and caressed him, feeling his back, the muscles of his thighs, his buttocks. Her eyes touched his manhood, standing stiff and proud with his passion for her. The sight of it brought an ache between her legs.

"Touch me," he moaned, guiding her hand. At the soft caress of her fingers, he shuddered. He pulled her under him, his weight nearly crushing her.

"Oh, Wynne, Wynne," he breathed. Again he kissed her, her mouth opening to his probing tongue, his soft full lips. It was as if they had been created each for the other, so well did they fit together. Valerian trailed hot kisses across her neck and breasts, his hand gently exploring, probing and caressing the hidden core of her being, setting her aflame. Her arms cradled his head to her breasts, his mouth torturing the swollen peaks.

Gently Valerian parted her legs and plunged deep within her. Wynne gasped, breathless with pleasure. Their bodies moved together like a summer storm, wild and sweet. He stroked her hair, murmuring words of love, sending shivers of delight through her.

Wynne gazed into his eyes and felt as if they

were joined in spirit as well as in flesh. She loved this Roman, loved her enemy.

At last they lay entangled, drenched with the dew of their love, and fell fast asleep.

Much later Wynne opened her eyes and smiled as she beheld her lover, the smooth muscles of his chest and arms. She noticed a scar on his shoulder and gently traced it with her finger.

"I killed during the battle where I got this wound," Valerian said sadly. "Celtic blood is on my hands. How I hate it. It's as if you can never get the blood off your hands after that."

"A warrior must kill," she answered softly.

"Perhaps, but killing is so often senseless. Blood begets more blood, until we drown in a red sea of our own making."

She started to speak, but he silenced her. "Don't talk. I want to love you. I need you so. I've wanted you for so long. I've dreamed about you."

"And I about you."

He cupped her face with his hands. "You have gone through so much for our love." He kissed her softly, his mouth sweet yet firm on hers.

Wynne put her arms around him and clung to him, urging him back down upon her body; her senses whirled and soared as he again covered her softness with his hard strong body.

"Love me again, Valerian," she whispered breathlessly.

With a groan he took her. She moaned and dug her fingers into his flesh as wave after wave of ecstasy washed over them. They were one, joined, forged—like iron. So great was her pleasure that it seemed to her that surely she must die, that she had gone beyond this world to the realms of the gods. She whispered his name over and over again as Valerian held her close, sharing her passion.

Wynne lay together with Valerian in their warm tangle of arms and legs, savoring the sweetness of their lovemaking. Valerian moaned and stirred, reaching out to caress her. Suddenly his eyes flew open and he was fully awake.

"Severus. I had forgotten. He will be here in two days with his legion." He sat up, his heart beating wildly. He had been so caught up in the enchantment of their lovemaking that he had closed his mind to all else. And Wynne, he realized, must return to her camp before she caused worry.

She understood his anxiety. "I must go," she whispered with regret. Now that she had found him again, she did not want to be parted, but she still had a deer to kill, and dusk would soon be approaching.

"Wynne. Wynne. You must make your people understand that they must offer the Romans peace, for if they do not, they will be slaughtered. The Romans far outnumber your warriors, and although I do not doubt that they are fine fighters, they cannot win against the might of Rome."

"No," she said stubbornly. She rose and stood

before him, her body gleaming like a marble statue in the light.

Quickly he got up, coming behind her and putting his arms around her slim waist. This was going to be more difficult than he had imagined, but he had to make her understand. "Many of your people have made peace with the Romans, retaining the Celtic chiefs who were their leaders. The only difference is that they become Roman officials."

Her eyes held such a fury that he was taken aback. "I spit on them. They are not Celts. They dress like Romans, talk like Romans, worship gods of Romans. Not Celts."

Valerian had to agree with her, yet even though he knew that her people would be greatly changed under Roman rule, he still had to protect them from the slaughter he knew would occur. Better Roman than dead. He recalled what Severus had told him about the northwest tribes that had refused to listen to the voice of the empire or to lay aside their native habits and warlike ways. Still he admired such courage.

"Trust me, Wynne," he said, looking deep into her eyes. "The Romans will soon leave and you will be free to do as you will. There are many tribes which have done so." He felt guilt wash over him, for he knew well what would happen. They would become Romanized, and a certain amount of freedom would be gone. It would be only a matter of time before the fiery Celt would be changed into the orderly Roman citizen.

Wynne's eyes mirrored her trust. Valerian would not hurt her people; he must be speaking the truth. Perhaps if the Romans were as fierce as he said, it would be better to be their friends. Her tribe had lived in peace for a long while now; they were not really prepared for the war which was to come.

"Perhaps we make peace, but must keep old gods, cannot make gods angry." Her chin jutted out with her defiance.

"Yes," he agreed, hoping that he could convince Severus to allow them to keep the Druid priests. He knew in the fruitful plains of the southeast where the Latinized Britons were concentrated, many of the gods had been blended eventually, many couples formed by the association of a Roman god and a native goddess, a sort of marriage between the beliefs.

Wynne smiled at him, showing her even white teeth. He gathered her into his arms and kissed her. "Now I go," she whispered.

"Yes, before I no longer have the power to let you escape from me." He patted her playfully on the behind to start her on her way, watching her dress, caressing her with his eyes. "You will speak to your people?"

"I will talk with my father, convince him to let me sit at war council. Women can do so. It is the custom of our tribe." Valerian gave a relieved sigh, happy that this worry that had plagued his days and nights was now to be lifted. He would hurry with his legion, search for

Severus, and give him the news. There would be no war.

"I will meet you here tomorrow for your tribe's answer," he said, "at the setting of the sun."

"Tomorrow. At dusk," she repeated, putting her arms around his neck and kissing him in farewell. She left the cave, glancing back at him from time to time. Valerian watched her go, knowing that this time when he left he would take her with him. He could not leave her again. If need be, he would take her father back with him too. He would see that the bard was well cared for.

"The world is beautiful!" he declared happily, whistling merrily as he left the cave to return to Burrus. Wynne would make her people understand the need for peace. He would convince Severus of the same thing. All would be well. And when he left, returned to Eboracum, he would have the woman he loved by his side.

Sloan awaited him not far from the cave, and Valerian mounted the horse to make his way back to his legion.

Twenty-six

In the lodge of Adair, Brenna paced back and forth. Where was Duncan? He had promised once and for all to get rid of the girl. Had he bungled the job as the giant had? She thought of that hulking kinsman of hers. Too bad she had been forced to kill him, but she could take no chances. She was high priestess of the followers of Domnu, Domnu of the Darkness. She had told Duncan Wynne would be out in the forest hunting. How could he miss finding her, with that mane of golden hair glowing in the sun?

Duncan had best be able to tell me when he returns that my husband's daughter is safely within our grasp, she thought with anger. How she had hated Wynne, right from the first. And then that night at the ceremony when she had so eagerly awaited the sacrifice of the handsome

Roman, only to find that the golden-haired chit had cut his bonds. Brenna had ordered that the dark-haired Roman be given a potion of white bryony and nightshade—belladonna—for the mating ceremony. He would have been a powerful lover, she knew. And afterward she would have given him as a sacrifice to the goddess Domnu herself, a blazing offering at the festival of the Feast of Five Fires.

Brenna could hear the snores of her husband as he slept on his bedshelf across the room. How she hated being tied to him now. Of course, before his accident he had been a fine lover, but no more.

You helpless old man. Why didn't you die? she thought vehemently. Well, perhaps once his daughter was safely out of the way she would see to his death also. She would not be forced to care for him.

Brenna was jealous of the power Adair had always had. Perhaps that was why she had become the priestess of Domnu.

Men. So foolish in their puffed-up pride. They are so easy to manipulate. Their brains are always in their manhood, she thought with scorn. Who were they to say that a woman could not hold the priesthood? It was just one more way in which they controlled a woman's destiny, made her a servant to their desires, a brood mare to bring forth their seed. She laughed as she remembered how eagerly Adair had awaited the birth of a son from her loins, little knowing that she had carefully used her herbs to bring on the heavy flow of her monthly time and to make herself infertile, because the demons of the night, the dark ones, decreed that a priestess should be barren.

She looked down at Adair as he slept, his face ravaged by his despair at the uselessness of his legs. True, he had once been a strong man and a forceful lover. She would never forget their wedding night. But those days were gone forever. Duncan pleasured her now, and if he was not as handsome, well, he would do for the time being.

A sudden impulse to wear Adair's Druid robes overcame her. She would have made such a fine Druid priestess, she was so strong and cunning. Giving in to her temptation, she gazed down at Adair; he still slumbered as soundly as one dead. She walked to the silver clothing chest where he kept his sacred garments and slowly opened the lid. How different would his white linen robe feel from her own coarse black priestess robe. Was there magic in the robes, as she had heard tell?

She slipped the robe over her shoulders, un-aware of the eyes which watched her in bewilderment from across the room. Adair had awakened and thought at first he still dreamed as he watched his wife. Surely she must know that it was forbidden to don the sacred robes. He was tempted to cry out to her, but a sixth sense warned him to keep silent.

Brenna was disappointed once she had put on the mystic garments. They felt no different from any of her other clothing. They were lighter weight than her dark robes, but she felt no surge of magic power from them. A sudden fear clutched at her heart. Domnu would be angered by her actions. Tearing the robe from her body, she began chanting to the offspring of Chaos and Old Night, the deformed ones, gods of the darkness; demons of night, darkness, death, barrenness, and evil. Then in a final act of atonement she tore the garment in two and held it up as if it were an offering to the goddess.

May the gods protect us, Adair thought in sadness as he heard her evil incantation and beheld her sacrilege. What vile evilness is this? Had he been a whole man, he would have leapt from his bed to take retribution on her for her treachery, but he was helpless. All he could do was to warn Wynne when she came back to the lodge to watch out for Brenna. She was acting as one demented—she could not be a member of the darkness cult, not the wife whose body he had entered, whose love he had cherished. It could not be true. So thinking, he closed his eyes and returned to the safety of his sleep.

When Wynne returned to the lodge, Brenna greeted her with such a look of surprise that Wynne was alarmed.

"What is it? What is wrong? Father is not ill, is he?" she asked fearfully.

Brenna found her voice at last. "No . . . your father is sleeping. He is fine. But you—your clothing. I . . . well . . . did you have any luck?" Her thoughts were in turmoil. So Wynne had escaped capture again. She cursed the girl and her father for their cunning, and felt a tingle of fear. Had they perhaps suspected what was afoot? Was that why Wynne had dressed herself in that strange costume?

"I brought home a large buck," she answered proudly. She felt triumphant and content.

"Well, it certainly took you enough time to bring the animal down," Brenna retorted scathingly, envious of the young woman's success.

Remembering the moments of love she had shared with Valerian in their hideaway, Wynne blushed. Thinking of Valerian brought to mind his words concerning the Romans, and she pushed past the dark-haired Brenna to talk with her father. She wanted to tell him all that Valerian had told her and ask his advice. She could only hope that he would not be angry when he learned that the Roman was back. Brenna followed hot on her heels, as if afraid to let her out of her sight. Wynne found Adair sleeping.

"That's about all he does now," Brenna said sarcastically.

Wynne ignored her cutting words. Bending down, she gently brushed back the blond hair from her father's face, the face she so dearly loved. If only there were something she could do to give him his legs again. She had prayed to all the gods, but her prayers had not been answered. At the feel of her cool hands Adair opened his eyes and smiled.

"So, you are back, my daughter," he whispered. "How was the hunting?"

"I brought back a large buck, Father," she answered proudly. No son could have done better, she knew.

"I was certain that you would. You are an unusual young woman, Wynne. I am proud of you." He struggled to sit up, and she carefully helped him. "Wynne . . ." he choked, looking in the direction of his wife and remembering all that he had watched her do. Perhaps Wynne with her second sight could tell him why Brenna had been acting so strangely.

"Be careful, Father. Do not strain yourself. You have not yet fully recovered of your strength," Wynne scolded, casting Brenna a glance that told the woman that she wanted to be alone with her father. Stubbornly Brenna refused to leave, but a stern nod from Adair changed her mind. He was still the head of the hearth and a leader of the tribe. She could not willfully disobey him if he wished her to be gone. Crossing the room, she engaged herself in cooking the night's meal while straining to hear what went on between father and daughter.

"I must tell you something . . ." Adair began, looking in his wife's direction and deciding that she would not hear him.

Wynne silenced him with a hand to his lips. "There is something I must tell you first. It is important. The Roman is back!"

Adair's eyebrows drew together as he frowned. "He is here?" The fear that the stranger would take Wynne from him washed over Adair. "What does he want?" he asked.

"The Roman came to talk peace." Wynne took his hand in hers and squeezed it tightly, as if by doing so she could make him understand her feelings.

"Peace! Ha! The Romans do not want peace. They want to wipe the Celts off the land so that they can expand their mighty empire. Your Roman is no different."

Wynne shook her head. "Yes, he is different! He *does* want peace. Father, we cannot let our hatred blind us. There are Romans who are greedy and cruel. But is it not true that there are those of our race who are the same? Should we be judged by the deeds of the darkness cult?"

"No!"

Quickly she told him all that Valerian had said, careful to avoid any reference to their lovemaking, for fear of alienating her father once again.

When she was finished with her story, Adair scowled. "How do we know that we can trust this Roman?" he asked with suspicion. "I have been to the lands of the South and seen what the Romans have done. They are like maggots swarming over the carcass of a dead animal. The Romans have little love for us."

Avoiding his eyes lest she betray all the love that she felt for her Roman, Wynne answered, "I know we can trust him, Father. He would not lie to us. What reason would there be to play us false?"

"Ambition. Greed."

"Valerian abhors all the bloodshed. He wants an end to the fighting between our peoples. I felt as you do now at first, but I see the wisdom of his words. We are not prepared to fight. The Romans will crush us like a beetle beneath their heel."

"But to give up without a fight. That is not our way. We are not afraid to die, Wynne. We are not cowards. Death is but the blink of an eye between this life and the next." Again he struggled to sit up, loudly cursing his infirmity.

"Perhaps we could prepare ourselves to fight at a later time if need be, if the Romans play us untrue or rule us too harshly. Then could we overthrow their hated rule, when we were strengthened. What is the wisdom in fighting a battle we know we will lose?" At her father's silence she continued, "I promised that I would talk with the warriors at the council this very night. I vowed, Father. I cannot go back on my word. Please, can you be there with me? Can you arrange such a meeting?" She bent her head in submission to his will, her lower lip trembling, her eyes closed.

Adair could deny her nothing, not even this. His hatred for the Romans ran deep, but his love for his daughter was even deeper.

"What harm can come of talk?" he answered. With his hand he tipped up her face so that he could meet her eyes. "I must warn you, however, that the council will think as I do. If they do not agree to peace, there will be nothing either you or I can do to sway them, nor would I want to do so."

"I understand."

"Still, I will be there with you."

"Thank you, Father." She knew how much strength it would take for Adair to do as he promised, and loved him more at that moment than ever before. Hugging him to her breast, she could hardly contain her excitement. She hurried off to see about the preparations for the council before Adair could tell her about Brenna.

Twenty-seven

The veil of night fell over the village as Wynne awaited the time of the council with great anxiety. She sought to still her trembling hands, for now she must be strong, could show no sign of weakness. To be among the Druids and warriors at such a time, to speak at council, was in itself an honor. Not even Brenna's envious eyes and sharp tongue could dampen her pride.

Wynne took great care choosing her garments for the meeting. Looking into the polished silver mirror her father had brought back from one of his trips to the Southland, Wynne studied herself. She had chosen to wear scarlet and white, symbolizing war and peace; the underskirt of white, the overgown of scarlet. The gown had long close sleeves and she wore a sleeveless bodice of fur. The glow of her jewelry shone in the light of the fire, the large ornate earrings with their great golden hoops, the large gilt bracelets which covered both her arms, the bronze belt which carried a scabbard for her sword, a gift from her father for the occasion. Her hair was left hanging long, a golden circlet adorning her head. Wynne carried in her left hand a bronze shield emblazoned with a maze of curving tendrils. She looked imposing in her finery, just as she had intended.

Adair too was imposing in his purple tunic and black braccae. He wore a sleeveless overtunic and a fur cloak over his once-strong body and looked like the leader that he indeed was.

Cedric, the chief of the tribe, had come with his son Edan to carry Adair to the council. Edan looked at Wynne with admiration in his eyes.

"You are beautiful, Wynne," he said in awe. "As beautiful as a goddess."

She smiled her thanks, taking his hand in a gesture of friendship. Cedric and Edan carried her father in a wicker chair, and Wynne followed close behind them to the sacred oak grove.

The full moon shone brightly down on the earth. Wynne could see as they approached the fire that the warriors were all wearing their round bronze helmets with horns on either side or with a comb of bronze in the center. The faces of the warriors were stern, causing Wynne to feel cold with fear.

Tonight there was to be a feast of deer meat. Wine and mead flowed as freely as after a battle. No doubt the men would call for her father to

sing his lays of the ancestors and songs in praise
of their own valor.

"Why must there be wine and mead?" Wynne
asked with annoyance. Whenever there was
drink, there was likely to be a quarrel. She knew
that sometimes the smallest pretext could pro-
voke a duel, which was often fatal. Death meant
little; it was just a moment of transition.

Adair laughed for the first time in a long
while. "Ah, just like a woman to question," he
said. "Men need to feel relaxed when important
business is at hand. They want to feel the blood
course through their veins."

Wynne snorted in disgust. "Well, I hope that
they remain sober so that we can discuss the
matter at hand." She well remembered the last
time she had sat in on such a meeting. It had
soon turned into a near-brawl.

There was little cause to worry, however, as
Wynne was to find out, for after eating, Cedric
raised his hand and the council was started.
Wynne knew from experience that each warrior
had a vote. She would have to convince the
majority of them of the wisdom of keeping peace
with the Romans, and that would be no easy
task. At the end of the night the vote would be
taken—javelins pointed with the tip to the ground
would mean a vote for war, javelins pointed
upward a vote for peace.

Standing, with her hands clutched tightly in
front of her, Wynne began explaining what the
Roman had told her.

"The Romans have the mistaken idea that

our peoples still indulge in human sacrifices," she said. "They ask of us only that we abolish such practices, which we have done already, long ago as a matter of fact." Wynne knew that in the far North there were still a few tribes that practiced human sacrifice, though most were civilized. It was too bad that the Romans saw all the Celts as one people and were unaware that they were made up of many tribes and customs.

One weathered old warrior stood defiantly in front of her. "And what else do these Romans ask of us? Far more than a promise to change our rites and customs, I'll wager."

"They want us to lay down our arms to them, give them our swords and our shields."

"Let them shear us of our weapons as the shepherd shears the sheep? Never!" Edan shouted from out of the darkness. His fists were clenched in anger as he glared at Wynne. Gone was his look of admiration.

Wynne stared into the darkness, seeking his face. "The Romans want peace. Their chieftain in Rome wants peace. Can it harm us to talk with them?"

"No doubt our brothers in the South listened to the Romans' false words. They were butchered and the sacred places burned. So much for the Romans' talk of peace," Edan cried out. The knowledge that Wynne's words were uttered out of her love for a Roman was like gall in his mouth. How could she be so blind?

Wynne fought to maintain her calm. "We are

not prepared to fight. We have been at peace too long."

"We are growing soft!" came the voice of the old warrior, angry at her words. "Someday this peace we wallow in will be the death of us all." With a snort he walked to the outer circle of the council, leaving behind him an uproar of discussion.

Wynne looked at her father, begging him to intercede for her, but he merely nodded his head as if to tell her that she was doing well. Twelve flickering torches danced in the night as Wynne stood by and watched the warriors in their talk. Finally one of the younger warriors spoke.

"Is it not true that the Romans will govern us as they do in the lands to the south?"

All eyes were upon her, waiting eagerly for her answer. "You are right, Maddock," she answered the red-haired warrior. "Our chieftain, Cedric, will become an official of the Roman Empire, reporting to Rome."

At her words turmoil broke out, shouts of anger that no Celt would ever agree to such a thing, threats to slit all the Romans' throats and hang their heads on the walls as the great ancestors had done. Wynne cursed herself for a fool for not weighing her words more carefully when so much depended upon this night, but all was not lost yet. If the vote was taken now, however, she knew well that the vote would be for war.

She was surprised when Cedric himself put up a hand to motion silence. He stood up from his place at the fire, tall, strong, red-gold hair gleaming in the firelight.

"I understand your feelings," he said sternly holding his head up with the dignity which befitted a leader of the people, "but we must think carefully before we decided what to do." With powerful strides he walked toward the fire, and taking his sword, drew upon the hard ground a rough map. "The Romans now are the rulers of a vast empire. Even here in Britain they occupy nearly one-third of the lands." He sliced at the map like one would an apple. "Here," he said, pointing to the area north of Humber and Trent, west of Severn and Exe, "is the area where the Roman soldiers have their great fortresses, here at Eboracum and at Caerlcon. And here"—he drew a host of lines through the map—"are the roads which they have built like a web through our land."

Wynne could see that the warriors were restless. A rumbling sounded through the night.

Cedric continued. "Wynne is right. We cannot win in our battle against the Romans. We are not prepared for war at this time. We have grown soft. Therefore I advise that we make peace with these would-be rulers of the world. There is much we can learn from them. And if they are as ruthless as some fear, we can use their own strategy against them. In the meantime, we can again make ourselves strong."

Again the red-haired Maddock stood up. "No. We must not bend our necks to the Roman yoke. We have been slaves to no men. I will not be one now!"

Each warrior took his turn to say his piece, some arguing against Wynne and Cedric, others speaking for peace. Long into the night the arguments raged. Looking over at her father, Wynne could see that he was wisely weighing every word before he took his turn. Finally that time came about.

"I have listened to all of your words," he said. "I too have pride. I, like you, would not want to see us as vassals of the Roman Empire, but I feel that to declare war is folly . . . self-sacrifice. I propose to you that we listen to the words of the Roman soldiers before we decide what course of action to take. What harm is there in listening? I suggest that we put our trust in the honesty and honor of this tribune who rides upon us. Show him that we will talk peace with him, if that is his desire. Then, if we can come to no understanding, we will turn to warfare, but first we must listen."

Wynne drew strength from her father's words. He was so wise. When it was her turn again, she suggested that as a symbol of goodwill they lay down their arms, for no soldiers would make war upon unarmed people.

"I will take back our answer to the centurion tomorrow at dusk," she said. There was silence as the moment of the voting drew near.

"Maddock, what is your vote?" Maddock, as Wynne had suspected, stuck the point of his javelin in the ground. "Cedric." His was a vote for peace. "Edan." War. "Adair" Again peace. The next three warriors buried the points of their javelins in the earth. War.

Thirty-six warriors were to vote that night, three circles of twelve. When the count was taken, twelve were for war, twenty-four for peace.

So be it. My answer to Valerian is that the Celtic people, my people, agree to talk peace, Wynne thought with relief. This should have made her content. It was the answer she had hoped for, and yet suddenly she was nearly overwhelmed by a vision of mayhem and slaughter.

For one brief moment Wynne was tempted to heed the warning of these bloody images, to caution the warriors. But she did not; logic told her that no harm could come of seeking peace, and she shook her head to clear away these distressing pictures.

"So, daughter, you have been granted your request for peace," Adair said proudly. "No warrior could have done better."

"Yes, Father. Let me not live to regret it," she answered, taking his hand and walking beside him as Cedric and Edan lifted up his chair and carried him back to his lodge.

Twenty-eight

Before daybreak, Valerian was up and about, anx-
ious for the Celtic campaign to be over. He
prayed to all his gods that the answer Wynne
would bring with her would be for peace.

The earth was covered with a mist which gave
the land a magical appearance, as if they had
been transported to the land of the gods. Valerian had learned from soldiers in his camp who
had been several years in this country that it
was often thus in this boggy land.

His men all seemed to be of good cheer,
grateful for a chance to rest after their long,
tedious journey. The countryside abounded with
wild game, so they were well fed.

"So, centurion. I see that you have returned."
Burrus smiled at Valerian's appearance, which
told the young soldier not only that the mission
had gone well but also that the handsome centu-

rion had spent the hours away in the arms of a passionate woman.

"Yes, and I have much reason for joy," Valerian answered.

"Then we are to have peace?" Burrus asked, relief washing over him like a tide. He was so sick of killing.

"Tonight at dusk I will know for certain, but I feel in my heart that the answer will be to talk of peace."

Together Valerian and Burrus made plans to ensure that Severus kept his word. They would seek him out just as soon as Valerian got his answer.

"We will ride southeast to meet his legion," Valerian decided. "Prepare the men to break camp at dawn tomorrow. We will ride like the wind ahead of the foot soldiers so that we may intercept Severus in plenty of time to counsel with him."

The day progressed so slowly that Valerian thought he would go mad. He longed to see Wynne again, not only to find out her people's decision but also to feel again the rapture of their lovemaking. She was all he had ever wanted in a woman—beautiful, wise, brave, kind, and she had a passion which sparked his own desire. What a wife she would make, and he *would* wed her, for he wanted to spend his entire lifetime with this lovely creature.

Valerian's thoughts turned to Severus. Would he be disappointed to learn there would be peace? Even Severus would not command his men to attack unarmed men, and Valerian would make certain that he informed Severus of the peaceful intentions of the Celtic peoples in the presence of several of the other centurions so that no mistakes could be made as to orders.

Had Valerian been able to see the face of his tribune at that moment, he would not have felt so optimistic. The tribune and his soldiers were camped much closer than Valerian would have ever dreamed, only a mile or so from Valerian's own camp, on the ridge of a hill. From where Severus now stood, he could see the distant figures of his centurion's army and cursed Valerian under his breath.

"He thinks to strike first so that the glory will be his. No doubt that golden-haired slut I saw him cavorting with is his spy and has told him the secrets which will help him to be victorious." His beady eyes gleamed with his hatred for the dark-haired centurion. He had always had everything he wanted—a powerful senator for a father, money, good looks. It had always been so easy for Valerian; hadn't he always gotten his way? Well, no more. Severus would not let the young upstart wrest this glory away from him, not when he, Severus Cicero, had been forced to work so hard to get where he was now, groveling before the rich and powerful in order to become a tribune.

What would be Valerian's battle plan? Surprise, no doubt, for his small century would be outnumbered by the Celtic warriors, he imagined, and they were ferocious fighters. Yet if they were taken unaware, before they had the chance to band together with other tribes, they would be vulnerable.

"At dawn. Valerian prepares to attack in the early hours of the dawn," he said in triumph. "But I will have already won my victory by then." He began to laugh uncontrollably. It was all to be so easy. What better way to ensure victory than to strike down a warrior while he was at ease, attending to his dinner?

"At dusk. We will attack at the setting of the sun. We will slaughter them before they have a chance to arm themselves, then we will burn down the oak trees in their sacred groves so that there will be no place on this earth where those savages can hide."

He smiled his toothy smile as he thought of the pleasure he would get from the sight of Valerian's expression when the centurion learned how Severus Cicero had bested him.

"And then I will derive extreme pleasure from separating his handsome head from his shoulders," he cried aloud, hugging his arms about his chest like a small boy. "I will put him to death for the traitor he is."

With a frenzied urgency, the tribune made his way down the hill to his tent, his heart drumming in his breast. He must prepare his men for their evening onslaught, his victory!

Twenty-nine

The shadows of the afternoon were deepening as Wynne rode Tara through the forest. Looking up at the sky, she was alarmed by the commotion of the birds, squawking and flying to and fro as if something had disturbed their peace. She veered off her chosen path in order to investigate the clearing for any signs of danger, thinking perhaps that the creatures of the sky sensed the presence of the darkness cult about, but she could find no trace of any humans near the area. Still, she had an uneasy feeling as she rode onward to her meeting with Valerian.

Approaching the cave, she was delighted to see Sloan standing before the entrance, regal and proud. It had been so long since she had ridden on the animal's back. She had missed him so. Slipping from Tara's back, she secured the mare tightly to a tree, fearful lest the animal stray, and ran over to where the large black horse stood grazing at the grass in front of the cave.

"Sloan," she called. The animal raised his head and nickered in greeting. Wynne patted his head, then looked around for Valerian. She would ask him to let her ride the black horse just once before she left this night.

"He has missed you," she heard a voice behind her say. Valerian came toward her from out of the forest. In his hand he held a bouquet of wildflowers. "For you," he said, thrusting them into her hands.

She smiled her thanks at him, breathing deeply of the fragrance of the flowers. His gesture touched her.

"I found some violets for you," he whispered. "You always smell of violets." He looked at her as if he would devour her, and Wynne was strangely shy. She lowered her eyes.

"I love violets," she answered.

"They will always remind me of you." He took her hand and gently led her into the cave. Valerian's lips moved to hers, his mouth warm and soft. He began to remove her clothing, but Wynne fought to stop him. This was neither the time nor the place. First she must tell him about her people's decision.

"I feel within my soul that the answer you have brought me is that there will be peace between our people. Is that not so?"

"Yes," she breathed, taking his hand and telling him about the war council. He felt his chest swell with pride for her. She was brave and eloquent, this lovely creature, and she was his.

"Tomorrow at the first rays of the sun my soldiers and I will ride out to meet Severus Circero. Even he cannot make war when there is a truce." Valerian spread his cloak upon the ground and gently tugged at her hand, pulling her down upon it. "Tomorrow at dawn I will ride out and will be gone for several days, but I will come back for you."

Wynne started to say that she could not leave her father now, could not go with him when he returned, but he silenced her with a kiss. He was right: they had only tonight. This time when he reached up to take away her garments, she did not stop him. Her beautiful body glowed in the dim light like ivory, so lovely was she. Valerian caressed every part of her, his lips devouring hers.

"We were meant for each other—do you know that, my pretty Wynne?" he breathed huskily. "I knew it the moment I saw you bending over me like a goddess. My flesh, my heart, my soul, belong to you. Without you I am as nothing. . . ." He stripped off his clothing, longing to become one with her.

Wynne's eyes and heart, her very senses, were filled with him as he stood naked beside her, as a god come to earth. His chest and arms were powerful, his waist slim, his skin tan and smooth. Wynne felt flames of desire consume her. As he bent down, she reached for him.

Valerian caressed her breasts, murmuring

words of love in her ear. His lips branded her flesh as he kissed her stomach and thighs. Wynne reached out to caress him also as they were swept up in the fire which ignited their love.

"Love me, Valerian," she moaned. His touch was driving her mad with her need of him. More than anything else she wanted to feel him inside her.

Valerian plunged into the sweet soft depths of her being, shuddering with excitement.

"We are a perfect fit, like a sword in a scabbard," he whispered. It was as if a bolt of Jupiter's own fire struck them, so wild were they with the rapture of their loving. Wynne had never known such abandon, such ecstasy.

When their passion was spent, Valerian moved away from her slightly, but Wynne did not want him to leave her. They fell asleep entwined, fulfilled, and content.

Valerian sat staring at his fair lover, marveling at the effect she always had on him. "I never have enough of you, goddess," he whispered, watching the flutter of her eyelids as she slumbered. He reached out to stroke her soft silken hair.

"You will be my wife. I vow it," he said, then wondered what the customs for marriage were among her people. In the Roman world a woman could not marry or dispose of property without the consent of her father, brother, son, or guardian, and after she was married she in turn became the ward of her husband, for the family was patriarchal, the power of the father and the husband nearly absolute. Would Wynne have to have her father's permission to marry him? Could he ever convince her father to let her marry a man from a different land?

"Surely the gods could not be so cruel as to let me glimpse what life is like with your love, the happiness we could share, only to take you away from me!" No, it must not be so; he would have Wynne to wive.

Gazing down at his beloved, Valerian was alarmed to see that she had suddenly gone pale, and was now tossing and turning and moaning in her sleep. Was she ill? He reached down to gather her into his arms, but she pushed away from him, her eyes wide open.

"No. No . . . please . . . don't let it be true," she cried out, her eyes wide with fright.

"What is it? Wynne, what is wrong?" he asked, again reaching out for her. This time she sought the safety of his arms.

"The voices . . . they told me . . . danger. Fire . . . death . . ." She told him how they had also warned her of the danger he was in that night when first they met. "I must go back!" Quickly she donned her clothing as Valerian watched, feeling panic rise in him as well.

"Let me go with you," he demanded, reaching out for his own clothing and dressing himself with trembling hands. What was happening? What terrifying sight had her dreams brought her?

"No. I must go alone," she insisted. "There is danger."

"All the more reason for me to go with you," Valerian answered firmly. He followed her out of the cave determined to go with her, but she raced to her white horse and sprang upon its back.

Seeing that she would soon be out of his sight, Valerian called after her. "I will come again for you in a month, in one cycle of the moon. Do you hear me, Wynne? I won't let you go!"

Turning for one brief glimpse of him as she rode off, Wynne felt as if a dagger were thrust into her heart. How could she live without him? Closing her eyes for an instant, she felt the tears trembling upon her lashes.

"Good-bye, Good-bye, my Valerian," she sobbed.

Valerian mounted Sloan and started off for camp, but suddenly he heard a shrill sound far off in the distance, the sound of trumpets.

"No. It can't be," he exclaimed. The sound was all too familiar, the signal for attack. With a scream of anger and anguish he turned the giant horse around and headed off in the direction of Wynne's village, but he soon became lost in the forest, not knowing exactly which way to go. He had to find Wynne before she reached her tribe, for he too now knew what was to happen.

"Great Jupiter, let it not be so!" Why had he not been more wary of Severus? How could he have trusted his word? The man was a serpent, a vile heartless beast, and Valerian was certain that it was of Severus that Wynne had been warned.

"I'll kill him. I'll kill him," he shouted, racing through the forest on Sloan's back like a furious centaur. He would find his way out of this maze of trees, he had to, for his very life, his soul, depended on it.

Looking towards the sky, his eyes beheld a flock of crows. He could hear their voices clattering as if to mock him, and he shuddered. The crows were an evil omen. Their presence heralded disasters.

"May the gods be with me that I will not be too late," he cried, hurrying off through the trees.

Thirty

The approaching horses sounded like a distant roll of thunder to Adair's ears, yet he knew instantly that this was not the rumble of the sky's fury, but of men at war. He longed to get out of bed, walk to the door of the lodge, and look out upon the night, but he knew that he could not. How he hated being helpless. If not for Wynne, he would end this miserable existence. If not for Wynne.

"Brenna!" he cried out. But his voice echoed in the empty room. He touched the amulet hanging around his neck with reverence; it was the image of the earth goddess with her three faces, one facing frontwise and two side profiles representing the cycle of birth, life, and death.

Wynne. I have got to warn her! he thought with panic. As if with superhuman strength, he pushed himself from the bed with his powerful arms. Dragging himself along, he worked his way slowly across the dirt floor and managed to maneuver himself to the doorway of the lodge. It was as he feared. *The Romans.*

They thundered down on the village, the infantrymen marching and brandishing their swords. Already blood was flowing, homes were being put to the torch.

"Unarmed! We are unarmed," he wailed mournfully. What foul breed of man would talk of peace and sneak upon their opponents like thieves in the night? At this very moment his daughter would be returning after promising them peace.

Adair could hear the cries for mercy but knew there would be none this night. He could hear the Roman voices babbling in their strange tongue.

Visions of Wynne being put to the sword tortured his soul. Why, oh why, were these Romans doing this to them?

Brenna—where is my wife? he asked himself. She had scorned him lately, belittled his manhood because he could no longer walk, but still he loved the wife of his heart. And what of Isolde, Tyrone, their children, and Edan? He did not have to wonder about Cedric's fate. Their chief would be slaughtered on the spot.

"A curse on all their kind," he cried out.

Valerian rode on, whipped by the wind as it swirled around him. At last he had let Sloan have his head, knowing that the animal would take him to Wynne's village. Onward they rode, like an avenging god on his immortal stallion. The shelter of the forest lay behind him, and the rolling hills lay before him like the waves of the ocean.

In the ebbing light Valerian could see them now, the ranks of soldiers stretching before him, pillaging and killing. The cavalry was stirring up the dust of the ground like a fog.

"Oh, Wynne. How can you ever forgive me? Will you ever understand that I had no part in this? That I have been betrayed as surely as have you?"

Even from this distance he could hear the screams and the pleas for mercy, see the bright scarlet of blood everywhere. Dazed and exhausted, sick with disgust at his countrymen, Valerian dashed on.

"I have to reach Wynne!" he cried, praying to all the gods at once that she was not already among those slain. If only he had kept her with him at the cave or gone with her to die by her side! Valerian would rescue Wynne, or die trying.

Sloan galloped on at a merciless pace.

Wynne arrived back at her village horrified by the sight which met her eyes. It was what she had seen at the war council, what the voices had warned her of; all was death and destruction. Frantically she tried to fight her way to her father's lodge, but it was no use. The Romans were as thick as the trees of the forest, forming an impassable wall. She dismounted and walked aimlessly, looking about her.

The embers of the fire of life faded and died as Wynne watched, helpless to aid her people. About her was a tangle of dead bodies and broken weapons. Death was everywhere, the strength and pride of her people gone, drained out with their blood on the ground.

Desperate to reach her father, Wynne wept. "Valerian, Valerian, how could you have betrayed me? You told me there would be peace, that we should lay down our arms, yet all the time your words were lies, your promises false as you plotted to take us unawares. And I trusted you!"

When her tears were spent, Wynne's only thought was to protect her father, who had not the power to help himself.

"Father!" she cried, moving in the direction of the familiar dwelling. She could see the tall strong figure of Tyrone as he tried to fend off Roman soldiers, using one of their own swords, which he must have confiscated in the battle. Wynne screamed a warning, too late as she saw her dear cousin ruthlessly run through from the back, his lifeblood pouring upon the ground.

"May he move to another life quickly," she prayed, making the symbol of the circle of life with her hand. "May all his other deaths be painless."

Her heart nearly stopped in her breast as she saw the same group of soldiers who had so callously cut down Tyrone now head toward her father's lodge. Would they be so cruel as to murder a helpless man in his bed? She knew that the answer was yes; these ruthless, honorless barbarians who would ask for peace with one breath and in the next instant swoop down upon an unarmed village, hacking and killing, would be capable of any crime.

Heedless of her own safety, Wynne pushed through the throng of soldiers, searching for a sword and finding what she sought. Like a Goddess of War she again mounted Tara and rode among the warriors, swinging her sword with a crazed vengeance powered by hatred and grief. Fighting passionately and victoriously, like the finest warrior, she worked her way to the door of the lodge. But, like all the bravest among her people, Wynne was outnumbered.

Seeing the avenging goddess astride her horse, a band of cavalry came upon her from behind while she was busily engaged in battle. The sword was struck from her hand, and she was torn off her mare.

"I haven't had a woman in months," shouted one man.

"By the gods, this one is a real beauty," said another.

Terror overcame Wynne, yet she fought valiantly against her attackers, biting and scratching those who held her, but it seemed as if a hundred men assaulted her, their intent in their eyes. She was to be a prize of war, vanquished by the most cruel of acts.

"She's a tiger," laughed one man who held her. Looking into his face, Wynne could see the grin of a wild beast of prey. She struggled even harder, yet against so many strong men her energy was wasted. There was no chance of escape.

Wynne felt herself being carried off toward the granary and closed her eyes to block out the hated faces above her. Could she ever wipe from her senses, her mind, the sight, smell, or sounds of this day? Would all the water and fire in the world wipe from her the filth of these blood-spattered hands?

She heard the soldiers arguing over who would be the first to enjoy her body, and cursed the day she had ever set eyes upon the Roman lover who had brought her people to this end. The sound of his language was now hateful to her ears.

Out of the corner of her eye she could see Isolde upon the ground, fighting with every ounce of her being against the assault to her body, crying out in her humiliation and pain, in her rage at the sweating, stinking, thrusting Romans who were defiling her, who had killed her husband.

"Isolde!" Wynne sobbed, trying with all her might to break free so that she could help her cousin, knowing that the same fate awaited her.

She was silenced by the strong hands of one of her captors as another Roman fumbled clumsily at the neck of her tunic, tearing it from her body, leaving her bruised flesh bare to the waist for evil eyes to feast upon, grasping hands to defile. Closing her eyes, weakened by her struggles, Wynne felt the hem of her tunic being lifted by yet other hands, and awaited the final humiliation, the fierce entry into her body, longing for death to take her first.

A cry of outrage and anger broke through the darkness of her nightmare as she felt the hands on her breasts go limp. Opening her eyes, she saw Edan and cried out his name. His hair looked like flames of fire, his eyes wild with rage as he fought like a wild boar to save her, striking fierce blows at his Roman foes.

"Leave her alone, you heathen scum!" he shouted as he cut down two of her tormentors.

Determined to aid him, Wynne struggled anew, springing up like a wildcat.

"Wynne, get back!" Edan thundered, fearful for her safety. But Wynne would not listen; her hatred for the Romans now too fierce. She fought like one possessed, lashing out wildly, kicking, using every muscle of her body against her enemies, moving with the grace of a deer. She did not see the Roman soldier come from behind her.

A searing pain tore through her head and she moaned in pain, reaching her hand up to her temple as she collapsed, trying with all her might to swim through the blackness swarming before her eyes. She struggled to remain conscious, not wanting to leave the world yet. Her efforts were in vain as she was engulfed in icy darkness, and she gave herself over to the mercy of the gods.

Thirty-one

"Wynne, Wynne," Edan sobbed. His tormented cry rent the night as he bent over her still form. All else was forgotten as he ran his fingers through the silken tresses of her hair, pausing to touch the area around her temple where the side of a Roman sword had struck her. His accusing eyes sought out the one who had dealt the blow. He lay on the ground weaponless, babbling in Latin.

"You killed her!" Edan said, taking his vengeance upon the soldier, then turning again to the still form of Wynne. The anguish he felt was like a sword wound in his belly, burning upward to his heart. He looked at her. Her eyes were closed, her face pale. She was not moving, and did not seem to be breathing. Frantically he felt for her pulse and found none. Gathering her into his arms, he wept like a child.

A soft moan brought Edan from his mourning.

Not daring to believe in miracles, he never the less looked at her face, felt the breath of her life stir against his cheek.

"She is alive!" he exclaimed, hugging her to him again. "She has not entered the world of the spirits yet." Her body was so lovely, so strong, and yet also so fragile and soft. Removing his own cloak, he wrapped it around her, then lifted her up in his arms to take her to safety, away from the fighting, to the outskirts of the village.

"You will be safe here, Wynne," he whispered, wishing that he could stay with her. But he could not; his duty was to fight these cursed Romans until he had no more strength left, until he was either killed or captured.

With a last lingering look at the unconscious golden-haired woman, Edan made his way again back to the fighting. He heard the sound of horses' hooves as more Romans swooped down upon his people, heard the shouts and cries of his kinsmen as they fought on bravely, and knew at that moment he had never hated so fiercely as he did now.

Like the war god Mars himself, Valerian rode into the fray, searching frantically for any sign of Wynne. His eyes were nearly blinded by tears at this senseless bloodletting. His heart was grieved that his own people were the agents of such brutality. What had happened to the Roman dream of civilizing the world so that it could live in peace? The truth was all too plain to see. The empire thought no price too costly for its own glory. He hated not only his country but himself as well for all the times he had allowed himself to be used as a pawn to further the ambitions of men like Severus.

Fearfully he searched among the dead, feeling blessed relief that he could not find Wynne among them. She must then be alive, but where was she? His instincts told him that she would return to her father. But where was Adair's lodge? Would she be there?

Fighting against his own men as well as against the Celts, to whom he was the enemy, Valerian, still astride the black stallion, made his way through the throng of flying swords and hurled rocks and thrusting javelins, approaching a hut that fit Wynne's description of Adair's lodge.

Oblivious of all else but his need for finding the woman he loved, Valerian grew careless, not seeing the hate-filled eyes that watched him. Recognizing the magnificent horse Sloan, and thus knowing the identity of its rider, Edan vented his rage on the man he knew to be responsible for this day of death and treachery. It was the Roman, the one who had possessed Wynne, had brought destruction and death with his lies to her.

"Roman swine!" shouted the large red-haired man. His long hair flew wildly about him as he ran forward, shouting his harsh battle cry, pulling Valerian down off Sloan. Locked together in combat, the two men rolled upon the ground.

Freeing himself from the Celt's grip, Valerian stood back. "I don't want to harm you," he said, panting. But Edan only looked at him in puzzlement. Not knowing any of the Roman's words, he supposed the Roman to be gloating over his victory. Valerian turned and walked away.

With a bellow of rage, Edan lunged again, his sword upraised, his eyes wild with hatred. As the sound of the Celt's sword whistling through the air, Valerian ducked just in time, and the blade found a tree trunk instead of his neck. For that he whispered his thanks to the gods, but the Celt was undaunted. He let out a battle cry and threw himself once more at Valerian. Again he swung his sword, and again he missed Valerian, this time by only a hairbreadth. Edan was no longer thinking clearly and was charging like a madman.

"There has been enough killing this day. I don't want to shed your blood," Valerian cried out. His words were useless, for clearly the Celt was intent upon his death. Reacting to the warning of his senses, his sword arm swinging forward, Valerian blocked his attacker's thrust. Edan's sword fell to the ground, yet he would not give up the fight, but dealt Valerian a deadly blow to the stomach which made him curl up as if still inside his mother's womb.

Valerian fought against the blazing pain inflicted by the Celt. Panting as he gathered his strength, he carefully aimed a kick which caught the red-haired Celt in the head. Edan staggered and fell to the ground, watching through a red haze as his enemy again made his way toward the lodge of Adair. He struggled to get up, but before he could regain his footing, he was taken prisoner by Roman soldiers and marched at sword point toward the Roman camp.

So intent was Valerian on finding Wynne, he did not see the soldiers approaching him until it was too late.

"Arrest that man!" he heard Severus shout at his back in a voice thick with hatred. "Strip him of his arms and bring him to me. He is a traitor."

Valerian ignored the soldier who had come to take him, and continued his forward stride, but a soldier blocked his way.

"Here, take my sword," he exclaimed, throwing it upon the ground at the soldier's feet. "I have no use for it now. I don't want to be a part of this carnage." In disgust he tore off his helmet and threw it too upon the ground.

Valerian's eyes met those of the young soldier whose duty it was to subdue him. He saw such devastation there, such unbearable self-loathing, that he had not the heart to say more. This young soldier was experiencing the same disillusionment, realizing the cruelty of war and feeling the guilt of striking down unarmed people.

"Please, before you take me to your tribune, there is someone I must find. I must know if she is safe and unharmed," Valerian pleaded, hoping to find sympathy from the young man.

He could see the uncertainty in the eyes of the soldier, who could not have been much older than his friend Burrus. Before the young man had a chance to make a decision, however, Valerian again heard the cold, cruel voice of Severus at his back.

"Bring that man to me at once!" he ordered.

Valerian was seized by four men and dragged off to meet his judgment. Forgotten now were the discarded sword and helmet, which now lay like relics of the past in the dirt.

Under cover of darkness, Brenna crept out of her hiding place like a serpent from under a rock. She felt no sorrow for the fate of her people; on the contrary, she had long sought the destruction of the tribal leaders. Now it would be so easy to pick up the pieces of this shattered band, become their priestess at the right arm of Duncan, who would be chieftain.

Entering the lodge she had shared with her husband, Brenna was surprised to find him lying by the doorway. So he too had been killed. With a gesture of impatience she kicked at the body with her foot in an effort to move it out of her way, then drew back as a moan escaped his lips.

"What is this? Is he alive?" she asked herself. Was she never to be rid of the burden of this cripple? In alarm she realized how the people of the tribe would flock around Adair, hungry for the leadership and wisdom of the Druid. She knew in her evil heart that she could not let Adair live for even one moment longer.

Brenna remembered the sword that had gleamed from the ground not far from the lodge, that Roman's sword. With all the deaths, those armored demons had caused this day, how simple it would be to lay one more death upon their heads. With a laugh she ran out into the night to retrieve this shining weapon and rid herself of her unwanted burden. Without a thought of remorse, she plunged it into the body of the man who was her husband.

Adair felt the searing pain of the sword in his side, felt it drive into his very soul. He lay gasping on the ground, looking up at his assailant.

"You," he moaned in disbelief. Killed by the very hand he had so loved, for he knew the wound to be mortal. As a Druid he was not afraid of dying, merely of leaving Wynne to the fate he knew awaited her.

Without one word Adair slipped into his final sleep, the sleep of death.

The last rays of the day faded into the darkness of the night in the clearing, the sacred grove of the oak trees, as the seven white-robed figures joined in their circle to thank the gods for their prosperity. Unaware of the brutal slaughter of their people, these Druids rejoiced in the beauty of the world. The silence of the grove was broken only by the singsong of the voices raised in praise to the gods and goddesses. But soon another sound overtook the chanting as their fate approached them, marching toward the grove.

Doom was thick as fog in the air. They were trapped, with nowhere to run. Terror gripped them as they looked into the eyes of their vanquishers. With horror they watched as their sacred trees were hacked down before their very eyes, then set aflame.

"A curse upon you," the oldest Druid threatened, only to be put to the sword as soon as the words were past his lips.

Just as Severus had threatened to do, he had destroyed the great stronghold of Druidism, and soon the very word "Druid" would disappear from all Roman writing and thought. But this brutal act of terror would never be forgiven or forgotten.

Thirty-two

Wynne awoke, her head throbbing; she was confused. She could tell by the slant of light that it was early morning. But where was she? Why was she here? Putting her hands to her head, she tried to remember what had happened, and shuddered as the memories came flooding back to her. She felt a wave of relief that her body had not been violated by the Romans. Edan had saved her; had he been able to save himself? And her father, what of him?

She tried to raise herself up but her bruised and battered body was too stiff and cramped to move. Tears of anger sprang into her eyes as she began to curse the Romans in their own tongue as she lay there, helpless. She could see the fires of their camps close to the wreckage which had once been her village, and was overwhelmed by hatred for the Romans. How could she ever have been so foolish as to trust one of them?

"Because I loved Valerian," she whispered to herself, feeling anew the grief at his betrayal. As she wept, part of her, deep inside her heart, wanted to believe that he had loved her, that there was an explanation for what had occurred, that he had not lied to her. At first her horror at what was happening had clouded her mind, but now she felt that she must talk to Valerian and give him a chance to explain to her what had gone wrong. Why had his soldiers swooped down upon her village, killing and burning? *Why?* She had to know.

Struggling to her feet against the pain which ravished her, Wynne looked around her. Everywhere she saw the mask of death. As if in a trance she walked closer and closer to the center of her village. She was hungry and thirsty, yet at the same time knew that it would be a long time before she could force anything to pass her lips.

She was filled with fear as she neared the lodge of her father, her home. Was her father alive? What about the others of her tribe that she loved? Tyrone was dead, she knew, for she had seen him fall with her own eyes. And Isolde, poor Isolde. She would live forever with her cousin's screams as the Romans ravished her.

"Isolde!" she sobbed, wondering if the woman who had been so kind to her was alive. What of Edan? Had he rescued Wynne only to endanger himself? And Cedric—what had happened to the chief of their tribe? As if in answer to her question, she looked in horror upon the dead body of Cedric, who had been hacked to pieces by a Roman's sword. Wynne looked away in horror, ravaged by her grief. She swore vengeance on these hated killers who had so callously wiped out a people with no more thought than if they had been stepping upon a hill of ants. Tears were streaming down her face as she made her way to the lodge, walking in an agony of sorrow and pain.

Reaching her home, she walked through the door, praying to the gods for her father's safety. Moving toward where he lay, she called to him, but he did not move, did not greet her.

"Your father is dead," Brenna said coldly.

Wynne stared at the lifeless form upon the bed. "Father!" she screamed, not wanting to believe. There was no answer. Throwing herself upon her father's body she sobbed her heart out, clinging to Adair and whispering his name over and over, telling him how much she had loved him, how much she would miss him, wishing him a quick return to the world in a new life. Her eyes sought solace from the hated Brenna, her only comfort now. They would be companions in their grief.

"Who did this to him?" she demanded, turning at last to Brenna when her tears were spent. "He will not escape my wrath. What kind of creature is it that strikes down a helpless, unarmed man?"

Brenna eyed her stepdaughter triumphantly,

seeing at last the chance to even the score on a hundred imagined slights over the years. "I saw clearly with my own eyes the slayer of your father," she answered.

Springing to her feet, Wynne was on Brenna, shaking her by her shoulders in her frenzy to know the identify of her father's murderer. "What did he look like? Tell me. I must know. I will search the entire camp of the Romans to find him and strike him down so that my father can find peace in his new life!"

Brenna pulled free of Wynne's grasp, wanting to avoid her eyes. "He was a tall, dark-haired young Roman," she said clearly, remembering the Roman who had escaped her clutches that night so long ago, saved by the hand of her husband's daughter. She would never forget his face. "His eyes were of an amber hue, his cheekbones high, his nose finely chiseled. He had a cleft in his chin, like so." She pressed her thumb hard into her stepdaughter's chin.

"There must be many Romans who look the same," Wynne whispered, ignoring the icy ball of foreboding she felt in the pit of her stomach at this description.

"He was a leader of his people. A centurion," Brenna continued. She managed to calm her voice, closing in for the kill. "I heard the other Romans call him Valerian." How many times had she heard her husband's daughter cry out that name in her sleep.

"No!"

"Yes, Valerian. Your lover!" Brenna said triumphantly.

"Brenna, you are lying," Wynne cried. "Tell me the truth or I swear—"

"I speak the truth." With icy control Brenna met Wynne's eyes with her own, to give the force of truth to her words. "Why would I lie to you?"

Wynne knew that Brenna had no love for her, but that was no reason for her to lie. Surely Brenna too would want to see Adair's death avenged.

Seeing her stepdaughter's confusion, Brenna continued. "I tell you the truth. I heard the Roman himself speak his name, Valerian. I heard him argue with your father, telling him that he wanted you to be his concubine, that he would provide for Adair as long as he found you desirable. He said he would take your father with him to his camp to assure that you would freely grant him your favors. Your father vowed that as long as he was alive he would keep you from the hands of such as the Roman. In anger he struck your father down."

"No. Valerian would not do such a thing!" Wynne cried.

"Oh no? Your precious Valerian murdered my husband, talked of peace with his serpent's tongue, playing you false while all the time he plotted to use our defeat for his own glory."

"No! No!" Wynne screamed, holding her hands over her ears. "I will not believe you. He would never strike down an unarmed man, and not my father!" Wynne was bewildered. How would Brenna know about the Roman, his eyes, his face, the dimple in his chin, unless she had seen him? And how had she known his name?

With a smug smile on her lips, Brenna went to retrieve the sword. How fortunate for her that she had witnessed the capture of the Roman by his very own men, had seen where the sword fell. By blaming the Roman for Adair's death, she would be taking all chance of discovery from herself. No one would ever know that she had killed the Druid herself, and besides, it was such a sweet triumph to bring Wynne such pain.

"Here is the Roman's sword," she said, thrusting it into her stepdaughter's hands.

Wynne examined it carefully, remembering the feel of it in her hands that night when she had wielded it herself. She remembered the hilt, the unusual markings, like no other, the small nick she herself had made in the sword as she had fought with the hulking giant who had sought her death. It was Valerian's, of that she was certain. Still, in her heart she could not believe that he was responsible for this foul deed, the murder of her beloved father.

Brenna perceived the doubt in her stepdaughter's eyes. "Is it because he said that he loved you that you doubt the truth of my words? Did you perhaps believe him because he used your soft white body to quench his desires? Did he promise you eternal faithfulness? Oh, Wynne. You fool. Men are all alike. They say soft words of love while their manhood is stiff, but by the light of the day those words blow away like the wind."

Wynne could stand no more. Sobbing hysterically, she fled the lodge to seek solace in the trees of the sacred grove. She ran as fast as her feet would carry her, oblivious of her bruises and her wounds. But the sacred grove was no more; in its place were charred stumps, among which lay the slain Druids. "You could not even spare us our sacred groves!" She poured out her heart to these gods and said a prayer for those who had died.

"May all who have fallen here be brought again to new life, moving through all the next lives without fear, without pain," she intoned. "Death and birth in their never-ending circle, move quickly before our eyes." With her right hand she drew an imaginary circle in front of her face, the sign of life eternal.

Sinking to her knees, Wynne felt as if she herself were one of the dead, for surely the woman that had once been was gone forever, killed by the Roman's lies and treachery.

"Vile Roman!" she raged. "Liar." She rubbed her hand across her mouth to remove the feel of his kisses.

A sound behind her caused her to start, but it was only Edan. "I mourn for your father and share your grief," he said sadly. "He was a great man and will be missed."

Wynne stood up and ran to him, relieved to see that he still lived and that he was free of the

Romans. "Oh, Edan, you are alive! So many have died that I feared for you." She buried her face in the shelter of his arms as she had done since childhood.

"Yes, I'm alive," he said bitterly. "No thanks to your Roman. Would that I had been able to kill him, to avenge our dead." The sunlight shone upon his red hair, making it shine like a glowing fire.

"Why did the Romans do this?" she sobbed. "They have even ravaged our sacred grove."

Edan gently brushed back a lock of her hair. She was so very dear to him, he had always loved her so. "Because they are like animals, yet they deem themselves to be our betters. How I hate them. All of them, especially your Roman. He mocked me in his babbling tongue as we fought."

"You fought with him?" Wynne broke away from the secure warmth of his arms to look into his face.

"Yes." Taking hold of her arms, he sat her down and told her his story of their battle. How he had recognized Sloan, had pulled the Roman from the horse, how they had fought. "He was intent upon going into your father's lodge. I tried to stop him and would have had I not been taken from behind by a group of his fellow Romans. But I soon broke free again."

His words were like a dagger to her heart. "Then it is true. He did kill my father."

"He murdered Adair?" Edan exclaimed, aghast at this news. "I had no idea of the depth of his treachery. Ah, my poor Wynne . . . to be so betrayed."

Wynne could stand the torment no longer. She had to be alone with her grief. "Please leave me," she whispered, looking at him with pain-filled eyes. Understanding her feelings, he did as she bade him.

Wynne beat her breast in grief, tears of rage and sorrow filling her eyes. She had loved Valerian, loved him more than life itself, and he had betrayed her, rewarded her love and her loyalty with murder. She had saved his life and he had taken the life of her father.

"I will avenge my father," she vowed. "Some-how, someday, I will see justice done." So saying, she fell upon the ground, giving vent to her anguish.

Thirty-three

Wynne's eyes were dry at her father's funeral. She had cried out her soul these last few days; there were no more tears to shed. For her people death was usually a time for celebration, not grief, a time when the spirit moves on to a new life; yet there was no joy this day. How could the spirits of the dead go peacefully to a new life amid the ruins of what had once been such a peaceful village?

The death toll had been taken: thirty had been killed, including all twelve of the Druids. Among the dead were Cedric, Tyrone, and Adair. Many had been wounded. If the gods were kind, they would survive.

Dressed in her tunic of red—the color of death and of life and blood, symbolizing the return of the spirit to the fire of life—Wynne looked down upon her father for the last time.

"I will avenge you, Father," she vowed, with her hand on her dagger, "if it takes me eternity to do so. You will be revenged."

Following Celtic custom, the bodies of the dead wre cremated in a round barrow, the ashes scattered to the winds to speed the dead on their journey to a new life.

Wynne saw Brenna standing nearby and noticed she was wearing her father's amulet. Wynne approached her and yanked the charm from around her stepmother's throat.

"That is mine by right of law," Wynne said firmly, and turned her back.

Brenna put her hand to her throat, her eyes blazing with fury. "You will pay for this insult, Wynne. That I promise you," she hissed.

Wynne sat numbly before the ashes of the fire of life, staring at the place which once had symbolized the soul of her people. Never would she forget the atrocities she and her people had suffered.

Feeling a hand touch her shoulder, she jumped, and a scream started in her throat as she imagined that she was once again to be assaulted by the filthy conquerors.

"It is only I, Isolde," came a voice she knew so well.

"Oh, Isolde," she wailed, gathering her cousin into the safety of her arms. She had not spoken with Isolde since that terrible day in the granary. They had always comforted each other, even as children when one of them had been punished or frightened in some manner.

Now Isolde gave vent to her sorrow, weeping her tears of grief and humiliation, then stepped back to look upon Wynne's face.

"We have both suffered much. It is as if I too died that day . . . my spirit," Isolde cried.

"How I hate the Romans," Wynne replied, creasing her brow in anger.

Isolde shook her head. "Hate is a feeling which destroys," she said softly. "Don't let your feelings destroy you, Wynne. What is done is done."

Wynne looked at her with incredulous eyes. "How can you not feel loathing for these barbarians who have killed your husband?"

Isolde's eyes were filled with her sorrow as she bent her head. "I loved Tyrone, but he would not want me to let the worms of evil rancor eat away at my heart. I will mourn him, but I will not give in to my hatred, and you must not do so. There is much to be done now, rebuilding, taking care of our wounded."

Wynne knew that her cousin spoke the truth, yet it would be hard to put the past behind her. Bidding her cousin good-bye, she left the fire of life to wander back toward the lodge. She could hear the shrill sound of Brenna's laughter cut through the silence of the night. Turning in the direction of the sound, Wynne could see the buxom woman who had once been her father's wife, surrounded by Roman soldiers. Indeed the dark-haired woman did not seem to remember that it was by their swords that her people had been so savagely murdered. Clenching her fists in anger, Wynne looked up to find Edan staring down at her. She fought long and hard against the tide of fury which threatened to engulf her. Her father had not been dead long, and already the woman was playing the traitor.

"That woman will use all her wiles to turn our tragedy into a victory for herself," Edan said thoughtfully, sharing her loathing for Brenna.

"She seeks to gain power and favor with our new masters," Wynne added scornfully. "Yet when you are chief . . ."

"If she has her way, I fear that I will not be chief after all."

"Not be chief? But it is your right as son of the slain chieftain. Even the Romans dare not take this honor away from you, though you will no doubt have to bow to their yoke." A voice inside her head seemed to tell her that Edan was right. The Romans were the masters now, and all their lives, their fates, were in Roman hands.

Edan tightened his grip on Wynne's shoulders. "How I wish that I would be chieftain with you by my side." His voice was gentle and husky.

Wynne pulled away from him. "No. It cannot be," she said, her voice quavering with fright. She could never give her heart again.

"Is it because you still love the Roman that you deny me?" Edan asked sorrowfully.

Wynne whirled upon him then, eyes blazing. "I do not love the Roman. He betrayed me and murdered my father. Were he standing before

me now, I would take his life and be glad of it."
She ran quickly to the door of the lodge. Edan
deserved much better than a woman who was
hollow, soiled, and had bedded another. At the
door she paused. "Someday you will find a
woman to love, who loves you, Edan. One who
will make you forget me."

"I will never love another woman as I love
you," he answered.

Unable to bear the pain on his face, she sought
the safety of the familiar dwelling, sinking to
her knees in her own sorrow, for she knew that
she too would never love. That in spite of all
her words, all that he had done, it was true—
she still loved the Roman. As she recalled with
anguish his loving face, his tender touch, she
suddenly thought it odd that she had not seen
him with all the other Romans these past days
in the village. Was he gone? Yes. No doubt now
on his way back to his chieftain's city, to Rome
and his glory.

Thirty-four

Manacled and chained like a slave, Valerian was brought before Severus in his tent. The beady eyes of the tribune swept over him with amusement and triumph.

With a shove Severus humbled Valerian, pushing him so that he sprawled at his feet. "So the mighty Valerian, the brave centurion, is here to answer to my justice. No power on earth can save you now," he taunted.

"You murdering swine!" Valerian shouted, his eyes blazing, heedless of the danger. He was already destined to be executed; what more could Severus do to him?

"I would be careful what names I let tumble from my lips, centurion, lest you lose your tongue as well as your head."

"You slaughtered unarmed men, men who wanted only place. They were going to lay down their arms and talk with you. Your victory could have been had without a drop of blood spilled." Valerian pulled at his chains, anxious to come upon this grinning baboon and tear him limb from limb, but he was securely bound. He managed to stand up, but Severus struck him with his sword hilt, nearly knocking him senseless. Still the hatred continued to glow from the centurion's eyes. He would never grovel before this murderer.

"You expect me to actually trust the word of the barbarian Celts, a people who sacrifice men by the dozen to their pagan gods at their fire festivals? They are animals, uncivilized brutes." Severus snorted, reaching for his cup of wine and gulping it greedily. Wiping his mouth with his bare arm, he sneered again at his prisoner.

"And what are we? You call murdering men civilized? What about our gladiators, or the Christians whose death amuses our emperor, or the executions which take place every day, or the murder of helpless slaves?"

"That is different. It has to be done in order to keep the peace! The priests of these people burn large wicker baskets filled with humans. They draw omens from their death agonies. Rome may not always be merciful, but our gods themselves must be horrified by this brutality."

"You don't understand these people. I do. Not all of them practice human sacrifice. The people you just slaughtered do not. Not all of the tribes have the same customs."

"But you yourself were nearly made a sacrificial victim," Severus answered uneasily, wondering for an instant whether he could have made a mistake.

"Not by the people you murdered! To think I trusted you, while all the time you planned to use me. You didn't want peace. My eyes were blinded because I wanted peace!" Valerian fought hard against losing all self-control.

"You lie! You wanted the victory for yourself. Well, the only victory you will have is being allowed to keep your head—temporarily." He turned his back on Valerian, not wanting to look into those tortured eyes. He motioned to the guards. "This man is to be taken back to Eboracum to await his execution. I want to witness it personally, but first I have some business to finish here."

"I'll see that the emperor Nero himself learns of what you have done!" Valerian threatened.

Severus paused for a moment. He did have to think about Valerian's father and what he would have to say to him concerning his son. The senator was close to Nero and could seek his downfall if provoked.

Motioning the guards to leave the tent, Severus faced Valerian alone. "Your father will be told that you suffered an unfortunate accident in the midst of battle. Perhaps I will say that a Celtic spear cut short your life."

"You will be a liar then," Valerian said, "as well as a coward."

"I am a man who has had to live by his wits. In this world, Valerian, there are the weak and the strong. I am one of the strong, and there is nothing I won't do to maintain my power."

"And what do you intend to say to my men about why I have been made a prisoner? It was no secret that I was following your orders in seeking to bring about peace."

Severus grinned with the leer of the victorious. "They will be told that you went against my orders, that I never sought peace. A good soldier learns soon enough never to question the word of one in command. You are merely a centurion; I am a tribune. Whom do you think they will believe? Are you so foolish as to imagine that they will want to suffer punishment at your side?" Again he summoned the guards.

"What about my men?" Valerian asked as two guards stood on either side of him. "They must not be made to suffer for your hatred of me."

Severus shrugged. "I will have your century brought here to be under my command until I decide what is to be done. I need their goodwill. I won't risk losing it by punishing them for following your orders. I hold you totally responsible. Now, go!"

Valerian was relieved at that and wondered what Burrus must be thinking of now. He longed to see the young soldier again, his only confidant. If only he could talk with him now, he would plead with him to find out what had happened to Wynne. He had to know if she still lived.

"If Wynne is alive, then I will move the heavens and the earth to escape from here, but if she is dead, then I will go to my own death easily," he whispered to himself.

"Come, prisoner," the guards ordered harshly. "Make ready for your journey." The guards pushed and shoved Valerian to the stables, where he was set roughly upon a brown mare.

"Please. I ask you to let me take my horse with me, the black stallion. I must return it to its proper owner one day."

The guard looked at him warily. "Well . . . the tribune didn't specify what was to be done about your horse. I . . . I . . . don't imagine there would be any harm done."

"My father will reward you for your kindness," Valerian promised, holding his gaze steady.

"All right." He pulled Valerian from the mare and led him over to where Sloan stood pawing at the ground. The stallion sensed that something was wrong.

"Thank you." Valerian murmured, mounting the black stallion and soothing him with his calm words.

"My name is Marcus," the guard said boldly. "Marcus Titanus. Don't forget me." A sudden grin spread over his face. He liked the centurion, no matter what it was that he was said to have done. He could not say the same for the tribune.

"I'll remember, Marcus," Valerian called back over his shoulder. Surrounded by soldiers, Valerian began on his journey, a journey that might end with his death.

Thirty-five

It did not take long for Brenna to ingratiate herself
with the conqueror of her people, the tribune.
She praised and promised until she convinced
him that she would be a worthy priestess of the
new gods. What did it matter to her that hence-
forward the gods would be Celto-Roman?—Mer-
cury and his consort Rosmerta, Apollo, Mars,
Minerva, Vulcan, Jupiter, Hercules. While the
Romans occupied the land, she would do their
bidding, but as soon as the invaders had left,
she would bring back the old gods, the gods
that demanded sacrifice and obedience.

She was able to communicate with Severus
quite well, since he had learned to speak her
language during his long campaigns in Gaul.
She in fact knew the Latin tongue as well, but
thought it best to pretend otherwise. Hence she
was able to listen to the tribune's plans without

his knowledge. As for Severus, he thought Brenna the perfect priestess and trusted her more and more as time went on. She had cunning and ambition, traits which he understood well and admired. He was sure she would come to be more valuable to him as time went on.

Although the people clamored to have Edan declared chieftain, Severus took the advice of Brenna and made Duncan the chief, even though he was not of the immediate tribe. Now Brenna and her lover were all-powerful, although Brenna began to worry that Wynne would recognize Duncan as one of the priests of Domnu and expose him.

"I will have to get rid of Wynne soon. I can only keep Duncan out of her sight for so long," she mused. What if she were to make Severus believe that Wynne was a Druid priestess, a danger to his power? She would bide her time until the moment was right, and then she would seek the revenge she so craved.

Sitting before the fire, Wynne looked across the room at Isolde, whose hearth she shared. It had been impossible to live under the same roof with Brenna, particularly since she was now so friendly with the Romans. Besides, the lodge of her father had held too many memories for her. Now that Isolde was a widow with three small children to tend, she felt her cousin needed her.

As a conquered people, the tribe's entire way of life was changing. Before the Romans had come, all lands were cultivated in common; no one man could claim ownership to any ground. All possessions were shared. Now, however, the Romans sliced up the territory like pieces of cake, giving out land to those they favored, those who sought their friendship. Women, who had shared most of the privileges of their tribesmen, now had no rights at all; they were the chattel of their brothers, husbands, fathers, just as the Roman women were. The Romans demanded that the line of descent be traced for written record through the father. It was as if women had ceased to have value.

"Will these Romans never leave our land?" Wynne cried out. "They know nothing of our ways. Why do they insist upon forcing their own laws and customs upon us?"

Isolde shuddered. "What frightens me is the way their warriors look at us with lustful eyes, as if we were theirs for the taking."

Poor Isolde, thought Wynne; even now her cousin trembled with fright anytime she was forced to endure the company of the conquerors. "Were I to have to suffer their foul touch again, I would kill myself!" Wynne vowed. "Better to leave this life and enter upon a new one than to have the dirt of their touch upon us."

Tears stung Wynne's eyes at the memory of Valerian's betrayal, and she hurried to brush them away. As long as she lived, she would remember the Roman and his lies. She had tried to be generous in her thoughts, to forgive, to find an explanation for what had happened.

But what Brenna had revealed was convincing. The evidence of the sword was damming. Valerian had used her, taken her love, lied to her, and worst of all, had taken her father from her. Rising to her feet, she paced back and forth as her memories tormented her.

She felt a gentle hand on her shoulder. "You love him still, don't deny it. I can read your thoughts, Wynne, as if they were my own," Isolde whispered sadly.

Wynne whirled around to face her cousin. "No! No. I hate him. How could I love him after what he's done to us? I curse the day I set eyes on him."

"Wynne," Isolde said, "things are not always as they seem." The pain of her own loss was reflected in the depths of her eyes. "We both know that Brenna is selfish and evil—why, then, do you trust her word about the death of your father?"

"Because I saw the Roman's own sword stained with the blood of my father. And Edan himself saw the Roman running toward the lodge. He killed my father, and for that I could never forgive him, never."

Suddenly the two cousins were interrupted by the raucous calls of Roman soldiers just outside their lodge. Wynne could feel Isolde's trembling and sought to comfort her, but Isolde broke away and went to the doorway.

"What do you want?" Isolde asked, trying to mask her fear. The soldiers eyed her ripe beauty and then turned to look at Wynne, who had joined Isolde in the entryway.

"Which of you is Wynne, daughter of Adair the Druid?" one soldier asked. He clutched at his sword as if to convey his authority to the unarmed women.

Stepping forward, Wynne lifted her chin proudly. "I am she," she answered. Immediately she was surrounded by the Romans as if she were a dangerous warrior.

Forgetting her fears in the face of danger, Isolde pushed her way past the solders to take her place by Wynne's side. "This is my lodge. I have a right to know what you want with my cousin," she demanded.

"She is to be brought before Severus Cicero, the tribune, this very night," was the reply from one of the soldiers, a grinning, balding man.

"Why? What does he want of me?" Wynne asked, trying to hide her apprehension. She had done no wrong, had obeyed the Romans' laws, kept the peace.

"I don't know. I was only told to bring you," the man answered gruffly. His eyes roamed over Isolde and his expression left no doubts as to his thoughts. Isolde shrank back in fear, afraid to say anything else.

Smiling, looking like a goddess, Wynne stepped forward. "Let us go," she said, gliding forward like a queen. She would not give these Romans the satisfaction of bullying her; she would show them Celtic courage.

Surrounded by the Romans, Wynne made her

way to the tent of Severus, her heart beating in her breast. Little did she know that Brenna was taking her vengeance, and had begun to work her evil that very day.

Thirty-six

Wynne was taken to the large tent, the tent of the Roman tribune who was called by her people the "demon rodent" because of his large protruding teeth and small colorless eyes. Wynne had seen him only from afar, yet she knew that he was not to be trusted. He stood with his back to her in the dim glow of the candlelight.

Severus turned abruptly, surprised by the beauty of the young woman before him. The priestess Brenna had warned him that the woman standing here was dangerous, a Druid priestess, daughter of a Druid holy man; but she had not mentioned how lovely the girl would be. As if appraising a fine sculpture, he walked round and round her, eyeing her up and down and licking his lips. He lifted a strand of her golden hair, enjoying the softness of the silken threads on his fingers. Wynne started as if she had been burned.

"Don't touch me!" she said hotly. All too recent was the memory of other Roman hands touching, bruising, pinching.

Her eyes were full of hatred, yet somehow her look excited Severus, and he wondered what this young beauty would be like to bed. Would she fight like a tiger or be gentle as a doe?

"It is my right to touch you," he taunted, grinning at her and reaching for her hand. He fondled her soft, slender fingers as Wynne fought the urge to slap his face. In that instant he made his decision. The usual punishment for indulging in the old rites of the Druids was death by the sword. He had told Brenna that this would be the girl's fate, but he could not bear to let such beauty go to waste. No. He had other plans for this golden bird.

"What do you mean, it is your right?" she asked in his language, much to his surprise. So she knew how to speak some Latin; that would be an advantage. An interpreter could always be of use.

He reached out to touch one of her full ripe breasts, and again Wynne drew back, her eyes searching for a sword, a dagger, anything to use. Severus knew her intent—to first kill him and then herself; that was the way with these heathens. He would have to make certain that she was always watched closely, all weapons out of reach of her slim fingers. Her defiance so excited him that he thought perhaps with her he could be a man, could once again enjoy the pleasures of a woman's body.

He reached for her amulet, examining it in the light. The three faces intrigued him. What did they mean?

"Beautiful," he said with double meaning.

Her eyes stared into his, wary and frightened. Now she reminded him of a small rabbit caught in a snare, and he smiled at her in an effort to befriend her.

"What is its meaning?" he asked.

"It belonged to my father," she answered. "It is a symbol of the life cycle." She was not afraid to speak the truth; there was no law against wearing the symbols of the old gods, merely in the practice of sacrifice to them.

He let the figure drop from his hand and returned his attention again to her hair, so soft. Her lips were full and he had the urge to kiss her right at this moment, but did not. Something about this girl was familiar; he had seen her before, but where?

"And was your father a priest?"

"He was a Druid. He was a holy man of my people," she said proudly, ravaged still by grief at his loss.

"And you? Are you also a Druid?"

"No. Among my people women cannot hold priesthood," she replied; then, remembering Brenna, she added, "At least, not until now."

Curiosity overcame him. She understood Latin very well, although she could not speak it fluently.

Obviously she had known how to speak Latin long before he came.

"How is it that you know my language? Who taught you to speak my language so well?" he asked, noticing the blush which came to her face at his question. She who had stared so boldly at him with such defiance now lowered her eyes from his.

"I ... I ... learned it from one of your people," she answered. "And my father knew the words of your land."

"One of my ..." It hit him like a battering ram: *Valerian*. This was the woman he had seen with his centurion. He began to laugh. This was just too good to be true.

The sound of the tribune's high-pitched laughter frightened Wynne. *He's mad*, she thought. Why else would he react this way? With an instinct of self-preservation she ran for the door of the tent; she had to get away from this lunatic. He was quicker than she, however, and with two large strides had her by the wrist.

"You will stay if I command it," he ordered. "You are mine. My property!"

She looked at him with large questioning eyes. "What do you mean, your property?" she asked warily.

He drew her to him and his bony hands grasped her waist so hard she could barely breathe. Her breasts crushed against his chest, she could feel the beat of his heart through the coarse linen of his tunic.

"You are my slave. My property. From now on I will do with you as I will."

"No!" The word was a sob.

"Oh yes, sweet beauty. You will be sent to Eboracum, where you will await me." He placed his wet hot lips against the base of her neck and sucked as an infant would at its mother's breast. Wynne was repulsed by him. She tried to draw away, but she was imprisoned by his lustful hands. It was all she could do not to scream out in terror and disgust. She closed her eyes, awaiting the assault which she thought was to come, but as quickly as he had grabbed her, the tribune let her go.

"You are a cold wench, but I will teach you how to please me," he said.

"Never. You may own my body but you will never own my heart or my soul," she answered defiantly.

Severus called for his guards. "I grow tired of you," he said peevishly. He instructed his guards to house her in a tent near his own, with constant watch. "You will be my concubine," he said. "In the meantime I suggest that you learn how to please a man, for only as long as you please me will I let you live."

In her own quarters, Wynne put her knees up to her chest and rested her head on her knees. Slavery was worse than death; still, she had reasons to live now: she would make that vile beast Severus pay for what he had done to her people, and she would find

Valerian, no matter where he was, and make him suffer also for the death of her father. "On my father's death I so pledge," she vowed quietly. "Only by the death of these two Romans will I be revenged." Until then she could bear any torture.

"Valerian must die," she whispered. Yet the idea of his death brought an ache to her heart. To see those amber eyes closed forever, never again to feel those lips upon hers—her loss caused her physical pain, as if her body itself were grieving.

"Father!" she cried, as if he still walked the earth. "Help me, help me to be strong, to do what must be done!" Collapsing upon the ground, she sobbed her heart out upon the dirt of the earth goddess. She would no longer be able to see her loved ones, walk on the grass in the spring, view the sunrise through the trees. She would be in a foreign land among her foes. Her life here was over and a new life was beginning, a life of hatred and saddness and grief.

II

THE DARKNESS BEFORE THE DAWN

Eboracum

Walk while ye have the light, lest darkness come upon you.

—John, 12:35

Thirty-seven

The fog-misted nights of summer gave way to crisp, cold evenings as autumn approached. Meghan shivered as she stood, clad only in her tunica, looking out the small tent opening across the hills for any sign of an approaching band of men. She had heard the whispered news that Valerian was returning, not in glory but in chains, a prisoner of Severus.

"Oh, my sweet lord, my kind master. What could have happened to have brought you to such a cruel fate?" she moaned. Valerian had been so very kind to her, saving her from that monster Severus. Never once had he forced himself upon her, but treated her rather as a daughter or a sister than as a slave.

Meghan tensed at the distant sound of trumpets. Was it the soldiers with Valerian? It had to be. Valerian had returned. Donning her palla, she wrapped it tightly around her, covering her head from the chill of the night air, and ran from the tent to await the arrival of the soldiers. She ran quickly by a small group of men who boldly leered at her as she passed. She could hear a few words of what they were saying amid their raucous laughter, and being fluent in Latin, she knew what they meant.

"Fine-looking piece of goods, she is," said one.

"Yes, and with her master Valerian soon to be parted from his head, she'll be up for grabs," said another.

"Don't be too certain. Old Severus will surely decide to take her to his bed. What a waste. I hear that he has long been impotent. Now, me, I could keep a pretty little thing like her happy."

Meghan shuddered. I will not let that disgusting old man touch me! she vowed silently as she continued to the area where the soldiers would arrive and hitch up their horses. Slipping behind a supply tent, she waited patiently for them to emerge from the cloud of dust in the distance which the pounding hooves of their mounts had created.

The soldiers numbered five-and-twenty and in their midst she now saw the familiar shape of Sloan with Valerian on his back. The sight of the haggard face of her master brought her to tears. He looked as though he had lived several lifetimes and experienced a visit to Hades and back. Even so, he was still the most handsome man she had ever seen. It was all she could do to control her temper as she saw two of the men push him to the ground, laughing at his fall from power. With his chin held upward in defiance, Valerian would not be humbled, even though death awaited him at the end of this journey.

"What's to be done with his property?" Meghan heard one of the soldiers ask, hoping obviously that the centurion's belongings would be drawn with lots.

"Can't touch them till Severus comes back, that's all I've been told. He's to be kept in the prison tent, chained like an animal, and guarded night and day until then." The voice of the soldier could not hide his disappointment. It would be a long while until the tribune finished his duties in Northwest Britain and returned to Eboracum.

Meghan carefully noted the location of the prison tent. Under cover of night, she would pay her dear master a visit so that the two of them could decide how he was going to make his escape.

Ibu, she thought suddenly, remembering the black slave boy whom Valerian had also saved from Severus. Ibu will help me. He too owes his very life to my lord.

With a smile she made her way back to her quarters, secure in the knowledge that all was not yet lost.

It was a cloudy night and the moon was hidden from sight as Meghan hurried to the tent where Valerian was to be held prisoner. To blend with the night, she wore a dark cloak and had tucked her red-gold hair underneath the hood. At a sound behind her she ducked hurriedly behind a tent, but it was only one of the large wild dogs which roamed the camp scavenging for scraps of food. Reaching into her leather pouch she quickly fetched the beast a piece of lamb that she had stolen to bring to Valerian. Knowing how the prisoners were treated, she feared that he would not be given proper food.

"Here, take this and be quiet," she whispered gently to the dog, which wolfed the morsel down greedily and then came back for more. Anxiously Meghan threw another scrap some distance so that the dog would have to chase after it.

Not five feet from where she stood a soldier stuck his head out of a tent. "So, it's only that mangy hound again," he said with a laugh, and went back inside.

Meghan waited several minutes before continuing on her journey. She did not want to be caught without an escort by one of these jackals called infantrymen, for she would be raped for sure. The entire camp would know by now that she was without a protector, and there would be no one to fight for her.

As she approached the prison tent she saw that, as usual, and as she had hoped, the soldiers on night duty were drinking and gambling at a small distance from the tent. They had a fire going, which would make it nearly impossible for them to see anything beyond the ring of its light. Meghan carefully tugged at the flap of the tent, ducking underneath as quietly as she could. It was black as pitch inside, and she paused to let her eyes adjust, then crept slowly toward the voice she heard moaning softly in sleep. She knelt down beside the man, gently touching his shoulder.

"Valerian, Valerian, it is Meghan," she whispered. "I have come to help you."

She nearly screamed out in fear as a hand grabbed her wrist. Fear overcame her that this was not Valerian after all, but another man. Her breath caught in her throat as she struggled to her feet.

"Meghan, Meghan, is it really you?"

"Yes, my lord, it is. Ibu and I are going to free you as soon as we can."

"Free me? Oh, that you could." His voice was toneless, as if he had given up hope. He did not sound like the Valerian she knew.

"Ibu has a way to get the key to these chains, and I will make provisions for your journey— food, weapons, clothing, and of course Sloan."

Her presence, her words, seemed to bring him comfort. "Yes. Yes, I have to get away from here. I have to find out about her," he went on in a near-delirium. "If she is alive or dead. I have to make her understand that it was not I, not I."

Meghan was confused by his words. What was he talking about? "You must escape and travel to Rome to seek help from your mighty king," she said sternly.

"Nero? He will take Severus' side. I fear I will get no help from him." Valerian ran a hand over his dirty bearded face. But his father—perhaps if Severus' treachery were known to his father's friend, General Cassius Quintus, something could be done.

"Master, you must try. You cannot let them kill you! I will never care for another master as I do you. You have been so kind." Valerian's manner, his voice, spoke of his heartache and his grief. What had happened during the campaign to make him so listless? "If not for yourself, at least try to escape for me. Redeem yourself for my sake, for if you do not, I will again be given to Severus."

Valerian gently took her hand and held it firmly in his own. "That will never happen. You will never be given to that beast. Tomorrow I want you to bring me quill, ink, and parchment. I will arrange for my friend Burrus to protect you. No matter what happens to me, you will be safe with him and away from the evil hands of the tribune."

Meghan lifted his hand to her cheek where he could feel her tears. "Thank you for thinking of me, master, but you must also save yourself."

He was touched by her loyalty. "I will do as you ask, little Meghan. I will go to Rome if it means so much to you, although I have little desire to stay in the legion after all that I have seen. First, however, I must go north again."

She gasped. "But that is where Severus is. You will again be taken. Why must you do such a dangerous thing?"

"I have to take my chances. There is someone there whom I love very much. I must find out if she still lives. I promised long ago that I would return for her and take her with me as my wife. May the gods will that I may do so." His answer was filled with such passion that for an instant Meghan was struck with jealousy. Oh that she could find such devotion and love.

Far into the night Meghan and Valerian went over the scheme for his escape, working out the smallest details. If Ibu and Meghan were to be discovered aiding a prisoner, they would be flogged within an inch of their lives, and that he could not have borne. When at last their plans were finished, Meghan rose to leave.

"Wait," he called out softly, and taking her hand, gently kissed the palm. The touch of his lips made her tingle. Was this what love was all about? If so, then a part of her heart regretted that she had not shared her master's bed. "Thank you, Meghan," he breathed. Letting go of her hand, he strained his eyes to the darkness to watch her leave. "Be careful!" he called out to her as she walked away.

"I will," she answered quietly. "May the goddess Rhiannon, the Great Queen, protect you until the next rising of the sun."

Valerian felt his heart beating faster within his breast. For the first time since his capture, he felt hopeful. He would see Wynne again, he felt certain. "In two days' time I will be on my way," he said beneath his breath.

Thirty-eight

The time passed slowly for Valerian as he awaited word from Meghan. As if somehow they guessed that something was about to happen, the guards assigned to watch Valerian seemed to hover about with their eagle eyes. Valerian paced the prison tent like a caged animal. He had been given a length of chain double his height so that he could walk about the tent and tend to his personal needs. The guards would not allow any visitors. His meals consisted of gruel, which was slaves' fare, watered-down wine, and cheese.

By afternoon Valerian could stand the suspense no longer and yelled for one of his guards, a young soldier who had shown him a measure of compassion.

"Guard, I must see my slave Meghan at once."

The young guard was used to taking orders, and the tone of Valerian's voice made him start.

"I have my orders, centurion, that you are not to be allowed to see anyone."

Valerian clenched his fists in anger. "And how am I supposed to settle my debts, tend to my properties, and make ready to die peacefully when I am not given the opportunity to even talk with my slave?" He pulled at his chains impatiently, causing the young soldier to draw back in fright. Chained or not, the centurion was imposing.

"I'm sorry," the soldier answered, regaining his composure. "But I have been so ordered."

Valerian laughed. "Perhaps that is it. My dear tribune, Severus does not want me to settle my life before I die. But I am still a Roman citizen and as such demand my rights. He has not the power to steal from me." He walked as close to the young soldier as the chain would allow, and reached out a pleading hand to him. "For the love of the gods, let me talk with the captain of your guards about this."

The young guard hastily left, and after a few minutes was replaced with the captain, a short muscular gray-haired soldier whom Valerian knew was half Greek and half Roman, a survivor of the Gaulish campaigns. He looked at Valerian with stern yet compassionate eyes, and Valerian began to suspect that the man held no great love in his heart for the tribune.

"You demanded to see me, centurion?" he asked, surprising Valerian by the use of his title, which would soon be stripped from him.

"Yes, I want to make provisions for my female slave Meghan, and so far, that has been difficult. I must see her. I would like her to bring me some writing supplies so that I might direct that she be well cared for upon my death."

"I have been ordered—"

"I know about your orders! What I want to know is why I have been denied my right as a Roman to see to my personal affairs. Were my father to hear of this treatment, I am sure that he would seek retribution for such actions."

The captain of the guards smiled, and Valerian could see that his front teeth were missing. "I have heard of your father. He is, as I recall, a personal friend of General Cassius Quintus, is that not so?" Valerian nodded. "Perhaps I could relax your watch somewhat to permit you to see the girl. A man about to die deserves at least a kiss or two before he meets his fate."

"Thank you," Valerian answered, returning the other man's smile.

"And as to the girl, I would hate to see her in the hands of the tribune. He is a cruel man. I will help you there. I have a daughter about her age." With that he left the tent and Valerian knew that the captain would be true to his word.

Meghan arrived soon upon the arm of the young guard, whose eyes swept over her with longing.

"Here is that which you have requested," she said, kneeling at his feet and handing him the writing materials she'd brought.

With annoyance Valerian looked up to see the guard standing nearby, feasting his eyes on

Meghan's beauty. "Guard, can I not be left alone with my slave?"

The young guard eyed Meghan with suspicion, then shrugged and smiled. She certainly did not appear to be strong enough to break the centurion's chains, nor did her innocent eyes betray any cunning. He left the tent wondering if he would ever get a chance to bed anyone quite so lovely as the centurion's slave.

As soon as he had left, Valerian grasped Meghan's hands. "How goes it?"

"Ibu has not been able to get the key. He has tried everything from drugging the guard's wine to gambling with him, but to no avail. We both believe that the guard is suspicious, for he poured the wine on the ground, making it appear to be an accident. While they wrestled, the guard kept the keys secured safely upon his person. Ibu says that perhaps he will have to resort to violence to obtain the keys."

"No!" The word was a command. "That would endanger not only Ibu but also you, and that we must not risk. I'll see to the keys myself." Hastily he scrawled on the parchment, tearing it in half when he was finished. He gave one piece to Meghan.

"What is this, master?" she asked scanning the writing and wishing desperately that she could read.

"As soon as Burrus arrives back in camp, I want you to give this to him. It is to be sent by courier to my father in Rome. It explains to him all that has happened here. I only hope that he can see as I do the danger Severus presents to the empire. And this," he said, handing her the other piece, "entrusts you to Burrus in my absence or upon my death."

Meghan's eyes flooded with tears. "I want no other master but you."

Valerian gently cupped her face with his hand and looked into the depths of her jade eyes. "You should have no master at all, little one. You should be free. One day, if I survive all of this, I will see that you are. In the meantime, you could find no better guardian than my friend Burrus."

She smiled up at him, tears trembling on her long lashes. "If you trust him, then so shall I."

Entering upon this tender scene, the guard coughed to announce his presence. "It is time for the girl to leave," he said an an effort to be stern, though his trembling hands gave him away. The slave girl stirred something in him and made him feel giddy with desire.

"Take care, Meghan," Valerian whispered, conveying with his eyes that she was to risk no harm to herself for his sake. He thrust the piece of parchment into the young guard's hands. "This is to be given to my good friend, the soldier Burrus, and to no other. Have you any word as to when he will arrive?"

"Your century will arrive by week's end," the guard answered. "We received a message today. He will be escorting Severus' new concubine here to Eboracum."

"New concubine? I do not envy the poor woman," Valerian replied dryly. "Who is she?"

"A Druid priestess, I hear, of great beauty. The rumor goes that Severus was going to have her killed, but one look at her face stayed his hand. He had best watch her, lest she enchant him or work some evil upon him."

"I doubt that she would do such a thing," Valerian responded. "You have much to learn about the people of Britain. I would instead be concerned for her. I pity anyone who is a prisoner of Severus Cicero Plautius." As the guard turned to leave with Meghan, Valerian said, "You will see that Burrus gets that note?"

The guard nodded and Valerian felt in his heart that the young man would be true to his word. Valerian's eyes held Meghan's as if asking her the same question, and her own eyes assured him that the letter would reach his father.

Thirty-nine

Meghan stood in the shadows outside her tent, listening to the sounds of the night. Nervously she clutched at the small key stolen from the guard by Ibu. Ibu had managed to play on the guard's love of boys; pretending to seduce him, he lulled the man into complacency, and once he'd fallen into a drunken stupor—unable to act on his desires—Ibu had snatched the key away. Hopefully he would be able to return it before it was missed.

Looking up at the crescent moon shining overhead, Meghan felt suddenly calm. All would be well; the gods and goddesses would protect a man like Valerian. They had to.

Such a peaceful night, she mused, looking about her. She started to walk briskly, as if going for a stroll, glancing back now and again to be certain that she was not being followed.

Gone were the weakness from her limbs and the trembling of her hands. She was composed, as if, once the plan was under way, the excitement became an antidote to fear, as if confidence took command. The prisoners' tent loomed up ahead, surrounded by shadows in the dim light of the partial moon. Two days had passed since her last meeting with Valerian. The black horse he loved so well was well provisioned and hidden in a clump of trees not far from the soldiers' camp.

Meghan slowed her pace, ducking behind a bush, as she heard the sound of laughter behind her. No doubt it was a few of the soldiers at their drink. She crept along on hands and knees, scarcely noticing the scrapes and bruises in her concern for Valerian. When she was sure there was no one about, she stood up again and continued on her way.

This night Valerian had been fortunate, for this was the one day when the guards indulged in their own desires, which meant that there would be fewer guards around the prisoners. Tonight these Romans would celebrate the end of the campaigning season, a festival to the war god Mars. After Jupiter, Mars was the most important of the Roman dieties, a symbol of the military might of the Roman Empire. Much wine would be consumed this night. If all went according to plan, Ibu would have been able to slip a sleeping drug into the wine of the guards, thus removing even the slightest risk of being caught at their task.

Meghan came to the first guard post and smiled as she heard the sound of loud snoring.

So, Ibu has been successful, she thought, taking a deep breath and walking toward the next post. Here the two guards were sprawled on the ground where they had fallen next to their drugged cups of wine. Meghan slipped quickly past them, gasping in alarm as one of the guards stirred, mumbled in his sleep, and clutched at her fleeing skirts. Looking back, she could see that his motion had been only a reflex action. The guard was again completely asleep. Holding tightly to the key, Meghan slipped into the tent.

Valerian knew that it was late. How late he had no way of determining for in the dark one hour dragged into another. He had been sleeping, falling into fitful dozes now and again.

Valerian's heart lurched in his breast as Meghan appeared. "So, you have made it. Good. Have you the key?"

In answer she slipped it into his hand. Quickly Valerian worked at the locks that held him chained. When the task was done, he questioned Meghan as to how the key had been obtained, and gave a sigh of revulsion when she answered him.

"Clever Ibu. If the gods will it and I am successful in my attempts to regain my freedom, my good name, I will make it up to him. He is more than a faithful slave, he is friend to me."

Frantically she tugged at his arm. "We have

to hurry, for I do not know how long it will be until the guards are roused from their stupor."

"Let's go, then," he answered, taking the heavy dark cloak she offered him. When they were outside, he breathed in the cold, damp night air as if it were an elixir from the gods themselves, savoring it in great gulps.

Following close behind Meghan, Valerian ran until he heard Sloan nicker in greeting as he sensed his master's presence. Meghan helped him gather up the supplies where she had hidden them nearby. Mounting the horse, Valerian felt a surge of strength come to him.

"Meghan, I do not know how to thank you."

"I want no thanks. To see you safe is reward enough both for me and for Ibu."

"I only pray that you will not be suspected for what has transpired this night. If the gods will it, I will see you again!" He leaned down and gently stroked her red-gold hair in a gesture of fond farewell. "Now, get back to your tent and remember that you know nothing of this night's work."

With a firm hand on his stallion, Valerian rode off into the night.

Forty

Wynne lay upon the cloak which was spread beneath her on the hard ground as her makeshift bed. Her entire body ached, from her head to her toes, a result of the difficult journey to Eboracum she had been forced to undertake. She was used to riding, but not for so long nor so far. Already they had covered fifty miles, but they had hundreds of miles left to travel.

Her guards had been kind to her, to her surprise, particularly the young man named Burrus. Severus had ordered them never to leave her alone, and being constantly watched had begun to wear on her nerves. Only the veil of darkness gave her respite from the soldiers' ever-watching eyes.

Wynne considered herself fortunate, for Severus had not touched her since that day in his tent, and then he had only embraced her and nuzzled her neck. His touch had made her sick with revulsion, and she wondered how she would ever be able to bear bedding him when she was forced to do so once he himself arrived in Eboracum. She wondered at his haste in seeing her off on the journey; it was as if he wanted to hide her—but from whom? And what had become of Brenna? she wondered. How she had dreaded seeing the hate-filled eyes of her stepmother, witnessing her shame, yet, strangely, she had not seen the evil woman since being summoned to the tent of the tribune.

So many questions left unanswered, she thought, letting the tears fall freely now in the darkness. She had managed to keep from crying in front of the soldiers, sitting proudly astride her horse, neither frowning nor smiling. It had earned her the nickname of "ice princess" from the soldiers, but she could tell from their eyes that they admired her spunk. In the solitude of the night, however, she gave in to her frustrations and her sorrow.

Slave! Slave! The very word haunted her nights and rang in her ears. She was Severus' slave, his concubine, his woman. *No, I'm not his. Never will I belong to anyone but myself*, she thought vehemently. Yet she had wanted to belong to someone once, to Valerian. She had wanted to be his wife. Oh, why couldn't she get that murdering, lying Roman out of her thoughts?

A hand on her shoulder caused her to wince. "Are you all right?" a voice she recognized as belonging to Burrus asked.

"Yes. Yes, I'm fine . . . just . . . bad dreams," she answered in her halting Latin. She could thank Valerian for one thing. He had taught her to communicate with these Roman dogs, and day by day she was becoming more proficient in their tongue.

"I'm . . . I'm sorry that you must be treated like a prisoner," Burrus said.

Turning, she could see his face in the moonlight. He was handsome, though not as handsome as Valerian. At the thought of him and his treachery she wanted to scream out in rage, yet she held her emotions in control. After a moment she again looked at Burrus, his kindly deep-set eyes, the strong chin, the full mouth.

Why he is even younger than I am, she thought in surprise. It was the first time she had looked at him so closely, and the knowledge of his youth was startling. It made her feel strangely protective. She who was his prisoner, his enemy.

"You are so young," she said to him.

"I am older than I look," he replied. It seemed that his smile lit up the night, his teeth straight and white. He ran his fingers through his dark brown hair, untangling the wavy strands, then again touched her arm.

"Why are you kind to Wynne?" she asked suddenly, her eyes meeting his.

"Because . . . because . . . well, I admire your courage," he stammered, glancing away.

"I am just a slave, no longer free," she whispered sadly. "Will I be safe . . . on journey?"

She felt the hand tighten on her arm in a

gesture of reassurance and was surprised to feel affection for this gentle young man. He was not like the others. She could tell that he had no heart for the life he was living.

"You are safe here. No one will harm you," he promised. And she believed him, for he was the temporary leader of the century, until a new one could be chosen at Eboracum.

"Thank you," she answered, reaching up to touch his hand. The thought entered her mind that Valerian too had been a leader of these Romans, a centurion such as the one she had heard about who had been sent away from his men in disgrace. Oh, why must everything remind me of him? she scolded silently to herself, lying back down upon her bed and trying in vain to sleep. The sounds of the night became louder, the blowing of the wind assailing her ears. Curling up on her hard pallet, Wynne shivered.

"You are cold," she heard Burrus say, and felt the heavy touch of a warm woolen cloak spread over her body.

Somehow the thought that she at last had a friend soothed her, and Wynne fell into a deep, untroubled sleep at last.

Before the first light of morning appeared, Wynne was roused from her sleep to set out again upon the rough terrain. She was given her ration of bread and porridge and then told to mount her horse for the journey. How she longed for a chance to wash her hair, to rid herself of the filth from the road, but there was neither the time nor the place to bathe, and so with a sigh she climbed on her horse's back. Since a slave could own no property, Wynne's white horse had been given to one of Severus' soldiers, and she was riding a gray mare.

The crisp early-morning air was invigorating. Wynne's cheeks glowed pink from the cold whipping her face, and she enjoyed the ride this morning, no matter where they were headed.

"I see that you are feeling better this morning," she heard a voice behind her say. Looking back, she saw the now familiar figure of Burrus. His brown eyes were looking at her with admiration, his dark brown hair ruffling in the breeze.

"Better, yes. When I ride, I feel free, at one with the earth." She smiled at him then. It was the first time he had ever seen her smile, and he was dazzled by her beauty. He hated himself for being the one to take her to the confines of the camp at Eboracum. She deserved far better than Severus, though he dared not let her escape or he would face the same fate as Valerian. At the thought of his friend, he winced as if struck. There was little doubt that the tribune would carry out his threat of beheading the centurion.

Noticing the sad look in the young man's eyes, Wynne cocked her head to look at him closer. "What is wrong?" she asked.

"Nothing. I . . . I was just thinking of my centurion. We were friends, he and I, and I fear he has been unjustly sentenced to die. You see, you are not the only one who has been wronged by Severus Cicero."

"Your centurion, what was he like?" Wynne asked in curiosity, carefully managing her horse so that she rode beside Burrus' own mount.

"Honorable, peace-loving, strong, brave. All the things I want to be. He hated war and the violence and death it brought, and for that he has been punished." He looked at her, his brown eyes mirroring a sadness, a disillusionment of hopes and dreams, which struck a sympathetic chord in Wynne. The world was not the place he had imagined it to be; it was cruel, hard, and lonely.

"This centurion of yours does not sound like a Roman to me," she answered. To her, most Romans were heathen dogs, animals who enjoyed bloodshed.

Burrus grinned. "Oh, he is Roman, all right. I can vouch for that." The young centurion focused his eyes upon the horizon. Alarm coursed through his veins. "Halt!" he ordered, seeing before him in the distance the black specks of an army, looking like ants. In this area of the country, Celto-Iberian tribalism survived in its more primitive forms, and he feared an attack.

Seeing the drift of his senses, Wynne looked also in that direction. "Brigantes," she said.

"Brigantes?" Burrus repeated, ashamed at the fear he was feeling. "Are they peaceful or are they warriors?"

"Enemies of Wynne's people," she answered. "Fight them many times. They are heathens—

take human sacrifice. Wynne's people do not spill human blood!"

"They make human sacrifices?" Burrus asked with a shudder.

"They worship the god Taranis," Wynne continued, "god of thunderstorms."

"Jupiter!" Burrus exclaimed. "They worship our god of thunderbolts, our supreme god, then. Why, surely they could not be heathens if they do so."

Wynne shook her head impatiently. "They take heads," she said. "Dangerous. Must keep out of sight."

Burrus had heard about the custom of taking heads, the warriors attaching them to the necks of their horses to later be embalmed in cedar oil and displayed on the walls of their lodges as trophies. Wisely he veered his men off in the opposite direction from the Brigantes. It was only a few years ago that the Romans had been killed in great number by the tribe of the Iceni in the southeast of Britain. He knew all too well how one incident could lead to another, until both sides were guilty of great wrongs. He would avoid any chance of such a thing happening today.

"Retreat," he ordered, leading his men off to the right. This moorland half of Britain was the chief area of military occupation, patrolled by some forty-thousand men, with great fortresses at Eboracum and Caerleon, yet it was miles away to the nearest legion. He could afford to take no chances.

Riding like the wind, Wynne struggled to keep up with the cavalrymen. A sudden urge to escape overtook her. It was now or never. The men were so concerned with their own welfare that they were paying hardly any attention at all to her. Heart beating wildly, she crested the top of a hill; there was no army behind her now, nothing but grass and hills before her. Urging her horse onward, she plunged ahead to freedom.

Forty-one

Behind her Wynne could hear the thundering sound of hooves as she plunged down the hillside. The taste of freedom was like sweet wine to her senses. No one could catch her now.

"Stop! Stop!" Burrus shouted as he followed in hot pursuit. He could not let her escape, not now, not when there was danger. There was no telling what might happen to her at the hands of the Brigantes. It was better for her to be safely among his men than to be sacrificed to some heathen god. He forgot all else but the golden-haired woman riding on so far ahead of him.

The wind tore at her face as Wynne rode onward. She had no thought but escape. It did not matter that she could not go back to her people for fear of being captured again by Severus or that she had nowhere to go. She only knew that she could tolerate the bonds of slavery no longer. Heedless of the rutted landscape, she rode faster and faster, looking back from time to time to see if the young soldier still followed her. She was amazed at his horsemanship as he pursued her.

"Look out!" came his hysterical warning, but Wynne was too preoccupied with her escape to heed his warning until it was too late.

The horse lurched suddenly and Wynne felt herself falling. Images of her father's accident flooded her memories and she screamed in fear and pain.

Hearing her cries, Burrus rode toward her like one demented.

"Let her be alive," he groaned, feeling a strange kinship with her. She was so proud, so brave. She didn't deserve the fate which had been dealt to her.

He spotted the gray mare and breathed a sigh of relief to see that the horse was uninjured; perhaps, then, the Celtic girl had also escaped serious wounds. He whistled for the horse, but the animal, still frightened by its fall, galloped out of sight. Cursing, Burrus let it go and rode on through the trees until he saw Wynne lying still and silent on the rocky ground.

Dazed and shaken, Wynne desperately tried to get to her feet, terrified that she would be helpless as her father had been after his fall. To her relief she realized she was bruised and scratched but no bones were broken. Her ankle throbbed, but she was sure it was just a sprain.

Looking up, she saw a horse and rider approaching her.

"No, I can't go back, I can't," she murmured to herself. Heedless of the pain, she hobbled forward, struggling to escape from her captor, but she was no match for Burrus. She felt strong arms lift her up onto a horse and cried out her anger.

"Let me go! Let me go!" she shouted furiously, her arms flying about as she fought to be free. It mattered not that it was the kindhearted centurion holding her thus. At this moment he was the enemy and the only obstacle to her liberty.

Burrus struggled with the Celtic girl, nearly losing his balance and falling from his horse. In her rage, she was as one panicked while drowning, her hair flying wildly about, stinging his eyes. Try as he might, he could not subdue her.

"Forgive me, Ice Princess," he whispered, and hit her a stinging blow to the chin that knocked her unconscious.

Wynne opened her eyes slowly and looked around. She was lying on the ground in the Roman soldiers' camp. The ropes which bound her bit into her flesh as she fought frantically against them.

"Don't struggle," she heard a voice say, and looked into the eyes of one of the older Romans.

Her jaw was aflame where she had been hit, yet she would not give vent to tears. She would not give up! Never! She would try again to get away.

"You have cost us a horse," the man said with anger. "It escaped into the wilderness. From now on you will have to either walk or ride behind one of the soldiers."

"And if I cannot?" she asked, motioning to her injured leg.

"I will put you out of your misery as I would a horse," he said with a malicious grin. "I despise you and your kind. You have cost me many a comrade during battle."

Wynne gasped. "But I am not a horse, to be killed for a hurt leg."

"Do not try me, Celt, for I am not as soft as the centurion Burrus!" He gave her a sour look and then stalked away, leaving her stunned and horrified. These Romans were worse than the Brigantes. At least the Brigantes would not hurt women.

"You Roman dog," she whispered beneath her breath, "I will get away from you. Oh, how I hate you!" Even Burrus, whom she thought to be her friend, had hurt her. Angrily she turned her head away when she saw the centurion approaching her.

Burrus knelt down and offered her some bread and wine, but she ignored him. When he touched her shoulder gently, she cringed as if he had burned her.

"I'm sorry that you are angry with me, Ice Princess," Burrus said softly. "I did what had to be done. As much as I like and admire you and wish you could be free, you are my prisoner and, for now, the property of my tribune. I could not let you go. And what would have happened to you in the hands of the Brigantes? Please try to understand."

At these words Wynne faced him, her lovely face marred by her scowl. "I understand that we are enemies!"

Burrus shook his head. "No, we are not enemies. Whether you know it or not, I am your friend. Someday I will be able to help you to be free, but now is not the time. Trust me, Ice Princess."

Wynne's eyes softened; she longed for his friendship and needed an ally among these Romans, yet she had trusted a Roman once and he had betrayed her. She remained silent.

Burrus gently touched her chin. "I hope I did not hurt you too much. Believe it or not, it caused me anguish to do what I did." He could see a dark bruise on her fair skin.

Wynne turned haunted eyes to him. "Please, let me go," she said softly. "I would rather be dead than Severus' slave."

Burrus clenched his fists and closed his eyes. "The gods know that I would if I could, but I cannot."

Remembering the words spoken by the gruff guard, she motioned toward her foot. "They will kill me, like a lame horse."

"No, no one will harm you," he answered, amused until he saw the fear in her eyes.

"He said if Wynne could not walk he would kill, like animal." Her eyes strayed in the direction of the soldier who had told her this.

Burrus fought to control his rage at the other man. "While I am alive, no one will touch a hair on your head! He merely said that to frighten you. You will not be killed, Wynne, but if he ever comes near you again, I want you to let me know and I will reckon with him. Now, if you can promise me that you'll not try to escape again, I'll leave your hands and feet unbound."

Wynne was silent for a moment as she considered whether she could honestly agree not to run again.

At last a smile spread over her face. "All right," she said. Burrus was her friend; he had proved it this night. "Thank you, friend," she whispered, closing her eyes and trailing off into sleep. That night for the first time in a long while she slept without nightmares to haunt her slumber.

Forty-two

Six days of exhaustion and pain had passed before Wynne reached her destination. She had been forced to walk part of the way, but the rest of the distance had been astride Burrus' horse, riding together with the young centurion. He had been kind to her, letting her ride his horse alone while he walked. Food rations had begun to dwindle and the soldiers had no time to hunt, and thus Wynne often felt the pangs of hunger, but so did the rest of the party.

Now, looking to the horizon, Wynne could see the tents of the camp at Eboracum. From the distance they appeared to be bright-colored flowers in bloom. She was bone-weary, but the worst of the journey was over. They would reach the camp before nightfall.

Wynne had grown used to the friendship and talk she shared with the young Roman soldier.

He had seemed to enjoy teaching her new words and phrases in his language, and praised her for her efforts. Soon, he promised, she would speak his language like a native.

"What are you thinking about?" Burrus asked, coming up close behind her as she walked along. He stopped so that she could climb on the horse behind him. The tilt of her chin reflected her pride as she gazed off in the distance.

"Wynne hates to arrive in camp dirty, smelling of horse," she said with disgust, running a hand through her grimy hair. "In my father's village I bathed in lake often."

Burrus understood her plight. His eyes searched for a stream. "There in that stream. You can clean yourself there," he said, leading her off in that direction.

Wynne blushed shyly as her eyes strayed to where the men waited upon their horses.

"I'll make certain that they don't watch you," Burrus promised. "You will have your privacy." He led her to a clearing by the stream which was sheltered by a grove of trees, still green from the summer rains.

"Will you watch?" Wynne asked with suspicion.

"No. Not if you give me your word once more that you will not flee. Will you?"

Wynne nodded. In spite of all that had happened to her, all the Romans had done, she liked this young man. She would not lie to him. Besides, her reason told her that there was really no place for her to go.

She took off her cloak and tunic and hung

them from the branch of a tree and put her foot coverings with their untanned leather and soft fur lining on a flat rock. She found a shallow place in the stream and waded into the freezing cold water. Standing in her underskirt, she bent down to wash her face and hands, then her arms, and last her hair, swishing her golden mane about in the frothy current. She squeezed the water out of her hair and let it dry in the noonday sun. It was a warm day for this time of year, and Wynne thanked the goddess for this blessing. Using a twig, she soon had the tangles out of her hair and gloried in the feel of its silken threads against her bare back as she walked to the shore.

Untying the drawstring of her skirt, she lifted it over her head and stood naked in the warmth of the sun. She laid her underskirt in the sun to dry and again waded into the water, deeper this time, splashing water up over her body until her skin tingled. Never would she let herself be dirty again.

When at last she was dressed again, she walked back out to where Burrus awaited her. If he had thought her lovely before, he knew her to be beautiful now, with her hair blowing about her shoulders like spun gold. Careful, Burrus, he cautioned himself. He must remember that she did not, could not, belong to him. She was Severus' slave.

"Let's go," he said curtly, trying hard to hide his true feelings; and together they walked to where the soldiers of the century awaited them, once more to start out to Eboracum.

Burrus' pace quickened as they reached the outskirts of the camp. He was anxious to be rid of Wynne; it was torture for him to feel her breasts against his back, her arms enfolding him, without being able to make her his.

Riding into the camp, they were greeted by three men, their faces grim and unsmiling.

"How goes it?" Burrus asked, to be met with a surprising answer.

"Terrible. The tribune will have all our heads," a short gap-toothed cavalryman replied. At Burrus' look of question he explained that the centurion they had imprisoned had escaped several days ago, and although they had searched near and far for him, he had not been recaptured.

It took all Burrus' self-control not to smile at this news, for he admired Valerian above all men, but he managed a frown. "He must be found," he said.

"We have looked for him everywhere, but he has vanished like the wind," the soldier replied, eyeing the young woman who rode behind the new centurion. He was not bold enough to ask who she was, but his instincts told him that she was the new concubine for Severus Cicero. Surely the tribune had all the luck to have found this one.

Burrus got down off his horse and gently lifted Wynne from her perch atop the stallion. "We are here," he said softly.

With frightened eyes Wynne took in the camp, the soldiers, so many of them. She had not seen so many armored men since the attack on her people that fateful day. Sensing her fear, Burrus inquired as to where she was to be lodged, and then escorted her to the large comfortable tent where she would stay to wait for Severus' return. Here were all the comforts of a Roman villa: curtains of silk, pillowed couches, fine rugs to keep out the damp of the ground and to keep in the heat from the small portable wood stove.

Looking around her, Wynne shuddered. To her it was a place full of foreboding. She could almost envision Severus sitting upon the pillows, and clutched Burrus' hand tightly.

"I do not like it here," she said simply.

He comforted her as one would a child, patting her hand and murmuring soothing words.

"Excuse me, sir" a young guard interrupted, handing Burrus a small roll of parchment. "I was to give you this immediately upon your arrival."

Drawing away from Wynne, Burrus scanned the missive, his eyes large with his surprise.

"So, I am to have a slave," he said as he read Valerian's words. "No doubt she is an old hag who he fears will be left to starve without a master. Well, bring her to my tent immediately. I will meet you there," he said; then, thinking again, he called back the guard. Perhaps this slave could befriend the Celtic woman; perhaps a friend, a motherly woman would benefit her. "On second thought, bring her here."

Burrus set about trying to make Wynne feel at home in her new surroundings, reassuring her all the while and explaining that she was to have a companion, one of her own people. Hearing a rustle behind him, he turned around, astonished at the sight of one of the loveliest young women he had ever seen before—as charming a vision, in her own way, as Wynne. His eyes appraised her curly red-gold hair hanging down below her shoulders, the large lash-fringed eyes, like the costliest jade in a perfect setting, the full, nearly round face, and the small turned-up nose. Then his eyes took in her tall and graceful body with slim hips and small, high breasts.

"I am Meghan," she said with a slight bow. "Your slave."

Burrus smiled. "Perhaps, lovely Meghan, my stay here will not be as lonely as I once thought."

Wynne's eyes met Meghan's and both women sensed that they had met a friend. The two smiled warmly at each other, utterly unaware that they were connected not merely by their similar plights, but by their memories of the amber-eyed Roman, Valerian.

Forty-three

Holding Sloan's bridle in his hand, Valerian walked about the clearing as memories overwhelmed him. Here was the magical cave where he had first made love to the golden-haired Wynne. Here they had been safe from prying eyes. He would rest the night in this haven and then with the dawn seek word of Wynne. He would have to be doubly cautious, for he well knew that Severus and his legion were still in the area, and capture would mean certain death.

Lying down on the hard ground without even a straw mattress or the soft grass to pillow him, Valerian sought sleep, but it was long in coming. His mind was tortured by the thought that perhaps he was too late to save Wynne. Yet his soul cried out that if this were true he would somehow know it, feel it in his heart. No, Wynne had to be alive.

The night seemed to be the coldest he had yet experienced on his rough journey, and he shivered, clutching his cloak tightly about him. Valerian spent the night in relative comfort, dreaming of another time, another warm body pressed against his own.

When the first light streamed into the mouth of the cave, Valerian opened his eyes. He squinted into the sunlight as he tried to remember all that Wynne had told him about the customs of her people. It was, to his reckoning, nearly the time for the feast of the Samhain, as she had called it, the autumn equinox. Soon the fires would be burning brightly on earth at the very time that the fire and heat of the heavens had begun to wane. If he was right in his timing, Severus would have his hands full trying to keep his new vassals in line, away from these fires and the influence of the Druids, who even beyond their graves would call upon the hearts of the Celts.

It is far easier to throw down idols than to destroy the inner force of the spirit, Valerian mused. The sacred places of the ancient Celts might be invaded, altars and oak groves thrown down, priests slain, but the hearts of the people should still seek their gods and their freedom.

Valerian left the cave in search of his breakfast and found it—two small goose eggs which he ate greedily, along with a handful of berries. In a nearby spring he sponged cold water over his body in a quick bath. If he were to find

Wynne, he wanted to look his best. Thus refreshed and fed, he set out upon his quest.

From a vantage point on the hilltop, Valerian
could see the Roman soldiers swarming around
the village like bees around a hive, and cursed.
How was he to enter the village with so many
infantrymen around? His eyes searched for
Wynne's lodge. From so far away, it was difficult to tell which one it was.

All day long he stayed at his post, fearful lest
he be detected by the eagle eyes of the scouts.
His heart ached for the plight of these proud
people who had now been reduced to servitude.
He could see women and children working hard,
bending their backs to their Roman foes as they
struggled to please them. He could see them
flee at the first sight of the cavalry, screaming in
fright at those who entertained themselves by
frightening them with threats and abuse. Even
the older villagers were forced to labor, stumbling on their frail legs as they went about their
tasks. Valerian was not proud to be a Roman
this day.

Searching in vain for sight of Severus, Valerian repeatedly saw the figure of a dark-haired
woman walking about in her finery like a queen,
gesturing and calling out loudly to the workers.

Who is she? he wondered. He recalled Wynne's
description of her stepmother and wondered if
it could be she. Dared he to hope? His eyes
scanned the area continuously, hoping for a
glimpse of Wynne. Would she be among the
workers, or perhaps working inside the lodge?

He could not take the chance on going down into the village, not yet. Still, if he could only talk with the dark-haired woman, perhaps he could find out Wynne's whereabouts.

"If I have to wait here all night, all day tomorrow, and the next, I will," he said to himself.

That evening Valerian was rewarded for his patience. In the quiet darkness a mist came up, cloaking the earth in an eerie veil. Valerian quietly made his way down the hill into the village.

Crawling on hands and knees, scarcely daring to breathe for fear of alarming the guards, Valerian crept closer, armed only with his sword and his cunning against an entire legion. He made his way to the lodge in the middle of the village, hoping that he would find Wynne safely sleeping inside. He would find her, wed her, and return with her to Rome.

Sliding through the doorway of the small dwelling like a lizard from the deserts of the Nile, Valerian slowly made his way past the strange fur-covered benches upon which he could see the figures of sleeping Celts. The light of the moon gave him aid as he searched for the familiar golden hair of the woman he had come so far to find. But he did not see her here. Was he in the wrong hut? With disappointment he retraced his path, intent on leaving this dwelling and searching another.

A noise warned him of danger. Looking behind him, he found himself staring into the face of the dark-haired woman he had seen from afar. Armed with a dagger, she had stolen up on him from behind. He met her eyes in surprised recognition, for who could forget that face!

"You!" he whispered in shock as she lunged toward him, intent on his death.

Forty-four

Valerian drew back to dodge the fatal blow; the blade burned a ribbon of pain through his shoulder. Brenna turned to strike again, anger making her careless. The centurion grabbed the wrist holding the weapon and twisted it behind the woman, holding her against him as prisoner. The dagger fell to the floor, and with a quick kick of his foot Valerian sent it skidding across the room.

Struggling furiously, the woman threw herself at him, her free fist striking the wound in the Roman's shoulder, sending a flash of pain through him. Fearful lest their fight rouse the others or that she scream out for help, Valerian lashed out, his blow sending her unconscious to the ground. He flung her over his uninjured shoulder and quickly stole out into the night with his burden.

The fog was beginning to lift, and Valerian realized his danger, yet his only hope of finding Wynne lay in his questioning of this woman whom he knew to be the high priestess of the darkness cult which had nearly claimed his life.

His shoulder burned unbearably as he dragged his prisoner along. He was loosing blood from his wound, but his only thought was to get to the cover of the forest.

By the time he reached the edge of the village, the fog had all but drifted away. He would be visible to the Roman guards unless he could find a place to hide or divert their attention. As if in answer to his prayers, a large stag came from out of nowhere, running in confusion into the throng of Romans. With shouts of challenge and laughter, the soldiers gave chase, each wanting to claim the trophy for his own. At that moment Valerian summoned up a final surge of strength to pull both himself and the woman out of sight of the legion.

Ripping the leather laces from his boots, he bound the arms and legs of his still-unconscious captive, then used his baldric to secure her to a tree so that she would not be able to escape. Only then could Valerian see to his own welfare. Tearing frantically at the hem of his tunic, he at last stanched the flow of blood from his wound. His head whirled, and patches of black floated before his eyes as unconsciousness finally washed over him.

*   *   *

When Valerian awoke, the eyes of the dark-haired woman were upon him, blazing their hatred. He struggled to sit up, not wanting her to realize how weak he was.

"It seems you are my prisoner," he said with false bravado, putting his hand to his sword.

She snarled her defiance at him, pulling at her bonds. "Do you understand my language?" he asked, wondering at her silence. "If you answer my questions, I may think about releasing you." He moved toward her slightly, eyes boring into her own.

"I speak your language," she answered finally.

"What is your name?" he asked, knowing the answer before it escaped her lips.

"Brenna, high priestess of the Celts," she answered proudly. "I answer only to the tribune Severus. My power is great!"

So, he thought, she is already in league with Severus. I must watch her even more carefully than I thought. "I remember you well. Once you held me prisoner and would have had me sacrificed if the gods had not been merciful to me."

"The gods had nothing to do with it—only the interference of the girl took you from me." She spoke with such hatred of "the girl" that Valerian felt fearful.

"That 'girl' saved my life, and for that I will be eternally grateful," he answered, trying to remain calm. "Are you the wife of the bard Adair?"

A shrill laugh bubbled forth from her throat.

"He is dead, Adair. No longer the bard, no longer a Druid."

"Dead? Adair is dead?" Sorrow for Wynne filled him. He knew how much she had loved her father. "How . . . when did he die?"

"Your Romans killed him. Yes, murdered a helpless cripple and slaughtered many of my people." A smile crept over her face. "Yet I have gained from their brutality, for now I have the power the Druids once possessed."

"With the help of the tribune, no doubt. Well, I am not surprised. You are surely two of a kind." His meaning was lost to her as she continued to smile.

"Someday they will be gone and I will rule my tribe," she exclaimed proudly. "Woman can rule better than man. She is wiser, more cunning. Men—ha. All they think about is war and killing."

Valerian rose to his feet but sat back down again as a wave of dizziness struck him. It was several moments before he could talk, for the pain from his wounded shoulder again stabbed through him. Looking up, he could see the brown eyes regarding him with triumph.

"You will die if you do not let me free. I can help you. I have herbs which will heal you. Let me free and I shall help you," she crooned to him.

Valerian shook his head violently. "I do not trust you. Why should I? You would have had me killed once before."

"You have no choice," she answered, staring at him as if to hypnotize him with her eyes.

"No! You will stay where you are. I cannot take the chance of your treachery." Groaning, Valerian sank down on the ground to rest awhile and regain some of his strength. After a moment he sat up again and asked the question he had waited so long to ask. "Where is Wynne? Where is the daughter of your dead husband?"

"Gone," she answered simply.

"Gone?" he repeated, his heart beating like a drum within his breast. "Gone where?" She did not answer him, merely smiled at him with malice. He struggled to get close to her, wanting to wring the answer from her if she did not tell him, yet not having the strength to do so. "Tell me, you evil crone, where is she?"

A smile played about her lips. "She is dead."

"Dead?"

"Yes, she is dead."

Valerian covered his eyes with his hands and swayed back and forth on his knees. It couldn't be true. It couldn't. . . . The woman was lying. He fought with his emotions. "But you said she was gone."

"Gone to the land of death to await a new birth," she answered.

The sob that tore from Valerian's throat was such a mournful sound that even the heartless Brenna was stunned. Eyes filled with tears, the centurion gave vent to his sorrow. How would he live without her?

"How did she die?" he finally asked.

"She was beheaded, as all those who refuse to

give up the old gods are, and I am not sorry she was killed. I hated her."

He could have strangled the woman there and then, but it would not bring Wynne back from the dead. Still, Brenna's hatred of the woman he loved reminded him that this was his enemy, now even more than before.

"Who killed her?"

"Severus, the tribune. He had her killed."

"When . . . when did she die?"

"A few days after our people were attacked by the Romans," she answered.

Heedless of his injury, Valerian rose to his feet, crazed with grief. "I will kill him. I will kill him," he shouted, stumbling as he tried to walk back toward the village, but his weakened body could stand no more strain this night. Valerian sank into the black pit of senselessness as he collapsed, the sound of sinister laughter ringing in his ears.

Forty-five

Valerian came to a long time later to find someone standing over him. It was Brenna, fumbling for his sword. Somehow she had escaped her bonds and now had it in her mind to kill him.

Let her do it, Valerian thought. Let it be over. I have no fondness for this life with Wynne gone. Yet his inner soul would not let him die this way. Just as Brenna had the sword firmly in hand, Valerian's instinct for survival took hold of him. With a scream of outrage at both her and the man who had murdered his lover, he tumbled sidewise, kicking upward as he did so. Brenna clutched at her stomach, dropping the sword to the ground. Valerian lunged for the weapon, using every bit of strength left to him, grasping it firmly as if in a handshake with a faithful friend. Brenna drew back, eyes wide with fright. Such a fearsome look did the centu-

rion have upon his face that she turned on her
heel and fled.

Valerian did not have the strength to follow
her, even though he knew that she would now
expose him. He wondered just how friendly she
was with Severus. Would Severus try to capture
him when he found out? No matter the answer,
Valerian knew that he had no strength left to
fight. His only chance was to hide in the cave
until his wound was healed sufficiently to enable him to travel.

Gasping in pain, Valerian made his way
through the forest. He was thirsty, as if all the
bodily fluids had seeped out of him with the
loss of his blood. His lips were parched, his
tongue swollen. A hundred times he staggered,
falling to his knees, unable to go on. But just
when it seemed that all hope was gone, he would
somehow find it in himself to push forward
again.

When at last he came to the clearing by the
cave, he dropped to the ground before the spring
of water. No wine had ever tasted so good to
him as he gulped it down. With his thirst
assuaged, he cleansed his wound and bound it
with a fresh piece of his torn tunic and splashed
the water over his face. Dragging himself to the
mouth of the cave, he whistled for Sloan and let
the horse pull him the rest of the way. Pain-
racked and weary, he dropped to the floor of
the cave, safe at last.

* * *

Several days of sorrow and anger passed before Valerian began to regain his strength. During his long, healing sleeps he saw Wynne's face before his eyes again and again in his dreams and he cried out to her. But Wynne was gone from him forever.

Valerian had been lucky; his wound had remained clean. He had seen many a soldier lose either his life or his limb through a festering wound. He was able to sustain himself with berries and the small game that passed near the cave. Day by day he felt his health return as his blood seemed to renew itself.

The day finally came when he knew that he could no longer stay in his forest hideaway, that he must return somehow to Rome. He couldn't help but wonder what his father's reaction would be to what he told him about Severus. Would he help him fight the tribune and clear his name?

Leaving his cuirass and armor behind him so that he would be able to travel at a faster pace, Valerian mounted Sloan in the darkness of the night.

He rode quickly through the forest, heading southeast. The path was deserted, as he had hoped it would be, no sign of the soldiers anywhere, nor of any travelers. Apparently the Celts did not want to risk running into the Romans in the darkness of the night. Hearing a noise behind him now and again, he would hide among the foliage, only to find that the sound had been caused by a flock of birds or a wild animal moving around in the dark.

It was not until the fifth day of the journey that Valerian realized that he was being followed. From his vantage point high on a hill he could see them, their bright scarlet cloaks billowing in the breeze, helmets gleaming in the sun with their horsehair crests ruffling like the feathers of birds in flight. They were a few miles behind him, but gaining steadily as they forged onward.

"So, Severus knows that I am near," he said. It amused him that so many men—he counted nearly thirty—had been sent after him. "No doubt he expects me to head in the direction which I now take southeast toward Eboracum, but I shall fool him. I shall go west toward Deva." It would be a dangerous trip, he knew, for uncivilized Celtic tribes, hunters of human heads, populated the land there, as well as the heathen Picts. Still, were he to have to choose between death at their hands and being taken captive by Severus, he knew he would prefer a quick death at Celtic hands.

"My fate is in the hands of the gods," he said, looking up at the sky.

Thus began a long, hard journey across the moorlands, toward the western seacoast, where Valerian hoped to find a ship—merchant or war ship, he cared not—which would take him safely back to Rome.

Forty-six

The early-morning sun caught the gleam of golden hair as Meghan carefully combed Wynne's tresses.

"Hold still!" she scolded, trying with difficulty to arrange the blond hair in a fashionable chignon high on the back of Wynne's head.

"I'm sorry," Wynne answered with a mischievous smile. "But I do not like just sitting. There is so much to be done." How she longed to go riding, but she was watched night and day, awaiting Severus' return. The lack of activity had not been wasted, however, for she had been studying Latin and was now almost fluent.

"I know. Neither do I," said Meghan. "It is hard to get used to the Roman way of life. They are so idle, always eating and enjoying their concubines."

At the word "concubine" Wynne winced. "Oh, I do not want to be that vile old man's mistress.

His touch makes my flesh crawl." She gasped in pain as Meghan pulled at a snarl of hair.

Meghan attached four narrow plaits of false hair to Wynne's coiffure and the front of false curls arranged in three rows on a framework, then stepped back to view her handiwork. "You look beautiful," she breathed in awe, wishing she were as lovely as this golden-haired woman. Perhaps then Burrus would look at her with eyes filled with love.

I must not be jealous of Wynne, she scolded herself. She is so kind and has been my friend. Still it hurt her to realize that to Burrus she was only a child, a pretty young untouchable girl.

Seeing the expression on the red-haired girl's face, Wynne asked, "Meghan, what is wrong?"

"I am a woman. Why can't anyone see that!" she answered peevishly.

"Ah, you are thinking of the young Burrus," Wynne said with a smile. She liked the young centurion. To her he was like a brother, a friend. Since her rough treatment by the Roman soldiers that fateful day, Wynne could not bear to be touched by any man. Even the touch of the gentle Burrus made her jump with revulsion.

Meghan blushed crimson to the roots of her hair. "Is it so obvious?" she asked, reaching up to adjust her own coiffure.

"No. But I too was once in love, and I know how it feels. All I have to do is see the way you look at him to remember my own illusions of love."

Meghan slipped her stola on over her head

and belted it with a finely woven cord. The linen material clung to her budding figure and made her look like anything but a child. Running her hands down over her body as if to assure herself of her maturity, Meghan was lost in her dreams, imagining the hands to be those of Burrus. Wishing to look her best when he came to visit later, she wound a string of pearls in her hair and put on several rings and bracelets. Wynne's laughter brought her back to her senses.

"Not too many jewels, lest you look too much the matron," she chided gently. Wynne stood before the silver mirror clad only in her undergarment, her strophium. These Roman garments felt so foreign to her. She was so much more comfortable in her gowns, but she had been forbidden to dress in her Celtic clothing. With a sigh she too dressed in a long, flowing stola of pale blue.

Meghan gently tugged at Wynne's arm. "Is this better?" she asked, having removed most of the bracelets. With her large innocent eyes she looked so vulnerable in her white stola that Wynne had the urge to gather her into her arms and guard her from any more heartache. Instead, she merely said, "Yes, you look lovely. Burrus would have to be blind or insane not to fall in love with you."

Meghan could not help but notice the sadness in her friend's eyes, and felt guilty for being so selfish as to only think about her own hopes and dreams, when Wynne had been through so much. "Do you still love your Roman?" she asked.

"No!" Wynne answered too quickly not to give lie to the answer. "He used the love I bore him for his own gains and killed my father!" As if to block out the sight of the handsome face of Valerian which even now haunted her, Wynne put her hands up to her face.

Meghan put a gentle hand on Wynne's shoulder, her eyes mirroring her sympathy. "Perhaps you will love again."

"No. I will never give my heart again, not ever," Wynne said angrily.

"What is it like, making love?" Meghan asked suddenly, her voice soft, her eyes wide with curiosity.

Wynne shuddered. "It can be the most brutal thing that can happen to a woman if she is taken without gentleness, with only lust." For the first time since it had happened, she poured out her heart to another, telling Meghan about that awful day when she had been seized and nearly violated by the Romans. It was as if a terrible burden had been lifted off her heart.

"Oh, Wynne, I had heard that you had been used vilely, but I had no idea how terrible it had been for you. Had you ever made love with your Roman before that time?"

"Yes. It was the most wonderful thing that has ever happened to me, like the flowing together of two waves. . . . If only he had not betrayed me, I would have been happy for the rest of my life with the memory of having loved him." She felt a stab of pain in her heart as she thought about Valerian.

"Excuse me, ladies," Burrus said, coming into the tent with a shy grin on his face. His eyes swept over Meghan, but he scolded himself for the thoughts in his mind. She was only a child, barely sixteen, and Valerian had entrusted her to him. To seduce this fair creature would be nearly a sacrilege. He turned his attention to Wynne, not really certain in his own mind just how he felt about the two women. In a way he loved them both. Proud Wynne with her blazing eyes and spirit—each time he was with her, his emotions were in turmoil. She was no stranger to love, he was certain, yet she acted as if she hated all men. And Meghan—what were his feelings for her? She was so lovely and pure; she too touched him deeply and stirred him.

"It is good to see you, Burrus," Wynne said with a gracious smile, proud of her fluency. He complimented her on her progress. To him she was no slave, but the ice princess, and as such, he greeted her like one would royalty, kissing her outstretched hand.

Meghan fought to control her tears; she thought that Burrus had not even noticed her. Little did she know how much self-control it took for him to ignore her, knowing that he would get lost in those jade-green eyes if he dared to let down his guard even for a moment. Feeling like a naughty child who had been punished, Meghan left the tent before the tears gave her away.

"Severus is to return at the end of the week,"

Burrus told Wynne, reading her face for her reaction.

"Oh, no," Wynne gasped. She had been nearly happy these past few weeks with Meghan and Burrus around her. Unlike some of the other slaves, she was not forced to do hard work or wait upon others, but instead led the pampered life of a concubine.

Without realizing the effect she had on Burrus, Wynne reached out to him, needing his comfort. Surprised at this gesture, he misread her, thinking that she wanted him to hold her and make love to her.

Burrus gathered her into his arms. Wynne did not struggle, but instead enjoyed the warmth of the embrace. He was her friend. He understood her terror at being owned by the tribune, or so she thought.

Before she understood his intent, Burrus' lips descended upon hers as though he wanted to devour her. She struggle against him, memories of other, brutal kisses flooding her mind. His hand was on her breast, his tongue darting into her mouth. So tightly did he mold his body to hers that she feared she could not breathe.

"No," she moaned, writhing against him in an effort to be free.

Overwhelmed with desire, Burrus kept up his assault, caressing her breasts, and lifting the stola up at the hem so as to be close to her bare flesh.

"Please . . . please let me go," Wynne sobbed, but her words were muffled by his kiss. Would he never stop? she wondered, feeling panic take hold of her soul.

Burrus pushed her down on the pillows, covering her body with his own. It was then that the images of the pain and the horror of that day sent Wynne over the edge and she screamed in mortal terror.

As if he had been doused with ice water, Burrus drew away from her. Wynne cringed from him, sobbing and whimpering as if he were some flesh-eating animal.

"Wynne, what's wrong? I only want to love you. Let me, please let me," he whispered.

"I . . . I . . . can't. . . . I can't bear to be touched like that," she cried, shaking with her sobs. Weeping hysterically, she told him all that had happened to her and to Isolde. Burrus listened to her story, feeling ashamed of himself for thus intruding on her when she trusted him so.

"I didn't know, Wynne, I swear it. I'll never touch you again, never. I promise."

Burrus had put a comforting arm around Wynne's shoulders to make up for what he had done, when he saw Meghan come back into the tent. Wynne's head was bent, her eyes closed, in thought. But for Meghan one look at the two of them shattered all of her young dreams. It was true, then, that Burrus loved Wynne, not her. Feeling as if her young heart was breaking, Meghan again went out into the cool air of the dawn.

Forty-seven

After the incident in Wynne's tent, Burrus avoided both the young women. He was ashamed of his behavior with Wynne and haunted by Meghan's sad eyes. Yet he did not know what he had done to harm the girl. Hadn't he always kept a distance from her, treated her respectfully, like a sister?

No doubt she is as disgusted with me as Wynne is, and as I am with myself, he thought with self-loathing. Compounding his shame were the images of Meghan that kept coming to him unbidden—Meghan opening herself to him like a flower, Meghan in his arms, Meghan loving him.

"Damn you, Valerian, for putting such temptation in my path," he swore. "How did you have the strength to turn away from this sweet and lovely woman? Was it because of the Celtic woman you spoke of whom you so loved?"

Perhaps, then, another woman would be the answer for him as well. A tall young Egyptian camp follower had been giving him the eye lately. He would take her to his bed.

Wynne too noticed the sad look in Meghan's eyes, but she suspected the cause. No more did she hear Meghan's laughter about the camp. After Burrus let it be known that he had taken a concubine to his bed, Meghan's spells of moodiness grew even worse.

I'm certain that he cares for Meghan as much as she cares for him, Wynne thought. She could not understand men.

But Wynne did not have much time to ponder male perfidy, as she had her own problems. A messenger sent from the South came to inform them that Severus was on his way and would be at the camp the next evening.

I will never let him bed me, she vowed. Let him punish me as he will, and kill me if he so desires. It is better to let the vultures pick the flesh off my bones than let such as him defile me.

Frantically she sought to lay hands on a knife or a dagger, anything that could protect her virtue from his grasping hands, but she was carefully guarded against just such an intent. She would have only her own bare hands with which to fight him off. That and her pride.

The sun seemed to fly across the sky that day as she waited with dread for the tribune's return.

She tried to keep busy, but there was very little to do except try to still the beating of her panicked heart.

When at last the legion was spotted, Wynne fought against the urge to run away into the wilderness. She would have it out with this Severus. She was no weakling, no coward to run away. She was a Celt, and she was proud of her heritage. She would face him like a warrior.

When Meghan came to fetch her, her face ashen with her fear for her golden-haired friend, Wynne held her head high.

"He is here. Severus is here," Meghan cried. "And he is asking for you. You are to meet him in his tent right away. Come."

On trembling legs Wynne followed Meghan to meet her fate.

It was a greatly aged Severus who met her at the entrance of the tent which they would now share. The days spent among the Celts, the worry over the escape of his prisoner, all had taken their toll. But Wynne could find no sympathy in her heart for this man. He was and always would be her enemy.

He had filled the tent with his personal belongings. No longer would this be a safe haven for her, her home. It now would be a place of horror to her, where she would have to suffer this madman's touch.

Severus forced a smile in an effort to win her affection, but it seemed to her nothing more than a sinister leer. He was sitting on the pillowed couch and now gestured for her to come forward. Little did he know the effort it took for her to do so. Her mouth was so dry that she could not speak. She glared at him with defiance.

"So I see that the weeks you have spent here have not softened you. You will no doubt fight me to the end. Well, so be it. I am used to fighting." He gestured for her to sit beside him. She did so, warily. The first sign that he was going to touch her would send her fleeing from this tent.

"I have thought of you often these long weeks," he said softly. "You do not know how I have longed for a woman's softness—a willing woman's that is."

Wynne thought that this creature had no doubt forced himself upon many of the unfortunate girls of her tribe, and her eyes flashed at him. If he expected her to be compliant, to let him have his way without a fight, then he did not know much about the Celts after all.

"I will never come to your bed willingly," she finally answered with a voice filled with scorn.

A wicked smile lit his face. "Willingly or unwillingly, you will do as I want. You are my most cherished possession." He reached for her hand, but she scrambled away.

"I am not your possession. I do not belong to anyone!" she hissed at him.

He stood up then and roughly grabbed her. "You are mine," he said, holding her wrists so tightly that she feared they would snap in two. Suddenly his hold on her loosened as he again tried to be genial. "It won't be so bad. You might even find you like it. You look to me to be a passionate woman in spite of your words."

"I loathe your touch. You are vile. I hate you and all your kind."

"Do you indeed?" Suddenly his hand whipped out and grabbed her hair, pulling it savagely. "I am sorry for your sake that you feel this way, for I intend to have you, whenever I desire you. All your pleading will do you no good."

He pulled her to him and kissed her roughly, heedless of her struggles. In spite of his skinny build, he was a very strong man. He kissed her as if putting upon her his seal of ownership. Wynne could not escape his grasp or his mouth.

Savagely he ripped at her stola, pulling it from her body and leaving her in near-nakedness. She sprang at him, kicking, biting, scratching, but he finally managed to pull her close to him, pinning her arms to her sides and holding her still.

"Oh, little tigeress, if you only knew that your struggles only add to my desire!" With a final tug he had stripped even her strophium from her, so that she was completely naked. His hand roamed freely over her body, caressing her full breasts and traveling down. Wynne gasped at the intimacy of his touch. Her hatred for him was even deeper than before. She tried to protect herself, but her arms were firmly held at her sides. With his one hand he disrobed, his bony body pressed against her own. In terror

Wynne looked down and was amazed to see only a small limp organ.

So he is among the men who cannot please a woman, she thought with relief. Indeed the tribune was no threat to her after all.

In anger and frustration, Severus seemed to sense her thoughts. "Touch me . . . there . . ." he ordered, hoping that this time he would be able to be a man.

"No," she answered.

"Damn you, woman, for your insolence!" he shrieked, pushing her violently away from him. Reaching for his tunic, he dressed himself and called for the guard.

"Take this woman out and give her twelve lashes, but be careful not to mar her skin. Whip her with her clothes on."

Wynne was encircled with the guard's strong arms and pulled from the tent, her eyes resting upon Severus as she went. He was a pitiable creature, this Roman. Let him whip her. Let him kill her. She knew in her heart that he would never have victory over her. The victory was hers.

Forty-eight

Lying facedown on the pillows, letting her tears flow freely, Wynne cursed Severus. She could not believe what he had done to her these last few days. She had been whipped and beaten and starved and made to endure all sorts of degradations in an effort to break her spirit.

The welts from her whipping still burned a trail of pain across her shoulders. She had refused to cry out and give the Romans the satisfaction of seeing her agony. Her bravery would have made Adair proud of her.

"Father!" she cried out. "Wherever you are, hear me. These Romans will pay for what happened to you and for their treatment of me."

Wynne's stomach growled with hunger. Severus had refused her all food except for bread and water until she agreed to do his bidding. He expected her to pretend that he was a great lover, to writhe and moan under him in the throes of make-believe passion. The man was insane and what he asked of her degrading.

"I thank the gods that he is unable to function as a man," she said beneath her breath. She knew that his pride would not let him turn her over to another of his soldiers, for he would want it to be thought that he was plunging into her body.

She hated these Romans more and more each day, except for Burrus, sweet kind Burrus. He had comforted her with his eyes, with soft words, and had smuggled food to her more than once.

"Someday I will kill him for what he has done to you," Burrus had said with such hate in his eyes that Wynne was shocked.

Tomorrow she would again be called before Severus. He no doubt thought she would now do his will—stroke him and pleasure him in unnatural ways—but he was wrong. She would die first.

"Pssst . . . lady . . . beautiful lady," she heard a voice rasp from behind her. She tried to get up to see from whom the voice came, but she was weak with hunger and instead fell back among the pillows.

"Who is there?" she asked in a voice tinged with fear. Had Severus thought of another torture for her?

"It is I, Ibu," the voice answered.

"Ibu?" She had heard of Ibu from Meghan. He was the black slave boy who had befriended

Meghan, although she had never seen him in all the time she had been in the camp.

She heard the rustle of footsteps moving closer to her and saw the faint glow of an oil lamp. Turning her head, she saw him and drew in her breath at the vision he made. His teeth were gleaming like pearls as he smiled; his skin was the same black as Sloan's coat. Wynne had never seen a black person before and his beauty fascinated her.

"I brought this to help soothe and heal your back," he said, bringing forth a bottle from inside his tunic. "It is an herbal salve used by my people."

Shyly he stepped toward her, knelt beside the pillows, and pushed down the fabric of her gown. "I too have felt the lash," he said, stroking the cool ointment upon her skin. It was as if she were bathing in a cool mountain stream. The hurt melted away with his smooth fingers stroking, touching, healing.

As Ibu worked his magic he told her all about himself. That he had once been a prince in the land of Numidia and was loved and cherished by his parents. How his uncle had become jealous of Ibu's father and arranged his murder, then sold the boy to the Romans. In her turn Wynne told him how the Romans had slaughtered her people and how she had been taken into slavery by the tribune Severus. She learned that Ibu was twelve years of age and that he had been a slave for over four years.

"I hate these Romans!" she said between clenched teeth. "They are all evil."

Ibu shook his head. "No, they are not all bad. Master Burrus is kind and gentle."

"Yes," she agreed. "He is, but he is the only one."

"Oh no, indeed he is not!" Ibu argued. "My friend the centurion was also a very kind man. He tried to save me from being whipped and later kept me with him as a stable boy to stop Severus from abusing me. If only he could have been my master, I would have not minded slavery so." He stopped massaging Wynne and stared off into space. "I only pray that now he is safe, wherever he is."

"He is not here?" Wynne asked.

"No. Severus was angered with him, imprisoned him and would have had him beheaded. I helped him to flee. I owed him that for his kindness to me." He smiled sadly.

"So he managed to escape." Wynne was intrigued. Perhaps it was not impossible to get away from Severus' clutches after all.

"Meghan and I helped him to do so," he whispered. "If Severus were to find out, we would both be punished." His eyes suddenly held fear.

"I will never tell, Ibu," Wynne promised. "I think you were both very brave to do such a thing."

"We both loved master Valerian very much," Ibu said with a grin.

Wynne stared at him. "What did you say?"

"I said that Meghan and I both loved master Valerian very much," Ibu said again.

"Valerian. Your centurion was named Valerian?" she stammered.

"Yes. Valerian Quillon Tullius."

Wynne got to her feet, heedless of her pain. Grabbing the boy's shoulders, she gently shook him. "What did he look like?"

Ibu broke away from her, afraid, staring at her as if she had suddenly lost her mind. "Dark hair. Brown eyes," he answered, backing away.

"Is his hair curly?" Ibu nodded yes. "Are his eyes the color of amber?" Again he nodded yes. She pressed her finger into her chin. "And his chin—like so?"

"Yes. Yes. It is all as you say. The centurion Valerian is very handsome. How do you know him?"

"He murdered my father!" she sobbed.

Ibu shook his head in disbelief. "No. No. He would not do such a thing unless he was forced to do so to defend himself."

"My father could not walk. Your centurion murdered him." Wynne could no longer stand, her legs were trembling so from weakness and from her emotions. She sank down upon the pillows and looked up at Ibu.

"I know that you must be wrong," Ibu argued. "Master Valerian could not be guilty of such an act."

"No. I am not wrong. I saw his sword caked with the lifeblood of my father, and for that he will pay someday." Her answer was a sob.

Realizing that she would not change her mind, Ibu fled from the tent to escape the accusations against his friend. He would have to watch the Celtic girl carefully if Valerian were to return, to make certain that she did not harm him. It was strange the way she had acted. Her words spoke of her hate, yet her eyes gleamed with love, as if she were at war deep within her soul.

Alone once more in the tent, Wynne tried hard to shut out the memory of Valerian, his lips, his face, his hands. He had been here in this very camp. Had he slept on this same bed? What had happened to him? No doubt he and Severus had quarreled over who was to be the lord over the vanquished. She had thought him all the way to Rome by now, perhaps seeking the favor of his emperor, but instead he had been held prisoner. A voice inside her head told her to question Meghan—he had been her master. But Wynne's stubborn side refused. She would not let his name pass her lips again until he had paid for his treachery.

Later that night when Wynne traveled to the land of dreams, she beheld the handsome Roman through the mists of a fog and stretched out her arms to him. He came to her, kissing her, caressing her, stroking her silky hair. Together they rolled about, locked in an embrace as they made love. She called out his name over and over again as she was shaken by swirling pleasure.

With a start Wynne opened her eyes. She had been dreaming, yet it had all been so real. In shame she covered her face with her hands. She had yielded to him in her dreams, had wanted him to love her, had dreamed that he indeed did. And why did this image seem less like a memory of their joining than a premonition? Weakness, such a weakness. She still loved him. What could she do?

"Will I never be free of you?" she cried.

Forty-nine

*Tossing to and fro, the merchant vessel forged on-*ward through the raging storm, destined for Gaul and then Rome itself. Aboard the ship Valerian Quillon Tullius, centurion and fugitive, lay on his pallet in the ship's cabin. The rain drummed hard on the cabin roof.

So I am finally on my way to Rome, he thought, rising from his bed. It was so stuffy in the cabin with the humidity of the storm. It was as if there were not a breath of air left.

Valerian went out on the deck. There a single horn-shielded lantern hung from the rigging, shedding its light on the deck. He walked along a little farther and leaned over the rail to watch the water froth and foam below him. He had been aboard the *Vesta* for three days now and was finally becoming accustomed to the rolling of the deck beneath him. He thanked the gods that he was not prone to seasickness.

The wind slapped at his face like a hundred small fingers, stinging his skin. A sudden clap of thunder split through the sky like a fire, one of Jupiter's lances, no doubt.

As he had so many times before in the last few days, Valerian thought about Wynne, and the memory of her caused him physical pain, like a knife thrusting into his heart. He wondered if he would ever be able to love again, and knew the answer was no. No doubt his father would marry him off to some Roman girl of fine family, but he would never be able to feel for any woman what he had felt for the golden-haired Celtic girl. He looked down below him at the figure of Vesta on the prow. The figurehead's blond hair, her ice-blue eyes surveying the sea ahead, reminded him of Wynne.

"Oh, how I loved you," he whispered softly, wondering if Wynne had entered on another life as she believed.

Valerian stared off in the distance, recalling his journey to Deva. He had come close to being caught by Severus' army. It had not taken them long to realize that he had changed direction and was heading toward the sea. Sloan had been magnificent, however, keeping up a fast pace and leaving the Roman soldiers far behind. The first few days of the sea journey, Valerian had scanned the horizon for any sign of a ship following behind the *Vesta*, but so far had not spotted any.

On his journey he had been befriended by several of the people of Wynne's race. Some had given him shelter for the night, or food. Although fighting seemed to be the heart's blood of the Celts, although they were often savage warriors, he found the honesty and straightforwardness of their spiritual outlook compelling. They honored their women more than the Romans, who viewed them as property. They were hospitable to strangers, sharing food and drink, telling their stories around the fire. Perhaps, having no large cities, they had not become corrupted by luxuries or the decadence that material things could bring. They were an outdoor people, loving and understanding the ways of nature.

A touch on his shoulder startled Valerian out of his musing.

"Can't sleep, eh, centurion?" a tall elderly sailor asked him kindly.

"No. I can't. The pitching of the ship made sleep impossible for me."

"Well, this storm should be over shortly, and then we will see smooth sailing ahead of us. What worries me is pirates, though. They have been spotted in this area."

"The pirates?" Valerian asked with surprise.

"You haven't heard of them? Ex-gladiators, they are, rogues who have taken to the sea in order to survive. We will be lucky if we don't have to flee from them, or worse yet, fight them."

"Fighting doesn't frighten me," Valerian answered. "I am used to such dangers. It is the killing of the innocent that haunts my soul."

The old sailor grinned. "Well, then, you don't have to worry, son. The last word I would use to describe these pirates is 'innocent.' They are truly bloodthirsty."

As the wind shifted, abruptly swinging the square sail around to catch the breeze from a different direction, Valerian was nearly sent flying overboard. The ship pitched and rolled as the waves tossed it about like a toy. The spray stung Valerian's eyes and drenched him to the bone.

As if the storm were not enough burden, Valerian looked into the old sailor's eyes and read fear clearly written there. His eyes followed the old man's line of vision.

"There, look there," the old sailor said, pointing with his long bony finger.

Three ships, their sails billowing in the wind, were silhouetted on the horizon.

"May the gods protect us!" the old man shrieked. "It is the pirates!"

Fifty

Valerian's heart sank, for more than the pirates he feared Severus. "They are Roman ships," he shouted. "They fly the purple sails of a Roman galley."

"No, they are pirates, all right," answered the old sailor. "Purple used to be used for only galley ships, but now more often than not such sails signal pirates. Their oars are silver-plated, I am told, and their masts gilded."

The captain was now barking his orders; the crew swarmed on deck readying for battle. Valerian himself clutched at his sword. If he had to die, it would be while fighting.

Below him Valerian could hear the sounds of wood striking wood as the oars were put in place. How many were there? he wondered. A dozen, twenty, or more? The wind was blowing against them from the south. It would take all the manpower available to outrun the pursuing ships.

"We will be killed," a young sailor cried, his eyes crazed with fear.

Valerian had no doubt he was right, for not only did the pirates capture and loot merchant ships, but killed both crew and passengers unless their captives were rich. Would he himself be held for ransom if they fell to these thieves?

"Will I never get to Rome?" he exclaimed in anger.

The captain of the vessel scanned the horizon, and Valerian stared with fascination at the ships in the distance. "We are outnumbered," the captain confided to his passenger. "If only the wind would change. It is blowing against us, holding us still, and our oarsmen number too few to be able to outdistance the pirate ships with their many manned oars."

From below the deck the rowing master beat his drum so that the oarsmen would row in rhythm. It was a nerve-racking sound and Valerian fought the urge to cover his ears with his hands, but at least the ship was moving now, and pulling off to the starboard away from the course of the pirate ships.

"We need more oarsmen," the captain shouted. His eyes scanned Valerian's face as if to ask him how much his life meant to him. Several passengers came forward, perhaps thinking it safer to be below deck when the pirates boarded, but the captain refused the paunchy bejeweled merchants. He needed strong men—men like Valerian.

"I will go below," Valerian finally volunteered, although he would much rather have stayed above to help fight. Following his example, five other sailors volunteered.

The galley was ill-suited to outrunning the pirate vessels, which may have had as many as a hundred oars to move them onward. Instead of rowing benches there were only cleats pegged to the planks on the deck for the oarsmen to brace their feet against as they moved their burden. The ship had no supports for the oars, merely holes in the railing. Taking off his cloak and tunic, clad only in his loincloth, Valerian bent to the task, pulling and pushing, pulling and pushing with all the strength he possessed.

All around him he could smell the sweat of fear as the men struggled against the waves.

"Row faster, faster, you bastards!" shouted the rowing master, beating his drum faster, frenzied with terror.

"I had vowed to my wife that this would be my last voyage," said one of the sailors sadly. "Little did I know how right I was."

"Stop talking and move that oar," shouted another oarsman, "or your prophecy will come true."

Frantically they rowed, even as the sound of scuffling feet sounded above them. It was torture for Valerian not to know what was happening, where the pirates were at this moment and if they were gaining on them. He looked at the sword at his feet; if worse came to worst, he would be prepared.

"They are preparing to ram us. I can see the battering ram even from this distance," they all heard a voice above them shriek. "May the gods save us."

Valerian knew that it would not be long now before the other ships would be close enough to fire a rain of arrows upon them. As if refusing to admit defeat, he pulled and pushed even harder on his oar, clenching his teeth with his determination. He did not want to die!

With a panicky scream the man nearest Valerian dropped his oar and jumped to his feet. "We don't have a chance," he wailed. "We are as a gnat outrunning a bird, three birds. I don't want to be sold as a slave."

In an instant Valerian was on him, knocking him unconscious and gesturing to the rowing master. "You take over his spot."

With eyes wide in his head, the rowing master refused. Picking up his sword, Valerian threatened him bodily if he did not obey. "We, every one of us, must do his part or we are certain to die," he said.

With reluctance the man took his place. Hardly a beat of the rhythm was lost, so quickly did Valerian act. Dropping his sword, he too rejoined the oarsmen.

A flurry of sound overhead came to their ears. A shouting so joyous that Valerian was puzzled. What was going on abovedeck?

"May the gods be praised. May the gods be

praised!" shouted a young sailor, running down below to fetch the others. "The wind has shifted. Haul up your oars. It is blowing from the north."

Bounding to his feet, Valerian raced up on the deck. The sails had been unfurled. The ship was fairly skimming across the water. Being lighter by far than the three pursuing ships, it did not take long for the *Vesta* to be far ahead of the pirates. Looking back, Valerian saw the ships grow smaller and smaller as they outdistanced them.

"We have won this day," he said. "Let us hope that our voyage will be watched by the gods and that they will protect us all the while."

Even through the aching of his entire body he felt joyful. He would make it to Rome; of this he felt certain.

"And when I do, you will pay, Severus. I vow you will pay for what you did to Wynne," he whispered.

Fifty-one

Severus reclined on the couch in his tent, drinking wine and gazing at the sleeping blond-haired Celt. What was the nickname the soldiers gave her? The ice princess. Surely it was a suitable name for the cold bitch. Try as he might, he could not force her to work his will, yet he wanted to keep her with him for the sake of his pride. He wanted his men to be eaten away by jealousy, thinking what they might. None would ever know the truth, that Severus Cicero could not make love to this woman.

Yet she went freely enough to Valerian's bed, he thought sourly, rage festering in his soul. It was as if the centurion's every action mocked him for his frailties, and now this Celtic woman was a reminder that Valerian was a man and he was not.

Overcome by his anger, Severus strode to the

couch where Wynne lay sleeping, wanting to hurt her for insulting him with her stubbornness. His eyes fell on his dagger. He could freely slit the bitch's throat and none would say him nay, but the pain would be over too quickly. Torture seemed not to affect her, for she had withstood every punishment he had dealt out to her, all the while mocking him with her eyes.

Of course, a grin spread over his face, why hadn't he thought of it before? The other Celtic girl, Meghan—he could use her to tame this one. It was obvious that she was overly fond of the red-haired child. Besides, Meghan had been his and Valerian had tricked him into giving her to him. At every turn he seemed to be bested by that damned centurion.

Severus gazed down at Wynne, who looked like a vestal virgin in her slumber. He laughed. Slowly, deliberately he tipped his cup so that wine sloshed down on her, waking her abruptly. Jumping up and wiping her face with the hem of her short sleeping tunic, Wynne eyed him with contempt. Never had she hated anyone more than she hated this monster. She could never forget that it was his legions who had slaughtered her people.

"Forgive me for my clumsiness," Severus said to her in mock gallantry. "I do hope that I have not disturbed your dreams." His mouth spread in a toothy grin which Wynne had learned from experience meant that he was about to do something cruel to someone.

"You are forgiven," she replied icily, holding herself as erect as a queen.

"I wanted to inform you that I intend to give a small banquet tomorrow evening for a few of my officers. It is my wish that the little red-haired slave dance for us." His laugh was full of malice, and the look on his face made Wynne's blood run cold.

"You have not the authority to command her. She is now Burrus' slave and his to command. Meghan does not belong to you," she said.

"She is a slave; Burrus is mine to command. If he wants to please me, he will not interfere in this matter," he hissed at her. It was at this moment that a messenger arrived, his eyes wide with fear as he saw the expression on the tribune's face. He turned to leave, but Severus ordered him back into the tent.

The messenger eyed his tribune warily, afraid of the reaction to the news he had to tell him. Nervously he twisted his fingers together.

"Well, what is it you have to say?" thundered Severus in irritation at the man's silence.

"It is the centurion Valerian. He has been spotted," he blurted out.

Wynne's heart seemed to stop beating in her breast.

Severus poured himself another cup of wine for celebration. Soon, soon he would have the centurion within his grasp. "Tell me where he is so that I may send a century after him," he exclaimed. Oh, Valerian had been so tricky, changing direction in an effort to outwit Severus.

The messenger swallowed hard. "He is on his way to Rome aboard a merchant vessel," he managed to say.

Severus nearly choked on his wine. "Rome. He is on his way to *Rome*? How do you know?"

"One of the empire's spies is aboard the ship and sent a message to us by pigeon when the ship was a half-day out to sea."

In a fit of anger at this news, Severus threw his cup to the floor, shattering it into a hundred pieces against a rock. "Send a message back and tell the spy to kill him. Kill him!"

The messenger shook his head. "He is a spy, not an assassin. Besides, there is no way to get a message to him, for the ship is far out to sea and most likely has reached Gaul by now."

Severus' eyes were angry slits in his face. "Get out of here!" Valerian had bested him once again.

In spite of all that he had done to her, Wynne smiled at the news that Valerian was safely out of reach of Severus' anger. The thought of his having won a victory over the hated Severus was sweet. She was not aware that the tribune saw her smile until he seized her roughly by the arm.

"You are happy for your lover, eh? Oh yes, I know about you and the centurion. I saw you spreading your legs for him like the whore you are, but it did you no good, did it!" He slapped her hard across the face.

Wynne's eyes blazed their hatred. If she had

been armed at that moment, she would surely have struck him down.

"He still betrayed you," he said with a laugh, noting her expression change. "Betrayed your people for his own glory. But I was too smart for him. I knew he intended to subdue your tribe and claim the victory for himself. I followed him and struck first. For that you cannot blame me. If not me, it would have been him." So the bitch did not know of Valerian's noble efforts to save her people. Severus hardly believed that story himself. If he could make her hate the centurion, perhaps she could prove to be a valuable ally. Did her tears mean that she longed for her lover, that she still desired him? Well, he would put an end to such feelings.

"If you only knew how he laughed at you. He thought you an ignorant heathen who could be manipulated. Oh, yes, you no doubt believed his soft words, that he loved you, while all the time his Roman lover awaits his return."

Severus' barb hit its mark. The thought of Valerian in another's arms tortured Wynne as no physical punishment could. But Severus' words merely echoed all that Brenna had said. She could no longer hide from the truth. Valerian had never loved her. She had been merely a tool to be used against her own blood. And now he was on his way back to his Roman lover. She had been so foolish to trust him. Her face was a mirror of her anger, and with a chuckle Severus continued his assault.

"All the while you were giving your body to

your lover, he was planning to conquer your people. As much as you obviously hate me, my sweet ice princess, Valerian has earned your hatred more." Savoring his triumph, Severus spun on his heel and left Wynne weeping on the pillows of her silken prison.

Fifty-two

Already the men in the tent were drunk. Wynne could hear their laughter as they awaited the surprise Severus had promised them—Meghan.

Severus has no quarrel with this innocent child she thought sadly. It is only because of the love that I hold for her that he seeks to harm her. Yet she had begged him not to make the girl dance before his guests. She had even promised to do as he wanted her to do, but Severus had only laughed in her face, certain that now he would even the score with her.

Meghan looked beautiful with her long red-gold curls falling down her back. Severus had ordered that the girl be clad only in the sheerest veillike material from the East.

"I'm frightened, Wynne," the gentle girl whispered, looking down at her sheer tunica with disgust. "I don't know if I can bear this. If I were forced to let any of those men touch me, I think I would die of shame! If only Valerian were here."

At the mention of the centurion's name, Wynne shuddered. Too fresh in her mind were Severus' accusations. She had longed to confide her feelings for Valerian in Meghan, but each time she opened her mouth to speak, she remembered the girl's loyalty to her former master and remained silent. She would be true to her vow not to speak his name again until she was revenged on him.

When Burrus entered the tent, Wynne felt pity for him, as well. She still wondered if her instincts were correct and if he loved Meghan. There was such a fury in the young centurion's eyes that Wynne worried at the outcome of tonight's banquet.

"It wasn't bad enough to torture you, Wynne," he said. "Now he seeks to force his attentions upon Meghan. And I . . . I am too much the coward to be a man," he added with self-loathing.

"There is nothing you can do, Burrus," Wynne whispered gently. "Severus has the power to do as he wills. The only thing he may not do is take her to bed. That at least is forbidden him by the law. Is it not?"

Sadly he shook his head. "I do not know, for here Severus makes his own laws. I can only promise you that if he abuses Meghan I will kill him!"

At his words Meghan smiled. Perhaps Burrus

did have some affection for her, she thought. Maybe she was more to him than just a slave. Dared she to hope and dream?

Her smile was sweetness itself, and Burrus fought against the temptation to gather her into his arms. She had bloomed like a rose these last months. If she were only a free woman of Roman blood, he would seek her hand, but he would not be allowed to marry a slave.

"The slave girl is requested to dance for us now," a tall soldier announced. His eyes feasted upon Meghan in her scant attire, and she blushed, covering herself with her hands against the assault of his eyes. Instinctively she sought for Burrus' strength, clinging to his hand, longing to throw herself into his arms and beg him to take her away from this wretched place.

"If I cannot save you from this humiliation, at least let me escort you to your doom," he said dryly. Wynne walked along behind them.

Inside the banquet tent Severus was flushed with wine as he plucked playfully at the strings of a lyre that one of the slave girls held within his reach. The girl was naked, as were several of the officers of the legion who sat inside the tent. Wynne wondered how they could stand the cold, for it was nearly winter and the weather had cooled to near-freezing. No doubt the drink had warmed them and clouded their good sense.

A juggler stood before the soldiers, tossing about his many-colored balls. The crowd roared with amusement as he made an obscene gesture at his crotch and reached for Meghan as if to ravish her. She pulled away from the clown just in time to keep him from grabbing her breast, and stood in the corner as if to become invisible. But Severus had seen her enter and now bade her to begin her dancing.

With shaking limbs, Meghan began to sway to the music of lyre, harp, and drum, averting her eyes from the leering crowd.

"The red-haired slave dances like a novice!" a low booming voice said.

"No doubt she is frightened. Her trembling and terror make her dance like a beginner," echoed another voice. "She should be whipped. Perhaps that would make her move faster." Laughter filled the room.

Severus scowled at Meghan as she danced before him. Her modesty infuriated him. "Give the girl some wine," he ordered. "Perhaps it will warm her blood."

Burrus furiously watched as the tribune made Meghan drink cup after cup of wine, until she was slightly drunk. Not too gently she was pushed back before the throng. Severus ripped at her sheer tunic as she walked by him, leaving her standing nearly nude before the crowd.

"Now, begin again," Severus ordered.

This time Meghan's dancing was more provocative as she felt the warmth from the wine engulf her. Her eyes met those of Burrus, and it was as if she danced only for him. He reached for her, but drew back his hands when he beheld the look of anger on Severus' face.

"Come now, don't be selfish with your slave,

my dear Burrus. You have ample time to sample her charms," Severus ordered, motioning Meghan to continue the dance.

Her shyness was completely gone as she moved to the beat of the drums. Imagining herself being loved by Burrus, Meghan writhed before him. Faster and faster she whirled as hands reached to tear the last of her veils away. She was dancing completely naked now, her small firm breasts and lithe body a glory to behold. She was tall and slim and golden; long-legged and perfect. As she danced, her red-gold curls glinted in the light of the torches.

All around the room the desire of the men for this lovely girl was apparent. Burrus to his shame, was no exception. He fought against his rising manhood, but it was no use. He longed to plunge into Meghan's sweet depths. To quench the fire in his loins, Burrus drank until he was senseless and had to be carried out of the tent and put to bed. Worriedly Wynne looked around. There was no one to protect the young slave girl now, as it became evident from the soldiers' faces that soon Meghan would fall victim to the lusts of the Roman barbarians. The poor innocent girl was helpless to defend herself.

With indrawn breath she watched as one of the soldiers picked Meghan up and whirled her around, pressing his naked body against hers. Pushing her to the floor, he attempted to mount her, but Wynne flew at him like a tiger defending its cub. Diving for the soldier's sword, she held it out before her.

"The first man who dares to touch her will find himself without his manhood!" she threatened, and the look on her face enforced her words. Too drunk to be of much danger, the Romans held back. Only Severus was not as docile.

"I will punish you for this!" he shouted. "I will flay all the skin off your back myself and feed you to the lions when I take you back with me to Rome."

"Do so. I care not," she retorted. All fear of him was gone now as she hovered to protect Meghan. "I would prefer death to being forced to keep company with an animal like you any longer. This girl is not your property. By the law she belongs to the centurion Burrus. You have no right!"

"I have every right. I am a free man of Rome. You, both of you, are nothing but lowly slaves," he shouted, taking a step forward.

Her eyes blazing with hatred and fury, Wynne raised the sword. "I will kill you if you take another step." The look in her eyes cautioned Severus, and he stood his ground with an angry growl. Wynne took hold of Meghan, maneuvering toward the entryway.

"If you leave this tent, you will answer to me!" Severus yelled, losing all self-control. "I am the ruler here." At his words several of the soldiers looked uneasy. Truly Severus had taken more power upon himself than was his due. He was, after all, only a tribune, not a general. If he had taken advantage of the weakness of the general who controlled the area for his own gain, that was one thing, but to act as if he were Nero himself was another matter entirely. Someday he would be brought low for his arrogance.

Not wishing to cause any further commotion, Wynne put her arms around Meghan and dragged her from the tent to a small clearing of trees where they would be safe at least for a time. With a start Wynne realized the feast of Samhain had passed without celebration, the time when a new fire was kindled by her people, welcoming in the new year.

"I am becoming as heathen as these Romans," she said softly, begging the gods to forgive her her weakness. But so much had happened, and it seemed that the old ways were gone.

Meghan looked at Wynne with sleep-glazed eyes. The wine was having its full effect on her now. Leaning against a tree, she fell fast asleep, feeling secure with Wynne guarding her.

As if to appease the gods, Wynne built a small fire, a miniature of the sacred flame, and sat in silence and prayer. No doubt she would pay for her actions on the morrow, but she could not let the soldiers brutally rape the young red-haired girl.

When the fire died down, Wynne looked around her, wondering how far she had wandered. The stone walls of the fortress of Eboracum surrounded them, another reminder of the changes the Romans had waged on her land.

The Romans have tortured this land as well as my heart, she thought sadly, remembering

Valerian. She wondered just what the punishment would be for tonight's transgressions. Never had she seen Severus so furious. I will worry about it with the coming of the dawn, she thought, leaning back to enjoy the pleasures of slumber.

At first light Wynne opened her eyes, expecting to be called before Severus, but the gods were smiling on her this day. In the distance she saw a flurry of activity—the soldiers were tearing down the tents and breaking camp. Why were they making ready to leave? she wondered.

She approached a young soldier and inquired as to the reason for their hasty departure.

"We make ready to travel to the southeast," the freckled soldier told her. "To the city of Londinium."

"Why?"

"I know not. I only heard that the Emperor Nero himself has commanded it. Last night at the banquet the tribune received the order that we must leave with the light of the sun." He laughed. "It will be good to be in civilization again, where there is decent lodging in villas and a man can have a decent bath."

"Londinium," Wynne repeated, feeling the name somehow boded well. Perhaps once she was there she could escape the foul Severus and take Meghan with her.

And so, once again my life changes, she thought.

III

THE FLOWERING DAWN

Southeast Britain

Two souls with but a single thought,
Two hearts that beat as one.

—Von Munch-Bellinghausen,
Ingomar the Barbarian

Fifty-three

A *blanket of snow covered the ground, shining* in the light like sparkling jewels. Winter had come to Britain, bringing with it a bitter cold.

Wynne stood in the atrium of the Roman villa where she lived with Severus, gazing on the mosaic floor that depicted Mars, the Roman god of war. Wynne could not help thinking that the god looked fierce and unyielding, like the Romans who worshiped him.

The villa was not at all like the lodges she had lived in as a child, which had seemed closer to the earth with their dirt floors and roofs of dried straw. Only in the cold of winter had her people kept inside their homes, preferring to be outdoors mingling with nature. The Romans, however, seemed to be overly fond of spending their time in idleness, cooped up in the brick boxes which made Wynne feel even more like a prisoner. A gabled roof shed rain and snow, and the many windows let in whatever sunshine might break through the clouds.

The entire interior of the villa had mosaic floors. Wynne could not understand why these Romans did not want to keep their feet on the earth, which was soft, and yielding under the feet. Perhaps the only thing about the villa that Wynne liked was the central heating. A hard black rock was mined from the surface of the Southeast and used to warm these villas. Wynne had learned that this coal, as it was called, was burned like wood in stoves which were connected to hot-air conduits in the walls and floors.

The Romans' baths, too, impressed her. In the corner of the room was a gigantic marble tub sunk deep into the ground like a small pool. It was large enough for six large Romans to enter at the same time.

These Romans are trying hard to become as gods, she thought. It was as if they were trying to best the Goddess of the Waters and make their own lakes inside their villas. They were wasteful in their use of water as they were in everything else they touched. Wynne's people, on the other hand, knew how precious the gift of the goddess was and used it sparingly, taking only sponge baths when they were not able to plunge into the depths of the lake. Besides, there was always the danger of taking a chill when the fires of the sky were sleeping their winter slumber.

At first Wynne had refused to bathe in these

Roman pools, but finding that she did not catch the chill and that the water was warm and soothing, she soon began to indulge in them frequently.

Already Wynne had been in this villa for two cycles of the moon. They were long days of boredom, for all Severus wished her to do was look beautiful and adorn his home.

Severus was gone for the time being with his troops to a distant part of the land. He would most likely return soon, but Wynne did not fear him any longer. Since he had been ordered to Londinium by Nero, he had become a changed man. He had even neglected to punish Wynne for her interference at the banquet the night she had saved Meghan from ravishment. Why? What had frightened him? she still wondered, for she knew that only the base emotions—fear, greed, lust—motivated him.

Wynne missed seeing Meghan, for Burrus and the slave girl were housed far from Severus' villa.

Sighing, Wynne let her undergarment slip to the floor and pinned up her golden mass of hair. The water in the bath was perfect now, not too cold. She liked this room with its murals of trees and flowers. When she closed her eyes, she could imagine she was again back home bathing in her lake. Reclining in the bath, letting the water wash over her, she felt tranquil and at peace.

A voice from the doorway startled her. She looked up to see the face of the same messenger she had encountered at Eboracum, who had brought news of Valerian.

A slave girl ran in after him. "I told him you were alone, not to come in here," she cried.

"It's all right," Wynne said, trying to contain her alarm. "Just bring me my robe."

The girl held up a cream-colored linen wrap, and Wynne stepped out of the tub and drew the soft fabric around her in such a way that her body was continually shielded from the messenger's sight.

"Now, what is it?" she said, turning to the flustered young man.

"I wish to see the tribune Severus," he said, his eyes darting, hoping for another glimpse of Wynne's lovely body.

"He is not here," she answered.

"I have a message for him. I must find him," the young man stammered.

"He won't be back tonight, nor the next," she said hotly, piqued by the young man's manner. "What is the message you have to deliver? I will give it to the tribune."

The young soldier wondered just how loyal this concubine was. She must be held in some esteem if she had slaves at her beck and call. He had been told to give the message only to Severus, but how could he, when the tribune was not there? He did not want to wait until the tribune returned. Still, he did not want to anger Severus by talking to the wrong person. He glanced warily at the slave girl. Wynne made a gesture of dismissal.

"Well," she said impatiently when the girl had gone, "what is the message?"

"It is the centurion Valerian Quillon. He has returned from Rome. The ship is even now in the harbor. The tribune wanted to know the minute we heard."

Valerian. Wynne turned away idly, as if this information were a matter of indifference to her. In fact she was afraid her face would reveal her tumultuous feelings. When she had composed herself, she faced the messenger again. "When will he arrive in Londinium?"

"On the morrow. He is traveling with General Cassius Quintus himself," he said.

The idea of seeing Valerian again played turmoil with her senses, but the memory of his treachery hardened her heart.

This time when I see him I will be prepared for his lies, she thought bitterly when the messenger had gone. No more will I listen to his soft words. I know him for the dog that he is.

Her father's face swam before her eyes. She remembered that he had been helpless to defend himself against the sword of the centurion and recalled the sight of the familiar sword stained with blood.

"Valerian," she cried out, her voice choked with a confusion of grief and rage and thwarted love. She must do it. She must avenge her father so that he could enter upon his new life with peace and contentment.

"I must kill Valerian. Yes, I must kill him,"

she whispered, feeling as if a part of her had died at that very moment. In her heart she knew that once Valerian no longer walked upon the earth she too would no longer wish to dwell in this life. No matter. She must find a dagger and then find the courage to do what must be done.

Fifty-four

From the deck of the Roman galley, Valerian could see across the bay to Londinium. The city had recently risen to economic and military importance as a port on the Thames River and hub of radiating roads. Valerian had no doubt that soon Londinium would be the Roman capital of Britain instead of Camulodunum.

Excitement rose within him as he looked at the city. Soon, very soon, Severus would pay for the atrocities he had committed.

The voyage to Rome had been rough, but he had arrived safely and had been greeted warmly by his father, who had already received his message. Meghan had done well.

His father had greeted him with news of his family, which he was glad to receive. But another bit of news had interested but not surprised him. He had been betrothed to his cousin Marcia, a girl of fifteen. With Wynne dead, he had no reason to oppose the engagement and so planned to marry her upon his return to Rome in a few months. She was a pleasant dark-haired girl whose family influence was even more powerful than Valerian's. With her he would raise a family and have a docile wife.

After family matters had been settled, Valerian had detailed to his father the events of the Celtic campaign under Severus. He had told his father all, including the slaughter of the unarmed tribesmen and his efforts to bring peace. It turned out that Severus was already being watched by Rome, for it was not the first time he had displayed his cruelty and his ruthless ambition. But in sentencing Valerian to death, he had really overstepped himself. Only a general was empowered with that authority. It was obvious that Severus was establishing his own little empire in Britain, thus challenging the Emperor Nero himself. So Severus had been called to Londinium to await the arrival of Cassius Quintus, who brought with him a new order. A new tribune—Valerian Quillon Tullius—would take the place of Severus, who would return to Rome.

"Well, Valerian, we are nearly to Britain," a voice said behind him. Looking up, Valerian found himself staring into the eyes of his general, Cassius Quintus, a handsome man with silver-streaked dark hair. "Tell me, what did you think of these Celts?"

"I found them very much like any other

people," Valerian answered with a slight smile, remembering the spirited Wynne. Such fond memories. "The same fighting spirit and need for freedom. The Celts you will meet these days in Londinium though, are Romanized. Some are even citizens of Rome, worshiping our gods and living in our villas. The world is getting smaller day by day."

"Oh, no. I feel that there is always new territory to be had for the glory of Rome, lands across the many seas that we do not even know about yet," Cassius Quintus answered thoughtfully, gazing out across the ocean. He turned again to Valerian. "When we arrive in Londinium, we will go to the villa of Severus. That will be your new home."

"Severus will no doubt be livid," Valerian said with a laugh, enjoying the thought of seeing the tribune's face when he heard the news. "Will he take his slaves back with him to Rome?"

Cassius Quintus thought for a moment. "Ordinarily he would be entitled to keep all his property. In this situation, however, I would like to see all of Severus' property, with the exception of his clothing and personal belongings, transferred to you, including his slaves. I have heard that his concubine is a rare beauty—a Celtic priestess, so the rumor goes—so you should benefit largely by my decree."

"I am not particularly interested in his whore. One woman is as good as another, isn't that right?" They both laughed at this, and Valerian felt a pang at the realization that without Wynne he really did feel this way. He wondered what kind of woman would allow herself to be possessed by such a man as Severus. He did not covet her, and he supposed she must be the kind of woman who used her body to win trinkets and favors. Still, it was cold in Britain and it would be pleasurable to have a woman to warm his bed.

"Well, you decide whether or not you want to keep her. If she is not to your liking, I will have her sent home with Severus and find you another to take her place. Let us say that it will be compensation for all the suffering you endured at the hands of that fool."

"I will not be needing a concubine for long. I am soon to be a married man. My father did not want to wait much longer." Valerian chuckled. "My only hope is that my wife will not be too displeased with the weather here in Britain. She has been a sheltered young woman, and, I fear, a trifle spoiled."

"All they need is a firm hand. Let her spin and tend to your children. Her main function after all is to supervise the slaves and keep the home orderly. In return she will be rewarded by you with profound love and respect. I have been happily married for twenty-five years and speak from experience."

Valerian looked upon Cassius. He was an imposing figure of a man. No doubt he did rule his wife with a firm hand, but somehow Valerian wished he could have a more spirited woman, one like Wynne.

The metal of the general's breastplate with its Medusa's head reflected the rays of the sun, which was at its high point in the sky. They were nearly at their destination and would arrive ahead of schedule. He wondered if Severus would be there to greet them or if the tribune were on campaign somewhere massacring more defenseless Celts. This night he had only one desire—a hot bath and a good night's sleep on a soft bed.

"Let Severus' whore wait. I have no need for her charms this night," he thought, gazing once again across the water.

Fifty-five

The soft glow of moonlight illuminated Londinium
as Valerian and Cassius walked down the ramp
of the ship. Although it could not compare with
Rome's glory, still it had a rustic beauty.

"I see that many of the buildings have been
rebuilt since last I was here," Cassius stated, his
eyes sweeping over the horizons. "A great deal
of the city was burned to the ground by the
Iceni."

Valerian scowled. "Another instance of ambition and stupidity where a Roman military leader
was concerned. From what I have heard, Boadicea was treated very badly and her daughters
raped by soldiers. It is no wonder that she rose
against the legions of Rome."

"A remarkable woman. She came close to driving us out of this land. It is too bad she poisoned herself in the face of defeat. Perhaps

someday we will learn how to ally ourselves with such leaders instead of alienating them."

"As long as we have commanders like Severus, that day is far off," Valerian answered grimly. They walked along the dock as their belongings were unloaded and put on a wagon.

"The horses will be stabled here at the dock until we are ready to move out on campaign," Cassius said, seeing Valerian's eyes following his black stallion. "Except of course for my chariot horses. I hope that meets with your approval."

Valerian nodded his head in assent. "I'm sure that Sloan will get the best of care," he replied, anxious to get to the villa, to bathe and get some rest.

As if sensing his thoughts, Cassius took his arm and led him to his finely wrought chariot. It was led by four matched brown geldings and was the pride and joy of Cassius, who had driven it in the chariot races in the Colosseum.

"I was practically born in one of these," the general laughed, taking the reins in his hands. He skillfully managed to avoid all the bumps as he drove the horses onward at a speed which rivaled the wind. Valerian was amused at the curious faces of the onlookers who ran out of the buildings to watch as they drove by. He must remember to tell Cassius about the war chariots he had seen driven by the Celts during his campaign. No doubt they would be difficult to beat in a race.

When they arrived at their destination, Valerian jumped down, his eyes searching out the tribune he had come to replace. He saw no sign of him.

"And where is tribune Severus?" Cassius asked, noting an absence of soldiers in the area.

"Perhaps he heard that we were arriving and decided to make good his escape," Valerian answered dryly. In asking the household slaves, he found that Severus was indeed gone on campaign.

"Tonight the villa belongs to us." Cassius laughed, relieved to be able to spend a quiet night without going through an unpleasant confrontation. He gazed around him. "Not bad. Smaller than those villas we are used to in Rome, but comfortable."

"I only hope that Severus has plenty of food." Valerian laughed. "After all this time at sea, I could eat a horse." Seeking out the kitchen, he learned that the larders were well supplied with food and wine. Grabbing a bottle of the wine, a cold breast of pheasant, and an apple, he sought out the softness of one of the couches and set about nourishing his tired body, heedless of the awed looks of the household slaves. These slaves soon had the household abuzz with the news: a new Roman would now be their master.

So it was that Wynne first heard the news that the man whose face had haunted her dreams for so long was finally within range of her wrath.

Fifty-six

The torchlight flickered against the wall as Valerian relaxed in the bath. The warmth from the water soothed his aching muscles as he leaned back, nearly dozing, unaware of the wide blue eyes that watched him from the shadows.

Wynne clutched her dagger. It had not been difficult to procure it from a Celtic citizen of Rome who sympathized with the slaves. It seemed to burn her hand like a live coal, this weapon which would take the life of the man she had once loved. Her heart ached as she regarded his cheekbones and fine chiseled nose. His thick dark curly hair was wet from the bath and she longed to touch it once before she must do this terrible deed.

As if sensing a presence, Valerian opened his eyes and turned in her direction. She wanted to call out, to have him come to her, put his arms around her, love her as he had once in their forest cave. She wanted to kiss his mouth and give him her forgiveness.

"He murdered your father, a helpless cripple!" shouted a voice in her ear.

Her breathing was unsteady as she looked upon her dagger. So many nights she had thought of this moment, and now that moment was here. Softly she took a step forward. He was all alone, she would bury the dagger in his breast and no one would know it had been by her hand that he was slain.

By the laws of my people it my right to avenge my father. As his nearest of kin I may kill this murderer, she thought over and over, agonized by the turmoil of emotions inside her head. Wynne covered her mouth with her hand to muffle her sobs. But as she looked at Valerian, it was as if the dagger had been thrust in her own heart.

"I love him still. I always will, no matter what he has done. Oh, that I had died that day along with my father. It would have been better than to suffer this agony," she whispered. Her hands were trembling violently. With a sob she let the dagger fall to the floor and ran from the room as quickly as her legs could carry her.

"Who's there?" Valerian shouted, rising from his bath. For a moment he had feared Severus' treachery. The tribune was not in Londinium, however, so it could not have been his eyes that he had seemed to feel burning hatred into the back of his head. Severus' henchmen, then, or perhaps his concubine, wondering what her new master would look like. With a scornful laugh he nestled again in the warmth of the water.

It was strange that he had not been greeted by the woman Severus bedded. It was an affront to the laws of hospitality. She should have met him at the door, fed him, helped him bathe, shown him to his sleeping quarters.

I will have to talk with her about her manners, he thought with anger. She could learn a great deal from Meghan. At the thought of the young slave girl with the red-gold hair, Valerian let his mind wander. He wondered what Burrus had thought of Meghan. No doubt he had fallen madly in love with her by this time, as he had with Wynne—lovely, lovely Wynne.

If only I had taken her with me that very first time we met. We could have been together forever. I know I could have convinced my father to let me marry her. Many a Roman has married with a Romanized Celt. By the gods, I should have listened to my heart.

Rising from his bath, Valerian dried his body and dressed himself in a plain white toga. He walked barefoot across the cold tile floor to seek out a bedchamber. How long had it been since he had slept with a woman? Not since Wynne had he done so, he realized. So long had he mourned, but now his strong healthy body yearned for the softness of a woman in his arms.

"I will see this famous concubine of Severus' first thing tomorrow," he said beneath his breath.

Finding a sleeping couch in one of the small rooms, he lay down on it, burying his body in the softness of the pillows. Soon he was fast asleep.

Long into the night Wynne tossed and turned. Vengeance was a two-edged sword, as they said. She had thought of nothing these past months except to avenge her father, and when she had the chance, she had wept like a little child and run from the room. She had not even had the courage to face Valerian, fearful of what she might do or say. Would she still be like soft clay in his hands, easily molded to his desires?

"Oh, that I had never met you!" she cried aloud, sitting up in bed and tossing a pillow to the ground in frustration. Yet had she not met him, she would not have known how sweet love could be, even when that love was not returned with a whole heart.

"I would be married to Edan by now, with a flock of children tugging to my skirts, instead of crying my heart out if I had not met you, Roman," she whispered to the darkness. But she could not really regret those moments spent in the Roman's arms.

One thing she knew. She could not face him and did not want to see him again. She must hide away until he was gone. He could not stay in the villa forever. When he found out that Severus was not due back for quite some time, he would give up waiting. Until then she must blend with the shadows and keep out of sight lest her heart betray her.

Tomorrow I will leave this place, she vowed, thinking perhaps she could stay with Meghan and Burrus until these Romans had left. Valerian would never look upon her face, never be able to chide her with his scornful words—never again in this life.

Fifty-seven

With the first rays of the sun Wynne was up and
dressed, a cloak wrapped securely around her
so that she would not freeze in the cold morning air. She had few possessions, so it did not
take her long to gather them together in a small
sack. With dismay she saw that there was a
dusting of snow on the ground. How she longed
for the warm shoes of her own people. Her feet
would soon be wet and cold in these Roman
sandals she had been forced to wear.

In a daze she walked to the door. There was
so much she needed to think about to drive out
the agony tearing her in two. Perhaps she would
feel better when she was far away from Valerian.
She pushed open the door, but a hand reached
out from behind her and grasped her tightly by
the arm.

"Are you trying to escape, slave? Does the

thought of belonging to the tribune Valerian frighten you so much as that?" came an unfamiliar voice to her ears. "I would think that he would be more desirable to a young woman like you than that old man you have slept with."

Turning around slowly, Wynne met the eyes of a stranger. He was wearing a uniform different from any that Wynne had seen so far, a short scarlet tunic covered by a breastplate embossed with a woman who seemed to have snakes coming from her head instead of hair. Wynne shuddered at the sight.

"Have you lost your tongue, woman?" the man asked, shaking Wynne by the shoulder. "You cannot leave. You are a slave, the property of the tribune." He reached for the bag that she held tightly to her breast. "Have you also been stealing from your master?"

She threw him a defiant look. "This sack is mine and carries my belongings. I would not steal from Roman dogs!"

The gray-haired man laughed. He admired her spirit. Too many slaves whimpered and cringed like animals. She might prove to be interesting. In a way, he envied Valerian this woman, who was no doubt a passionate lover. He wondered how Severus had been able to please her, for he knew at one glance that this beautiful woman had to be the concubine.

"All right, I will believe you were not stealing, but I want to know why you were running away," he said less harshly.

Wynne didn't know what to do. No doubt

anything she said would reach Valerian. She could not let him know how she feared that her own treacherous body would betray her and send her into his arms.

"I want to be free. I do not like slavery!" was all she could think to say. It was the truth.

Cassius Quintus chuckled. "No slave does, young woman, but that is the way of the world. The strongest enslave the weakest. It is for the good of the empire."

"I am not weak. It was by treachery that I was enslaved," she answered hotly. She stood looking at him with her shoulders back and her chin up. "Severus is an evil man!"

In spite of himself, Cassius Quintus felt a flash of pity for this young beauty. He had heard of the brutality of the tribune.

"So I have heard, but you will not have to worry about Severus any longer. In my wisdom and kindness I have given you to the new tribune."

"New tribune?" she asked, her eyes wide with surprise. It could not be true. The gods would not be so cruel as to deliver her into the hands of her enemy. . . .

"Valerian Quillon Tullius. A handsome, virile young man, not an aging fool like your former owner. That should please you." He smiled and gently tipped her face up to look into her eyes, wondering why he had such a strong impulse to please her, this mere slave. But the look he read there was not one of gratitude.

"No, no," Wynne was whispering, horrified at her new plight.

Cassius Quintus turned his back on her, puzzled by her behavior. Was the girl weak-minded? It would be sad if it were so. She was so very beautiful.

"It will be up to your new master to determine your punishment for trying to run away," the general said. "I would suggest that you go and make yourself beautiful for him and hope that he finds it in his heart to be merciful. If he decides that he does not want you, I will send you with Severus to the land far across the ocean where the sun bakes all the moisture from your skin until you are old before your time." He left her, tired of talking and anxious to find some breakfast. He would put a guard on the Celtic woman. She must not be allowed to get away.

Wynne walked back to her room, fervently praying to her gods for strength. She felt thoroughly shamed, her slavery a bitter draught to drink. Must she now bear this humiliation also? It was true that she had hated Severus and did not want to go with him to that hot land the stranger had spoken of, but was the alternative to live out her tortured days with Valerian until he tired of her?

Hurriedly she made her way to bed, burying herself among the blankets like a caterpillar in its cocoon. She tried to cry but the soothing tears would not come. "I will not bed him. I will not let him make me his whore!"

Even if he whipped her and starved her, she would not submit meekly to Valerian. She had given him his life twice now. She did not owe him anything more. To let him know she loved him would give him the means to destroy her. Soon he would make her his concubine, submissive to his every desire. She could not let him further debase her.

"No matter how much I love him, and I do," she sobbed, "he must never know."

Valerian awoke with a start, his heart beating wildly. He had been dreaming of Wynne. He had thought himself finally over the tragedy of her death, yet she continued to invade his dreams as she had once invaded his heart.

In the dream she stood before him dressed in virginal white, her long blond hair flying about her shoulders. She had started toward him with a look of ecstasy on her face, calling his name softly. But as soon as she had gotten near him, she had started to scream, fighting him and trying to escape, as if he were some sort of demon.

"So you are finally awake, eh?" Cassius called from the doorway. "I thought surely you would sleep the day away. Your days away from soldiering have made you soft."

"You should have awakened me."

Cassius laughed. "No, sleep while you can. In a few days it will be early to bed and early to rise again." He started to leave the room, but turned back. "Severus' concubine tried to run away. I caught her at the door early this morning."

"Run away?"

"I hadn't told her that you were to take his place as her master yet, so don't feel too slighted. Still, she must have had some reason for wanting to get away." Cassius shook his head in puzzlement.

"Perhaps she fears that I will not want her."

Cassius looked deep into his eyes. "If you do not want her, then you are either blind or a fool. She is the most beautiful woman I have ever laid eyes on, and I have traveled the world for many years and looked upon many lovely women."

Valerian felt an odd sense of excitement rise within him. "She is that beautiful?" he breathed.

"Yes, enough so to nearly make me want to break my word to you and take her myself. However, lovely or not, I would suggest that you summon her to see you as soon as you are up and about. If this sort of thing is not punished immediately, you will no doubt have a slave revolt on your hands. She must be punished."

Valerian put a hand to his tousled hair. "I do not like to punish women," he said, feeling a twinge of sympathy. To be a slave must surely be a terrible experience, especially for a woman. He would be gentle with her no matter what she had done, although he would chide her.

"I do not like to lay a hand on a woman in punishment either, but these Celts . . . well, the bastards have to learn their place as conquered people and you cannot let this woman be immune from your wrath." With this said, he strode through the door, leaving Valerian scowling behind him.

"Thus I am to have a beautiful, spirited woman on my hands after all. Well, she will soon learn to obey my words." He arose from the bed to start the new days with a surge of exhilaration.

Fifty-eight

The splendor of the morning sun streamed into the courtyard as Wynne looked into the silver mirror. What would Valerian think of her? Would he find her changed? Would he still desire her? Would he lie to her again and tell her he loved her, or would he shun her now that she was no longer necessary to win his victory?

Wynne set about the task then of making herself presentable, knowing that Valerian would call her to him today. She had taken the suggestion of the stranger and dressed in her finery. A rich golden stola adorned her slim figure, and her hair was done up in its false curls. She wore a gold necklace around her throat. She outlined her eyes in kohl and painted her lips. If she must act the part of his whore, she would look the part as well.

"The master summons you," a young male slave said in the doorway.

Wynne turned from her mirror to follow him, her heart in her mouth. They entered the atrium and then went up a narrow hallway to a reception room. Wynne forced her trembling legs to support her. At the open doorway she paused, her heart rapidly beating. Valerian stood with his back to her. She had forgotten how wide his shoulders were, how trim his waist.

"Why did you seek to run away from me?" he asked, still without turning. "I will not punish you this time, but if it happens again, I assure you I will have to do so."

"You can never keep me here willingly. Every chance I get, I will try to escape from you—you . . . you Roman." She spat the words in a raw whisper.

"So I see we must begin as foes," he said, turning around to face her.

By the gods, but she looked so like Wynne. She was a vision, a man's dream. The gold of her gown set off her wide blue eyes and fine complexion, her hair golden in the sunlight, a cluster of curls atop her head. It was not fair for another woman to look so like Wynne and to haunt him with things that might have been. He was speechless before this golden beauty.

Wynne's legs went weak. She feared that she would shame herself by collapsing in a faint at his feet, but she strove to maintain her composure, smiling stiffly in mock greeting.

"So we meet again," she breathed.

"Wynne?" His voice whispered a question he dared not believe, yet in the next instant he knew it to be her. "Wynne, is it really you!" For a moment their gazes locked in silence.

She started toward him, but memory rose like a wall between them—his treachery, her father's death. Her eyes turned cold as her expression filled with scorn.

"By the gods! It is you." He hurried to her and gathered her into his arms, holding her stiff body close to his own. The gods had brought her back to him, back to his arms. It had been an eternity since he had kissed her and held her close.

"You are even more beautiful than I remembered," he said softly. "I have missed you more than you will ever know."

He started to kiss her, but she struggled free from his embrace. "You missed me, Roman? Words are meaningless. It is deeds that tell the story."

"I thought you dead!" he said.

"The woman you knew once *is* dead," she replied.

It suddenly dawned on him that she was speaking perfect Latin. They were conversing fluently in his own tongue. "You have learned my language well," he said.

"We slaves have been taught well," she said bitterly.

She must think that he had betrayed her people that blood-filled night. How would he ever show her the truth? But she must believe him, after all they had shared; their love would show her the truth. He had so many questions to ask her. How had she escaped? Why had Brenna said she had been killed? What was she doing here? Yet he could not seem to begin to form the words.

The sight and smell and touch of her was intoxicating. His eyes feasted on her beauty. "I much preferred your hair flying about your shoulders," he whispered, reaching out for her and pulling out the pins. She did not cringe from his hands, merely stood like a statue. In an instant he had removed the false curls. Her own blond hair cascaded like a silken waterfall across her shoulders, and he remembered the first time he had seen her, his goddess.

Wynne could read the desire in his eyes. "No!" she gasped evading his arms, her voice full of horror.

Valerian drew back in alarm, confused by the stark fear in her eyes. "Wynne, what is it?" he asked.

"I can't abide your touch," she answered.

Her words were like a sword piercing through him. "What?" he exclaimed, all his dreams shattered.

She turned her back to him, no longer able to meet his eyes without sobbing her heart out. "Please leave me alone," she whispered. Her eyes were filled with tears. She reached up to brush them away, lest he see them.

"Oh, my Wynne. You *do* think I betrayed you, don't you?" With shaking voice he told her what had happened, how Severus had tricked him, how he had wanted peace with her people, had sought to avoid bloodshed. He told her how he had searched for her that fateful day, only to be captured by Severus and brought back a prisoner.

"I did not want to see your people slaughtered. You must believe that, Wynne," he pleaded. "I had no idea that Severus planned an attack on the village."

She wished she could believe him, yet she had been tricked once before and it had cost her dearly.

"You are a liar!" she spat at him. "Like all Romans. I hate you and all your kind."

"Oh, Wynne . . . Wynne . . ." he groaned. "Do you really hate me so much?" He gently ran his fingers up and down her arm, finally reaching out to caress her soft breast.

Against her will her body responded to his touch. A warm tingling swept over her, the first stirrings of desire at his nearness. In spite of all that had happened, she still desired him. In her panic she reached out and slapped his face.

"You are no better than Severus," she said scornfully. "All you know is forcing your will upon a woman. Lust, not love, guides your hand!"

"Severus. What has he to do with you and me?" he asked in confusion. His hands were clenched helplessly at his side, powerless.

Like the dawning of the day, Valerian suddenly remembered why she was here. It was no accident, and not the will of the gods to reunite him with his beloved. Wynne. Wynne his lover, his life, his own beloved, was the concubine of the tribune. More than her angry words, the truth of this knowledge nearly destroyed him.

"You . . . you are Severus' concubine?" he asked, hoping against hope that she would deny it.

"Yes," she answered, backing away farther from him, her back against the wall.

His eyes grew hard with jealousy and he sought to hurt her too, to lash out at her, to wound her as he had been wounded.

"I see. Then I won't try to make love to you again, Wynne, ever again." He could see her tremble and longed to comfort her, gather her into his arms, but the scorn in her eyes angered him even further.

"Then I am free to return to my room?" she breathed.

"Yes. I have no desire for Severus' leavings. You may go back to your room to dream about your aged lover!"

She started toward him then, wanting to tell him that Severus had never possessed her body, but before she had time to say anything, he hurled a further insult at her.

"No doubt many men have touched you since last you gave your body to me. I can see it in your eyes."

His words stung her. It was as she thought: he would think her sullied by all those Roman hands. She tried to speak, but all that would come forth from her mouth was a sob.

"How many Romans have you lain with since we parted? Ten or twenty? Have you earned your precious trinkets with your body?" He looked at the golden necklace as if it were a serpent wound around her neck.

"I have been enslaved. How can you say such things?" She wept, covering her face to shield it from his gaze. Did he know that she had nearly been raped? Had he witnessed her shame that day without even lifting one finger to help her? How could he be so cruel now, to fling such harsh words at her?

Jealousy had made Valerian deaf to her words as he reached out to take her arm.

His touch brought back all the old fear Wynne had tried so hard to bury. Remembering the pain she had suffered, the ugliness of that day, Wynne turned white. All thoughts of revenge were gone now. She only sought to flee from the look in his eyes.

"So now you are Severus' concubine, quite an honor," he said sarcastically, goaded on by her rejection of him and his own jealousy at the thought of her bedding another man. "You talk like a Roman and now you look like a Roman whore with your painted face. You even think like a Roman—just what you claim to hate. Oh, that you were still the girl that I remembered."

Wynne could stand his scorn no longer. Turning, she fled the room, eyes brimming with tears. In his fury Valerian did not even try to follow her.

"You are right," he said angrily. "The woman I once knew is dead."

Fifty-nine

Valerian awoke the next morning sick with remorse for how he had behaved toward Wynne. It had been his jealousy which had spoken, that and his pride. "Is it any wonder she hates Romans, with all that has happened to her since seeing her people killed before her eyes," he told himself now. He had to admit, though, that as deeply as his words must have wounded her, so had her refusal to believe him innocent of the atrocities committed that day.

I must give her time, time to learn to trust me again, he thought. He loved Wynne, loved her strength of character, her pride, and her bravery. Damn his temper. He felt like a beast for acting as he had toward her just because she no longer loved him. He would win her love again, he had to.

That Severus had been her lover was a torture to his heart. The thought of her perfect marble-white body beneath that loathsome old man poisoned his mind and kept him from seeking her out.

And Wynne. Wynne too was brokenhearted. She would never forget the disgust in his eyes when he thought her Severus' lover. Why hadn't she told him the truth? How many times had she been punished for refusing to caress Severus and give in to the vile things he asked of her? Had she somehow wanted to get revenge by wounding Valerian's pride? Since their bitter words Wynne had kept to her room. It was not like her to be such a coward, and she knew she could not hide for the rest of her life in her sleeping chamber hidden among the pillows.

Dressing in a pale blue stola, her hair flowing free, her face unpainted, Wynne left her sleeping chamber for the triclinium, or formal dining room. If she found Valerian alone, she would ask him to explain again what had happened that terrible night and would confront him with the evidence surrounding her father's death. She would let him know that she had not been the concubine of Severus but that she also would not be his whore either. She would tell him how much she once loved him, how her heart had been broken by his betrayal. Also she would tell him that she wanted to make her peace with him. More he could not ask of her.

Wynne stopped at the door to the dining room as she heard the sound of two male voices.

"How did you fare with your new slave?" she

heard the older Roman ask. "Is she as passionate in bed as her actions suggest?"

"I don't know. . . . I . . . I haven't bedded her
yet," came Valerian's reply. An embarrassed silence followed.

"Haven't made love to her yet? By Juno, were
it me, I would have been between her legs the
first night I was here, with or without her
consent!" Again the voice of the general. "What
ails you? Is it because you pine for the love of
your betrothed in Rome? She is far away. You
will soon tire of your empty bed."

Wynne's heart nearly stopped. Betrothed? So
Severus had not lied to her about Valerian's
Roman lover. More deceit, more betrayal. How
could she have hoped it might be otherwise?

Valerian spoke so softly that Wynne could
not hear his answer, no matter how hard she
tried. Was he telling the general how much he
loved the Roman girl, how soft her skin was,
how he loved to kiss and caress her? Tears
spilled down her cheeks.

All lies. He told me he loved me and that he
tried to find me, but he lied to me about that, as
he has lied to me about everything else. She had
been a fool to want to believe in love. Shedding
tears of outrage and shame, she fled to the
courtyard, where she paced until she was too
exhausted to do anything but stand looking up
at the sky and wishing that she could fly like a
dove away from here to freedom.

*   *   *

Sitting before the warm fire talking with Cassius, eating the last of their honey cake, and sipping the watered-down wine, Valerian continued his conversation. He needed the advice of a friend. He told him the story of his first meeting with the Celtic girl, of their love, of the death of her people, how he had been taken captive by Severus and had thought her dead. He was not aware that the woman herself was crying her heart out right outside the walls of that very room.

"If you love her, you should forget about Severus," Cassius advised. "I have little doubt that she was forced to bed him. Think you that she would desire that skinny old man? Why, I would be surprised if she got much joy out of their coupling."

Valerian clutched his cup of wine tightly, enraged with himself. Of course Cassius was right. Wynne had most likely been forced to share the tribune's bed—but had there been any others? "I cannot help but wonder if she has bedded anyone else," he said with a frown.

"And are you completely pure yourself, Valerian?" Cassius laughed. "Besides, the woman is a slave who cannot command her actions, not your wedded wife. If you are man enough and treat her right, to rule her with a firm hand, she will want no one else. Then when you tire of her you can sell her to someone else. In the meantime, forget about the past. It will only serve to torture you."

"I don't want her to be my slave. I want to

free her, to marry her," Valerian answered. Cassius was right about the past: already it had put a wedge between them.

"Free her and ruin a good thing?" Cassius roared his laughter. "Then she will put a ring in your nose, my dear friend. And as to marriage, I doubt that your father would approve such a thing. What value would there be in such a match? No. Bed her, but don't wed her."

"She has suffered enough shame already. She deserves her freedom. She was never meant to be a slave," Valerian said, defending his desires. "And as to marriage, I care not what my father will say."

Cassius put up his hand to motion silence. "You are young and foolish, Valerian, but think on this. If you free her now, with her hating you as she does, thinking you guilty of the death of her people, how long will she stay here with you? An hour? A day? A week? Think, my friend, on that if you will." This said, he stood up and walked to the doorway, leaving a disturbed Valerian behind him.

Deep in thought, Valerian had to admit the truth of the general's words. He would eventually free Wynne, for the gods knew how much he owed her—his very life, as a matter of fact— but for now he would keep her tied to him as his slave until he could make her love him again.

Sixty

Valerian had never been so tortured in his entire life as he was now, having Wynne beneath the same roof with him, without having her love. Time and again he sought her out with the determination of setting things right between them. He wanted to tell her that he was sorry, to tell her that he would never love anyone as he loved her, and that it did not matter that she had been forced to bed Severus. He had to make her believe once and for all that he had not been responsible for the slaughter of her people. But each time he approached her and had the chance to be alone with her to tell her all these things, she avoided him as a young deer avoids the archer, and with the same frightened look in her eyes.

Wynne took Valerian's dark gazes in her direction as contempt for her, not knowing the turmoil that was raging inside him at her very nearness. Once when she accidentally brushed his hand while they were passing in the hallway, he pulled away as if she had burned him. The touch of her skin on his nearly made him lose his head. Wynne was wounded by his reaction, not realizing how he yearned for her.

He acts as if I will contaminate him, she thought with anger. Their violent conversation on that first day echoed through her mind. How could he possibly think such things of her, that she would share a man's bed for trinkets?

As the days passed, the wall between Valerian and Wynne grew thicker as each misunderstood so many things about the other, but at the same time certain routines were established. Wynne began seeing to Valerian's household, since he had no wife with him. This pleased him. He spoke no more angry words to her, but neither did he try to approach her again to touch her or caress her. In his heart he hoped that she would come to him. Every time he looked upon her, it was a torture not to be able to take her in his arms. He was not blind to the looks other men gave to her tall slim beauty. He could not help but wonder if any of these men had bedded her, and this question ate upon his heart.

As for Wynne, she was oblivious of her effect. Even Cassius was drawn to her, though he would not even think of betraying his friendship with Valerian now that he knew of the young man's feelings for the girl.

When Wynne could stand the tension between

them no longer, she asked him to give her her freedom. With her chin held high, she stood before him in the atrium, the light making her hair look like spun gold. "I must ask you to free me," she said.

"No," Valerian said firmly. "You belong to me now, Wynne." At the pain in her eyes his voice softened. "I will try to make it as pleasant as I can for you here. You will not have to work, nor share my bed."

"I beg of you—give me my freedom," she whispered.

But Valerian was adamant about keeping her tied to him, lest he never see her again, and he dismissed her.

"Why don't you take what is yours, Valerian?" Cassius asked later that week. "It is your right as her master. Her body is yours. You even have the power of life and death over the woman."

"I want more than her body. I want her love," Valerian answered, looking thoughtfully out of the window at the falling snow. How he longed for the summer again.

"Love? Love? There is no such thing. There is only respect for one's wife and lust for one's mistress!" Cassius stood peeling an apple with his dagger, wishing instead for the tart grapes he was fond of. As he talked, he punctuated his words with jabs of the dagger.

Valerian shook his head. "No. You are wrong. Love does exist. I had it once. Wynne loved me. This I know."

"And what if she never loves you again? Are you willing to wait forever? Take my advice, and if you don't want to force yourself on her, then find yourself another concubine. At least until the Celt comes to her senses and realizes that you are a much better protector than Severus ever was." Cassius looked up to see Wynne coming through the door, laden with foods for the evening's entertainment—a banquet he was throwing to honor the new tribune.

As usual Wynne averted her eyes from Valerian's as if trying to pretend that he didn't exist. His refusal to let her have her freedom had deeply hurt her; it chafed her pride to think that he considered her his property to do with as he would.

Cassius hurriedly left the room, leaving the lovers alone, eyeing the tribune as if to say: Take what is yours.

"I appreciate the trouble you've gone to for tonight's festivities," Valerian said.

"That is a slave's duty, master," Wynne responded haughtily, busying herself with an arrangement of pine boughs.

He ignored the iciness in her voice and continued trying to win a smile from her. "Let me see what you have brought. Ah, shellfish, eggs"—he touched each of the items as he spoke moving closer and closer to her as he did so—"capon, truffles, apples, dates from Rome." He grinned at her. "I fear we will all be fat as bulls when this night is through." Inadvertently her eyes met his and he whispered intently, "Do you still hate me so much, Wynne?"

"I do not hate you, *master*," she said. "It is my duty to please you in all things—except one." No doubt, she was thinking, he lusted for a wench to share his bed when the festivities were through and for that thought her good enough. Had he so soon forgotten about all the other men who—according to him—had sampled her body, or didn't it matter when a man's staff was swollen with desire?

"Don't call me 'master.' My name is Valerian. I am sick to death of your calling me that! Do you understand?" He was torn between his rage at her aloofness and his excitement at her proximity.

"As you wish, Master Valerian," she replied coldly, again emphasizing the word "master" as if it were an insult.

Valerian could control his temper no longer. He had held himself in check all these long days, but now his emotions were like a dam about to burst. With furious energy he gripped her shoulders.

"Let go of me!" Wynne cried. She struggled against him, but he was strong and his anger made him even more powerful.

"No. By the gods, I won't. Not unil you admit that you do still care for me, that you have forgiven me, and that you want me as much as I want you." Savagely he pulled her to him and pressed his mouth to hers in a brutal kiss, his hands tangling in the golden mass of her hair, his other arm about her slim waist.

Wynne fought him in earnest, remembering all too well the pain a man's body could inflict upon a woman. Gone was the memory of how precious his kisses had once been. Now he was only another panting, sweating, lusting Roman. In a moment of panic she bit down savagely on his lower lip, and he reeled away from her, his mouth dripping blood.

"Why, you bloodthirsty little heathen," he cried out, forgetting his protestations to Cassius about wanting Wynne's love and not just her body. Anger made him foolish. "Were you so ruthless to Severus, or did you melt in his arms? Should I shower you with jewels to win your favors, as he no doubt did?"

"How dare you say such things to me? You are vile!" she sobbed. "You of all people should know I am not a whore. A woman cannot help it if her body is used against her will." She drew back and in fury pulled the shoulder of her stola down, exposing the scars from her whipping at the hands of Severus. "This is what I got from Severus," she said. "Because I would not bed him. I never slept with him, never. I would as soon have bedded with a snake."

He stared at her then and regretted to the depths of his soul his angry words and actions. "Oh, Wynne, I'm sorry, truly sorry," he stammered. "I should not have said such things to you." He took a step forward, but she broke free of him and ran from the room.

"Valerian, you imbecile!" he shouted at himself. "Now you will never have her love. Your temper has killed it."

Overwhelmed with remorse and tenderness for her, he remembered their first meeting and how she had fed him, clothed him, and given him Sloan. If there was any way to make up to her for the terrible things he had said, perhaps it was with Sloan. It was his only hope. If she still hated him, refused to forgive him, then he would give her one more present: her freedom.

Sixty-one

Valerian had been looking forward to the evening's banquet, but he had hoped that by now Wynne would be at his side, as his equal, his beloved. But it was not to be. All through the dinner she avoided him, unless serving him, and even then averted her eyes. Her scorn was a thorn in his heart, embedding itself deeper and deeper within him each time she came near.

Wine flowed freely, as did conversation. The assembled guests had removed their shoes and had taken their places on the couches, reclining before movable tables. In Rome the room would have been decorated with flowers, but here in the dead of winter, Wynne had decorated it with evergreens and colored cloth.

The meal had three courses: the appetizer of boiled eggs and shellfish in a wine sauce; the main course, a roasted boar, with truffles and apples; and for desert, honey cakes and nuts.

"Eat heartily, Valerian," Cassius urged him. "Soon you will be eating simple soldier's fare again." Washing his hands to prepare himself for eating his dessert, he threw Valerian a wolfish grin and reached for a honey cake.

Valerian tried to enjoy his meal, but the food seemed to stick in his throat. A sudden desire to order all his guests to leave overwhelmed him. Usually one to abstain from drink, he soon was in his cups, hoping that this would dull the pain in his heart.

Seeing his friend's unhappiness, Burrus made his way through the throng of laughing soldiers to Valerian's side. They embraced warmly, as the comrades they were.

"There were so many here that I have not had time to greet you properly," Burrus said, watching as Valerian reached for another goblet of wine. "It seems to me that you have much to tell since last we met."

"Yes, that is true. The gods have favored me. They spared my life and have given me much. If only the goddess of love were as kind."

"Ah, Valerian, how much more favored could you be than to have such a beauty as Wynne in your household? She is not only beautiful, but brave as well."

Valerian turned to his friend and gave him such a look of anger and jealousy that Burrus drew back in surprise. "What is it? What have I said to upset you?" he asked.

"You know her?" he asked, then realized that—of course—Burrus had been with Severus at the same time as Wynne.

"Yes, I know her," Burrus answered in a choked voice. "I think perhaps you had better put down your goblet, my friend. Drinking seems to make you quarrelsome." He reached to take it away, but Valerian held it firmly.

" 'Tis not the drink which affects me so. It is the suspicion that perhaps you have sampled my slave's charms, taken her to your bed. I am not blind to the looks which have passed between you this evening, nor the smiles which she has shed upon you. Would that she looked at me thus."

"You insult her," Burrus replied. "I have never bedded that lovely woman, though the goddess Venus herself knows that I would have tried to had she shown the slightest interest in me. She is a rare jewel, that one. She withstood every torture Severus could think of—beatings, starvation, being mauled, insults, threats. All the while Severus proclaimed her his alone, never once did she bow to his will. Never did she willingly let any man touch her."

"Never?" Valerian asked, his voice growing softer as his anger died.

"Never," Burrus answered. With sorrow he related all that he had heard from Wynne's own lips of the horrors she had experienced that day when Severus had so brutally swept down upon her tribesmen. How she had seen her people slaughtered before her eyes, and how a Roman she trusted with her life itself had murdered her father. "She was nearly raped by many of our kind before the day was through. For a time she hated all Romans, until I was able to befriend her. It made me sick to admit that I too was Roman after hearing her story," Burrus said.

Valerian's eyes were wide with shock. Never had he suspected that she had been through so much debasement. "My poor Wynne," he moaned. He saw her across the room and was not surprised to find her giving him an icy stare. He deserved all the scorn she heaped upon him after all that he had said in his jealousy.

"Ever since that day, she has been unable to abandon herself to passion, though I know that before that time she was deeply in love with someone." Burrus looked up then and was taken aback by the look on the tribune's face, as if Pluto himself had beckoned from the under-world for him, as if death were at his door. "Valerian, what is wrong?" he asked fearfully. The tribune's face was as pale as if he had seen Cerberus, the three-headed guard dog of the underworld. "Are you ill?"

"I wish that at this moment the earth would swallow me up, that I could disappear forever and sleep the eternal sleep." He put his hands to his chest as if he would die at that very moment. "I am as one dead now, for I have killed that which was more precious to me than this life itself." He told Burrus then all that had happened between Wynne and himself since he had been reunited with her. He told about all the hateful things he had said to her, how she blamed him for the death of all those she loved, and her slavery itself, how he feared she would never forgive him.

"Then Wynne . . . Wynne is the Celtic woman you loved, the one you went to see that day to talk about peace? The one who has haunted you these long months."

"Yes. Once she was mine, but now I have lost her." Valerian hung his head in order to hide the unmanly tears which spilled from his eyes.

Burrus opened his mouth to speak, to try to comfort his friend, but before he had the chance, another friend stepped between them, slapping Valerian on the back.

"So there you are, hiding in this corner. Come, come, the entertainment is about to begin." The intruder tugged at the tribune's arms, and Valerian found himself once again in the middle of the room as the dancers and acrobats began their antics, but his eyes were blind, his ears deaf to anything but his grief and what Burrus had told him.

Wynne lay in her bed listening to the sound of the drunken laughter of the soldiers. It had been good to see Burrus again. She hoped that before he left the next day she would be able to talk with him.

She wondered how things were between him

and Meghan. Had love been kinder to them than it had been to her?

Her pillow was wet with her tears again this night, as it was every night since Valerian's arrival.

"Oh, why does he refuse to give me my freedom?" she cried aloud. "O Goddess, beloved Mother, why does he hold me to him and thus break my heart?"

She supposed by now he had found one of the other slave girls or dancers to share his bed. The thought tortured her with visions of his hard muscular body entwined with another's softness. And yet she had denied him.

"Oh, that I could find it in my heart to forgive him, to forget all the horror of that day, to be able to give myself to him as I did so freely in our cave. I know now that I do love him. I love him so much I can hardly bear it!" Sobs racked her body as she gave in to her grief. "Even if he does not love me, I would be happy in his arms if only I could be a woman, but I cannot, for as long as I live, I will be but half a woman, a shell." She shivered suddenly and pulled a coverlet up about her body. It was a long time before she slept, and then she was plagued by dreams. She seemed to see Valerian standing by her bed whispering words of love to her, begging her for forgiveness, bending down to touch her shoulder and stroking her hair. Through her haze of dreams she could feel the warmth of his hand and smiled.

Little did she know that it was no dream, that

Valerian was actually in the room with her, looking down at her sleeping form and adoring her with his eyes. When he could no longer refrain from touching her, he gently ran his fingers through her silken hair, then turned and left the room.

Sixty-two

Valerian wakened slowly, opening his eyes to the harsh morning light. His head felt like a ripe melon, his stomach churned, the pain at his temples threatened to drive him mad. He remembered all the wine he had consumed the night before and cursed himself for his gluttony.

His first thoughts were of Wynne. He remembered all too clearly all that Burrus had told him last night. No wonder she had flinched when he had asked her how many men had fondled her lovely body.

Valerian got out of bed, moving slowly so as not to cause his head to throb any more than it already did, and dressed in his tunic and toga. Soon he might have to wear two undertunics, as the weather was growing colder.

I must find Wynne, he thought. There is so much I have to say to her, to make up to her.

Now more than ever he knew he must give her the freedom she so desired, knowing full well that he would never see her again. He would go first thing this morning to fetch Sloan, and after he had given the horse back to her and told her all the things that needed to be said, then . . . then he would give her her freedom and see that she was escorted safely back to her people, where she belonged. The idea of making Wynne happy was a balm to his soul, and for the first time in a while he felt at peace. He left the room.

Stepping out of his bedchamber, Valerian was not surprised to find some of the celebrants sleeping off their intoxication of the night before. No doubt there would be many other throbbing heads around the villa this morning. He tooked for Burrus to tell him what he was about to do, but could find the young centurion nowhere.

"Well, it makes no difference, he will find out soon enough," he said to himself, heading for the stables and mounting a large gray mare.

Wynne opened her eyes to find the familiar face of Burrus staring down upon her, and smiled.

"Hello, Ice Princess," he said with a grin that made him look younger than his years.

Wynne sat up in bed and reached for his hand, grabbing it and holding it tightly in a treasure of friendship. "Burrus! Burrus! It is so good to see you again. I have missed you and Meghan so."

"As we have missed you." He kissed her lightly on the forehead and was pleased when she did not draw back from him as she usually did from any man's touch. "How goes it with you, Celt?"

She battled bravely to hide her true feelings. "All goes well. Severus is gone. Soon the winter will turn into spring."

Burrus lifted her chin and forced her to look at him. "And your new master? How fare you with him?" He scrutinized her face as he waited for her reply.

"He does not beat me as Severus did. All is well," she answered softly, turning away her head.

"No, all is not well. You cannot lie to me. Think you that I do not see the tears brimming your eyes? I know all about Valerian."

Her eyes grew wide as she looked back at him. For a long time there was silence in the room; then she spoke. "What do you mean? What do you know?"

"About your love for each other."

She tried in vain not to let the tears gather in her eyes. "He loves me no more," she whispered, "and I hate him!" She sprang from the bed to flee across the room. In two strides Burrus had caught up with her, grasping her arm and turning her around to face him again.

"You do not hate him. I am no fool. Your eyes betray you. You love him, and it is tearing you apart inside. Why? Why won't you forgive him for a few foolish words he might have said?"

"Foolish words? They were hateful words. And you do not know what he has done to my people."

"He only spoke out of jealousy because he cares so for you."

"He does not care for me. He thinks me dirty because I was attacked by lusting Roman dogs who tried to defile me. Does he think that I didn't want to die at that moment? I fought them with every breath of my being." Her eyes blazed anger.

"Valerian does not think you anything but beautiful and brave," Burrus answered. He reached up to stroke the gold of her hair in brotherly fashion.

Wynne shook her head, relaying to Burrus her side of all that had gone on between Valerian and herself since his return, all his harsh words, his contemptuous looks.

Burrus led her back to the couch, where they both sat down together. So many misunderstandings between them. He sighed. "Oh, Wynne, you misunderstand. Valerian did not know about what happened until I told him last night. He did not know about how cruelly you were abused that day. I thought that he would break down and cry like a baby when I told him. Indeed, he nearly did."

"He accused me of trading my body for trinkets. How could he think that I would do so? How?"

"That was merely jealousy speaking."

Burrus told her the entire story of his conversation with Valerian the night before, how Valerian had nearly fought with him when he found out that Burrus knew her, of his efforts to find her, his torment at having found her only to think that she hated him and would never forgive him. "It nearly drove him insane to find out that you were Severus' concubine. He did not know that the old goat was unable to bed a woman, but I had heard it was so."

As Wynne's eyes grew wide with surprise, Burrus laughed. "Oh, yes, I knew that he was impotent and I thanked the gods every night that at least you were spared that torture."

Wynne laughed then for the first time in days. "Yes, I was spared that torture." Her laughter turned to crying as her emotions broke like an aqueduct. Valerian loved her, was jealous of her, and did not think her soiled by the touch of others' hands. Perhaps all was not lost after all. Perhaps he would be able to explain what had happened in the village. But a shadow passed over her face as she remembered something else.

"Valerian is betrothed. I heard it from the lips of Cassius himself," she said.

At this news Burrus drew back. He had not heard this. "That I know nothing about except that it must be some sort of mistake. I don't believe Valerian would take another woman to wive when he is so in love with you. Talk with him. Find out the truth of this matter."

"No." She was stubborn in her pride. "Besides, it matters not. That is not what really holds me from his arms. It is his betrayal. Valerian came to me with promises of peace while all the while he was planning to attack my people and win a victory over us for his own glory. For that and for the death of my father I will never be able to forgive him." She started to leave the room, but Burrus blocked her way.

"Listen to me, Wynne, and listen well. Valerian is not guilty of all these things you accuse him of. He did try to make peace between your people and our legion. I know. I followed him. He was my commander. It was Severus who was the bloodthirsty one. He broke his word to Valerian and attacked. He was not supposed to follow us for several days. We were going to make peace with your people and then ride like the wind to intercept the legions."

"Is this true?" Wynne asked, longing to believe him.

"It is true. I swear by the gods that it is. Valerian was sick unto death of all the killing and shedding of Celtic blood. When he learned that Severus planned to attack your people, he persuaded Severus to let him go on ahead and make peace so that there would be no fighting. He thought that even Severus would not kill unarmed men who sought peace; but he was wrong. Severus thought that Valerian wanted to attack your tribesmen first." Quickly he told her all that had happened and about Valerian's constant talk about the lovely Celtic girl he adored. As he spoke, Wynne's eyes filled with happiness at the thought that Valerian loved her and was not guilty of betraying her as she had supposed.

"And that is why Severus was going to have Valerian beheaded, for going against him. But Valerian escaped with the help of Meghan and a slave boy named Ibu," Burrus continued.

"Yes, I know the story." The memory of that day when Ibu had told her that Valerian was his master and of all the brave deeds Valerian had done came to her mind. But what of her father's death? Edan had seen him headed for Adair's lodge. Why had he slain her father? Had it all been some monstrous error? Could there be some logical explanation besides evil treachery? For the first time since she had heard Brenna's words, she allowed her doubt to begin to take hold— Brenna was capable of any lie, she knew.

Putting her arms around Burrus, she hugged the young centurion close against her. "Thank you, Burrus. Thank you for telling me and for being my friend," she said.

When at last they drew apart, Wynne's thoughts were of Meghan. It was only right that her friend be happy, even if she could not be. "How goes it with Meghan?" she asked. "Is she well?"

Burrus nodded. "She is growing more beautiful every day."

"She loves you, Burrus," Wynne blurted out with a smile. He blushed at her words like a young boy. It was obvious to Wynne that he felt the same, and his words confirmed her hopes.

"Yes, I know, and I love her. Sometimes I think that being near her will drive me mad, but I will not touch her until she is free. As long as she is considered my slave, I will not bed her." His eyes held the love he felt for the red-haired girl.

"Then I suggest you waste no time in seeing to it that she gets her freedom," Wynne teased.

"Free her?" He cocked his head to one side. The idea had never occurred to him, to free her and then to make her his wife. With a grin Burrus shook his head. "Good idea, Ice Princess. Good idea, indeed. I will speak to Valerian about it this very day."

For a moment Wynne felt sorrow cloud the happy moment as she too longed for freedom. She watched Burrus leave with a heavy heart.

Sixty-three

Valerian arrived at his destination in a little over an hour. He was hungry and tired, his head nearly splitting, but the sight of the black stallion made him forget his misery. Valerian greeted the soldier on guard, who was familiar to him though he wasn't sure where he'd seen him before.

"I'm going to take the black horse with me back to my villa," Valerian told the man as he left the stables.

"Will you be leaving the other horse here?"

"No. I will need them both. The black horse is for someone else," Valerian answered, wondering at the nervousness the stable keeper displayed; it was almost as if he were stalling for time. Still, one met many such strange, lonely fellows among these soldiers, many of whom had been away from home for years.

"Have you happened to hear any news concerning the tribune Severus?" Valerian asked, knowing that stablehands were often the first with news from travelers.

"No . . . no . . . no word at all," was the hasty reply. The soldier turned to leave, yelling over his shoulder at Valerian to be certain to shut the gate when he left.

Valerian went back inside the dark, foul-smelling stable to go about harnessing Sloan.

"Easy, easy, Sloan," he said, patting the horse on the neck. The animal seemed unusually agitated this morning, pawing the ground and tossing his head to and fro.

"You have been through a lot, haven't you, Sloan?" he said. "Well, from now on you will be back with the person who loves you, your rightful owner. I just borrowed you for a while." As if understanding his words, the horse nickered and fought to get free. "Easy, boy. We will be home soon enough." Laughing, he slipped the leather reins over the horses head.

Noticing that the horse appeared to be limping, Valerian bent to check the horse's hoof, and it was then that he heard the sound of metal striking wood above his head.

"What the—?"

He stood up and looked in the direction of the noise. There, embedded in the wooden wall, was a spear where Valerian had stood only moments before. Had he not leaned down, he would have been skewered on a spit like a leg of lamb. He ran to the gate, but there was no one in sight—not even the guard. The stables looked deserted.

Mounting Sloan, Valerian wasted no time in riding away, the gray mare in tow. He did not doubt for a moment that someone had tried to kill him. A thrown spear could be no accident. It had been deliberate. But why? And who?

Severus! he thought, for who else would want to see him dead? Was he back from his campaign in the North? That must have been why the guard had acted so strangely. No doubt the man was a spy for Severus. Valerian would have to be careful from now on, until Severus was on his way back to Rome.

When Valerian arrived back at the villa he carefully secured Sloan to a tree out of sight. He wanted to catch Wynne off guard and surprise her with his gift. Whistling like a small boy, he sat down to a meal. It was thus that Wynne saw him and wondered at the cause of his sudden joy. Burrus had told her that Valerian was devastated by her anger, but here he was looking unaccountably smug and cheerful. In confusion she turned and started to leave the dining room, but her hand brushed a goblet and sent it crashing to the floor.

Valerian leapt up to help Wynne pick up the broken glass. She protested, but when Valerian insisted, she was too flustered by his odd behavior to persist.

"I have something for you, Wynne," he said to her when they'd disposed of the shards of glass. She did not pull away from him this time when he took her arm, but instead went with him out past the atrium, across the back courtyard, to a grove of trees which reminded her of the forest she so loved. Wynne threw Valerian a measured glance, suddenly wondering what he had in his mind, not fully trusting him yet. Then she saw him.

"Sloan!" she breathed. It had been so long since she had seen the horse. Eyes sparkling with tears of joy, she darted to where the horse was tethered and threw her arms around his neck.

"Would that you were to greet me so," Valerian said with a smile, and was surprised to find his smile returned.

"Can I ride him, Valerian?" she asked, eager as a child. Her use of his name—instead of "master"—filled him with hope.

"You may do whatever you want to, Wynne," he replied. "I am giving him back to you. He was never mine. Never."

She eyed him with suspicion, but his expression was guileless.

"Oh, thank you, Valerian," she cried, and climbed on the back of the animal. In a moment she was galloping across the open field. It had been so long since she had felt so free, so alive. For a time she forgot that she was a slave, but guiding the horse back to where Valerian stood, she remembered, and as she dismounted, she bowed her head sadly.

"I cannot keep him. Slaves cannot own property." She looked up then and read the kindness in the Roman's eyes.

"You are no longer a slave, Wynne," he said.

"What do you mean?"

"I mean just that—you are no longer a slave. And you were never meant to be one. You are more a queen or a princess."

Wynne could not believe her ears. Was he giving her the freedom she had asked for? Did he no longer want her with him? Without knowing quite why she burst into tears. Valerian never had been more moved by a woman's sorrow. He gathered her into his arms, holding her tenderly, as if she might break. Her tears wet his tunic as he rocked her gently, his hands caressing her hair. It took a long time for her to stop, and all the while the sounds tore at his heart.

"Please, please, Wynne, stop crying. Oh, my love. Don't. I cannot bear it. Please forgive me for all the things I have said to you. I have so much to make up to you for. For my jealousy, my foolishness. They were of my own doing. Hush. Hush. I love you so!"

She looked up at him and her eyes mirrored his own words, love showing in their blue depths. Then Valerian's lips were suddenly upon hers. She did not shrink away from him in fright, but instead responded with all the longing of her heart. When at last they drew apart, they both started to talk at once, but Wynne held up her hand for his silence.

"You asked me once if I hated you, Valerian," she said. "The answer is no. I have always loved you. But a part of loving is trusting, and that I have not given you. I thought you guilty of deceiving me, but Barrus has told me what I had to know about that terrible day. I should have known that you could not ever be responsible for such a vile betrayal, for such a deed as the murder of unarmed people." She put her arms around him and kissed him then, and all the bitterness of the past seemed to dissolve like the ice and snow on the first day of spring.

They suddenly had so much to tell each other, so much to say. At last Wynne asked him the question which haunted her night and day.

"Did you kill my father?"

"Your father? Kill your father?" he repeated stupidly, not understanding what she meant.

"Did you stab my father with your sword—perhaps not knowing his identity?"

He was incredulous. "No. No. Of course not. Why would you think such a thing of me?"

The whole story—Brenna and Edan's accusations—tumbled out in a torrent of words.

"No wonder you hated me so and didn't want me to touch you." Valerian reached for her hand and held it tenderly in his own strong one. "Wynne, when I went in search of you, Brenna told me you were dead, murdered by the hand of Severus. I recognized her. She was the priestess of the darkness cult who had begged for my death."

"The darkness cult? Brenna?" She had always disliked the woman, but could she be truly evil?

"I know it was her. I would never forget that

face. She told me how much she hated you and that she was glad you were dead. She tried to kill me, to stab me with a dagger."

"And you did not kill my father?"

"No. I swear by the gods that I did not. When Severus had me arrested, I dropped my helmet and my sword. You say you saw them stained with blood, and I tell you that whoever killed your father used my sword to do so. May his murdering soul rot in Hades for eternity!" Again he gathered her into his arms. She felt so right there, so warm.

"So Brenna lied to me in order to hurt me, knowing no doubt of my love for you."

Valerian breathed deeply of the perfume of her hair, feeling desire stir deep within him. Yet, worried that he might frighten her, he held her a little away from him.

"If you want to go back to your people, I will see that you are escorted safely there. I will go with you myself if you so desire."

Wynne shook her head. "I want to stay here with you, now that I know the truth. You are my people, my life, and have been since I first saw you. I will be content to be your concubine. I will come to you of my own free will."

"Not my concubine, but my wife, Wynne," he whispered.

She searched his face and was satisfied that he was sincere. "And what about your betrothed?"

"I only agreed to marry a woman my father had chosen for me when I thought you dead. I knew that I would love no other in this life."

"I want to be with you. Come to me tonight, Valerian."

In answer he held her tightly to him. She could feel the hardness of his manhood, but with him she would know love and tenderness.

"Tonight," Valerian whispered, "will be the most beautiful of my life."

Sixty-four

Wynne lay on her couch, her eyes closed, her golden hair spread on her pillow and a smile on her lips. She looked to Valerian like the goddess Venus herself.

How could I have mistaken her for Minerva? She is Venus incarnate, the most beautiful woman in the empire, he thought as he looked down at her. With a whisper he breathed her name.

Wynne woke slowly. "Valerian?" she said softly, reaching out to touch the warmth of his firm flesh.

Valerian felt as though he would drown in the blue pools of her eyes as she gazed up at him.

"You are so beautiful," he murmured, his hand moving past the neckline of her tunic to her silken skin. He tugged at the fabric of her sleeping gown and slipped it off her shoulders, exposing her breasts. His breathing was uneven as he sat on the edge of the couch, reaching out for the softness of her skin.

Wynne felt her breast tingle and become firm with the gentle touch of his stroking fingers. Desire caught fire in her belly as he kissed her lips. She could feel him trembling with the depth of his passion for her.

Feeling her respond to his caress, Valerian removed her tunic, then with a single motion tore away his own. As she lay naked against him, he groaned with ecstasy and covered her body with his own.

"Don't be frightened," he whispered softly. "I won't hurt you, I promise. If you want me to stop, you have only to say so. I will not force you."

"I know," she whispered, looking deep into his eyes. For a long time they were transfixed by each other's eyes, and then he began caressing her again. His mouth sought her neck and shoulders, then once more teased her lips. Her own lips returned his passion as a fire began to build within her. With him everything seemed so right, so beautiful. She belonged to him and loved him.

We were made for each other, she thought. The gods must have created us just for this very moment. Her eyes closed as she whispered his name, begging him to love her, opening her legs to him.

She could feel his weight upon her, but felt

none of her old fear, only desire for him as he tenderly entered her.

"I love you," she breathed. Together they soared to outer realms. Wynne thought she would die from ecstasy and knew that she could die happily, a woman whole again, a woman loved. With a cry of joy she shuddered as Valerian thrust forward with one last triumphant motion, reaching his own fulfillment.

They fell asleep then, their bodies entwined, smiles on their faces.

Wynne moaned and awakened with the first soft rays of the morning sun. Opening her eyes, she knew that something was different in her life. Then she remembered that Valerian was here with her. He had loved her last night, not once but several times, and never had she known such joy.

Valerian leaned on one elbow. "You are lovely." He reached out and lightly caressed her breast with his fingertips. His touch warmed her, as did his gaze, making her feel beautiful.

"I love you more than my life itself," he whispered.

"As I love you," she answered. Her head was cradled against his shoulder, and she sighed in contentment.

With a smile Wynne reached over to tenderly caress her lover's strong chest, moving to his abdomen until he groaned with pleasure.

"Ah, Wynne, you drive me crazy with desire." Looking down, she could see that her fingers had awakened his manhood, and gently reached down to stroke it in fascination, remembering the pleasure it had given her.

"You want me again," she breathed.

"Yes. I want you," he groaned, taking her into her arms and kissing her savagely. His lips were hot and hard against hers, and as he reached out to caress her breasts and stomach and thighs, she gave herself up to the pleasure of his touch.

Valerian ran his hands from her breasts to her navel, to the golden mound between her thighs, exploring softly the petal-soft folds that had brought him such joy. As if she were drunk with wine, Wynne was enveloped in a haze of contentment; then she was consumed with need. She felt hot, trembling all over as she ached for him to again possess her.

"Love me, Valerian," she cried. Her arms went around his neck, pressing him close to her. Her fingers clutched at his back as he entered her. She was filled, completed, made whole by his presence within her. They were fused, inseparable, one being now and forever.

Sixty-five

True to his word, Valerian gave Wynne her freedom. He called forth a scribe to draw up the papers of manumission that very morning. According to Roman law, a liberated slave did not have the full rights of citizenship, but it was a step, and as Valerian handed the papers to Wynne he felt light of heart.

"You will always belong to me in my heart," he said, "but I want the ties that bind us to be the bond of marriage, not enslavement."

Wynne remained silent, happy about her freedom and forthcoming marriage but troubled too. In the midst of her blissful slumber that morning she had awakened from a dream that was more like one of the visions she used to have. But this made no sense—it was a battle not of Roman against Celt, but of Roman against Roman, soldiers of one army slaughtering their comrades. She shook herself to be free of these strange images and clung protectively to her beloved.

"I think you a fool, Valerian," came a booming voice from the doorway. Turning, he saw Cassius standing there, along with Burrus and other friends come to help them celebrate. "This woman could have brought you many gold coins, but freed, she is worth nothing."

"She will be the mother of my children," Valerian replied with anger, then noticed the sparkle in Cassius' eye.

"Mark you well then, tribune, lest she soon become your master. A woman needs a firm hand." He came up behind him and whispered in his ear, "I envy you, Valerian."

Cassius clapped his hands, and a young boy appeared whom Valerian knew to be the general's slave.

"Bring a flagon of wine and goblets. We have much to celebrate," Cassius ordered.

"As you wish, master," the boy said. Wynne looked sadly upon the child and wished in her heart that he too could be given his freedom.

Cassius toasted the young couple and then had other news to tell Valerian. "Severus has returned," he announced. "I have ordered him to report to me on the morrow."

Cassius looked at Wynne, wondering what her reaction would be to seeing the tribune again. No doubt Severus would be enraged to find his lovely woman free and safely out of his reach. "He has brought several new slaves with him.

Perhaps that will soothe his anger when he finds out that his golden bird has been given her freedom," he said. "I have been told that these slaves are from your land, Wynne. They are members of some demon cult who worship gods of the darkness and offer human sacrifices."

At this news Valerian's and Wynne's eyes met.

Cassius continued. "It seems that the priestess of this cult was once in league with Severus and that he himself helped her attain her power after the slaughter of the Druids. But the woman seems to have become drunk with her power and foolishly thought herself stronger than her Roman conquerors. Now she has been brought to this city in chains, snarling like a wild beast. I doubt that she can be made useful to any master."

Wynne closed her eyes as Brenna's face flashed before her. It could be no other. The gods had been just.

"I must see this priestess," she said to Valerian. "Can it be arranged?"

"I will see that you are escorted there. I do not trust that woman. Were she to harm you again, I would not want to live," he answered.

Wynne smiled at him, comforted by his love. The thought of seeing her stepmother again did not please her, yet she had to find out from the woman's lips who had killed her father and why Brenna had lied so viciously to her.

The room was soon buzzing with the conversation of Valerian's friends. Wynne was left alone with her thoughts. She could see Burrus and Valerian in deep conversation and could see

Valerian smiling and patting the young centurion on the back. No doubt he had asked for Meghan's freedom and had been granted it.

Suddenly, as Wynne was watching Valerian and Burrus together, the images from that morning flooded her mind's eye again; unable to ignore their warring any longer, she rushed to Valerian's side. At that moment a clash of swords and shouts of alarm were suddenly heard from outside.

"*Severus!*" Valerian swore. And there he was, rushing into the room with dozens of his followers armed and intent on death and destruction.

Wynne screamed as she saw one of Valerian's officers fall, a sword driven deep in his chest. He lay facedown on the mosaic floor, the blood from his wound making a dark stain on the white tiles.

With a warrior's instincts, Wynne picked up one of the small tables and hurled it into the throng of Severus' men. The general's soldiers followed suit, hurling goblets, bottles, kitchen utensils, and tables, all in an effort to disorient the foe and give themselves time to get their swords, which were outside the doorway.

Wynne's eyes sought Valerian, and terror gripped her as she saw Severus making his way toward him. Frantically, she ran to her bedchamber for her only weapon—her dagger.

Valerian looked up to see the grinning Severus bearing down on him, sword raised. He had not had time yet to retrieve his own sword, and he cursed himself for letting down his guard. A good soldier was always prepared for battle.

Severus lunged. Valerian dodged, escaping with a scratch. Dark eyes glared at him in hatred and rage. "I have long thought of your death," Severus said to him, his protruding teeth flashing an evil smile. "You cheated me out of your death once, but you will not do so again."

It was as if the scene before him was moving slowly as the cornered Valerian saw the blade bearing in on him for the kill. Suddenly Burrus stepped between them, taking the blow meant for him; at the same moment, Wynne came forward, her dagger in hand. She threw herself forward, striking at all enemies in her path in a valiant effort to get to her lover. She saw Severus fall to the ground, the lewd grin of death on his face. Cassius was standing over him, holding his sword.

With their leader fallen, Severus' troops were in disarray, some fleeing, some surrendering. Within minutes the villa was again in the charge of Cassius.

"Valerian!" Wynne cried, seeing a still form on the floor. But it was not the tribune; it was instead the noble centurion Burrus.

Sixty-six

"Is he dead?" The question was a sob as her eyes beheld his still form with its bloodly wound.

"No!" Valerian answered. "But he must be attended to. Sweet Juno, put himself between me and that foul Severus and took the sword meant for me. The gods can't let him die."

"I will do what I can," Wynne promised. "Our people know well the arts of healing."

Burrus opened his eyes, pools of misery. "Meghan, Meghan," he breathed. "I must see Meghan . . . there is so much to . . . say to her."

"Lie still, my dear friend," Wynne answered, binding his wound. "I will see that she is brought to your side, but for now you must save your strength."

"That vile monster Severus. Oh, that I had killed him long ago," Valerian mourned.

"It is too late to speak of what-ifs, tribune,"

Cassius said quietly. "What is done is done. We must now guard Burrus' life and see that no more tragedy comes from this day." He motioned to the household slaves to carry Severus and the other fallen soldiers away to await proper burial.

Valerian and Cassius gently lifted Burrus and carried him to a bedchamber. Wynne examined his wound carefully with her gentle hands, issuing orders like a general. "I must have myrrh and golden seal," she snapped to the household slaves.

The myrrh was brought quickly, but the slaves were confused at the mention of golden seal. Wynne realized then that she had called the plant by its Celtic name.

"The root is called yellow paintroot or eyeroot," she said, seeking the Latin name. She described it in detail, her heart thumping wildly in her breast as she fought against time. Burrus was now pale as death, and she feared for him.

An old woman stepped forward. "It is ground raspberry that you seek," she said. "I will find some for you." She hurried away, soon returning with what Wynne sought.

Wynne steeped the myrrh and the golden seal in boiling water and washed the wound carefully in this solution. She again bound the wound with clean linen when she was through cleansing it, having sprinkled a little of the powdered golden seal on the wound itself.

She tenderly stroked Burrus' forehead as he fell into a healing slumber. Turning to Valerian,

she said, "There is no more I can do here for
the time being. I will ride to bring back Meghan.
She is the best medicine he can have."

"Let me go with you," Valerian whispered,
fearful lest she run into any danger.

"No. I can travel faster alone. Sloan will carry
us both back—and I shall be careful," she added,
grateful for his concern for her.

Within minutes she was off like the wind to
Burrus' villa. Everywhere, she could see the mixture of Roman and Celtic culture as she rode.
The city had paved and drained streets, forums,
basilicas, temples, houses with stone foundations
and tiled roofs, public baths where hundreds
could bathe at once. And throughout the city
were statues of Roman gods entwined with Celtic
goddesses.

Burrus' villa was made of wood and smaller
than Valerian's. Jumping from Sloan's back,
Wynne ran to the door, little thinking what a
fearsome sight she made, her pale blue stola
covered with blood, her hair in disorder.

The slave at the front door drew back in
shock when she saw her. "Go away. Go away,"
the woman shrieked. "Help me. Help me. A
heathen!" The door was firmly closed in her
face.

In anger Wynne pounded the wooden door.
"I must speak with Meghan. I must!" she shouted.

The door was opened a crack and the woman
looked out again. "Who are you?" she asked,
her voice shaking with fear.

"Tell Meghan that Wynne is here to see her.

And hurry, please. Burrus has been wounded," Wynne pleaded.

When the door opened again, Meghan herself was standing there, her eyes wide with fear. "Wynne. Wynne. What has happened to Burrus?" Seeing the blood soaking Wynne's garments, she stifled a scream.

"He has been wounded," Wynne answered, grabbing her hand. "We have no time to talk. Come!"

Sixty-seven

Nearly as soon as Wynne reined in Sloan behind the villa, Meghan was off and running toward the courtyard, her red-gold hair tumbling about her shoulders. Wynne turned Sloan over to a slave and followed her. Meghan was flushed, her jade eyes wide with the fear that she would be too late. Through the chamber door they could see the bent figure of a white-haired Roman wearing the green toga of a physician.

"My Lord Burrus!" Meghan cried, rushing toward the pillowed couch where he lay and burying her face in his tunic.

Awake now, Burrus reached for her and held her to him with his uninjured arm.

"Don't die. Don't leave me. Please, Burrus," she whispered. "I love you. I love you so."

How he wished he had made this lovely young girl into a woman. Why had he been so foolish and noble, when they had both wanted to belong to each other in soul and in flesh.

"He will live," said the physician sternly. "Although I must tell you that the wound in his chest came very near his heart." He regarded Meghan appraisingly. "Are you the woman who bound his wound?"

"It was I," Wynne said softly.

"Even I could not have done better. The wound is clean, without even a sign of the illness which comes of a blade thrust. Where did you learn your healing art?"

"From my father."

"Was he a physician, then?"

"No, he was a Druid!" she answered proudly.

"Ah, yes. I have often heard of the wonders of their magic and herbs. There is much you could teach me about healing. Too often our methods are useless," he said with a scowl. "Rome has learned much from others, but I fear there is still much to be learned." He turned to give Meghan instructions on Burrus' care.

Wynne could feel the strong arms of Valerian around her waist and leaned back to rest her head against him. The knowledge that Burrus would live was a balm to her heart.

"You have been through much this day," he whispered, "yet as always you amaze me with your strength and wisdom. What a lucky man am I to have you. As beautiful as Venus and as wise as Minerva."

"And I am lucky too," she replied. "No woman ever had a man as kind, gentle, and handsome as you." His lips brushed her hair and she could feel a flash of desire run through her. Together they walked out into the courtyard. As they walked, Wynne's smile faded. "So Severus is dead—I am avenged. But I still wonder who killed my father."

"I have found out where Brenna is housed," Valerian said. "Perhaps now is the time to find out the truth once and for all."

"Yes. I must know, for only then can I be truly content." She reached up and put her arms around him, drawing him close. Her lips were soft and sweet as they mingled with his. "Perhaps when all this is over I can then give you my whole heart."

"Let me go with you. I too have a score to settle with that witch!"

"All right," she agreed. "I have need of your strength and your comfort." Together they made ready for the final confrontation, the one which would remove once and for all the last wall between them.

Sixty-eight

Wynne and Valerian were ushered to a small dank stone cell when they came in search of the slave named Brenna. The guard eyed them warily.

"Why do you want to see her?" he asked. "She is touched, that one."

"There is something I must know, and only she can tell me," Wynne answered, pulling her cloak tightly to her to ward off the dampness of the room.

"She is dangerous. Already killed one guard. She should be safely in the underworld, where she belongs!" Grumbling, he pointed toward a barred corner which was more like a cage than a cell. "There she is," he said.

Holding on to Valerian's arm, Wynne walked over to the cagelike structure, which was only big enough for a person to sit. She had seen wild beasts treated better than this. Huddled in the corner was the figure of a woman muttering to herself in Celtic. Her hair was matted and filthy, lice abounding in the dark tangles of her hair.

"Brenna? Brenna, is that you?"

At the sound of her name, the woman turned, and Wynne gasped in shock. The creature that stared back at her with glazed eyes looked like the mask of death. There was hardly a trace of Brenna's former beauty.

"The darkness that falls is heavy with light. The powers of hate are no longer strong," she babbled to herself.

Wynne shuddered. No matter what this woman had done—even if she herself had killed Adair—it was terrible to see her like this.

"Brenna. Brenna. It is Wynne. Look at me. Look at me," she cried.

"Life kills ... the earth is shattered by too much light," the woman crooned, rocking back and forth on her knees.

"She is hopeless, Wynne," Valerian whispered, feeling pity himself for this soulless woman. He drew Wynne back, intent on leaving the foul-smelling place.

"No. Not yet. Brenna, Brenna," she called again.

At last the creature turned to her, her eyes clearing for a moment. "You look like the daughter of Adair!" Brenna croaked. "But you are dead ... dead ... I myself saw that you were condemned to death." A burst of laughter came from her cracked lips. "I turned you in as a Druid priestess."

So it had been Brenna who had nearly destroyed her life.

"Strong and fierce are the wolves of the dark world," Brenna rambled on. "They rush on and tear at our flesh . . . be strong . . . be strong . . . power will win all . . . sons of the darkness . . . daughters of Domnu . . . arise!"

Wynne shook the bars in an effort to quiet the woman. The crazed eyes met hers. The face covered with dirt smiled. The woman held up her hand in greeting, and with shock Wynne could see that it had been severely burned.

"No doubt Severus' punishment," Valerian exclaimed. "No wonder the woman is insane."

"As well I know," Wynne breathed. Taking a deep breath, she closed her eyes and spoke the word "Adair." "What happened to my father?"

"Adair . . . Adair . . . Adair . . ." the woman chanted. She wiggled her head as if in rhythm to some unearthly music, then suddenly stopped and faced Wynne again. "Dead. He is dead."

"How do you know?" Wynne persisted.

"I killed him. My husband. Adair is dead." Piercing laughter cut through the darkness of the cell. "I killed him with the Roman's sword." Again the laughter. "My revenge was complete you see."

Valerian reached out to gather Wynne into his arms. "I thought as much. No doubt she used my sword to further hurt you and draw suspicion from herself. She is even more wicked than I suspected." Not waiting for any chance for Wynne to object, he drew her away from the cell and soon they were again outside breathing in the fresh air.

"Brenna murdered him. I should have known." Wynne's eyes filled with tears. "How often did she tell me that she was tired of being tied to a cripple."

"Hush, now. It is all over. From now on we will be together, and I swear to you that no one will ever part us again." Seeing a smudge of dirt on her face, he gently wiped it clean with his thumb, then cupped her face in his hands. Her lips tasted salty from her tears as he kissed her, and with his warm scalding kisses he melted them away.

"Come!" he said, putting his arm around her waist. "It is time to go home."

Sixty-nine

Wynne was completely spent by the time she and Valerian arrived back at the villa. It was as if all the months of pent-up pain and hurt had spilled forth like the waters of the ocean at high tide.

"You must try to forget all that has happened, Wynne," Valerian said gently, kissing her with all the tenderness of his heart and soul. Yet even Valerian's kisses did not seem to waken her from her lethargy. It was as if she were somewhere else at that moment, another place, another time.

"If only I had realized that she was capable of doing such a foul deed. If only I had stayed with my father that day. I should have sensed somehow that she might seek to do him harm. Indeed she once told me that his death would bring her freedom," she murmured softly.

"You saw no evil in her because there is no

evil in you. We can only torture ourselves by trying to relive the past." Valerian picked her up in his arms. "We have the future to think of now," he said, making for Wynne's sleeping chamber. "I am going to put you to bed. You are exhausted."

"No. No. I don't want to be alone."

Valerian ignored her protests and took her to the bedchamber and placed her on the bed. She looked up at him with frightened eyes, eyes which reflected all the months of bitterness and grief.

"What if I had killed you? Avenged myself upon you?" The idea made her shudder, and she prayed silently to her gods for staying her hand that day when Valerian had returned to Britain.

Valerian turned to leave, and she reached out to touch his hand. "Stay with me, please, Valerian. I don't want to be alone, not now." Her arms wrapped about him as he bent down to her.

"I won't leave you. I'm merely going to un-dress you and massage you and bathe you and love you." He helped her to lie back on the pillows of her sleeping couch. Calling for two slaves to see to her bath water, Valerian turned his attention to undressing her.

"Now it is time for your bath," he exclaimed, picking her up once again and depositing her in the warm water.

Wynne leaned back in the soothing water and tried to banish from her mind the thoughts of all that had happened this day. Could she ever forget the sight of Brenna's burned flesh or the vision of her crazed eyes? She remembered what Edan had once said to her, that hate can destroy. Indeed it was true, for it was hate and jealousy which had destroyed Brenna.

"So much bloodshed," she cried. "Why does the world have to be filled with so much hatred and killing?"

Valerian reached out to touch her cheek. "Perhaps someday the world will learn how to love and to live in peace," he whispered.

Her eyes caught his, and the love she felt for him was reflected in their blue depths. "Perhaps someday, Valerian. Someday."

"Until that day we must be content with the love we bear each other and our friends. There is much good in this world too. It is not all bad." He gently kissed her forehead, his passion increased by her vulnerability.

Wynne reached out and caressed his face, her fingers trailing down to the cleft of his chin. "I love you," she breathed. "Without you I would have no desire to live." His eyes told her that he felt the same.

Watching her in her bath had aroused Valerian. "Now it is your turn to wash me," he whispered, disrobing and joining her in the poollike tub.

Wynne hesitated a moment, then began to massage him as he had done to her, noting with pleasure the broad chest, the muscles of his abdomen, and now the throbbing manhood which proved his desire for her. . . .

"Enough of this torture," he groaned. He took Wynne's hands, and together they left the water.

Valerian dried her lush body and then went about drying his own.

"You told me once that your people believe in the purification of water and fire," he whispered. "Together we have purified ourselves of the past. Only the future awaits us now." He took her mouth then in a devouring kiss, bringing fire into her loins.

Valerian carried her to the bed and lay down beside her, caressing her with hands and lips. Wynne returned his caresses until the flame blazed within them both.

"Love me, Valerian. Love me now," she breathed.

With a groan of desire he entered her, filling her with such pleasure that she caught her breath. Together they found the perfect motion, pulsing with the rhythm of some primitive rite, taking them higher and higher toward the dwelling place of the gods. They were one now and forever, as if they had been one since the beginning of time.

"We were created for each other," Valerian sighed. "Without you I am as nothing."

As she took him deeper and deeper inside her, it was as if his love was a salve to her pain. The wounds of the past were healed by their love.

Later, as they lay in each other's arms, Wynne told Valerian of her people's belief in the circle of life and how she knew in her heart that they would never be parted.

"I love you so, my beloved conqueror," she whispered, knowing, with a sudden clear vision of the future, that they had not only this life to share, but many other lives as well.

ABOUT THE AUTHOR

Kathryn Kramer lives in Boulder, Colorado, where she is an executive secretary for an aerospace firm as well as a professional vocalist. History has always been of interest to Kathryn and is reflected in both her writing and her collection of 300 historically costumed dolls. *Love's Blazing Ecstasy* is her first novel.

Sensational Reading from SIGNET